A Poppy in Remembrance

Other Books by Michelle Ule:

Mrs. Oswald Chambers: The Woman Behind the World's Bestselling Devotional
Bridging Two Hearts

A Poppy in Remembrance

Michelle Ule

A Poppy in Remembrance

Cover design by Nicole Miller of Miller Media Solutions.
Editing by Jamie Clarke Chavez.
Author photograph by Elise Aileen Photography.

Oswald Chambers quotations used by permission of Discovery House Publishers.

Note: This is a work of fiction. Names, characters, places, and incidents are either products of the author's imagination or used fictitiously. All characters are fictional, and any similarity to people living or dead is purely coincidental. All historical characters are long dead and portrayed using adapted historical dialogue.

Published in the United States of America
Print ISBN-13: 978-1724569769
www.MichelleUle.com

To the memory of my parents,
Ben and Jeanette Duval

Chapter One

London, August 5, 1914

Claire Meacham opened the door over her mother's "Wait!" and exited before the chauffeur brought the motorcar to a halt. She had to find Peter before he made a decision they'd all regret.

She squeezed into the throng, her trusty leather satchel banging at her side. How would she find him in this mob?

"Don't push, miss," growled a Cockney voice.

She yanked in her elbows with murmured apologies. Before her stretched an ocean of men wearing hats: bowlers, straw, flat caps, and even a top hat worn by a dandy in a disheveled tuxedo. "Peter!" She hoped her voice would carry. "Peter!"

The warm morning air reeked from the sweat of work and the tang of alcohol. A place so far removed from Radcliffe's organized, hushed library would be hard to find. And yet there Claire stood, surprisingly tall among the British men, looking, hoping, and begging whatever God might be watching to find an earnest twenty-two-year-old with curling sandy hair, gray eyes, and rosy cheeks.

"Any sign of him?" Claire's mother caught up with her as the multitude parted with a polite doffing of headgear. Anne Meacham's refined dignity, along with her shining white-blonde hair under a proper hat, always brought out the best in people, no matter their station in life.

"He had a head start." Claire took her mother's arm as they shuffled toward the looming brick building two blocks ahead. She thought of Sherlock Holmes and Dr. Watson. They never worried about getting into Scotland Yard.

But then, they hadn't tried to visit on August 5, 1914. The front page of the *Times* proclaimed the problem in three bold words: BRITAIN AT WAR.

Newsboys held the paper aloft and shouted the latest information. Whenever Claire caught sight of the headline, her stomach flipped and she shuddered. How could the Meacham family have left sane, orderly Boston in time for a war? What was her father thinking?

No need to ask: the latest news and his empty bank account always commanded his attention.

That morning, however, Jock Meacham wanted his only living male relative yanked from the line before he did something foolish. Claire craned her neck. A six-footer like Peter should stand out in this crowd.

"Can I help you, miss?" A British bobby in a rumpled blue uniform appeared before her.

"We're looking for my cousin but so many people—"

"Men started lining up as soon as the king announced war." He rubbed the nape of his neck. "I've been here since midnight. Hundred have come through, thousands. They're keen to fight the Germans and kick the Kaiser back to Berlin."

A nearby military band struck up "Rule Britannia," and two sailors moved through the male sea bellowing: "Interested in the navy? Hove to the right!"

"We've the finest ships on the ocean!"

More roars and raised fists shook in the humid air.

Anne pointed after a handful of men drifting to starboard. "Peter's an excellent sailor; maybe we should try the Admiralty?"

Claire secured her spectacles and shook her head. "He adores biplanes now, he wouldn't join the navy." She put the ball of her French-heeled shoe onto a lamp post base, lifted her ankle-length skirt and hoisted herself up.

An approving male chorus eddied around her knees.

"What are you doing?" Anne grabbed at her hem.

At eleven o'clock last night when King George V declared war, the family had toasted each other with solemn faces. After Peter gulped down three glasses of champagne in short order, Claire tucked a red rose into her cousin's lapel as a civilized touch before the horror began. Then he and his childhood friend Edward left and did not return.

Amid the swell of dark coats, she hoped to spy the crimson flower.

"Do you see him?" Anne tried to shield Claire's legs. "Climb down."

"Peter!" She shouted again, and dozens of male voices took up the call, some in falsetto: "Peter! Oh, Peter!"

Claire slipped to the sidewalk and her hair toppled around her shoulders. "No sign of him." She rifled through her satchel—aha—then twisted the thick ebony curls into a knot and jabbed a yellow shorthand pencil through to anchor them.

A whistle caught her attention. Men turned and she glimpsed limp red petals. Claire stumbled through the crowd to a familiar face.

Peter glared at her. "You don't belong here. Do you see any other women?"

"Papa says it's too soon. There's no hurry and plenty to accomplish beforehand; you need to plan your actions strategically."

"Hey, Claire, they're not taking women yet!" Edward, her cousin Sylvia's beau, lifted a magnum of champagne to salute her. With tie askew and bloodshot eyes, his ruddy face nearly matched his hair color. He slung an arm across Peter's shoulder. "We're going together."

"Peter cannot enlist. His mother needs him." The line retreated at Anne's commanding voice. Several guffaws and a murmured "Mama's boy" made for a scoffing audience.

Claire didn't know much about men but understood her mother's scolding wouldn't work. "You have responsibilities. Your father's estate will be settled in another month or so and then you can enlist. The war only started last night. You have plenty of time."

"We'll beat the Boche by Christmas," Edward declared. "If we don't enlist now, we'll miss the whole thing."

She eyed him, appalled at his ignorance. An Oxford graduate should have known better.

"Uncle Jock sent you, didn't he? He couldn't be bothered to come himself but sent you two to find me?" Peter's nostrils flared in his mottled face and spittle flew from his mouth.

"That's uncalled for!" Anne cried.

Claire frowned. "Papa's reporting on the war."

"Aye, the war, a story, something else always needs attending to by Uncle Jock, nothing personal."

A heavy paw clenched Claire's arm. "Let the boy go. He don't need womenfolk dragging him back to the nursery."

"Take your hands off her!" Peter clenched his fists.

Claire wrenched her arm away. "I'm not saying he shouldn't defend his country. He just needs to put his affairs in order before he joins the army."

Peter looked back and forth between exuberant Edward and the working-class men surrounding them.

Claire held her breath as he weighed his options. A resplendent Union Jack sagged in the hot sun beside the arched doorway. Men in sharp new uniforms gestured to the crowd, beckoning them forward.

"Even if you don't come with me, Peter, I'm joining up. I'd never be able to face my father otherwise." Edward hiccupped.

Anne touched Peter's shoulder. "He's not your concern. Your mother needs you."

Peter crossed his arms and narrowed his eyes. "I need to go with my mate."

Claire's heart hammered so hard her chest ached. "Edward doesn't fly."

A murmur rose around them—"flyer."

"Them biplanes is dangerous," a burly man said with admiration. "Made of paper, they are."

Peter examined the overcast sky as if seeking an answer from his late father, then groaned and reached for Edward's hand. "I'm sorry, old boy, but not today. Claire's right, I need to resolve my responsibilities before I enlist. I'll be a few weeks behind you but I'm coming. What shall I tell Sylvia?"

The good cheer vanished from Edward's face. His chin trembled. "Tell her she'll be an officer's wife before Christmas."

"Good luck." He stepped out of line and took Anne's arm with a sigh. "How did you get here?"

"Mr. Able is waiting in the motorcar." Claire directed them to Whitehall Avenue, stumbling in relief. They walked several blocks in silence.

"You made the right choice. Your mother is distraught," Anne murmured as they settled into the soft leather back seat. It smelled of wealth. "I had no idea you were learning to fly."

Claire glanced at Peter. Her mother never missed anything.

"I didn't want to upset Mummy."

Anne stared at him.

"Home, sir?" the chauffer asked from behind the steering wheel.

"No. Take us to the Boston News Syndicate offices. It's time for me to deal with my uncle man to man."

Anne clutched his arm. "I don't believe that's a good idea. We never bother Jock at the office and certainly not on the day a war starts."

"The news is always king with Uncle Jock," Peter said. "Right, Claire? Isn't that why you're aching to become a newspaper reporter yourself? You're as bad as he is, always pushing your nose into other people's business to find out what's happening."

Claire gasped at his betrayal. She'd been waiting for the right moment to reveal her dream to her parents.

All her stenography training, history lessons, and language practice had one goal: preparation for becoming a foreign correspondent. But her mother wouldn't approve and Jock, Claire shuddered, would dismiss her goal as the fanciful dreams of a child.

"Really?" Anne leaned back into the seat. "We haven't known many respectable female reporters. We intend for you to be a history teacher. Why else did we spend all that money sending you to college?"

Claire looked out the window at suffragettes in Trafalgar Square exhorting men to enlist, and her confidence slipped away. Her parents kept no secrets from one another. If her father ridiculed her hopes, Claire's soul would shatter, just like her lost senior year of college. No home, no Radcliffe, no future; her shoulders slumped.

Peter shifted beside her and cleared his throat. She shook her head.

The motorcar crept past St. Martin's in the Field church, and Claire rallied to devise an answer as they headed east toward Fleet Street and Jock Meacham.

"Grandfather always said I was a born reporter," Claire finally said. "You know I'm a good writer."

"You are a good writer," Anne agreed, "but your grandfather's poor judgment is the reason we're living in England on my sister's charity while we pray your father doesn't lose his job."

Claire had no answer to the truth.

Peter waved his hands. "No charity, Aunt Anne, we're thankful you're here. My mother's spirits are much improved since you arrived. I'm sorry I spoke. I didn't mean to cause trouble."

Anne arched a brow. "So what are you doing now?"

He swallowed. "Setting things straight with Uncle Jock. He needs to understand I'm not a child. I'm a man."

Mr. Able stopped the motorcar before a gray stone building flying flags from several nations, including the United States. Peter opened the door and stepped out with Claire right behind him carrying her satchel. "Aunt Anne?" he stretched his hand to her.

She stared straight ahead. "Jock won't tolerate domestic issues in the office. If you're determined to confront him in the newsroom, I'll remain with Mr. Able. This has been an illuminating outing and I have much to consider. We will wait."

Claire and Peter entered a foyer of black and white marble tiles. Claire's head swerved as she took it all in. She'd not visited yet and longed to examine the newsroom where her father worked as a journalist and editor—assuming he didn't throw them out first.

"I say, Claire, I'm sorry. I thought you'd have told them by now."

She stopped at the lift gate. "I didn't know your flying lessons were a secret."

"You know Mummy." He squared his shoulders. "We'll face your father together. It can't be worse than the time we ran his sailboat aground."

Claire adjusted her satchel and blew out her breath at his usual optimism. If they didn't handle Jock correctly, this could go much worse.

Two years older, Peter had always been her hero. He'd taken responsibilities seriously those family summers in Newport, Rhode Island, teaching her to sail and warning her to ignore his sister's bossy ways. Her solitary childhood would have been much lonelier without those summers and Peter's letters from across the Atlantic.

Now she wasn't so sure about his judgment.

They rode the creaking lift to the third floor and exited into a hallway facing frosted glass doors marked with white letters: Boston Newspaper Syndicate. Peter blanched at the bold label. "A mate of mine from Oxford works here, Nigel Bentley-Smith, a copyboy. You'd like him; he studied history."

The rackety staccato of typewriters echoed from the office, and an echoing excitement welled in Claire. She ached to see her byline in a newspaper, particularly *The Boston Daily* owned by the BNS, and yearned to hear today's latest news. While she'd hoped to prepare a little longer before broaching her writing aspirations with her father, if she acted decisively, she might be able to lay the groundwork for an opportunity.

It was a long shot, but she'd fulfilled her father's order and deterred Peter from enlisting in the British Expeditionary Force. Surely he'd see her as responsible and competent, even resourceful like a good reporter.

Peter straightened his shoulders like a soldier, strode to the doors, and pushed them open with a bang.

Chapter Two

Few men noticed them over the typewriter din as they marched into the office, the air smoky blue from tobacco. A slight man with a tiny moustache over a frown stalked across the newsroom from a glassed-in office opposite the doors. He wore rumpled black trousers and a white shirt with sleeves held in place by black garters. "May I help you?"

"We're here to see Jock Meacham," Peter said. "It's a personal matter."

The man's eyes narrowed.

"Are you Mr. Conroy—the city editor?" Claire asked. "I'm Jock's daughter."

He sniffed. "Surely you know we're covering a war and families are not welcome in the newsroom, particularly on personal business. Is this an emergency?"

"Yes," Peter said, even as Claire answered, "No."

Conroy scowled. "Take a seat. He's watching the wire news. I'll see if he can be bothered."

They sat in straight-backed chairs along a wall lined with dusty bookshelves in the high-ceilinged room. Wood paneling, clusters of desks, candlestick phones, the smell of ink and newsprint were all familiar to Claire. She'd called upon her father in newspaper offices since birth—but always at his invitation.

Glass doors lined the south wall, the home of the clattering telegraph service. "Managing Editor" was painted in gold across the window of the southeast corner office overlooking Fleet Street. Empty teacups littered the busy journalists' desks, the only British distinction she observed.

The reporters ranged from squeaking callow youths to gravel-voiced men, all wearing a variety of facial hair and clothing similar to Conroy's. Four of the most youthful—copyboys—sat in the southwest corner along with an unoccupied desk covered in papers. In most newsrooms they typed, handled wire copy, and served as general assistants.

Cub reporters often started as copyboys, and that's where Claire wanted to be—in the thick of the newsroom and under her father's tutelage. A hum of joy pushed a smile across her face, even as her stomach roiled in anticipation.

Only then did she notice the absence of women.

Peter indicated an athletic man with high cheekbones in the far corner. "Nigel. I'll introduce you when we get a chance." He put up his hand.

His friend jerked his chin in response but kept typing.

Nigel had tied his bowtie at a natty angle and slicked back his fair hair. His long fingers stilled the flapping yellow paper in his typewriter automatically. His manner—confident, controlled, and focused—pricked her interest. "How well do you know him?" she whispered.

"Well enough. You interested? He grew up in New Zealand, a colonist like you."

Claire shook her head at the old family joke, but needed to concentrate on thwarting this potential disaster, not on a handsome man. She removed her glasses to polish with her handkerchief and to think.

The door opened behind Nigel and an auburn-haired young man with broad shoulders carried in a wire report.

This would be fresh news, possibly from the continent. Claire replaced her glasses and edged forward in her chair.

She heard Jock Meacham's distinctive Boston accent barking orders and asking questions. He strode through the doorway, a pencil stuck behind his ear and papers in hand. His handmade leather shoes squeaked on the wooden floor as he halted in the middle of the newsroom like a circus ringmaster, a handful of reporters jumping up to perform.

Seeing her tall father in his element—blue-black hair gleaming, tailored trousers fitting perfectly, ever-present pipe punctuating his words—thrilled Claire. Jock Meacham commanded every room with his vigor and personality while his dashing features—sky-blue eyes against swarthy skin—could not be ignored.

He fixed his piercing eyes on each writer as he outlined the latest information. He pointed at stories he wanted, waved off those unneeded for the five o'clock news cable to Boston, and snapped his fingers for the wire report. The auburn-haired man spoke in a flat American accent.

Jock's gaze raked the audience until he saw Claire and his black-winged eyebrows shot up. He handed off his papers and crossed the room in five broad steps. Claire and Peter stood.

He scrutinized his nephew, but spoke to Claire. "Where did you find him?"

"Scotland Yard recruiting office."

"You should not have sent Claire—" Peter began.

"It was mobbed," Claire said.

Jock faced her. "What do you mean?"

"The bobby told me men began lining up as soon as the king declared war. He'd been there since midnight trying to keep order."

Jock raised his voice. "We need this story. Any copyboy handy with a pencil and paper? Hodges?"

Claire pulled her pad from the satchel and released the pencil from her hair. "I'm ready."

"It's Hodges's job."

"I'll write down what I saw. It will save time."

"Uncle Jock." Peter began again. "If you wanted me, you should have come yourself."

Jock ignored him. "No need, Claire. Hodges will take down the information."

"I've got it right here." Claire scribbled as she spoke. This might be her only chance. "The sun beat down, the men stood in a line more than a mile long stretching to Trafalgar Square and blocking traffic. The honking of horns, cheering of men, and playing of the Royal Navy Band made for a raucous clamor."

"Good." Jock fumbled his pipe into the pocket of his fine jacket and rubbed his chin. "Are you getting this down, Hodges?"

"Not quite, sir," the American said.

"I've got it." Claire jotted as fast as she could, confident she'd stay ahead of him.

"What else do you know?"

"Mr. Meacham, women do not work as reporters at the Boston News Syndicate," Mr. Conroy said. "If you want a story on the recruitment drive, we'll send a reporter."

"No need if Claire has the information," Jock said. "Ready, Hodges?"

Hodges nodded.

Claire had already written several paragraphs, sticking to facts and the details she'd deliberately noticed, just as Grandfather had taught her. "Why don't you use my notes?

I can type them up myself." She flipped over the first page and scrawled more lines and curving notation.

The copyboy cleared his throat and she looked up. Deep brown eyes watched from a round, pale face as Hodges tried not to smile. "She appears faster than me, Mr. Meacham. She's already filled more than a page."

She heard Peter's exhale of irritation behind her, but catching her father's attention with news usually deflected his anger. She'd used the technique for years.

Jock thrust his hands into his pockets and jingled coins. "Okay, how many men?" He nodded to Hodges. "Take this down."

Claire wrote the answer on her pad. "The bobby said hundreds, maybe even thousands, enlisted this morning in both the British Expeditionary Forces and the Royal Navy. Featuring men from every walk of British life, many had been up all night celebrating the declaration of war. Some carried the effects of a night spent drinking, while others were sober and quiet at the enormity of their action."

"Stick to facts," Jock growled.

"Suffragettes manned tables at the base of Lord Nelson's column in Trafalgar Square. Transport crowded the streets as men answered their king's call to enlist in the BEF."

"By Jove, the young woman's a reporter," said a journalist seated not far away.

"She's learned from the best," Peter muttered.

"Here's the final question," her father said. "What happens inside Scotland Yard when a man enlists?"

Claire's mouth dropped open. She'd not thought of the question and certainly wouldn't have been allowed into Scotland Yard to find out. "He's examined by physicians," she said slowly.

Jock crossed his arms. "Hard to get the full story when you're not the right type of reporter, isn't it?"

She blinked rapidly, not sure where to look.

"The enlistee has to be at least five foot, three inches tall and between the ages of eighteen and thirty-eight," Peter said. "He's asked to sign up for a specific time period and often joins with his mates. Edward Henley and I went to enlist this morning. We wanted to serve together. Thanks to you that won't be possible."

The two men glared at each other. "Give Hodges your notes, Claire. He'll finish the job you started."

"But I've written it in shorthand," Claire said. "I should do this myself."

"You can read Pittman shorthand, can't you Hodges?" Jock asked. "Take Miss Meacham's notes and type them up."

Claire tore out the pages with a savage rip and thrust them at Hodges.

"Thank you," he said. "Will you review them so I can be sure I understand your hand?"

Hope flared and Claire lifted her head high.

"Quickly, Claire. Hodges has a job to do. Join us in the hall." Jock propelled Peter out the door.

Smelling of sweat and typewriter ribbon, Hodges had ink-stained square fingers. "I've been here all night," he apologized. "I'll be more confident of my accuracy if we go over your notes first."

He made several notations as she read. "You're very fast. Did you work as a stenographer in America?"

Claire shook her head. "I took down lectures in college. Writing notes verbatim helped me learn better."

"So I've heard. Were you at a women's college?"

"Radcliffe for three years, up until June." Disappointment at not finishing jabbed Claire yet again.

"War has a way of changing everyone's plans," Hodges said. "Thanks for your help."

Claire stepped toward the exit.

"Let me open the door for you," said a clear tenor voice with a different accent. "Nigel Bentley-Smith. I knew Peter at Oxford."

"So he said." Claire had to look up to him. "You're a copyboy?"

"At the present. Tell Peter I'll call at Belgravia soon. Magnificent trick with your hair and note taking. Very impressive." He opened the office door with a flourish.

Claire nodded at the handsome man with turquoise eyes and slipped out, mystified at his attention.

In the hallway, Jock lectured Peter. "An adult doesn't abandon his widowed mother and debutante sister without having a plan in place."

"I want to serve with Edward."

"If Henley is such a good friend, he can wait for you. The first men who enlist end up in the meat grinder. Take your time. If you're so keen on flying, get more training. The Germans aren't playing; they're shooting real weapons and many soldiers will die."

"You're an American, you can't understand."

"I grew up hearing my father's stories of the War Between the States. I covered the Spanish-American War. I know what happens when weapons are used. It's not pretty and this war isn't going to be over soon. You've plenty of time to get yourself killed; make sure your mother and sister are taken care of before you do so."

Claire stomped up to them. "How can you be so cruel?"

"You studied history; you know what's happened in Europe. Do you believe this war will be concluded quickly?"

"No."

"And what was that stunt in the office?" Jock demanded. "I sent you to find Peter, not interview people on the street."

Claire couldn't meet his eyes.

Jock's voice softened. "Thank you for your observations. We'll use them, but the newsroom is no place for a refined young woman." He touched her fallen hair. "Especially one as pretty as you. I can't have you distracting my copyboys."

"I meant to help, Papa."

Jock lifted her chin. "You did. Boston needs the news and I need to get it to them. See you at the house."

The door slammed shut behind him.

"That wasn't nearly as bad as running the boat aground," Peter said.

Claire pushed the elevator call button. Maybe not for Peter, but Jock had squelched her hopes.

Except, she thought as the lift eased up, she had plenty of time. The war had only just started.

Chapter Three

August 1914

Uncle Henry had left behind a muddle of business affairs and complex banking arrangements when he'd drowned last January. Starting August 6, Peter applied himself to the complicated task of winding up his father's estate. Every morning he packed up a briefcase, put on a bowler hat and strode out the door determined to resolve matters with the barristers as quickly as possible.

His mother, Anne's older sister, Sarah, thanked Jock for taking Peter in hand.

He lit his pipe. "Young people need a purpose. Peter simply needed to be redirected."

Why didn't her father think the same thing about Claire's empty days? When she volunteered to take notes at Peter's appointments, she'd been dismissed with an indulgent pat on the head like a pet dog.

"What's my purpose, then?" she asked. "What am I doing here?"

Jock laughed. "Why would a history major in London need to ask that question? If nothing else, get a reading card to the British Library. I'm sure your mother can come up with ways to fill your time." He banged out the door.

Claire grit her teeth.

A month after arriving in London, the Meacham women were still trying to find their role in Aunt Sarah's snowy-white three-story mansion facing Belgravia Square. With a bevy of servants awaiting orders, Anne and Claire had few responsibilities in the polished marble house filled with thick Turkish rugs, heavy velvet curtains, and the hush of loss.

Anne spent most days closeted with her only sibling, who mourned her husband with Victorian severity. Aunt Sarah's dayroom was a shrine of photographs, heavily scented flowers, and baskets of handwork. Sarah knit, wrote letters, and listened to her sister read aloud—when Anne wasn't urging her to get out and reclaim her life.

Claire sought refuge in Uncle Henry's library, still smelling of his cigars and brandy, the glassed-in shelves stuffed with leather volumes. His grand desk sat unused, the globe unspun, but the welcoming sofa and excellent lighting invited diligence. Claire practiced her shorthand, wrote up her diary, and read every newspaper and periodical that entered the house.

The rest of the time left Claire with her cousin Sylvia, a pert twenty-one-year-old debutante with precise diction and fashionable clothing. Oblivious to the war and busy arranging social events, Sylvia zeroed in on Claire's twenty-year-old flaws immediately.

"I know you've spent most of your life in dreary libraries," Sylvia murmured one morning at breakfast, "but my dressmakers can take you in hand. Clothing is more elegant in Britain; your Boston togs simply won't do."

Claire seldom felt comfortable in posh clothes requiring geometric precision to close properly. She preferred simple garments that didn't hamper her long limbs.

"Thank you for your suggestions," Anne broke in before Sylvia listed Claire's social failings yet again, "but we need to see how the war proceeds before we purchase new clothing."

Sylvia's delicate eyebrows contracted. "Indeed."

She shared Anne and Sarah's golden hair and liked to open her sapphire eyes wide in feigned innocence. Always garbed in finery designed to emphasize her long neck and slim figure, Sylvia sauntered through life in a cloud of French perfume.

Claire spent a lot of time at her side failing to be a good sport.

As the second week of war ended, Aunt Sarah was presiding over the lavish breakfast table when Jock hurried in to grab a meal. He'd been reporting nearly round the clock for a fortnight; dark circles bagged under his eyes. "I need to leave, Anne."

His wife insisted on a full breakfast but understood him well. "Claire, hand your father what he craves."

Claire provided the morning's papers. She rose early to read and mark the most significant news in red ink before a housemaid ironed the pages flat.

Jock chuckled. "I love a woman who understands what's important." He winked at Anne and opened the *Times* as he tucked into breakfast—two fried eggs, salted kippers, a baked tomato, and buttered toast.

Sylvia tapped the top of her hard-boiled egg with a sterling spoon while Anne poured tea from a Wedgewood teapot. The butler and a maid came with hot crumpets, the mail, and impeccable service, and then left.

"How is life at the office, Papa?" Claire sipped tea fortified the English way with milk.

"Madcap, the copyboys run all day long. I'm down to two and Hodges hurt his right hand."

Hope soared in a flurry, but she kept her voice casual. "Do you need help?"

He stopped chewing. Her parents studied each other a moment too long. Jock shook his head, Anne raised her eyebrows. He sighed. "How fast do you take shorthand, Claire?"

Her heart leapt. "One hundred seventy-five words a minute."

"So fast?"

Jock drummed the white damask tablecloth with his fingers. "Conroy will oppose your presence, but I don't see how else to get the cable out to Boston on time. I've lost reporters too. All I can offer is a front-row seat on history in the making and hours of dictation and typing."

"I'd love to."

"I don't know, Jock," Anne said. "Is the newsroom a proper place for your daughter?"

"I've been in newsrooms lots of times," Claire protested.

Jock snorted. "She'll be working for me, not hunting a husband." He turned to his sister-in-law. "I've lost half my copyboys to the army. How will society treat Claire if she joins me in the newsroom?"

Aunt Sarah pursed her lips. "This would help the war effort?"

"You're not a suffragette, are you?" Sylvia sneered.

Claire's mind whirled as she tried to devise the best answer for the most people sitting at the table. "I could free a man to fight."

"She'll be safe with Jock," Aunt Sarah said, "but could you manage without her, Anne?"

Anne picked up her teacup. "You run your home so beautifully; I believe Claire will be more useful helping Jock, as long as she's discreet."

Jock pointed at the clock. "We're leaving in ten minutes, Claire. Put on a plain garment—your female presence will be distraction enough without frivolous clothing."

Claire ran.

An indignant and overruled Mr. Conroy assigned Claire the desk between Nigel and Jim Hodges. "If you have questions, ask them. For the record, no flirting will be tolerated in this office. You serve your father, no one else, and I don't think you belong here." He stalked away.

"A princess joins the peasants." Nigel leaned back in his chair.

Claire smoothed down her shirtwaist's long white sleeves. "Hardly."

"I'm glad you're here," Jim said. "We need help. Do you type?"

The boxy black Underwood sat square in the middle of the oak desk, a basket of fresh paper beside it. Claire set her leather satchel in the bottom drawer. "Yes, though I'm better at shorthand."

"Good. Your father talks fast and he has a thick accent," Nigel said.

"We don't have an accent."

A cheeky grin. "Guess again, Yank. Jim is just as bad."

Jock called her into his office, closed the door, and indicated a straight-backed chair. "Take this down."

Jock described a meeting the night before with the First Lord of the Admiralty Winston Churchill. Claire easily kept up. When he pulled out scribbled notes from his pocket, she snickered. "You expect me to read this?"

He sighed. "I obviously need help. It's helpful to have an American who understands Boston's culture and interests."

Claire grinned.

Jock smiled back. "But don't forget, Conroy's watching. You don't want to cross him."

Claire avoided the city editor as much as possible as the days passed, and she took dictation, transcribed notes, argued with Jock's theories, and typed. She focused on her yellow pencil and tried not to picture the scenes as her father crafted his stories. Soldiers wearing spiked helmets marched into villages and billeted in civilian homes. As the guns roared across fields ripe for harvest, birds vanished and the smell of hot bullets singed the air. Casualties mounted in appalling numbers.

Her stomach knotted as she sharpened her pencils with her late Grandfather's silver pen knife. Sometimes the inky scent of the silk typewriter ribbon provoked nausea.

Jim Hodges stopped beside her one afternoon. "Are you feeling okay, Miss Meacham?"

"I tell myself to act like a machine, not a person. If I don't picture what the words describe, I can do my job." Her hands trembled.

"Perhaps the mechanics of it," he said. "But I pray you never lose your heart or your desire to know the truth."

"Is that possible?" Claire snapped the knife shut and dropped it into her bag. "The facts are repellant."

"But they're part of the job." Nigel lit a cigarette and blew out pungent smoke. "People need to know the truth about what's happening on the battlefield."

Jim crossed his arms. "Whatsoever things are true, whatsoever things are honest, whatsoever things are just, think on these things."

"How do you do that in a war?" Nigel muttered.

Claire tried to remember where she'd heard Jim's quote. "That sounds like a journalist's creed, hunting for the story."

"It serves the purpose." Jim restacked the papers on his desk.

"Such an interesting question." Nigel rolled a fresh piece of paper into the typewriter. "What is truth?"

"Pilate's question was cynical," Jim said. "He didn't want to know the truth."

Nigel raised an eyebrow. "Pilate preferred propaganda. Like the Huns."

Claire watched their verbal sparring with interest. The term copy*boys* did not describe Jim and Nigel. Unlike the teenagers who worked at the Boston BNS offices, they were mature men in their twenties batting issues and vocabulary between each other. She relished their arguments, thankful to be discussing meaningful events with knowledgeable men, rather than enduring Sylvia's endless chatter about haute couture.

"You must have reporter instincts in your blood," Nigel said. "What was it like to grow up with such a father?"

"Never a dull moment!" Claire laughed. "I've learned many tricks from Jock Meacham."

"Too right?" Nigel's New Zealand drawl teased. "Can you pull a rabbit out of your hat?"

She'd never received much attention from young men and certainly not from one as dashing as Nigel. Claire gave a brief thought to how Sylvia would respond.

It didn't matter. She wasn't allowed to flirt, even if she'd known how.

Mr. Conroy's eyebrows came together as he looked in her direction.

"You're not answering," Nigel said. "Do you need a hat?"

She picked up her pencil as an answer popped into her mind. "It's one of the oldest reporter tricks. You remain silent and wait for your interviewee to blurt out information. Thanks for providing a demonstration."

"Touché." Nigel stubbed out his cigarette and resumed typing; the key's *rat-a-tat* beat a healthy rhythm broken only by the mechanical zip of the paper carriage.

"Hodges and Claire, come in here," Jock shouted from his office door. Claire grabbed her notepad and pencil. She noticed Jim's untucked shirttail as they entered the office.

"Were you here all night, Hodges?" Jock asked.

"Yes."

"You've been working hard and the news should be quiet for a few hours." He held out a thick envelope. I want you to take this to Lord Northcliffe at the *Times*, his eyes only."

He'd been complaining about the British news censors all week.

"What are you up to?" Claire asked.

"We need to band together and figure out how to get meaningful information," Jock said.

He eyed Hodges. "After you're done there, take a couple hours off for a break. I'm sending Claire with you so she'll get some fresh air. I'm headed to Whitehall to meet with officials."

"But—" Claire sputtered.

"Conroy won't tolerate you in the office without me. I'll need you when I return from this appointment."

Claire leaned close to whisper. "Don't you know what this looks like?"

Jock crossed his arms. "Perhaps you'd rather sit alone in the tearoom at the Savoy Hotel?"

She touched her throat as she tried to fathom the social impropriety.

"Hodges, can I trust you to escort my daughter without any designs?"

Heat coursed through Claire. "But—"

"My intentions are always good, sir," Jim replied. "Perhaps we can tour the National Gallery of Art afterwards? We could inquire about their plans for the war."

"Fine, but no questions. You're not reporters. That good enough for you, Claire?"

"Miss Meacham can ignore me if she prefers." Jim's dark eyes crinkled at the corners.

This was getting worse.

She'd noticed Jim's helpful attitude in the newsroom. While Nigel teased her for not knowing how to replace a messy typewriter ribbon, Jim did it without a word. Maybe he'd regard this as another such task. "I'll go."

"Good. Get some air and see some art." Jock checked his newest prize, a watch strapped to his wrist. "Be back by three o'clock. The censors aren't going to pass us anything before then. They take a long lunch at their clubs."

"I'll get my coat." Jim left the office.

"I don't trust that Nigel—he watches you too much—but Hodges is harmless." Jock pulled a gold sovereign from his pocket. "Take a cab to the museum. That'll put Hodges in his place."

Claire accepted the heavy coin and collected her satchel and hat.

The late summer sun beat down when they exited onto Fleet Street and the city smells of oil and horse droppings assaulted the nose. Honking taxis and rumbling horse-drawn transport rattled past while Londoners filled the sidewalk. Three young men in new uniforms strutted before them, bragging in cracking voices of their plans for the German army.

"Everyone wants to go to war." Claire clasped her straw hat to her head as a breeze threatened to steal it. "How about you?"

"This isn't my war."

"Do you plan to enlist?"

Jim helped a woman's perambulator over a rut in the pavement. "No."

"What if America joined the fighting?"

"No."

They reached the *Times* building a dozen doors down the street and were ushered directly into Lord Northcliffe's office. The elder statesman of British journalism scowled. "Why didn't Meacham come himself if this was so important? Why send a chit of a girl and a grubby—what are you? A copyboy? And Americans both? Aren't British men good enough for the Boston News Syndicate?"

"They all joined the BEF. I'm taking a spot so a man can fight," Claire stuttered.

"A woman in the newsroom?" Northcliffe grabbed the envelope, scanned the note, and shook his head. "This doesn't even justify a formal response. Inform Meacham we trust the generals; they'll tell us what we need to know."

"Are they giving you the full story?" Claire asked. "Reporters need at least two sources."

He looked down his aristocratic nose at her. "We are in a battle for our lives, miss. I don't need an American girl telling me how to report our war. Improper information can be deadly."

"But if other countries think you're distorting the truth, they might question what else you're not reporting correctly. You could undermine the whole effort if you limit information." Claire couldn't believe she had to remind him of basic journalism ethics.

Northcliffe turned red and blustered, "You don't know what you're talking about!"

Jim spoke calmly. "I believe Miss Meacham is appealing to your sense of honor, sir."

"Both of you, get out of here. I could shut down the BNS for such an effrontery."

Jim tugged her away as the secretary slammed the door in her face

"This is not responsible journalism." Claire clutched her fists and stared at the door.

"I didn't realize you were a reporter," Jim said.

"Not yet, but my grandfather once owned the BNS and I've heard stories from him and my father. The British government's censorship is wrong."

"Perhaps they don't have a choice. England is not a democracy." Sweat beaded Jim's brow. "The press may not be so free."

Claire's mind whirled as she replayed the conversation. That fat old man wasn't a journalist; he'd become an army stooge. She touched her lips. She hadn't said that, had she? What would Jock say?

And what about Mr. Conroy?

Claire's stomach clenched. She had been rude and should have just delivered the message. But Northcliffe was wrong in choosing to side with the government. Her mother would have expected her to be more judicious when addressing a lord. Claire bit her lip. "Don't tell Mr. Conroy what I said."

"Certainly not. Shall we go on?"

Claire stopped at the street corner and pulled a London map from her bag.

Jim peered over her shoulder. "A clever way to learn the city."

"The only way, so far. I've money; my father said to call a cab."

He scrutinized her, then stepped to the street and raised his hand. She couldn't meet his eye, at the slight. Her stomach would not stop churning

The National Gallery of Art shimmered like a palace in the sunlight, but Claire remained distracted. They silently climbed the stairs through Corinthian columns guarding the entrance.

Jim's steps quickened. "Look who's here."

They met a welcoming couple at the entry. The youthful woman of medium height had merry blue eyes and wore her soft brown hair brushed into wings over her ears. "We missed you this morning, Jim."

"I spent the night with the telegraph. I've been given a reprieve for a few hours. May I introduce my colleague?"

Claire stood taller at his description and held her chin higher.

"This is Miss Claire Meacham. Claire, may I present Biddy Chambers and her husband, Reverend Oswald Chambers."

Claire shook the pretty woman's hand and tried to be polite as she turned to the tall, lanky man beside her. First a run-in with an officious lord and now a clergyman. Could the day get any worse?

Reverend Chambers wore a white clergyman's collar against his black suit, a genial smile crossing his thin face. Fawn-colored hair waved back from his high forehead, but what she noticed most were his deep-set marine-blue eyes. Amusement enlivened his features and he stretched out his hand. "Are you the new American with the excellent stenography skills?" His voice carried a lilt of Scotland.

"How do you know who I am?" Claire asked.

Jim colored. "Oswald is the principal of the college I attend. I told them how well you take dictation since Biddy is also a stenographer. She's faster than you."

Biddy laughed.

Claire didn't believe him. "How fast do you take down, Mrs. Chambers?"

"Fast enough."

"Two hundred fifty words a minute," Jim said.

Claire stared. "Faster than people speak?"

"And sometimes necessary for me if I start to ramble," Reverend Chambers said. "We're here to tour the gallery, would you care to join us?"

"May we?" Jim asked. "I know you're familiar with the paintings."

Claire sighed. She knew few clergymen besides the ones she'd heard preach in Boston and at glorious St. Paul's Cathedral in London. An Anglican like most of her set with only a perfunctory knowledge of the Bible, she couldn't imagine how a clergyman would react to art. "We don't want to bother you."

"We're here to see our favorites in case the gallery closes again with the war," Reverend Chambers said. "Join us. We'll start with this one."

Exactly as Claire expected, *The Mystic Nativity* by Sandro Botticelli featured Mary and Joseph, Jesus, and barnyard animals. A myriad of angels—several on the crèche's roof—cluttered the painting.

Reverend Chambers laughed, "This was one of John Ruskin's favorites. The name comes from his comment about its mystic symbolism."

"You've read Ruskin?" Surprised by the clergyman's reference to an art critic and not the Bible, Claire instinctively reached for her notebook and pencil.

"Go ahead," Jim whispered. "Oswald's a teacher."

Reverend Chambers described the history of the painting and the religious issues in Italy at the time. She'd only vaguely heard of Savonarola and jotted down the name for further investigation.

"Some of these concepts might be new to you," Oswald said. "I find it helps to brood on the unknown and let it sit it in your soul. It's particularly helpful for me when I struggle with Bible passages."

How novel, Claire thought, a clergyman who admits he doesn't always understand the Bible. She followed him with surprising interest as he moved to the next painting.

Claire recognized specific details when he explained them and pretended she understood their importance. After a half-dozen, she could contain her question no longer. "How do you know all this?"

"I trained at London's Royal Academy before sensing God's direction to be an ambassador for Christ. I like to sketch. And you?"

"I'm not artistic, though I've played the piano."

"I play the organ. It's wonderful to praise our creator with our artistic abilities, don't you think?"

Claire squirmed. "I've never considered it. What about you, Mrs. Chambers?"

"Call me Biddy. I leave the art to Oswald. I wanted to be secretary to the prime minister of England. That's why I studied shorthand."

Claire stared at her. The woman smiled and raised an eyebrow. "You?"

"To help me with my work," she said slowly.

"That's exactly what Biddy does," Reverend Chambers said. "We're a team. She takes down my words, runs the college and prays. We'd accomplish nothing without her."

"We all know prayer is the greater work," Biddy said and nudged her husband toward the next gallery.

They continued through the galleries, chatting easily. Oswald wasn't necessarily drawn to religious art, though

Jim gazed for a long time at a painting of Pilate confronting Jesus.

Caught up in the insightful explanations, Claire lost track of time. When an ornate clock chimed three, she gasped. "We're late!" They scurried to catch a cab to the office.

"You're late," Jock growled at their return, "but so are the censors. Why are your cheeks red, Claire?" He glared at Jim.

With her mind energized by Reverend Chambers' descriptions, Claire struggled to put into words what she'd learned. "We met a man who taught me how to look at the world differently."

"The world or paintings?" Jock lit his pipe.

"Does it matter?"

He puffed several times, watching her. "It very well could."

Chapter Four

The war came home at Sunday's luncheon on September 6. Seated beside Peter at the grand table decorated with lavish roses, Claire noticed her cousin barely touched the savory roasted beef and Yorkshire pudding. His right leg jiggled, and then he knocked over his water glass. "What's wrong?" she whispered.

Across the table, Jock divided his time between watching the clock and eyeing Peter.

"The office will call with breaking news," Anne reminded him. "It won't hurt to take an afternoon off. You're far too high-strung."

"There's a war on, Anne."

Claire passed her cousin the horseradish. "When will you finish with the barristers?"

He thumped down the crystal bowl. "I signed the final papers on Thursday. Mr. Black will oversee the business and Mummy and Sylvia's needs. Father's estate is in competent hands until I return at war's end." He pushed back the Louis XIV chair and stood. "Mummy, I've been commissioned into the Royal Flying Corps. I leave next week."

Aunt Sarah crumpled.

Anne went to her side. "Oh, Sarah."

Jock bolted up. "You fool. Lord Kitchener believes this war will last for years. You could have waited until they developed planes capable of crossing the Channel without fear of crashing. You didn't need to rush out and enlist."

"If you knew the value of aerial surveillance you'd be glad blokes like me are willing to take a chance and fly as soon as possible. All my friends have joined up. I'm practically the last one."

"You, the heir, are putting yourself at risk!" Anne cried.

"I have to go. Mummy, surely you understand?"

Aunt Sarah's native American accent overcame her cultivated British. "I'll never understand."

Sylvia rang the bell for the next course.

"I knew there'd be a scene. Why aren't you saying anything, Sylvia?" Peter gulped from his wine glass.

"I have good news. Edward and I are engaged. Finding my trousseau should take your mind off war, Mama. Claire can be my bridesmaid."

Aunt Sarah dropped her handkerchief.

"You want me?" Claire squeaked.

"It will need to be a small affair. If we put up your hair and lace you tight, you'll do. I'll take care of your dress."

Aunt Sarah's bewilderment vied with hope. "Peter cannot leave until the wedding."

"I start next week, Mummy. You can't control the army." Peter looked at Sylvia. "When did this happen?"

Sylvia displayed a diamond-encircled finger, facets glinting in the light. "Last night before he returned to camp; I thought a Christmas wedding. Will you attend?"

"God knows," he muttered.

"A better question is, will Edward?" Jock said.

Peter stormed away. His mother hurried after.

God knows.

Claire pondered Peter's remark as she prowled the garden behind her aunt's mansion. The morning's sermon at St. Paul's had been full of martial ardor, as if the Anglican bishop in showy robes recruited for the BEF. The mix of war and religion made her uneasy. German ministers must be preaching a similar message.

And now Peter would be a target in the sky.

Claire shuddered and searched the gray clouds for a ray of sunlight.

"Are you brooding, darling?" Jock stood on the granite steps, pipe in hand.

Reverend Chambers had used the identical term at the art gallery, advising her to consider an idea from different angles and see how it set. "Yes."

"You know the antidote. Collect the facts. Examine them. Apply information you know. Draw your own conclusions. What's worrying you? Peter?"

Claire touched the soft petals of her aunt's favorite pink rose and breathed in the heavenly scent. "I wonder what God makes of the war and why Peter wants to fight."

"What did you decide?"

"Leaders' evil hearts cause war." The daily news confirmed Claire's opinion. "Usually based on covetousness, surely war is greed on an international stage."

"Bah. The Serbs have been picking fights for years. Germany's helping them."

"Whose side is God on?" Even as she asked the question, Claire cringed. Rulers always invoked God's name to rally their troops. But the readings she'd heard that morning made Claire wonder if the God who loved justice, mercy, and humility wouldn't prefer one side, particularly when one nation invaded another.

Jock puffed on his pipe, a weedy scent in a florid garden. "I don't believe it works that way. Both sides call on the Almighty to advance their arguments. I'm not sure God, if one exists, cares."

"Of course he cares."

Jock pointed the pipe stem at her. "Show me the evidence. All I see are monarchs determined to fight. I don't see any God stopping them."

"Today's sermon implied the British cause was God's." Claire scuffed her shoe on the pebbled walkway.

He set his pipe on the banister and rubbed his eyes. "Religion provides solace for the ignorant; you can't mix it with political events. Simple people ask a priest, often the only educated person around, to explain events outside their control. It's a crutch; they're afraid. You don't need religion. You're a thinking girl who understands how the world functions."

"Do I?" In contrast to what she knew of battlefields, the garden throbbed with life: bees buzzed the flowers, ants prowled the path, and butterflies fluttered fragile wings.

"Don't be ridiculous. We go to church to be seen, not brainwashed." Jock's pipe smoke drifted. "Are you afraid, darling?"

Not two hundred fifty miles away, men waited for nightfall and a sky lit with aerial barrages. Peter would fly over the trenches eventually. His and other soldiers' souls teetered on eternity. Trying to make sense of the enormous casualties Jock suspected and wasn't allowed to report, Claire needed answers to quiet her own fluttering soul.

"If no God exists, where is Uncle Henry? What will happen to Peter if he's shot from the sky?" She whispered the forbidden question. "Where are my brothers?"

Jock stepped away, his eyebrows flexed with rage. "How dare you! Don't ever mention the boys to your mother. We can't endure her grief again."

Claire stepped on the line of ants and watched the survivors scatter. "There must be something beyond this life. I don't want to fear dying, so I need to know what will happen in eternity. How can you survive a war if you don't believe in God?"

He shrugged and looked away. A church bell tolled.

She bit her salty lip. "I need to be sure my life has purpose."

"Stick with me, darling," Jock finally said. "You don't need a God crutch. The BNS and I need your shorthand abilities. Your life won't be lived in vain, trust me."

She'd trusted him her whole life, but these days life seemed as delicate as an airplane wing and as easily ended as a footstep.

Claire no longer thought her father possessed all the answers. She'd need to find them for herself.

Chapter Five

She'd pondered the question all evening, unable to sleep for worry about Peter. Once assignments were set Monday at the office and Mr. Conroy had disappeared on an errand, Claire asked the two most likely to have an answer.

"Why do men enlist in the army?"

Jim straightened papers and cleared his throat. "To protect their families and homeland."

Nigel stared at his typewriter, his face a mask, his voice without inflection. "A man enlists because he has no choice. His nation demands it of him; his father suggests he's unworthy if he does not; and strangers bedevil him for cowardice. A man volunteers for a hundred reasons; few of them good."

Claire removed her glasses. "Are you enlisting?"

"You can't escape the army when you're twenty-three years old and your country is at war. You can only hope your intelligence lands you in a safe spot. How about you, Jim?"

"This is not America's war."

"You could join up anyway." Nigel reached for a cigarette; his eyes defiant.

Jim shook his head gently. "No."

"Why not?"

"No."

Nigel batted away the word with his lit cigarette and returned to the typewriter, pounding the keys with vigor.

Claire polished her glasses, uneasy, and turned to her notes: *who, what, when, where, why, how?* She'd spouted the questions since babyhood. According to what she'd just heard, young men felt obligated to enlist. This article for Jock provided information as to where: Scotland Yard; and how to apply. Recruitment posters hung everywhere in London, including one with a drawing of Lord Kitchener pointing a thick finger: "We want you!"

Jock had told her to rearrange and type the notes into related paragraphs. He'd mark up the copy with thick blue pencil and return it to Claire to fashion his arrows and circles into a coherent draft. Once done, he'd edit, pass it to Mr. Conroy, and shout for Jim to take it to the telegraph operator. He seldom reexamined a story after the second review.

"You enjoying the job?" Jock asked as he read her work on the recruitment story.

"I love it."

A quick grin. "Maybe your grandfather was correct; reporting is in the Meacham blood. You've done a good job organizing these facts. I've little to add."

A flush of pride. "Did you wait to write this until after Peter enlisted?"

"Yes. I saw no reason to help him make a bad decision."

She flinched at his tone. "But now you're providing information for others?"

Jock pulled out his pipe. "They're all cannon fodder; only the clever understand that. Still, the BNS wants to know what life is like over here. This story will tell them." He struck out a line. "My readers don't need Scotland Yard's address or hours; they're in Boston."

He touched the pencil tip to a sentence. "We'll see if the censor lets that one through." He scribbled "30" at the bottom, signifying "the end."

When she returned with the censored version two hours later—Jim had telegraphed it to the War Office, and they had sent it to their censors, who edited and returned it to the London BNS office—the line had been rejected.

"Now we know," Jock mused. "The censors don't like, 'War hysteria is like a sickness.' No surprise, they're all retired military officers. Remember how they rejected the Quaker story last week?"

"You think that was Lord Northcliffe's doing?"

He shook his head. "Northcliffe's in bed with the government and the army. He won't cross them, and if I get too close, he'll throw me out of the country. So I work the odd angles and Boston will get some news."

Jock always sought both sides of a story. It bothered him reporters only heard grotesque propaganda about the Kaiser's army. "Dastardly though it was to march into neutral Belgium, does it make sense an advancing army stopped to commit civilian atrocities?"

"Didn't that happen in our Civil War?" Claire asked.

"It became a tool to subdue the population later in the war when supplies were limited. This is the opening salvo." He leaned back his chair, put his long legs on the desk, and considered the colorful European map on the wall.

Three days earlier Brad O'Brien, a journalist friend, had dropped by and rearranged the pins on Jock's map. In his opinion, the Germans were headed to Paris. O'Brien returned to the United States with a letter from Jock to his boss, Josiah Fischer, detailing the censorship issues.

Now Claire asked, "Can you trust Mr. O'Brien's information?"

Jock nodded at the map. "Does anything else make sense to you?" He tapped his pipe on the desk. "Northcliffe says war is good business for newspapers because it not only creates a supply of news, but a demand."

"He's a fool."

Jock grunted. "You were rude to him, even if you were right. We can't afford to get on the wrong side of his office, so you won't go there again. I'm just glad you weren't talking to Conroy or you would have forfeited this job."

She moved to the window overlooking Fleet Street. News sellers stood on the corner hawking their papers. *WAR* screamed in such large bold letters above the fold she could read it from the third floor. "Can you call it news if you don't get the full story?"

He barked a laugh. "How can anyone get the facts sitting at a desk? When I interviewed Churchill, he pontificated, 'The war is going to be fought in a fog. The best place for correspondents will be in London.' He covered the Boer War for the *Morning Post*; he should know better."

"What will you do?" Claire used her fingers to calculate the distance between London and France on the map. Only the English Channel separated Dover from Calais twenty-five miles away.

"Fischer cabled this morning. He wants me in northeastern France tomorrow. We need real information instead of this nonsense the censors peddle. You can't come, obviously, and Conroy won't have you here."

Her heart sank. "What will I do?"

Jock rustled in his desk for pipe paraphernalia. "Make sure Peter gets off in good order."

She shut her eyes. "Of course."

A lit match, four puffs on his pipe, and his mood rallied. "Bandage roll with Sylvia, learn to knit socks, visit schools and meetings, admire art, and chat with the people you meet."

"By myself?"

"Just attend social events. Don't go anywhere dangerous. Check out Jim's college, for example. He's traveled a long way. What's the attraction? Keep your eyes and ears open wherever you go. Be careful if you attend a suffragette meeting; we don't want you to get arrested."

"Suffragettes? What are you asking me to do?"

"Take notes, of course." He lowered his voice. "It's time for you to learn how to spy like your mother. The best leads often come from innocent sources who don't realize the importance of what they've told us."

The sultry summer gave way to London's traditional gloom and rain as Peter packed his kit, kissed the womenfolk good-bye, and journeyed to the Salisbury Plain not far from Stonehenge.

Eleven years after the American Wright brothers first flew an airplane, the Royal Flying Corps was but a fledgling branch of the British army. They boasted only one hundred planes at the start of the war but were working hard to remedy that deficit. Before departing, Peter invested family funds in the Aircraft Manufacturing Company, Limited. "If the war goes on as long as Uncle Jock predicts, we could make a lot of money."

Dread as heavy as a sandbag weighed on Claire whenever she thought of Peter. The muddy conditions, limited visibility, and pilots flying without parachutes made his survival odds unthinkable. Claire didn't worry about her father tramping through France in search of a story. With his larger-than-life character, Jock could survive anything.

Pursuing a story had always been her father's salvation. Maybe it would be for Claire too. Setting a stylish hat borrowed from her cousin on her head and with her mind alert to potential story ideas, she joined Sylvia and her smart set of friends to roll bandages for the war effort.

The half-dozen women gathered around a long polished table in a sumptuous dining room hung with portraits of ancestors. Claire would have liked to inspect the paintings, but she'd come for a purpose. "Show me what to do."

"Wash your hands in the basin, stand at the end of the table and roll away," Sylvia said. She and a young woman dressed in similar layers of fine silk giggled together. Claire smoothed her hands down what she'd come to regard as her uniform: a white shirtwaist tucked into a black skirt and sensible shoes.

Four inches wide and the length of the banquet table, the soft, white, gauze-thin muslin rolled up easily. Claire wound the cloth as tight as possible, the strip slowly moving down the table in her direction. She tied off the three-inch thick cylinder with a piece of twine and started on the next long piece of muslin. Sylvia and her four friends worked at the table: two cutting the fabric into lengths, two laying it straight on the table and one joining Claire to roll.

The pace was leisurely, the conversation tedious: new officers ordering expensive tailored uniforms, questions about the coming season, whether silk would be hard to procure. Before she'd finished the fifth bandage roll, Claire knew she'd not return. Her notebook listed one question: "Do Sylvia's friends have any meaningful ways to spend their time?"

Their frivolity galled her when she thought about Peter daily risking his life to fly flimsy wooden biplanes.

At the other end of the spectrum, the hearty suffragettes were determined to help the war effort any way possible. A dozen women of varying ages rolled the immense pile of muslin in an hour, all the while debating how to get the vote before war's end. Far more educated than Sylvia's set, they applauded Claire for holding a job.

Of course the only reason she could attend the meeting was Conroy's refusal to allow her in the newsroom, Claire thought bitterly. Claire avoided personal questions, but the suffragettes fueled her determination to earn a byline as a bona fide reporter, no matter what her parents thought. Attending meetings such as these and writing up notes afterwards was part of her training. She'd win over her father by demonstrating her skills.

Knitting with Aunt Sarah went nowhere. "I don't understand why you can take shorthand, but keep tangling the yarn," Aunt Sarah said.

"I can't knit either," Anne said.

"You've never been patient," Sarah told her sister. "You're much better at the card table."

Anne winked at Claire. "Exactly. I serve my husband better by spying on the wives of powerful men in social gatherings."

"Be careful," Aunt Sarah said. "A word like *spy* could get you into trouble these days."

"Fact-finding," Anne declared. "That's what I'm doing, though Clemmy Churchill doesn't reveal much at the bridge table."

The two women shook their heads over the suffragette meeting. "I doubt the BNS would be interested in their ideas. Have you become a radical?" Anne teased.

"They make sense. Women should use their talents. I'm as competent in the newsroom as Nigel and Jim. Why shouldn't I work? War causes social upheaval, often for good reason."

"I wouldn't let your stenography skills go to your head." Anne pulled a crocheted shawl onto her shoulders. "Men aren't interested in professional women."

Claire shook her head. "That's immaterial for me right now."

"Don't you want to get married and have a family?"

"Yes." Claire sighed. "But I want adventure before I settle down, like you and Papa."

"We traveled through Europe together. Find a husband and you can do it too."

She echoed her father. "There's a war on, Mama."

"All the better way to meet one, then." Her heartiness faded into reflection. "Though I'd rather you marry an American, so you'd live near us. Just don't bring one home from that Bible place or we'll have trouble."

"I'm sure they're earnest and lovely people at the Bible Training College," Aunt Sarah broke in. "Ask them to pray for Peter and Edward while you're there."

"Of course." Claire had saved Jim's college for her final fact-finding mission. While she'd known he was a religious man and the principal a clergyman, she hadn't expected to visit a Bible school.

"Your father won't be pleased." Anne opened up *David Copperfield* to read aloud.

"He told me to find out why Jim Hodges came to London from Ohio for college. It's nothing more than a spying mission."

"Why don't you just ask him and spare yourself the trip?"

"I'd like to see Reverend and Mrs. Chambers again. Our conversation at the National Gallery was the most interesting one I've had since I arrived in England."

"I beg your pardon."

"Except for talking with you, of course, Mama."

Aunt Sarah paused her knitting needles. "My friends speak well of the Bible Training College. What can go wrong at a school for missionaries? Mr. Able can drive you this evening and wait. You'll be fine."

"Indeed." Anne picked up Claire's raveled yarn to wind.

Chapter Six

Aunt Sarah's chauffeur drove the motorcar past Big Ben and the Houses of Parliament over Westminster Bridge to the south side of the Thames River. In due time, parkland appeared. "Clapham Common, miss," Mr. Able said. "The largest park in London."

They traveled a road skirting the park's north side along rows of connected five-story granite mansions hedged by fragrant cedar trees. Midway down a massive line of residences filigreed with balconies and carved stonework, Jim Hodges sat on the steps of number 45 holding a small bouquet of red carnations.

Ivy covered the lower walls and windowed doors peeked out from an arched doorway. Jim stood when Mr. Able brought the automobile to a halt. "You're welcome to join us."

"Thank you, sir," Mr. Able replied. "I brought a newspaper."

"Shall I send out tea?"

"Thank you, sir."

Jim helped Claire from the automobile and presented the posy. "To remember your visit."

She touched the spicy petals, not sure how to reply.

"My mother liked to say, 'Flowers make a memory.' I hope you'll enjoy your first lecture at the Bible Training College."

"Thank you." Suddenly uncertain about spying on a friend, Claire sought a benign remark. "This looks like a mansion, not a college."

"The League of Prayer rented it for a Bible school. Twenty-three students and I live here along with the Chambers family."

They climbed eight stone steps and entered a vestibule. The comforting scent of warm bread and soup helped soothe Claire's unease. She clutched the flowers.

A door opened on the left, and Biddy stepped into the hall. "How lovely to see you again, Miss Meacham." She pressed Claire's hand with long smooth fingers. "Did you bring your notebook? You must sit beside me at the meeting tonight, and we'll compare notes."

Reverend Chambers walked carefully down the lovely curving stairway carrying a tiny girl who reached for the vivid flowers. Claire held them out for the child to touch. She grabbed the posy.

"It's a fine night to see you again, Miss Meacham. Did you mean this for my Kathleen?

"Who can say no to Kathleen?" Jim chuckled.

"She'll be to bed soon, and we'll return it." Reverend Chambers set down his daughter, and good humor lit his craggy features all the way to his piercing, deep-set eyes. "Please—join us for tea before the lecture."

Biddy escorted them into a large dining room filled with several long tables covered in simple white cloth. Groups of adults carried on lively conversations over their meal.

Dressed in a smocked white nightgown, Kathleen toddled between diners, her fair curls bouncing. Her father spoke to everyone while the women fussed over the child.

Claire focused on her hostess. "Tell me about your name."

She folded her hands. "My parents named me Gertrude, but Oswald has a sister with the same name, so he decided to call me 'Beloved Disciple.' He soon shortened it to B.D., or Biddy."

"He likes to give us nicknames," Jim said. "I call him OC."

Biddy brought cutlery, cups and plates. "He doesn't mind."

Reverend Chambers soon joined Jim and Claire. "My entertaining Kathleen has already supped and is soon to bed. May we sit with you?"

Biddy returned with a ceramic teapot and glanced at the clock. "Twenty minutes."

"It will be enough." He set Kathleen on a chair and tied a napkin under her chin. "Just in case."

Reverend Chambers moved with deliberation as the little girl chattered and waved. Jim and Biddy retrieved bowls of soup, a loaf of brown bread, and a cup of soft butter.

Claire picked up the bread knife.

"I'm hungry as well," Reverend Chambers said. "Shall we ask the Lord's blessing?"

She clasped her hands together and bowed her head, agitated she'd missed a social cue. Her stomach growled, and she hoped grace wouldn't take long at a Bible college.

"We thank thee for the food and for our evening together. In Christ's name, amen." Reverend Chambers passed her the bread plate. "Will you cut, Miss Meacham?"

Claire focused on the task. She could slice bread.

"I love flowers on the table." Biddy took the red carnations from Kathleen and settled them into a glass of water. "They make a meal more festive. Pick them up on your way home." She poured strong, fragrant tea into a china cup for Claire.

The thick bean soup reminded Claire of her childhood suppers; happy times when manners weren't scrutinized and Jock told her stories before going out for the evening. "Your home is lovely; have you been here long?"

"The college has been in this beautiful building since 1911. We're pleased to live and serve here." Reverend Chambers offered Kathleen a bit of buttered bread. She giggled and pushed it aside.

"Excuse me, Oswald, I must ask about something you said this morning." A scrawny, middle-aged woman began a lengthy theological discourse far beyond Claire's understanding or interest. She watched the man across the table listen and wondered why his soup didn't curdle under her onslaught.

When the woman finally paused for breath, Reverend Chambers put up his hand. "I understand you are having difficulty with this concept. Leave it for now and brood on it. The answer will come to you later."

She straightened her lips into a thin line. "That's it? You won't discuss it further?"

"We should let the Holy Spirit guide you to the answer. You need to spend time comparing what you believe with what the Scriptures say."

"Only because I trust you." The woman stomped away.

"How many instructors teach at the college?" Claire touched the napkin to her lips.

"Claire may end up a reporter like her father the way she asks questions," Jim said.

She stiffened. She hadn't mentioned her reason for coming.

"Fact gatherers are important," Reverend Chambers said. "Without them truth might be missed. While we welcome guest speakers here at the school, 'tis mostly me lecturing, and I direct the correspondence course. I love to hear Biddy speak; she's particularly good with the Psalms. More soup?"

Jim stood. "I'll get it."

Claire considered her empty bowl. Sylvia insisted a woman never ask for seconds.

Biddy reached for her daughter. "I must put Kathleen to bed. The clock."

Reverend Chambers passed his bowl to Jim. "One for me, please. And you, Miss Meacham?"

"No, thank you."

The rest of the conversation revolved around art, as he described paintings he particularly enjoyed. Claire took notes for her next visit to the National Gallery.

When finished, Reverend Chambers excused himself and set his empty bowl on a tray with other used crockery.

"What's the purpose of a Bible Training College, and why are you here?" Claire asked Jim.

"The answer's the same for both: to put biblical study and a relationship with Jesus behind faith."

"So it's not blind faith?"

"Faith is built on a confident relationship with the God who can be trusted: Jesus." His eyes flashed, but he remained relaxed.

The Sunday Peter announced his enlistment crossed her mind, and she remembered her questions about eternity and God. Claire squirmed. Peter would be at risk as long as the war raged. The need for answers hadn't diminished despite facts deleted by army censors.

"Did you come with personal questions or will you be listening through the filter of preconceived notions?" Jim stacked her bowl on top of his.

"I'm not altogether sure why I'm here."

"Fair enough." He set the dishes on a tray. "The lecture is this way."

The drawing room spanned the depth of the mansion and served as a lecture hall. Claire spotted a parquet floor beneath dozens of straight-backed student chairs. An oversized gilt mirror halfway down the western wall faced a marble fireplace. Tall windows lined either end of the long high room, the southern ones facing Clapham Common.

A pretty young woman with dark hair played hymns on a pump organ tucked into the far corner. Men, including two in uniform, and women paged through worn hymnals. A blackboard sporting a chalked outline dominated the front with a plain wooden table beside. Other than the overwrought ceiling fresco, a religious place less like St. Paul's Cathedral would be hard to find.

While it bore little resemblance to her college classrooms either, Claire took her preferred seating: last row, left side. Biddy sat beside her and opened a notepad. Claire did likewise.

Reverend Chambers set his large black Bible on the front table. He sang with gusto and waved his arms to encourage the singers.

After a simple prayer, Oswald Chambers began his lecture. "War. It's here. Is it of the devil or of God?"

Claire gasped.

"He goes to the heart, doesn't he?" Jim retrieved the pencil she'd dropped.

"It is of neither," Chambers continued. "It is of man, though God and the devil are both behind it. War is a conflict of wills either in individuals or in nations."

He referenced the Bible passage in which Jesus reminded his disciples "in the world you will have tribulation, but be of good cheer, for I have overcome the world."

Claire clutched her pencil as Reverend Chambers lectured with the easy authority of her professors. His thoughts were clear and concise, not overblown with grandiose religious language. She'd never heard a preacher speak with such easy confidence.

He didn't skirt the issues, but Reverend Chambers's facts affirmed. He seemed to know what God thought. "Jesus Christ did not say: You will understand why the war has come, but 'do not be scared, do not be put in a panic.' "

Claire could hardly think about the war without her heart racing and her palms sweating. Even now, her chest tightened and her breathing quickened. She pushed up her glasses.

"There is one thing worse than war, and that is sin. We get tremendously scared when our social order is broken up, and well we may. It's sin that produces pain in the heart of God, not the wars and devastation that so upset us."

He spoke as calmly as if discussing the weather, yet Claire had never considered God cared what she thought, nor how her sin might affect God. Her fingers jotted; her mind spun.

The Book of Common Prayer they used at St. Paul's always included references to confessing sin and sinfulness. She spoke the words but never applied them to her own life. Claire tried to be good and to obey her parents. Sin was what other people did in dark places.

Could her actions really cause pain in God's heart? How could the creator of the universe have time to be interested in what she did?

He finished with a short prayer, but Reverend Chambers's last line echoed: "Whenever we begin to calculate without God we commit sin."

His words had sunk deep, maybe even into her soul. Claire knew she needed to review the notes and think through the implication of his words. Sin was never discussed at home, and yet what else could have caused the evil actions that led to war?

She stared at the thin man. Perhaps Reverend Chambers had the answers she needed. As windows to her mind opened with new ideas, hope stirred. Maybe God did care about her in the midst of this war chaos. Deep inside, as if a bell chimed, Claire knew only God could get her through the war whole. If Jesus had overcome the world—an amazing realization—surely he could overcome the war.

Jim elbowed her. "A final hymn."

"It Is Well With My Soul" described her, Claire realized: full and content somewhere inside even as her mind struggled to process what Oswald Chambers had said. Claire met Biddy's eyes. "I didn't take many notes."

"May I see your pad?" Biddy easily read Claire's Pitman shorthand. "Sin, fear, war, tribulation—heavy words. Tell me what you fear."

"Death," Claire whispered. "My cousin's a flyer."

"I understand. We pray for soldiers most mornings at eight o'clock, particularly on Mondays. You're welcome to join us."

"Can you pray for my cousin Peter and his friend Edward?"

"It would be our honor. But as for you, do you own a Bible?"

"I can get one."

Biddy sat still, as if listening to a faraway voice. "Read and consider Jesus as portrayed in the Gospel of John." She smiled. "You will find him both a challenge and a joy. Good night."

Claire's mind raced as Biddy stacked hymnals. The Bible Training College might have answers to her questions, but she knew her parents would not approve. The beautiful building might look like Aunt Sarah's mansion, but the culture inside was foreign to her family's attitude.

But she wanted to be a foreign correspondent. Couldn't visiting Reverend Chambers's BTC be a test of her ability to ferret out and translate a different way of life?

She didn't understand how or why, but Claire liked the confidence displayed by Oswald and Biddy Chambers. The war continued, but God in relation to it—and to Claire—felt closer and personal.

She needed to figure out how such an intimacy with God could affect her peace of mind for an entire war, no matter what her parents thought.

Chapter Seven

September–October 1914

Mr. Able delivered Claire to the office at noon, then headed to King's Cross Station to retrieve Jock from ten days' news-gathering in the battlefields of Belgium and France. Claire anticipated a busy and exciting work day.

"Ah, the princess arrives after much too long a hiatus." Nigel sat on his desk, swinging a leg. "When will our king appear?"

"As soon as Mr. Able picks him up."

"Then we've time to fawn over you." He lit a cigarette and winked. With dark circles under his eyes and his tie askew, the normally fastidious Nigel exuded distraction.

"Difficult night?" She relished his banter; it made her feel like she belonged in the newsroom.

"I'm wrestling with a decision. How do you become the heir?"

"Birth," Claire said in a regal voice.

She ducked her chin and hoped she wasn't blushing. Nigel's warm voice prompted a happy response that left Claire uncertain how to react. She'd ask Sylvia for advice except her cousin would laugh at her.

Nigel's saucy grin sent her across the newsroom to help Jim arrange chairs. Jock liked an organized audience.

"Did you enjoy the BTC?" he asked.

Claire nodded. "Reverend Chambers and Biddy both gave me plenty to consider."

"Thinking is always good." Jim retrieved a thin paper from the city editor. "You'll want to see this War Department wire before Mr. Meacham arrives."

Claire flinched as she read the week's casualty rates. "Dear God."

"Exactly."

"Whose side is God on?" she whispered. The numbers of dead were incomprehensible and her imagination shied from picturing the carnage her father must have witnessed.

"His own."

She fled to Jock's office where she placed the wire on the desk and willed herself not to sob. She needed to behave like a professional. But why didn't God end the fighting? Flanders must be swimming not only in flooded lowlands, but in blood.

Once she gained control, Claire rejoined the journalists. Mostly middle-aged now that the young ones had enlisted, they smoked and chatted in clusters. Jim and Nigel hunched over their typewriters, rattling out copy.

The door slapped open. Carrying a filthy black raincoat, Jock drooped with exhaustion. His rumpled suit reeked of fetid mud, oil, but hopefully not blood. Jock tossed his coat onto the rack, rubbed his neck, and stalked into their midst. He nodded at Claire. "Take this down."

"The Allied armies may have won the battle along the Marne River in northeastern France, but the price they paid is difficult to comprehend." Jock described futile maneuvers, screaming horses, and suffocating clouds of artillery smoke. She clenched the pencil and refused to picture the words. When a collective gasp rose, Claire bit the inside of her cheek to not react in kind.

She heard the muffled drum of rain.

"Did anything positive come from the battle?" Jim finally asked.

"Don't be ridiculous." Scorn cracked Nigel's voice. "At least we repelled the Huns."

"People need hope," Jim said. "Any reassuring event to soften the horror?"

Claire liked that about Jim; he always sought the positive, even amid dreadful news.

Jock closed his eyes. The clock ticked. He spoke as if remembering a dream. "The French army ran out of transport and as the battle intensified, the roads filled with Paris taxis bringing soldiers to the front. There's your hopeful note, the indomitable spirit of French civilians."

"The Frogs didn't abandon the British?" Nigel asked.

"The armies fought hard; conditions are miserable."

Claire took dictation until her clutching fingers ached. When Jock announced, "Enough," she trailed him into his office while the reporters scurried to their desks. Typewriter clatter started immediately.

Her father absently pushed the wire report with his finger. "My father dragged me to every Gettysburg battle reunion. He never recovered from the abomination of standing on the ridge and watching Pickett order his men to charge. Your grandfather risked his life when he started shooting over the Reb soldiers' heads. He couldn't bear seeing brave men mowed down by his rifle finger."

Claire clutched the notebook. She tasted bile.

"It's like Pickett is advising the generals. They order waves of men to certain death and then call for more. What nation has enough men to see them slaughtered so?"

"Pickett went insane," Claire remembered.

"They're all insane, fighting a war with modern equipment that rips a man apart before he takes a step."

"You didn't say that in your dispatch."

"The censors won't allow it. Do you know British officers give their soldiers a jolt of rum before sending them over the top. They can only fight half drunk."

Claire closed her eyes and wilted inside. "Someone has to tell the world."

"Not if they want to work in Britain." Jock slid the wire into his desk drawer. "Do I really have a social dinner tonight? It's criminal to dine with wine and cigars when the Tommy soldiers burrow in the stinking dirt."

"Mama will call for you at six."

He loosened his collar. "I need a nap and a shower. Read me what you've got and then we'll head home."

"I'll stay to type up. Nigel or Jim can call a cab for me."

"Fair enough." He creased his cheek as if to smile. "Heard anything from Peter?"

"He's studying hard and loves the flying."

"Naturally." Jock rubbed his eyes. "What's he studying?"

Claire paused. Her cousin had sworn her to secrecy, warning that if what he wrote appeared in the newspaper, he'd never tell her anything again. "What you'd expect. Maps, weather, how airplanes work."

Jock scrutinized her. "I know there's more, it's all over your face, but I'll leave it for now. In the meantime, be kind to the young men. Take your time coming home if they need you. Read this one to Nigel and have him type it. Conroy can do the final edit."

Claire kissed him and returned to the newsroom where Nigel waited. He stubbed out a cigarette. "What have you got, princess?"

"I'll read while you type the story."

"I recognize power when I see it." He cranked in a sheet of paper. "I await your command, Nellie Bly. Start talking."

"Nellie Bly?" Claire blinked in surprise. Inspired by Bly's clever 1880s reporting techniques, she'd practically memorized *Around the World in Seventy-Two Days.*

"Isn't that why you're here?"

Claire's heart thumped so hard her chest hurt. She couldn't tell if he was making fun of her. His blue eyes, though, shone with the question.

"Fine. Don't tell me. Apples she'll be." Nigel placed his strong fingers on the round keys.

"What does that mean?" Claire asked.

"Don't worry about it, mate."

"We like independent women in America, particularly clever ones." Jim pulled the paper out of his typewriter, clipped it together with others and rose. "Surely New Zealand's pioneering women are made of the same stock?"

"Maybe. Read away, Nellie."

Claire opened her notebook and began to read, adjusting the order, correcting grammar, and simplifying verbs while retaining Jock's vivid descriptions. She read slowly, trying to avoid mistakes as Nigel typed. Jim volunteered to give him a break, but the New Zealander refused and smoked his cigarettes to the nub, the sweet smoke curling into the inky, humid room.

"Six thousand soldiers transported to the front line in taxicabs," Jim read over Nigel's shoulder.

Nigel tugged the final page from the typewriter. "At least the British sent double-decker buses to the Continent. It's a more efficient way to move men."

"But they're tall. They'll be easy targets," Claire said.

"Their height makes them easier to find among a taxi mob," Nigel barked. He brushed Claire's arm. "Do you know how to write words others can read, or do you only take shorthand?"

"Don't be silly. Why?"

"Just like Jim said, a bloke needs hope. Would you write to me?"

Her heart sank. "Where are you going?"

"I'm being commissioned next week. I'll be posted to Whitehall in intelligence, not far from Belgravia Square. Want to help celebrate?" His eyes were defiant, his chin up.

"After what you've typed, you're enlisting?"

"Thanks to Jim, I know if all else fails with army transport, I can call a taxi to take me to the front lines."

She reached for a handkerchief to polish her glasses.

Nigel straightened the typed papers and clipped them together. "Of course, an army of fighting Americans would be more helpful."

"You'll have to manage without us," Jim said.

"Why not you? You're here. Why don't you join up?"

Jim's face reddened. "I'll pray for you every day, Nigel, until the end of the war."

"Or I die?"

Jim cleared his throat. "You can possess eternal life."

"I'm not going to church." Nigel snapped shut his cigarette case.

Jim winced. "I'd hate to see a man as fine as you destroyed because of pride. Why don't you come one night? Claire's visited."

Nigel caught her hand. "Wouldn't you rather go dancing?"

Claire hesitated. This man left her flustered in an intoxicating way. She hated to disappoint. "Perhaps when you're in uniform."

"Soon enough. I'll hold you to it."

⚜ ⚜ ⚜

Jock scanned St. Paul's Cathedral while they waited for the service to begin several weeks later. He nodded to Winston Churchill, then nudged Claire. "See that woman veiled in black? That's ol' Bobby Lee's daughter."

"The general?" The Meacham family detested the late leader of the Confederate Army. "How old is she?"

"Ancient. She's been wandering around Europe for years. Got your pad? Let's get a few quotes from her after the service."

Of course Claire carried her notepad; a reporter needed to be prepared. "You're not supposed to work in church," she whispered.

"A reporter is always looking for a story. There's no time off. If you don't want to work, I'll take notes myself."

"I'll do it," she muttered.

Jock hummed, and she could imagine the questions swirling in his mind. They were churning in hers, too, but she needed to focus on God, not on chasing a story.

A choir of boys wearing scarlet robes and wide, rippled white collars sang the Charles Wesley hymn "Soldiers of Christ Arise." Claire sighed. She could never escape the war.

Jock scurried down the aisle at the final amen. By the time Claire caught up, he was speaking to the elderly woman draped in black. He scratched his right ear when he saw Claire, a signal to stand out of the way but within earshot.

Miss Lee's southern accent creaked and slurred as Claire scribbled her words. "My father used to say war is a terrible alternative and should be the very last choice."

"What would the general think of today's battles?" Jock asked.

"He said those killed in battle experienced a soldier's quick and glorious death. It's harder for those crippled and mangled who do not die. The world after the war doesn't understand them and has no place for them."

"You're anticipating what will come?"

She nodded. "I have been neutral. I have tried to heed President Wilson's advice in word and deed. My sympathy is with suffering wherever it exists, with the brave men fighting in the trenches, and the brave women waiting back home."

Jock appeared to wipe his eyes. "Thank you, ma'am."

"Your paper, sir?"

"*The Boston Daily*, flagship paper of the Boston Newspaper Syndicate."

"Yankee, then?"

"Yes, ma'am, but in this war, we're all Americans."

A tiny catlike smile appeared on her lips. "I believe you are correct in this. Good day."

He bowed and escorted her up the aisle.

Claire scrawled the remaining quotes and then headed toward the cathedral's main entrance. She'd catch up with the family outside. While Jock had given her the go-ahead nod to take notes, she felt guilty and wanted to avoid friends seeing her open notepad.

Two large hands waved at the end of the aisle, and Claire's heart leapt. Peter and Nigel made up the distance, laughing and triumphant.

She stifled a desire to spin in glee.

"I caught an early train home for the day and ran into Nigel on the street. I told him we'd find a good meal if we could locate you all. Is the family dining at home?" Peter kissed her.

"Yes. Your mother will be delighted."

The two soldiers carried themselves with brash confidence in uniforms boasting one star on their sleeves—signifying a second lieutenant rank. Both uniforms were tailored to fit well, particularly across their broad shoulders.

Their khaki tunics buttoned up the front with four pockets: two breast pockets closed with brass buttons, two larger ones under the snug wide belt at their waist. A thin leather belt crossed over the right shoulder to connect to the belt. Their trousers were tucked into shiny black boots, and they carried peaked hats.

Claire sighed in appreciation. She hated the war, but how handsome these young officers looked. She glanced around. Had anyone noticed they were with her?

"I'm still waiting for a letter written in American," Nigel said.

She put her hands on her hips in mock outrage. "Send me your address."

"Too right." Nigel took her elbow. "Anything exciting happening in the news business?"

Her toes wanted to lift off the ground. "We just interviewed Mary Lee."

"Who's she?"

Claire filled him in on the American Civil War before the family caught sight of Peter.

Peter was the center of attention, and his effervescent happiness spilled onto them. Jock tried to grill his nephew, but Anne hushed him. "Ask your military questions later."

His mother couldn't contain herself. "How dangerous are the flying conditions?"

"We're as safe as can be. When the weather's bad, we don't fly. We're grounded today and tomorrow, so here I am." Peter squeezed her hand.

Aunt Sarah's eyes filled with tears over her proud smile. Sylvia leaned against her brother's shoulder, her face guileless and shining with happiness. Claire savored the moment: all the people she loved in one place, safe and whole. Her knot of worry eased.

Luncheon centered on the lieutenants' adventures. Peter regaled them with tales of his fellow officers, rounds of drinking after flights, surprising ways to solve technical problems, and the trials of keeping a pillow dry in leaky quarters. He sounded too jovial to Claire, and she noticed her father's uncharacteristic silence.

She remembered a lesson from her grandfather. Sometimes a source talked too much. A good reporter used his eyes as much as his ears, paying close attention to the way an interviewee spoke and what they avoided discussing.

"Let me eat this delicious meal," Peter finally exclaimed. "Ask Nigel questions."

Stationed in Westminster near the houses of Parliament, Nigel claimed his job dealt with relations among the Commonwealth countries—he represented Australian and New Zealand interests. "We call the combined armies ANZAC." He described mundane paper pushing, officious senior officers, and pleas from mothers who didn't want their sons to enlist. "Pretty standard activities for headquarters, they tell me."

When Jock asked a clarifying question, Nigel referred to books and history.

Sylvia wanted to know the names of their tailors, and the conversation wandered off to uniform intricacies.

Peter couldn't sit still—his fingers tapped, he nodded, he shifted so often in his seat as to be fidgeting. He slid his water goblet back and forth on the tablecloth when not balancing the sterling cutlery on his fingers. Claire recalled how steady he'd always been while sailing in Newport, except for the one frenetic day they ran the boat aground.

She mirrored her father and leaned back to watch.

Nigel lit cigarette after cigarette until Claire needed her handkerchief to keep her eyes from watering. His long elegant fingers tapped too. She polished her eyeglasses. If men handled stress like this before they went to the front lines, what happened when they reached France?

"Have you taken over the office yet, Nellie Bly?" Nigel asked as the family adjourned to the library.

She glanced around for her father before answering. "We're busy without you. Mr. Conroy has hired two retired men to help with the typing, but they don't take shorthand, so Papa needs me even more."

"You must be happy."

"It's far more interesting than talking about clothing."

He laughed. "Tell me how you spend your time besides news-gathering. Peter and I are tired of the war."

"Hear, hear" Peter cried. "Let's discuss real life. Read anything good lately? Seen any shows?"

As Claire escorted Nigel to the door at dusk, he caught her hand. "Will you explore London with me when I get time off? I'd like to see the famous sites before," he faltered, "before I go home."

Claire tried to focus on his question, but his large, warm hands distracted her. "I'd like that. I'll dig out my copy of *Baedeker's London and Its Environs.*"

He kissed her hand and then saluted. "Next Sunday, then, after luncheon."

Later Jock approved the plan. "Enjoy yourself, be home for tea, and keep your ears open in case the lieutenant drops any newsworthy hints."

She squirmed. "Must my outings always be a hunt for news?"

Jock nearly dropped his pipe. "Why wouldn't they be?"

"He seems a pleasant young man, but be careful of your reputation." Anne rubbed her hands. "Wartime can bring out questionable behavior."

Peter tossed back the last of his brandy. "It's splendid as always to see him, but Aunt Anne is right. Be careful with Nigel."

Chapter Eight

November–December 1914

The BNS loved the Mary Lee interview, which received lots of attention in the United States. Jock paid Claire a sovereign extra, "since I know it was the Sabbath." She admired the coin, ran her finger along the ridged edge and dropped it into St. Paul's mite box. She'd rather not mix work with worshipping God.

Jock finally examined Claire's notes taken while he was in the Marne. "Other than this BTC sermon, you picked up interesting information and amusing quotes we may be able to use later. Remember to always double check your facts."

Such habits were necessary for a reporter, especially a foreign correspondent, and were the reason she'd studied French and German, European history, and geography. A reporter needed to understand ideas in their original language and be able to examine events within their historical and physical settings. She'd learned shorthand to facilitate information gathering. The BNS newsroom allowed her to observe Jock's interview skills and ability to write on deadline.

But while Jock unknowingly provided an apprenticeship, another subject had captured Claire's imagination through its primary source material.

It began when she read, as Biddy Chambers had advised, the lyrical opening words of John's Gospel in the Bible: "In the beginning was the Word, and the Word was with God, and the Word was God."

She knew the Word of God meant Jesus.

Odd she'd never given much thought to Jesus as a flesh and blood person. He had always been an icon: the baby in the crèche, the tortured figure on the cross. Half-remembered sermons were not lining up with the dynamic man striding through John's narrative. Jesus seemed unfazed by the traps and circumstances thrown at him.

Unlike Claire.

Jim's steady faith and the memory of Oswald Chambers's calm demeanor intrigued her as war tensions ratcheted. With Peter, Nigel, and Sylvia's fiancé, Edward, in the army, the casualty reports were a personal threat. Peter wrote of cracked up airplanes and young men killed in both foolish and tragic accidents. *Don't worry about me,* he said. *All those lessons from the summer taught me to respect the machine. I'll be fine. But keep this just between us.*

Claire didn't show his letters to her family, but the burden of knowing dangerous information they lacked weighed on her. As the rain poured and the temperature dropped, she imagined Peter's icy hands struggling to control a fragile plane in buffeting winds. Some nights the agony of worry made it impossible to sleep.

Biddy's invitation to pray echoed, and Claire wondered if visiting a BTC prayer meeting might soothe her anxiety. It couldn't hurt to go once and find out, even though Jock wouldn't approve. The idea grew into a yearning, and as the insomnia continued, Claire became convinced she should make another trip to Clapham Common.

She only wanted to double-check Oswald and Biddy's faith. Sort of like spying.

Getting to the BTC without telling her father presented a challenge, so she asked Sylvia to accompany her. Sylvia winced. "I'm not rising early to mutter prayers. I need my beauty sleep for Edward."

After thinking and pondering—praying really—Claire approached her mother and aunt, both of whom she found in Aunt Sarah's overstuffed sitting room.

"A prayer meeting?" Anne frowned. "We pray at St. Paul's. That's enough. Your father wouldn't approve."

A statistic they weren't allowed to report the week before steeled her determination: ten thousand casualties in a twenty-minute battle. "It's for the soldiers. People ask God for the safety of their family members. I'll be praying for Peter and Edward."

Aunt Sarah stirred the sweet-scented air with her fan. "What a comforting idea. Please pray for my son. I'll direct Mr. Able to take you and wait."

"Don't tell your father," Anne said. "Be home by nine-thirty for breakfast."

"Surely he wouldn't object to a prayer meeting," Aunt Sarah whispered.

"He's never forgotten," Anne muttered. "Nothing beyond church services. He's adamant."

Jim grinned the following Monday when she slipped into the BTC and sat beside him. Reverend Chambers, OC, opened the prayer meeting promptly at eight o'clock. They bowed their heads and many knelt on the parquet floor.

Claire had never attended a prayer meeting before, much less prayed in public. She expected the over-solicitous language she heard at St. Paul's, but Jim's OC surprised her with the simple declaration, "Good morning, Lord."

The slight, dark-haired organist, Eva, spoke with more emotion: "Oh, Lord, my God, I am bowed in thy presence this morning. I kneel in adoration and thanksgiving."

Claire knew only the formal appeals from *The Book of Common Prayer* and the child's ditty "Now I lay me down to sleep." For these people, however, prayer was more genial conversation than crafted poetry. They weren't asking for anything, merely telling God how they saw him—kind, benevolent, and merciful. Her mouth dried and her heart raced.

Jim touched her forearm and leaned so close she felt his breath on her cheek, which agitated her more. "You don't need to pray aloud unless you want to."

Several people read passages from the Bible. Claire recognized Psalm 23, "The Lord is my shepherd."

By the time prayer requests began, she breathed more naturally and her eyelids no longer fluttered. Her fingers moved as if taking dictation. Specific soldiers were mentioned, and Claire whispered to Jim, "Could you pray for Peter, Edward, and Nigel?"

When a lull came, he spoke their names.

OC ended with amen at 8:30. While the others headed to breakfast, Biddy lingered. "Did you enjoy the prayer time?"

"Yes."

Biddy indicated her chest. "And in your heart?"

"I feel better knowing God will watch over them."

"Good. Come again." She glided away.

Claire arrived home well before breakfast; Jock never noticed her earlier absence. She slept that night and the rest of the week. In relieved gratitude, Claire returned to the BTC the following Monday and then the Monday after and thus it went through the fall. The prayers succeeded. Peter survived upending his plane on a rough landing. Nigel confidently took to his role as a sub-lieutenant. Edward suffered only a sprained ankle jumping off a truck.

She prayed for Jock, who traveled twice to France without mishap. While he was away, Claire stayed for breakfast and brought a list of questions for OC from her Bible reading. He ate his porridge and answered with good humor and further references for her to check.

When Jim suggested using the book of Psalms as a template for prayer, Claire added a psalm to her now daily morning readings. Whenever grisly war reports sent her rubbing her eyes to staunch the tears, she whispered Psalm 23.

With OC leading, they prayed through the Battle of Ypres, the British blockade of Germany, German U-boat threats off the English coast, the declaration of war on the Ottoman Empire, and a wet December. When the war showed no sign of ending by Christmas, optimism sagged, but prayers continued.

Praying for the people she loved soothed Claire's gut-tightening fears and gave her something constructive to do with her emotions. Prayer took the edge off nightmare statistics and enabled her to work for the stoic Jock. She knew the source of peace and eventually could speak it aloud at the BTC: "Thanks be to God."

Sylvia married Second Lieutenant Edward Henley on December 20, 1914, in the drawing room of her mother's house. Claire stood by her side before the massive marble fireplace, praying the shaky groom would get the ring on her cousin's finger. Skinny, fair Edward looked boyish in his dress uniform, hardly the dashing soldier Sylvia made him out to be.

The sophisticated Sylvia, on the other hand, wore a flood of white satin tucked into a brocaded waist and trimmed with pearls and crystal-beaded fringe. Veiled in cobweb-delicate Brussels lace, her beauty dazzled Claire as much as Edward.

After the short service read by an army chaplain, Claire welcomed Edward into the family with a hug. "I'll be praying for you."

Edward pressed her hand. "I need all the prayers I can get. The war is terrifying."

"Are you trying to steal my husband?" Sylvia simpered.

"I'm adding him to my prayer list."

Sylvia grasped his arm. "I'll take care of my man, thank you."

Claire watched them move away in a blur and approached her father. He pulled her spectacles from his breast pocket. "You're beautiful with your glasses and without."

"The world is clearer when I wear them." Indeed, with the glasses returned to her nose, Clair's senses engaged; she could appreciate the hothouse flowers' scent, the stringed quartet's notes, and her royal blue dress's smooth silk. Claire spied her mother raising her eyebrows at Jock from several yards away.

Jock winked at his wife and lifted his drink. "Your admirer is here, darling."

Nigel raised his glass in reply. He looked as splendid as the others in his dress uniform, but a golden curl slipped over his forehead, and she saw a nervous tic under his left eye.

"Shall we invite him over?" Jock asked. "He watched you throughout the ceremony."

Her heart skipped. Witty and always smartly dressed, Nigel provided insightful historical comments on their

London rambles. But his jokes and stories often suggested a jagged intensity that left her uneasy, even as they amused.

Home on twenty-four hours' leave, Peter joined them. "I switched the name cards. Nigel wants to sit beside you."

Her father nudged her. "Told you."

"Claire's the type of girl who gets under a soldier's skin," Peter explained. "A pretty face and a listening ear turns us all into would-be heroes. Stay in London, you'd be deadly at the front."

"That's why women make the best spies," Jock said. "See if you can pick up any information. Drinking soldiers can be useful sources."

"You want me to spy at Sylvia's wedding?"

"Fact-gather. Your mother needs me." He laughed and crossed the room to kiss his wife

Peter watched. "There's a marriage to emulate. My father said they had a rum go in Egypt losing your brothers, but they're obviously still in love."

Claire ignored the familiar ache. "They refuse to discuss their time in Egypt with me."

Nigel spoke to her parents. Jock slapped him on the back, but Anne merely smiled.

"Aunt Anne is on to him," Peter muttered. "Listen, engage Nigel's mind and talk about anything but the war. Even better, bat your eyelashes like Sylvia. If you keep him entertained, he won't drink as much champagne." Peter brushed lint from his sleeve. "He's coming. I must circulate."

Nigel kissed her hand. "You look lovely."

She flushed.

"Do I smell French perfume?"

"A gift from Sylvia. How did your job go this week? I've been praying for you."

"You and Jim, I suppose." He sighed. "I can only hope my analytical abilities are sufficient to keep me from the front lines. It's brutal over there."

Claire nodded.

"Kitchener's keeping the intelligence folks close at the moment, so I'll remain in London. Will you attend the cinema with me Tuesday night? *Tillie's Punctured Romance* is playing at the Bayswater Theatre."

"Charlie Chaplin?"

"Too right. A mate needs a laugh, and Chaplin provides one."

"I'll check my calendar." Claire tried to still the butterflies inside as they strolled to the dining room glowing with candlelight.

Liveried maids circulated with champagne-filled flutes and tidy canapés on gleaming silver trays. The two-dozen elegant guests spoke in dulcet tones of money and power. Aunt Sarah had softened her mourning with a gray silk dress and seemed more like her gracious self as she conversed with Edward's stiff parents.

Nigel led Claire to their engraved place cards in a corner of the long table.

"Do you miss typing?" Claire asked.

"A clerk does it for me, now." He winced. "Those days at the BNS feel like ancient history. I liked watching you read the copy. You couldn't keep the horror out of your voice."

"I wasn't very professional. Here's hoping the stories improve."

"Unlikely." He finished his champagne and passed the glass to a maid. "Ever figure out why Jim's not enlisting?"

Claire fingered her pearl necklace. Jim might not be as intriguing as Nigel, but she liked and trusted him. She depended on his reasonable American practicality and attempts to find positive news as the war deepened. "Jim prays. You're among the first he prays for."

"Prayer. It's hardly enough, but I'll try it. I pray thee, will you take in a film with me?"

Claire adjusted her glasses. "Okay."

He snagged two glasses of champagne from a tray. "This calls for a toast."

"I..."

"Every bit of good news calls for a toast in a war. It's the only way to survive. Haven't you learned that yet?"

Over Nigel's shoulder, Claire saw Peter's lips flatten. "I'm still trying to figure out how to survive a war."

Nigel handed her a glass. "Drink up and be merry."

The sparkling bubbles rose through the pale champagne and popped into an acidic sweetness, but Claire shook her head. Life didn't seem so simple to her.

Chapter Nine

Winter 1915

Ambition goaded Claire as the work tempo increased and her responsibilities grew. With so many stories to write on a given day and office staff truncated, Jock often instructed her to listen in on a second 'stick phone while he interviewed sources from the office. "Don't breathe into the mouthpiece; they mustn't know you're listening. Put quotes together into a coherent story, type them up and bring them to me."

Jock used a thick blue pencil to edit her notes. He wrote in shorthand-like symbols, but once she understood an upward squiggle meant delete and the right angle drawn under a capitalized word meant new paragraph, she could correct the copy. Following the arrows and circled sections to where they belonged required detective skills.

How Jock simplified sentences and moved the most important information to the top of the story fascinated her. "It's like an information triangle aiming down," he explained. "You start with the crucial information. You add additional details until you're down to facts that may not make a difference."

"So beautiful prose isn't as important as pure information?" Claire circled a paragraph and drew a line moving it down the page.

"Exactly. Boston edits to whatever length they need for their space, cutting from the bottom up." He tossed the pencil onto the desk. He'd just edited a breaking news item about a zeppelin raid on the eastern English coast the night before. They awaited more news from the wire while Jock debated traveling to see the damage with his own eyes.

"You seem to be handling the grim news better. Your hands don't shake so much when you take dictation. Or were you afraid of Conroy?"

Claire shrugged. She avoided the editor as much as possible. "I guess you could say I've learned how to manage my reactions to the war news."

He snorted. "Who can adapt to this nightmare?"

"I pray and leave the war in God's hands."

"Don't be ridiculous."

Claire stowed away her notepad and pencil. Prayer had become a whispered ritual: "I give my worries to you, Lord, help me, and help them." On devastating news days, her prayers never ended.

"Remember what the bishop said at St. Paul's on Sunday, how God knows the number of hairs on our head and the length of our days? I can't protect Peter or Edward or Nigel, so I ask God to watch over them."

Out came the pipe. "What will you do when they're killed?"

Claire flinched. "You don't know they'll die."

"I know the odds; slim to none." His sulfur match smelled of hell.

"Papa!"

"A junior officer arriving in France today has a life expectancy of five weeks. You need to face facts and deal with them, not waste time mooning over a romantic notion God will protect the people you love."

Claire pushed up her glasses. "I need to be more optimistic."

Jock puffed at the coals. "Edward will be the first to die; he hasn't a brain to stay out of trouble. Peter's flying machine is a target of wood and canvas. Nigel might survive because he's the wily kind. He'll avoid heroics and stay in the rear as much as possible. The intelligence corps should be safe if it's nothing more than a desk job. He'd do well not to distinguish himself or they may send him to France."

"How can you be so calculating?"

He pointed his pipe stem at her. "It's the only way to outlive a war. You weigh the risk. You don't hide behind mumbled words to someone you never see, who may not exist for all you can prove. You're better off rolling bandages or knitting socks than praying."

"You're wrong." Claire shoved back her chair and stood. "Prayer is the only thing helping me. Your vaunted knowledge is terrifying. When I see a man on the street with a sleeve pinned up, I'm reminded of war's destruction on the personal level. You told me the army took away cameras and diaries so the soldiers couldn't document front-line horrors."

"How else could they get young men to fight, much less convince mothers to send their sons? We're only allowed to see the government's propaganda. War is brutal and it will only get worse." Jock's eyes narrowed. "You lack personal experience. Grab your coat. You're coming with me."

"Where?"

"East Anglia. You need to see what the zeppelins did. I'll bet someone there prayed last night."

They traveled by cab to King's Cross station and boarded a train headed north. Claire watched the crowded London suburbs change to rolling countryside as the train clattered down the tracks. After an hour, rain fell straight from dark clouds and made afternoon vision impossible. "How could the dirigibles ever find the town to bomb?"

"We'll ask questions when we arrive in King's Lynn. I'm glad you're thinking."

Jock spread the latest edition of the *Times* over the first-class carriage seat and read aloud. Details were sketchy. "We need more information than this for Boston." He checked his watch. "The January 22 paper at this rate. You'll get to experience the war raw today. We'll see how you like it."

Raw described the scene in the market town of King's Lynn. Rubble littered the flooded streets as the rain poured. Stunned survivors in black mackintoshes staggered amid the debris, picking through homes now slumped into piles of broken brick and sodden possessions. When Claire poked her head into a crumbling house, she smelled clean rain, stinking mud, and a tang of sulfur and petroleum. She pulled her cloak closer against the chill and tugged her new cloche hat down to her eyebrows. The weather made the appalling destruction worse.

Jock barreled into the ruins tossing questions. Eventually they met a constable whose thick accent sounded like soggy chewing. He indicated a coatless man soaked to the skin with a notebook. "He's from the *Sphere*, ask him."

The local reporter spluttered the names of the woman and teenage boy who'd died. "Percy lay there in his bed when the bomb fell through the roof." He indicated a twisted fin-shaped object. "Kid never had a chance. Real shame it were."

A hollow-eyed woman moaned beside her home, the front wall shorn off to expose a flowery wallpapered interior. "How do you feel about what happened?" Jock asked.

"Numb. Where will we go?" she wailed. "Nowhere be safe."

He asked a similar question at the next house before addressing Claire. "Are you getting these statements?"

Claire fumbled for her notebook. "She didn't say anything."

"She's numb. Write it down."

Claire peered at the rain. "How did they find this place to bomb?"

"The lights," an elderly woman said. "Constable Jones said the enormous balloon followed the train tracks along the coast until they came to the lighted city and dropped the bombs. I'll live in the dark from now on rather than be a target in the electric light."

Jock's eyes danced. "Did you get it? A great quote."

"Wasn't it raining?" Claire asked.

"Nay. 'Twas a clear night, the stars felt close enough to touch until they fell from the sky to destroy. Then the whole street erupted into smoke and flames."

Claire jotted. "What will you do now?"

"Pray I never live through such a night again."

Jock crossed his arms. "Will God listen?"

"I don't know anything except he got me through last night. That was enough for me."

A stunned woman with thin hair and sagging eyes, the dead boy's mother, huddled in a doorway with two young girls. Jock introduced himself and asked his questions.

"I heard a banshee scream as it tore through the ceiling. He lay in bed, a big boy of fourteen, and I asked if he were all right. When he didna answer, I saw my boy were dead."

Claire closed her eyes against the tears and forced the descriptions through her fingers. Hearing the mother's hopeless voice chilled Claire even more. But her father, usually sensitive about the death of children, kept probing.

Her toes curled up and Claire shuffled with tightened throat as he asked painfully intrusive questions. She finally tucked away her pencil and pad and wept.

"Thank you, madam, and please accept my condolences." He handed the mother a golden coin. "I don't know how to get over the loss of a child except through time. I hope this helps."

"You didna pay her did you?" The local reporter asked as they trudged to a pub. "I canna pay."

"No. I sympathized with her loss."

Jock bought the reporter a drink and picked his brain for details. Claire's pencil flew as they dried before a roaring fireplace.

"We heard the slow rumble, high above, like thunder only not so sharp or loud. Most did not know what it could be, and then a long gray-white cylinder appeared in the sky, dropping flashes of light. The bombs hit the ground and the noise, ach, the noise; it filled your ears and your mind and threw you to the ground."

He gulped. "Then the screaming. The air choked with dust and propellant smell. It was a miracle only two died, but that's little comfort to the families."

The reporter provided more facts about the countryside and general mood of the populace. Jock obtained statistics, shared a few stories from his past, and ordered food from the pub owner. When the savory meat pies arrived in a fragrant brown sack, he downed his drink and paid the bill.

Jock checked his watch. "We'll catch the next train to London."

Sagging with emotion and exhaustion, Claire trailed him out the door. "Why not spend the night at an inn?"

"We'll craft the story on the train and go straight to the office when we get to London. Come along, darling, this is the reporter's life."

Claire took down her father's musings as they powered through the dark night. He spoke, she wrote. The conductor brought hot tea. Jock finished dictating as the first London outskirts appeared.

"How could you ask those mothers such questions?"

Jock twisted the pipe in his hands. "You cannot let yourself be emotional when following a story. You get the facts, craft them into a picture, and report. You must tuck your heart away. If you don't compartmentalize your life into work and home, this job will crush you and render you useless."

"Surely the dead boy bothered you?"

He stared at the black countryside. "You can't take it personally. You get the story and push through. The time to cry is when it's all over."

"All over? The war? It could be years."

"You harden your heart and don't meditate on it. Do you need a whiskey?"

"No, thank you." Claire stared at her father. She had never seen him cry. Unimaginable.

She thought of Jim's prayer her heart wouldn't grow hard. It seemed impossible to detach emotion from experience, yet her father did it constantly. Isolating her brothers' deaths in Egypt must be the way he dealt with their loss. To him, the deaths of those young boys must be a narrative told long ago and banished to the corner of his heart where he hid grief.

Claire shivered. If this is what it took to be a reporter, she needed to learn how to detach her emotions from the facts.

The train slowed and wobbled as the first blurred suggestion of tall city buildings appeared. A soft drizzle fell on the black night. She wrapped her coat tighter around her neck. Her body slumped beyond tired, but her mind coursed with devastating images.

"I'm not a bad man, Claire."

"No."

"History needs reporters to bear witness and tell the world what happened. You can't report and cry. You stuff away your reaction and tell yourself an opportunity will come one day to be sad, but not this day, or you will fail the people who need you to tell the truth."

Speak the truth in love, OC advised. Claire contemplated how to frame the zeppelin story with love. She'd need to understand how the families felt and describe their agony with respect. She'd need to figure out how to answer who, what, when, where, why, and how without embarrassing those most affected.

Jock sipped his whiskey. "What's your opinion of raw journalism?"

"I can do it. I can write up what happened with respect and honor."

His eyebrows came together and he cocked his head.

Claire took a deep breath. "This is how I want to spend my life. I want to be a reporter like you."

"Preposterous. You're going to be a history teacher."

"No. I want to bear witness and provide facts for historians, not teach them long afterwards."

He shook his head. "You don't know what you're saying. You think tonight was difficult, try living in the field for days and weeks on end. Sleepless nights, long hours of waiting for events that may never happen. We didn't raise you for this life. A girl like you belongs in the classroom teaching students how to avoid the misery of daily news."

"I've grown up waiting for the story," Claire said. "I've spent half my life listening to you interview other people. You know I can write. I've been watching you and learning ever since we arrived in England." She gestured to her notepad and pencil. "These are the tools of my apprenticeship."

"I'll fire you."

Stung, Claire rubbed her palm across the notepad. Disappointed tears threatened, but her brain shoved back and reminded Claire of a crucial fact. She cleared her throat and stuck out her chin. "There's almost no one left in your newsroom. Who will help you report the news if you fire me?"

He downed the whiskey and scowled. The train halted at the station

"Gather up everything. We'll see if you have what it takes."

Jock hurried down the aisle toward the front of the train. Claire tugged on her still damp coat, thrust notepad and pencil into the leather satchel, and chased after him.

They disembarked onto a platform shared with another train. The steam from their locomotive dissipated into the foggy air, leaving a whoosh of warm, oily smoke. Claire straightened her glasses. "Why are so many people here in the middle of the night?"

Jock pulled her into a shadow. "Watch."

Orderlies bearing canvas stretchers approached the other train. The platform filled with a flurry of nurses in headdresses, doctors in dirty white coats, and husky servicemen in uniform, all converging on the carriage doors. One by one, soldiers were helped from the train, many with bloody gauze wrapped around their heads. Several limped on unsteady legs; others leaned on the sturdy arms of fellow soldiers. Bandaged eyes were common.

"Take this down," Jock murmured.

"They pour into the train stations late at night, when the casual traveler is least likely to see them. Men fresh from the battlefront are helped by their comrades, hoping to arrive at hospital before it is too late. Orderlies by the dozens haul stretchers of nonresponsive men. The whistle of the train, the moan of the men occurs nightly in London: dying warriors come home."

Claire couldn't see her writing in the dark, but she spooled the symbols as she'd been trained. She could decipher at the office.

Jock's voice continued low. Claire smelled dried blood and the haunting whiff of an unidentifiable sharp, sweet scent. When the last soldier limped away, she started to fold up her pad.

"Not yet. We wait a little longer. Step further into the shadows."

She shifted in her damp boots, weaving with weariness and dread. Once the station cleared, nursing sisters exited and directed more orderlies. The stretchers they carried bore silent and immobile men like statues wrapped in white.

"Bodies?" Claire whispered.

"Poor beggars."

"Hey, what are you doing?" an officer shouted.

Jock displayed his journalist card.

"No," the officer said. "No press. Move along."

Claire tucked away her notepad. Jock took her arm. "Let's get to the office. Boston needs the news. We can catch tomorrow's extras if we hurry tonight."

She knew a journalist's satisfaction: two good stories. Claire would reflect on what she'd seen and maybe throw up . . . tomorrow.

Chapter Ten

Spring 1915

The tendrils of spring unfurled slowly, as if waiting to see whether the mayhem would remain checked long enough for flowers to bloom. London's dank fog and rainy weather continued but gave way to startling hues of red and gold as tulips appeared. On Sundays Claire admired the flower beds at St. Paul's painstakingly cared for by elderly gardeners.

"It's hard to believe flowers still grow," Nigel said. "You'd think they'd pop up, look around, and cower back under."

Nigel's descriptions delighted Claire and she transcribed many into her diary. They'd fallen into a Sunday rhythm of church, dinner, and long chatty walks. Conversation flew across centuries and kingdoms, eddied around books they'd read, and then roared to reflections on current events.

Jock egged him on during Sunday meals spent with the family.

Another girl might complain of her father sitting long after a meal to drink brandy and chat with his daughter's friend, but Claire savored the opportunity to learn more about world events. When the men debated which army could outlast the other, Nigel referenced ancient battles fought in Sparta and Rome, while her father countered with experiences gleaned from American Civil War veterans and Teddy Roosevelt's

Spanish-American War. Anne listened with occasional pithy remarks. Sundays were instructive on several levels.

It helped take their mind off Peter, now flying above the trenches of northeastern France on "aerial reconnaissance." Claire knew he had memorized the topographic map of the country and was juggling a heavy camera that made the biplane tricky to land. He'd enclosed a tiny piece of flattened shrapnel in the last letter, without explaining why. Her prayers intensified.

Meanwhile, when Nigel could get a free night, he'd escort Claire to the theater or cinema. He enjoyed vaudeville shows; anything with physical slapstick amused him. He preferred loud music and bright lights but rubbed his eyes during a performance of Mozart's searing Clarinet Concerto.

"Perhaps he has a soul after all," Anne said after the concert.

One bleak Saturday night they'd met Sylvia and Edward at a dancehall. The newlyweds clung together as they shuffled across the floor; Edward would head to France in days and Sylvia wept continuously.

Nigel danced frantically and held her too close on the foxtrot. Claire squirmed, yet his manic pleasure excited her. She wanted to forget the war as much as he did. She couldn't imagine Edward's thoughts.

They visited the London Zoo on a breezy Sunday and laughed at the clever penguins, admired the giant elephant, and gasped at a North American porcupine.

"Fancy those spines!" Nigel said. "What happens when you encounter one?"

"I've never seen a porcupine before."

"Not even in the bush?"

The only animals Claire had seen in bushes were squirrels. "No."

Methuselah the ancient tortoise bore a message painted in white on his shell: “We can’t do without our shells.”

Nigel groaned. “Not fair using propaganda on an innocent animal.”

Claire pulled out her notebook. “This might make an interesting story.”

“Can’t you experience life without taking notes?” He took her hand. “I want to show you a fairy from my homeland.”

He led her to a darkened aviary room where nocturnal birds were kept. Once Claire’s eyes adjusted, she glimpsed delicate movement among the ferns. A tiny puffball with an absurdly long slender bill called in a high faint whistle and scurried in the dark.

“When I was a lad,” Nigel whispered, “I’d spend the night in the bush to watch for kiwi birds. They’re as sweet as can be.”

Claire loved this side of the man from Down Under.

While Jock encouraged the outings, Anne had concerns. “Does Nigel behave himself?”

Claire flushed. “Of course, what do you expect?”

“I expect a young man headed to France to seek any comfort he can get.”

“Mother!”

“It’s a fact of life,” Anne said. “Nigel’s a handsome man with many positive qualities, but he has weaknesses that could make life with him challenging. Do you want to marry him and spend your life in New Zealand?”

“Who’s discussing marriage? Doesn’t he deserve as much fun as he can before he faces the guns?”

Her mother closed her eyes. “The war won’t last forever. Guard your reputation and do nothing you’d be ashamed of in the future. Read anything lately?”

Between working in the office and meeting Nigel, she could scarcely finish a book in a week, where once she'd devoured one a day. Some Mondays she had trouble getting up in time for the BTC prayer meeting. "No."

"Darling." Anne took Claire's face into her cool hands. "The times may be extreme, but you mustn't allow circumstance to influence who you are. Enjoy yourself, yes, but in moderation. I don't need you to be as intense as your father; one Jock is enough for any household.

Claire hugged her. "Agreed."

She drew a line in her social life. Sundays with Nigel were sufficient with church, luncheon, and an afternoon outing. She'd spend the evenings writing notes in her diary or reading to Aunt Sarah—who often requested Bible passages.

However, on evenings when Jock and Anne attended social affairs, Claire waited until their departure and with Aunt Sarah's blessing and fare, caught a cab to the Bible Training College's evening meetings.

After months of reading the Bible and praying on Monday mornings, Claire's curiosity about God continued to grow. Her yearning to know her life had purpose found a respite in verses like, "For I know the thoughts that I think toward you, saith the Lord, thoughts of peace, and not of evil, to give you an expected end." Studying Jesus's behavior forced her to see religious belief as a conscious decision, not simpleminded acceptance.

Jim answered questions in hurried asides at the office and suggested passages for her to consider. Quick conversations with Biddy and seemingly random remarks from OC lodged in her mind and reverberated through the week. Even the hymns echoed and she found herself humming "Be Thou My Vision, O Lord of My Heart."

She longed to visit more often but her parents believed clergyman preyed on irrational fears, and Claire knew they would forbid her trips. Between Peter's letters and her time at the BTC, Claire balanced too many secrets but didn't know what else to do but carry on.

One morning after she had peppered him with questions, OC handed her a correspondence school pamphlet. "A more directed study of the Scriptures might help you. Write out the essays and I'll correct and return them to you by mail."

Claire opened the green pamphlet. "What is the attitude to our Lord Jesus Christ in the gospel of Mark?" She smiled. "I can figure this out."

"Pray first," OC said. "You'd be surprised how your answer may change."

One morning at the BNS office Jim passed on a prayer request. Claire eyed her father's office door, took a deep breath and entered. "I have an appointment with Jim when we're done this evening."

Jock didn't look up from the copy. "No flirting in the office."

"The lady supervisor at his college, Mrs. Chambers, burned her hand. I've volunteered to take dictation in her place tonight."

His eyebrows came together and he stared at her. "At the Bible place? Really, Claire?"

"I'm helping a woman in need. I won't be late." She fled.

Jim sat beside her in the lecture hall. He'd been a great help, translating the foreign concepts of the BTC for her. Never hurried or perturbed, Jim walked through the BTC and the newsroom with easy assurance. She could discuss anything with him, trusted his judgment, and knew he wished only the best for her.

Nigel, on the other hand, left her flushed and uncertain, excited but wary. If the men were books, Jim spoke confident fact while Nigel sang with allusion-fueled poetry.

That night Claire studied the black chalkboard at the front of the lecture hall and copied OC's precisely drawn diagram into her notebook. For what he called his Sketching Class, OC outlined an entire book of the Bible on the blackboard and then explained the basic message and application over the course of a week.

"Thank you for being our scribe tonight," OC said.

"I'm happy to help, but I wish I could come more often. I have so much to learn."

Those sunken, loving eyes blessed her. "You take in more than you realize. Much of what is taught requires real and deep experience. I see you struggling with these concepts in your essays. Brood over your questions and meditate on the Scriptures. You'll be surprised by how much is revealed and how much you already know."

"I hope you feel the same about my next essay."

His chuckle rolled out warm and friendly. She loved to give a man who wanted nothing a reason to laugh.

"God will not do for you what you can do for yourself, Miss Steno. He will give you the insight you need, but you must spend time seeking it."

"I'm trying."

"I give you Psalm 103 this night."

"Which verse?"

The smile spread across his craggy features and reached his twinkling eyes. "All of it." OC checked the clock. "Time to begin."

Jim opened his black Bible full of tiny handwritten notes in the margins.

"What does it say?" Claire checked her pencil lead.

" 'Bless the Lord, O my soul: and all that is within me, bless his holy name.' Read the rest. It's rich."

She made note of it.

Punctual as always, OC finished his lecture at 8:00. Claire gave her notes to Jim to pass to Biddy later. As they exited the lecture room, the busy kitchen manager approached. "Could you help us this evening? We've a day's worth of dishes to wash."

Claire drew away. "I never wash dishes. I could hardly be of help."

"Do you know how to wash dishes?" Jim didn't sound amused.

She stared at him.

"Don't you remember what OC said?" Jim tapped her notes "The real test of the saint is not preaching the gospel but washing the disciples' feet."

"I've just spent an hour taking dictation."

"Would it hurt you to wash dishes to relieve someone else of the chore?"

Claire's throat thickened. "You don't understand."

"I don't think you do. Are you the Meacham princess here? What is the attitude of your heart toward manual tasks?"

"I'm not a princess, but I don't do chores like dishes." She cringed even as she spoke.

"Why not try now?"

A verse from the lecture whispered. Jesus said, "Whosoever of you will be the chiefest, shall be servant of all."

Claire squirmed. "It's time for me to be on my way."

"Half an hour, Claire. Can you not wash dishes for half an hour?"

She thrust gloves, pencil, and the remainder of her note pad into her bag. "Fine. I'll dry dishes, but you'll need to escort me home. It's getting late."

He gestured downstairs to the kitchen.

Claire paused at a card thumbtacked to the wall: "All service ranks the same with God. You are requested to kindly do your part in keeping this room tidy. If you do not, someone else will have to."

She squared her shoulders and entered the steamy kitchen, warm and smelling of sour dishes. Claire wrinkled her nose and hesitated at the greasy pots before whispering a prayer of thanks Sylvia would never know. She picked up a drying cloth.

Ninety minutes later, Claire stomped down the Underground station steps. Jim found them seats on a car headed north and Claire closed her eyes.

Though she'd worn an apron, her shirtwaist and skirt were damp. Her shoulders ached and she shuddered at the carbolic soap smell clinging to her hands. They'd cleaned the entire kitchen, Jim doing most of the hard labor while Claire dried the mountain of dishes. Completely out of her element and incompetent, she'd broken three cups and a platter.

As the car jerked into motion, Jim touched her red hands. "Even though I know you're from a different class, I thought you should be willing to help. I apologize."

A different class? The Meachams' near-insolvency made his comment laughable.

"I apologize for my bad attitude," Claire stammered. "I'm embarrassed."

They swayed with the clacking movement of the subway car, their shoulders touching then slipping apart.

Claire twisted her fingers. "When my parents were first married, my mother ran the household by herself. My father hated how hard she toiled, particularly when her parents and sister owned large homes and employed servants. He wanted to prove himself capable of providing a better life, so he sought journalism assignments overseas. Living in Paris, Moscow, and Cairo meant he could afford help. By the time they returned to America where I was born, they employed servants. I've never done housework."

"Your father earned his standard of living."

Claire shrugged. "My mother could have washed those dishes in half the time it took me to help you. Some days I wonder if she might be happier living a simpler, more purposeful existence."

He nudged her. "You don't need to be poor to be useful to God. The apostle Paul spoke of being all things to all people. Your place in society isn't a surprise to God. Perhaps he means to use you where you're established. You should watch for opportunities."

"Spy, you mean?"

He recoiled.

"My mother calls it spying when my father sends her into society hunting stories for him. It sounds like you're suggesting I spy out opportunities to remind the people I meet about God."

He stroked his chin. "What an interesting idea. God could use such a skill. Don't you agree?"

Weary, Claire could barely shrug. She had no idea how to answer his question.

Chapter Eleven

Claire yawned. Last night Nigel took her to see another Charlie Chaplin film and they stayed out too late. She'd managed to arise in time but needed to pinch herself awake during Monday's prayer time.

Biddy motioned to her afterwards. "You're much distracted. What's on your heart?"

Claire squirmed. Biddy saw past outward appearances and went straight to soul-truth. Her no-nonsense honesty shone through all she did, and she did not let Claire off the hook spiritually or emotionally. Claire couldn't decide if she liked being so well understood.

She sighed. "I'm troubled about my father. He doesn't know I come for prayer, much less I'm taking a correspondence course. I'm guilty, yet I know I need to be here."

Biddy drew back. "How do you honor your parents in this way?"

Claire removed her glasses and rubbed her eyes. "My mother knows I come to pray. She doesn't know how frequently, but she agreed when I asked permission."

"From your father?"

"From my aunt in whose house we live. Mama knows I'm studying the Bible and always encourages me to read widely."

"Your mother sounds wise."

Anne Meacham personified a woman wise as a serpent while looking as simple as a dove. Claire polished her lenses. "Mama doesn't know I come to the evening lectures."

"Where do they believe you go?"

Claire perched her spectacles on her nose and Biddy's concern came into focus. "I wait until they leave before I come. They don't know."

She heard little Kathleen's singsong voice as she trod down the stairs. The large front doors opened and closed and a clatter of dishes announced breakfast.

Biddy spoke quietly. "Our Lord has no patience for sin, sham, or slovenliness. Honesty is the hallmark of Jesus Christ."

"You think I should tell them I come?"

Biddy lifted her palms to God. "We give this to you, dear Lord. Amen."

Claire waited; surely she needed a longer prayer.

"We must always be centered on God himself. I believe God." She kissed Claire's brow and stepped to the dining room. Claire's vision blurred. She sat quietly with Eva Spink during breakfast and left without saying good-bye.

As the trolley rumbled through the streets south of the Thames, she envied the crowds going about their business and wondered why their lives seemed so simple in comparison to hers. Food, clothing, shelter; each day they began another round of living within their sphere. Claire moved between three circles: the grandeur of the upper-crust home, the excitement of the newsroom, and the provoking consolation of the BTC.

Each beckoned. She just needed to figure out how to meld them together into a life approved by everyone.

It seemed an impossible task.

Claire exited into the flow of city life several blocks from the newspaper office. She paused on a corner to fish a half-penny from her bag to purchase a newspaper. The bold headline screamed "Hymns of Praise for the Kultur that Kills Woman." She read about the German propaganda decried in the headline and shuddered over zeppelin raids in southern London. The tolling bell at St. Clement Danes reminded her to hurry. Claire needed to reach the office before her father arrived from an early morning interview.

She didn't know how to tell Jock about the BTC. Biddy expected it of her. She knew, with sinking heart, God did too.

"I finally caught up. You ran out after breakfast." Jim's face was red.

Claire showed him the headline. "What's your reaction?"

"I'm outraged and disgusted."

"Does it make you want to join up?"

He shook his head. "What good would that do? The Germans need prayer as much as the Allies. Besides, this isn't our fight."

She stopped. "What if you weren't an American? What if you were from New Zealand like Nigel? Would you enlist?'

Jim took the paper and refolded it. "Would you like me any less if I said no?"

"I'd like to know why."

"Maybe I'll tell you one day."

Claire stuffed the newspaper into her satchel and quickened her steps. Jim's presence helped on days when the news weighed her down. Germany's U-boats now blockaded England and threatened to sink passenger ships. The BNS wanted a British reaction. Jock was at a breakfast meeting with government officials to get one.

"What's troubling you?" Jim asked.

"I need to be honest with my parents about my trips to the BTC. I'm afraid of my father's reaction." They passed the brightly colored Twining's Tea Shop and through the open door, Claire caught a whiff of exotic lands.

"You're an adult. Can't you make your own decisions?"

"I'm not yet twenty-one. My father supports me. I've never disobeyed him until now."

He steered her around a group of soldiers. "You underestimate yourself. With your office skills you're employable anywhere. You just need to figure out who you want to be."

"What do you mean?"

"Adults choose how they want to live and where. You could too."

"I can't become a reporter without my father's help."

"Is that your goal?" Jim grinned. "Good for you. You've the talent and sweet heart to be an excellent one."

"A sweet heart and reporting do not go together."

He tucked up his collar against the chilly morning and took her elbow. "Let the Lord be your guide. He'll keep you in perfect peace if you keep your mind focused on what he desires for your life. Your situation is no surprise to him."

Two women marched toward them with zeal in their eyes—which were fixed on Jim.

"My good man, you're not in uniform," the taller one declared in a haughty voice. She wore a sweeping hat decorated with spring flowers.

He paused and his face went expressionless.

The shorter woman spoke in a cultivated accent. "You should be ashamed of yourself. You need this." She handed him a white feather.

"What are you doing?" Claire shouted. "You don't know anything about him."

Flower Hat sniffed. "Young men should be in uniform. He's a disgrace to manhood."

"He's an American," Claire said.

The two women peered down their noses at Claire. "Perhaps your nation should join the cause, miss. Good day." Flower Hat nodded to her companion and they marched off to seek other prey.

"I'm sorry, Jim."

He tucked the feather into his pocket. "I'm getting quite a collection. This is number five."

"I apologize, I didn't—"

"God examines the attitude of our hearts," Jim said. "It's helpful to keep that in mind when we want to judge. I know your heart." He watched the women badger another man near Twining's. "He knows theirs too. Perhaps their loved ones are serving in the army, and this is how they deal with their fears."

She stared at him, wondering if she would ever be as fair-minded. Jim went out of his way not to take offense, and Claire struggled over every suggestion she might not be perfect. "They insulted you. How can you be so forgiving?"

He sighed and shook his head. "I'm not a saint, Claire. I've just learned there's more than meets the eye when people say ugly things. It's taken lots of prayer and confession of my own weaknesses."

She wanted to ask what weaknesses, but his bleak expression silenced her. She took his elbow this time as they trudged through the Fleet Street crowds.

Jock stepped out of a taxi as they reached the office and squinted. "How did you get here?"

They parted. Claire licked her lips. "Trolley."

"Hodges?"

"Good day, Mr. Meacham. I also rode a trolley."

"Are we done, governor?" The cabbie held out his cap. Jock tossed a coin into it, not taking his eyes off them. "Inside, the two of you."

Jim opened the door and the Meachams entered the marble entry. "Really, Papa, what is the matter?"

"Are you telling me you rode the trolley from Belgravia?"

She swallowed. "I've been riding the trolley and the underground for months. It's cheaper than a taxi and it frees Mr. Able to drive Aunt Sarah."

He glared at Jim. "Were you with her?"

Claire held her breath.

"No. I met her at the corner when she purchased the newspaper."

Several reporters stepped around them with puzzled expressions. Jock frowned at Claire and Jim. "I can tell something's up, but I'll deal with you later. Boston needs the news."

Biddy said she needed to tell the truth, but Claire's stomach roiled at her father's building anger. What would happen next?

News, of course.

Claire finished up by four and joined Jock in his office, where he puffed his pipe and stared out the window. When Jim entered to check out, Jock interrupted him.

"What are you intentions toward my daughter?"

"I admire your daughter, Mr. Meacham. She's a diligent stenographer and a well-meaning young woman. I consider her a friend."

"Claire?"

The only way to deal with him was to bluster, but she didn't trust the fire in his eyes. "Jim is my friend. I don't understand what you're insinuating. Have we missed essential news?"

"No? Where were you this morning?"

She raised her chin. "I went to a prayer meeting at the Bible Training College."

"After I told you not to?"

"I went to pray, Papa. No harm done."

"Then why bother?" His lip curled. "Your role, Hodges?"

"I saw Miss Meacham at the meeting. She left and I caught the trolley after hers."

"But you've encouraged her, haven't you? How often does she attend these meetings?" Jock turned the pipe over in his hands.

Jim remained calm. "I've seen her on many Monday mornings, sir."

"Claire?"

"Most Mondays." She beat him to the next question. "Since the fall."

"After I forbade it?" His voice rose.

The newsroom clamor slowed. Claire closed the door to buy time. "You never told me I couldn't go."

"I forbid you now."

"I don't care."

Jim sucked in his breath. Claire swallowed and realized the truth. She didn't care.

"Sir, perhaps you should visit the BTC and witness its positive effects."

"You're fired, Hodges. You've encouraged this insolence from my daughter and I don't appreciate you distorting her understanding of religion's role. Collect your paycheck and don't come back."

"How can you fire him for something I did?" Claire smacked her notebook on the desk. "You're not being fair!"

Jock pointed out of the office. "Good day, Hodges. I'm sorry it ended this way."

Jim stopped at the door. "Sir, if I may say one more thing?"

"What?"

"If I've caused a breach between you and your daughter, I apologize. I never intended to cause problems in your family."

"Fine words, Hodges, but too late. Get out."

Jim shut the door quietly behind him.

Bitterness surged from her lips. "How can you fire him? If you want to fire someone, fire me. Don't take out your anger on Jim. It's not fair!"

He rapped his pipe on the desk. "You should have thought of that before you involved him. You're the one at fault here. I made my opinion known and you disobeyed me."

"You're trying to control what I believe. Why don't you ask me what I think, instead of assuming Jim harmed you?"

"You're getting caught up in this odd religious group. I won't allow it. We're thinking, rational people and you do not need to spend your time at bogus prayer meetings."

She clenched her fists so hard her nails indented the skin. "How else can I handle the war? Giving my fears to God helps me. Your antagonism toward God is not mine. Maybe the problem is yours."

"How dare you?" He struck the pipe on the desk so hard, it broke in two.

Claire swallowed and resisted the urge to stamp her foot like a child.

The clock ticked. Her father stomped to the window. She remembered a verse she'd read advising to do whatever necessary to live at peace with others.

Claire bit her lip. Who was in the wrong here? Her father for demanding she be what he wanted her to be, or Claire for not telling him what he refused to hear? Most fathers would be thankful for daughters who read the Bible and went to prayer meetings.

But not Jock Meacham.

Jim thought her resourceful and talented. Biddy prayed for Claire.

"I'm sorry if I've disappointed you, Papa."

Before she could finish, he spun around. "I knew you'd see reason. Let's go home. I'm hungry." He swept the pipe pieces into the wastepaper basket. "I need a new pipe."

Claire gathered her possessions. Her father walked into the outer office and shouted for a new copyboy.

Jock obviously thought he'd won.

She'd show him differently.

Chapter Twelve

April 1915

Mr. Able had closed the motorcar door the following Monday morning, when Jock hurried down the front steps and climbed in beside Claire. "Thought you'd escape, didn't you?"

Claire cleared her throat. "I told you Monday morning prayer is important. Are you coming with me?"

Mr. Able settled behind the wheel. "Sir?"

"Take Claire where she wants to go," Jock said as he settled into the seat beside her.

The streets of fashionable Belgravia were quiet. Street sweepers brushed down the road and tradesman called on the staff downstairs, but the upstairs windows of the stately white mansions were dark. Only pink blossomed cherry trees added color.

Jock smoked his new pipe and drummed his fingers. His large presence made the seat warmer on the chilly April day, diminishing Claire.

"Have you considered returning to Radcliffe?"

So unexpected, she sat up straight and gasped. "Really?" But then she rallied her reporter-trained brain before he could crush her hopes. "You want me to cross the ocean during a war? With U-boats hunting ships? What does Mama think?"

"We haven't discussed it. I thought perhaps you'd be happier home among the books, preparing for the future." He stretched his arm across the seat.

"Where would the money come from? Besides, this is my future. I want to be a reporter, hopefully a foreign correspondent."

"Reporters are easy to find. You're my only daughter. You might be safer in America."

"You mean far from the BTC?"

Jock shrugged.

She stared out the window.

They traveled past the Royal Mews and Buckingham Palace along Birdcage Walk toward Westminster. Big Ben's hands indicated plenty of time to make the twenty-minute drive to Clapham Common.

Claire's emotions warred. She craved the BTC encouragement but worried what Jock would do.

When Mr. Able drew up to number 45, Jock exited.

"Are you coming to pray?" Claire asked.

"Isn't it open to anyone? Got your notebook?"

"Of course."

Jim's eyebrows climbed to his hairline when Jock entered the foyer. He shook hands with his former boss, who responded politely, and escorted him into the lecture hall. Claire trailed them with dread.

Jock took a seat in the last row and she and Jim joined him. OC softly played "When Morning Gilds the Skies" on the compact pump organ.

Jock hummed along.

She didn't trust him. Meanwhile, what could she say to Jim? "I'm sorry you lost your job because of me."

"God on the move; a better opportunity came up."

Jock snickered.

OC increased the volume and they sang the hymn full-voiced. After OC's "Good morning," the congregation of two dozen praised God and thanked him for a myriad of blessings.

With her father so close and sitting with arms and feet crossed, Claire could not focus on God. She tried to ignore Jock but didn't dare pray aloud.

When Jim mentioned Edward, Nigel, and Peter, her father grunted, "Amen."

Claire tried to relax.

Jock behaved himself.

After OC led them in a final prayer, her father sped across the room to greet him. By the time Claire collected her bag, the two men were in conversation.

Biddy detained her. "Your father? I am pleased he came."

"He's up to something."

Biddy chuckled.

Jock motioned her over. "Reverend Chambers has invited us for breakfast and has agreed to an interview. Shall we begin over the meal?" he asked OC.

"Certainly. I can give you one half hour after breakfast. I am a man under authority and must stay true to my schedule."

"Fair enough." Jock nodded at Claire. "Get this down."

He asked aggressive questions to which OC answered confidently, laughed occasionally, and took nothing personally.

"My American readers will want to know how your time in the United States affected your ministry," Jock said.

"I liked America. I taught in Cincinnati, Ohio, at a school called the Mount of Blessings, which describes it well. The students were open-minded and teachable. They studied the Scriptures without prejudice and with great pleasure."

Claire scribbled down their words while she sipped bracing, sugarless tea. The questions sounded benign, but she knew they wouldn't stay that way.

His head down, Jim barely touched his porridge. He was undoubtedly praying.

"How much did they pay you?"

"I received a sufficient honorarium to fund my trip to Japan." OC sipped his tea.

"You must have earned plenty if you could travel overseas. You only had to preach on Sundays to earn it?"

OC smiled. "There's a passage in the New Testament, the book of Luke, chapter 10, in which Jesus reminds his disciples 'the laborer is worthy of his hire.' While I am content to live as Christ has called me whether I am paid or not, I appreciated the gift given me by the people of Cincinnati."

Jim intervened. "He taught at the school, ordained ministers, and wrote articles. Reverend Chambers was busy from morning until night. Many sought him for prayer and counsel."

Jock focused on OC. "What made you go to Japan?"

"God sent me with a Japanese evangelist, Juji Nakada, a brother in Christ. I wanted to see missionary work and preach the gospel to the lost."

OC ended the interview promptly at 8:55. "I must teach a class. Come again, Mr. Meacham. I am happy to speak with you. We appreciate your daughter. Claire lightened the load by taking dictation for my Biddy when she was injured."

Jock rose with him. "One more question. Why do you think women are drawn to you?"

Biddy, collecting the teacups, stopped to scrutinize Jock.

"It is not me who brings the call," OC said. "All who come are attracted to the Lord Jesus Christ, motivated by the workings of the Holy Spirit to present themselves a holy and living sacrifice to God. We can do no less. Good morning."

Jock reached into his pocket. "You can't smoke here," Claire hissed.

He withdrew his hand. "May I have a word with you, Mrs. Chambers? I need a few facts."

Biddy set down the tray. "I will answer three questions, no more."

"Where did you meet your husband?"

"He spoke at a revival service at Eltham Park Baptist Church shortly after I was baptized in 1905."

Claire wrote down the answer.

"Did you fall in love at first sight?"

Her eyes sparkled and a smile played across her lips. "No."

"When did you get married?"

"May 25, 1910. Good day." She picked up her tray and left.

"Wait!"

Claire stuck her pencil and notebook in her bag. "You asked three questions, Papa. No one trifles with Biddy."

Jock said nothing as Mr. Able drove them to the office. He sent Claire to retrieve the wire copy, a task now falling to her with Jim's departure.

Mr. Conroy stopped her as she carried a sheaf of organized stories to his office.

"You're the reason I lost my best employee. That's why women are not welcome in the newsroom. How do you think I'm going to be able to replace him?"

"I am so sorry," Claire stuttered. She felt her face redden and didn't know where to look. "I didn't mean for it to happen."

His teeth set, the thin man leaned toward her and spluttered. "But it did. I'd like nothing better than to throw you out of here myself, but that's not allowed. You listen to me, miss. You stay in that office. I don't want you out here luring other men away from their jobs."

"No."

"And if you think I'll use your skills to help other men, you can toss that idea from your feminine brain. I don't want you here, and this is the reason why."

"I understand." Shaking, Claire fled to Jock's office where she placed the wire copy on his desk. He was cleaning his pipe.

"What took you so long?" he asked without looking up. "Take this down. An international evangelist with ties to the Holiness Movement in America runs a school in one of the tonier areas of London."

She didn't like the word *tonier*, and she didn't trust her father's hooded eyes and restless fingers. Claire looped the symbols, her eyes fixed on the page. As he spoke, she pushed the pencil lead deeper into the paper, and clenched her jaw. Her strokes were dark, legible, and clear.

Claire asked him to repeat sentences.

He finally looked at her. "I know you're faster than this. What's wrong?"

She threw down her pencil. "This isn't an honest story. You're twisting what Oswald Chambers said. You've made him out to be a charlatan preying on people for money. That's not who he is."

"You're too young to understand the ways of the world. Anyone could see through the pious Scot surrounded by female staff and besotted young men like Jim. You need to enter a story like this with an unbiased mind, Claire. Out of your fear, you've grabbed hold to his pie-in-the-sky myth God will watch over you no matter what happens."

Anger surged at both him and Mr. Conroy. Maybe the suffragettes had the right attitude about patronizing men.

"Pick up your pencil; this goes out tonight. The syndicate wants stories related to America, this will be perfect. Chambers is better known at home than I realized."

Claire thought of Oswald Chambers's even temper and humble manner. He referred to art, psychology, and history as he recounted items from books he'd read. He insisted they stick to the Bible whenever they presented a spiritual argument, and he prayed with a quiet assurance they tried to emulate.

"I refuse. I won't transcribe lies." Her stomach ached and her voice rasped. She'd never spoken to him in such a way. She'd never been so furious either.

"How dare you!" His eyebrows came together.

"How dare you malign a good man who seeks nothing but God's will!"

Jock pushed back his leather chair. "Everyone's biased. We report through the lens of our past experiences. You need to determine your preconceptions and try to counterbalance them. Everyone has one."

"You're biased against OC because of me. You're angry with me and taking it out on an innocent person, just as you did to Jim."

"You're wrong," he declared. "This time I've gone to the source. He's not innocent, he knows what he's doing running a school in that lavish building. Money must be coming from somewhere. He's probably fleecing the students."

Heat flashed through Claire. "Penniless students like Jim? A religious organization rented the building. The Chambers have no wealth."

"How do you know?" Jock demanded. "Because he told you?"

She raised her voice to match his. "Because I have eyes to see and ears to hear stories about him emptying his pockets to those in need. Biddy owns few garments; their time is given to God's call. Buying books is his only indulgence. How can you fault him?"

Jock went to the window. Claire rubbed her eyes and wanted nothing more than to sink through the floor with exhausting heaviness. Her nose tickled as he puffed on his pipe. Hands trembling, she paged through the morning's notes. Her father was wrong.

She tried to control herself by speaking quietly. "What did you conclude about Oswald Chambers the man?"

Jock replied from a cloud of tobacco smoke. "He's amiable and obviously well read. I appreciated his sense of humor, his choice of hymns, and how he didn't drone on forever when he prayed."

"Yet you'd write a story slandering him. You'd destroy a hardworking man of God because of your pride?" She couldn't help the bitterness.

"You're biased, too, only the other way." He faced her. "I give it to you. If you can do a fairer job, then you write the story." Jock tapped his wrist watch. "You've got two hours."

She blew out her breath and realized she couldn't go to her desk in the newsroom. Fury surged again, but boxed in, she turned her back on her father and sat at the table in his office.

"You're not going out to your desk?"

"No. I'll use the typewriter in here."

Fashioning an article about a person she admired took longer than Claire anticipated. She needed to remember her father's slant and put together an article melding both angles. Jock always said, "Truth is somewhere between the two extremes."

As Claire thought and examined her notes, she questioned herself. What facts did she know?

Oswald Chambers admitted he wasn't perfect. Biddy chided him for humoring his toddler. He taught too many students in his correspondence class to the detriment of his sleep. He acted with enthusiasm, even when his companions flagged from exhaustion.

They ate simply at the BTC and wore plain clothing. Neither OC nor Biddy showed signs of personal indulgence. Jim never complained. Students flocked around OC and famous Londoners sought him out. Even Aunt Sarah's friends spoke well of the man.

Claire wrote, rewrote, crossed out, reconsidered, quoted, and then removed the quotes. She'd typed eight paragraphs when Jock asked for her version two hours later.

He picked up the blue pencil and scrutinized the text, his pipe mercifully unlit. Jock marked the copy, drew lines, and scribbled notes of his own. "Not a bad start, darling. You need a few more facts and observations, but you've done well for a first attempt. This isn't half bad."

"I've learned from you." She released her breath.

"Perhaps. Let's craft it together."

They edited another hour, adding Jock's impressions and a few tidbits Claire remembered hearing from Eva and Jim. By the time they finished, on deadline, they both were satisfied.

"Will I share the byline?" It was worth the anguish if her dream could be a reality.

Jock laughed. "No."

"I wrote this article but nothing changed about my chance for a byline?"

He shrugged. "You never know when your break will come. That's the life of a reporter."

Chapter Thirteen

May 1915

Two weeks after Edward left for France with the British Expeditionary Forces, Mr. Able appeared in the breakfast room with a telegram. Aunt Sarah paled and touched her chest. Sylvia ignored the thin paper on the proffered silver plate.

"I'm sure there's a mistake. It must be for Uncle Jock."

Mr. Able shook his head. "The messenger said Mrs. Sylvia Henley."

"I couldn't."

"May I, darling?" Jock reached across the table.

Sylvia touched her lips with a napkin. "Please."

Anne moved to her niece's side while Jock slit the envelope with a silver butter knife. He read quickly. Sylvia didn't look up, but Anne met his eye. A curt nod.

Claire crammed her knuckles into her mouth. Aunt Sarah sputtered into sobs.

Sylvia stared straight ahead. "What does it say, Uncle Jock?" Her voice, usually so coy and full of life, sounded as ashen as sand.

"I'm sorry, darling, Edward is gone. He died on May 7 outside Ypres."

Sylvia clenched her brilliant diamond ring and rotated it at dizzying speed, light catching on the facets and spilling fractured rainbows around the room.

Anne stretched her arms around Sylvia's shoulders and pressed her damp cheek against her niece's.

Sylvia cleared her throat. "We'll bury him at his parents' estate in the country. It's what he wanted."

Jock inspected the telegram. "They've already buried him in France. His body won't be coming back."

Sylvia excused herself.

The thud of a dropped rucksack announced Peter's return two days later, and the family hurried to greet him. His cheekbones stood out of his haunted face and his hands shook. As Claire hugged him tight she tried to categorize what he smelled like: noxious mud, frightened sweat, greasy transport.

"The weather's miserable and we're not flying, so the command granted me leave to bring Edward's kit. Sylvia shouldn't have to go through it by herself."

His sister turned to ice. "Edward is gone. I don't need his possessions."

"Perhaps his mother would like them?" Peter suggested in a hoarse voice.

"Take them to her. It's too much for me. Tea?"

Jock poured a whiskey, which Peter gulped. They muttered a few exchanges in what Claire thought of as army-speak.

"How bad?" Jock asked.

"Division swamped; men incompetent and the Frogs incomprehensible, as you expected."

Jock rubbed his arm. "Wouldn't you rather be teaching flying in England?"

"Abandon my mates? No."

Nigel had known Edward at Oxford, so he joined them at the Henley family's ancient chapel in Kent for a memorial service two days later. Sylvia wore a precisely painted albeit stoic face behind her fashionable black veil. Peter, tall and resplendent in dress uniform with a new medal over the left pocket, sobbed.

He collected himself enough to read the lessons in an empty tenor. Claire focused on the jewel-colored windows and the waxy candle scent mixed with Sylvia's subdued bouquet. Jock moved his pipe in and out, in and out, hands riffling his hair and feet tapping to empty sighs. Anne moved among them with clean handkerchiefs and soothing words.

"Keep your eyes on Sylvia," she whispered to Claire. "I'm afraid she'll crack."

The young widow remained in control. After the service, they had a splendid breakfast which no one touched.

Sylvia rarely spoke of Edward again.

Claire wondered if her prayers had made a difference.

On Sunday the family motored to St. Paul's, where they sat facing the choir stalls. Cherubic boys sang the service in soaring voices echoing through the enormous cathedral. The airy dome circled above and light rays reached to the polished floor. Peter clenched his jaw. He jerked when Claire touched him.

"What are you thinking?"

"I must be in a dream. My real life endures a million miles away in mud and stench, where blood runs like streams. To sit in a place like this, clean and ornate, full of music and candles, seems impossible. Edward died in screaming agony while English life trots on."

She rested her head on his shoulder. "I'm so sorry."

"I don't know if anyone can understand who hasn't been there. At least I can take off into the sky and don't need to burrow into the ground like an animal. Of course, every soldier on the east side of No Man's Land who watches me wants me dead."

Helpless and bereft, Claire murmured, "Oh."

"Nigel's safe at headquarters but Edward never stood a chance." He rubbed his eyes. "I mustn't speak of such misery in the house of God."

"Where else should you talk of them, if not before God?" Claire whispered. "He, at least, knows and understands the ways of man."

"The army is full of animals, not men. We're disposable hordes."

Claire shuddered, suddenly cold. "Each of you is loved by God. You must believe me."

He sighed. "You believe it for me. I don't believe in anything right now."

The solemn service did nothing to dispel his gloom. The priest remembered Edward in his remarks and prayed long for the families of those lost when a U-boat sank the ocean liner RMS *Lusitania.* The German menace hidden under the water off the coast terrified both sides of the Atlantic Ocean.

After the service Claire spied Jim on the north side of the altar and hurried to greet him. "The family's mourning. Sylvia's husband died at Ypres."

Jim took her hand. "I'm sorry. I'll pray for your family."

She nodded. "How are you?"

"I'm following God's lead and heading overseas with the Young Men's Christian Association. I'll be ministering to soldiers."

Could she take any more war? "Won't you be in danger? Peter visits YMCA canteens near the front lines."

He shrugged. "I go where God sends. I volunteered to help the ANZAC troops at Gallipoli. I'll be out of headquarters in Cairo."

Claire's eyes widened. Her mother, a practical woman who managed whatever life threw at her with aplomb, cringed whenever someone mentioned Egypt. Having grown up with Anne's anguish, Claire regarded Egypt with more dread than the grisly ANZAC stalemate on a peninsula off the coast of Turkey. "I'll pray for you."

He smiled. "I hear Cairo's got plenty of taxis, but not the Dardanelles. We'll need your prayers. Will you write me in legible script? It's been an honor to know you and watch your faith grow, Claire Meacham."

"My faith feels tiny sending you off, especially now."

"Let me show you something." He led her to a nearby painting. Jesus stood before a wooden door, his right hand raised high to knock. Wearing a royal robe and a crown of thorns in a nighttime garden, Jesus lifted a lantern in his left hand.

Claire knew it. "William Hunt's *The Light of the World*."

"This painting has special meaning for OC and Biddy," Jim explained. "It's where they became engaged. They promised their mutual life to Christ's purposes on this spot. Wherever God sends them, they are willing to go. I feel the same. How about you?"

Claire pondered Jesus. She wasn't sure.

"'Behold I stand at the door and knock,'" Jim quoted. "'If anyone hears my voice and opens the door, I will come in and eat with him, and he with me.' That's what we're called to do, make Christ known to the world."

"Perhaps if you actually did something in the world, I might respect you." Nigel waited with crossed arms and a sour expression. "It's time to go, Claire."

"Nigel," Jim nodded. "Are you headed overseas soon?"

"It's not clear. But I'll certainly be in theater before a shirker like you. Received any white feathers lately?"

"You have no call to be rude, Nigel." Claire shook Jim's hand. "Thank you for showing me the painting."

Nigel propelled her to her parents waiting by the south doors.

"What's up with Hodges?" Jock asked.

"He's going overseas with the YMCA."

"Excellent. The canteens are invaluable. An optimist like Hodges would be useful."

Anne craned her neck. "Is he the young man you fired?"

"How can you be reasonable now?" Claire asked.

"You must learn to separate the personal from the professional. I never said I didn't like Hodges; I just didn't like his influence on you. There's a difference."

"Not to me."

"Then you'll burn out too fast. You must compartmentalize your emotions. This will be a long war. No one can afford to hold grudges. Where's he going?"

"Gallipoli."

Jock froze. "Give me your notebook."

"By George, I didn't know he had it in him," Nigel muttered. "Gallipoli's a charnel house."

Anne's fingers touched her lips.

Her father scribbled down words and tore out the page, retrieved an engraved business card from his pocket, and folded it into the paper. "Go ahead."

Jim knelt before the painting, head in his hands. As her father approached him and Nigel pulled her to the door, Claire wondered if she'd ever see Jim again—this side of eternity.

Chapter Fourteen

June 1915

Mr. Conroy knocked on Jock's office door. "An American is here to see you, claims to be a journalist."

Claire stood up when the bearded face of Mitchell Bellamy grinned over Conroy's shoulder. Jock beat her to him and hugged his old friend. "Where've you come from?"

Bellamy's eyes were on Claire. "My goodness, Annie, you're younger than the last time I saw you."

"I'm Claire and you know it." She hugged him.

"History teacher in the making, I hear," he said. "What're you doing in the newsroom?"

Jock grunted. "Claims she wants to be a reporter. I've been discouraging her."

Bellamy's face fell. "For good reason. I've just come from Germany. Can I wire a story to New York?"

"It will go through the British censors." Jock fetched his pipe. "What've you got?"

He pulled newspapers from an inner pocket and handed them to Claire. "Can you read these?"

"*Welt in Bild*," she read. "The world in pictures." She flipped through the pages as Bellamy told his story. With four other American journalists, he'd crossed into Germany and traveled through the country under German army escort.

Jock indicated the wall map. "Where are the lines?"

Bellamy adjusted the pins. "This was a week ago. Brits are flying over the trenches mapping them. I saw several planes shot down."

Claire stepped closer and caught her breath. Peter's last letter had come from that sector. He'd referenced how Grandfather Powell would have loved the views he'd seen. Claire had understood Peter meant he flew along the coastline, not far from where Bellamy pinned.

Jock's eyes narrowed. "Is that where Peter is?"

"Hard to know," Claire finally said.

"If it's someone you care about, you better hope not," Bellamy said. "Conditions are nasty. We'd heard stories of German atrocities in Belgium and wanted to prove them. Nothing."

"Of course not," Jock said. "You were with the Germans."

Bellamy put up his hand. "The propaganda mill is running overtime and it's British. I'm on my way to New York with the real story." He patted his suit pocket. "We saw no signs of nuns or children being brutalized."

Jock squinted, skepticism obvious.

"Belgians died, but the Germans consider their cause just. The Brits squeezed them politically and economically for years. If the war didn't come now, it would come later. It was only a matter of time."

"What's your reaction to that, Claire? You studied the economies."

"There's logic in what Mr. Bellamy says. They've been pushing at each other for years," Claire pointed to the Baltic coastline. "The British navy bottled up the German dreadnaughts in their ports; it's not safe for them to come out. She rules the seas and the Kaiser doesn't like it. He had no choice but to go underwater."

The thought of U-boats made her shiver.

"Good observation. Where'd you get your information?" Bellamy beamed at her.

"I studied applicable subjects at Radcliffe. I'd love to be the first female American foreign correspondent in Europe."

"Too late, honey, Mary Rinehart's ahead of you. She traveled into Belgium with the Red Cross."

"How?"

"She trained as a nurse before she published mysteries. The Belgian military invited her to tour hospitals and she traveled as far as the trenches before the command evacuated her. Maybe you can be the second?"

Jock reached for his hat. "Let's go to the pub for a drink; you deserve it. Finish up the dispatch, Claire, and ring your mother—we're bringing home a dinner guest."

"But I want to hear what he has to say."

The men exchanged looks. Bellamy shrugged.

"I'm not a child. I can handle it."

"You'll hear the stories at dinner," Jock said. "In the meantime, Boston needs the news." The men left.

If he'd hoped to dissuade her, Jock's plan had backfired. Claire now knew at least one woman had worked as a reporter in the war zone. She could make it two.

"What are you working on so locked away?" Anne asked as she entered Claire's bedroom a week later.

Seated at the table under tall windows, Claire handed over the green pamphlet. "It's a Bible correspondence course."

"The entire Bible?" Anne thumbed through the eight pages. "This is a thin syllabus."

"The BTC has six courses covering a variety of topics; this one deals with sanctification."

"Indeed. Which is?"

Claire checked her notes. "OC says 'sanctification means intense concentration on God's point of view. Every power of body, soul and spirit are chained and kept for God's purpose.' "

Anne grabbed Claire's chin. "I don't care what OC says. I want to know what you think. Use your brain."

"Sanctification means I can live a holy life with purpose and when I die, I won't disappear into oblivion, I'll go to heaven." Claire's hands turned clammy.

Anne relaxed into a bedside chair. "Since you know, why this Bible study? Why these prayer meetings? This man is luring you away from your family, trying to make you into a person you're not."

"I like OC and Biddy, but it's what I'm learning about God that makes a difference to me. I've never heard Jesus explained like this. It helps me make sense of the war."

"Society is in flux with the war," Anne said. "The news frightens. While calling on the Divine is a fine idea, you don't need to become obsessed about it."

"About *him*," Claire corrected. "Jesus is a real person."

Anne brought her graceful hands to rest on her lap. "Certainly, but don't you think you're becoming a bit zealous on this subject? Certainly it's admirable to study the Bible, but..."

Claire straightened her spine and gazed at her mother, who stared back.

The silence lengthened.

Her mother knew Jock's trick too.

When the tiny desk clock chimed four, Claire gave in. "I'm studying the Bible to better understand the type of person God wants me to be. The war is so awful; the Bible teaches me God has a purpose for my life and how I should live."

"As I suspected. You're afraid. You shouldn't hide in a book, sheltering from the world and listening to narrow church people. You've too much life ahead of you. Don't become a sober nun; embrace the world." Anne paced the room, muttering, "Even Nigel may be better than this."

Claire thought of the liveliness she'd experienced at the BTC: Biddy's kindness, OC's wisdom, and the friendly students. Laughter rang in the lecture hall, cheerful spirits and jokes prevailed; they'd welcomed her into their fellowship and made her one of their own.

Claire touched a floral card propped beside her diary, an encouraging note presented with a hug from Eva Spink. "What can I do to make you happy, Mama?"

"Act on your dreams. Studying the Bible is fine, but don't be distracted from your plans. Perhaps we should arrange a trip to Stonehenge or to Edinburgh to view the castle."

"I'm acting on my dreams in the newsroom. Can you be happy now?"

"Of course not. Reporting is dangerous work, long hours with little pay. Men aren't attracted to nosey women asking questions. You don't want to end up like that Nellie Bly: lonely, broke, and forsaken."

Claire swallowed hard. "You don't want me at the BTC and you don't want me in the newsroom. Do you think I'm better suited to roll bandages and fret over wartime fashion like Sylvia?"

Anne rubbed away the lines in her forehead. "What does your father say about your goal?"

"Didn't he tell you? He threatened to fire me."

Anne laughed.

Claire's throat tightened. "I reminded him I'm the only one left who takes dictation, so he changed his mind. I expect he's warming to the idea."

Anne rose. "Good luck. I'd pray hard if I were you." She hesitated at the door. "Do you know what he's up to now?"

Bewildered at the sudden change in subject, Claire shook her head. "If you don't know, nobody knows."

"You've not heard anything at the office? I know he's agitated about something. I recognize the signs."

Claire frowned. "He hasn't said anything to me."

Anne tied open the velvet draperies facing Belgravia Square. "Maybe a transfer?"

Claire joined her at the window where down on the street below Mr. Able helped Aunt Sarah out of the motorcar. "Where would he go? America?"

"He'd never leave the biggest story of his lifetime. I imagine it's Paris; we love Paris. I hope it isn't Berlin. I couldn't endure the Kaiser's court."

"Spying, you mean?"

She chuckled. "Fact-gathering's my job. I'd better brush up on my French." Anne made a face. "Maybe even my German."

Claire watched her aunt speak with an elegant gentleman carrying a fashionable cane. "Could you leave Aunt Sarah?"

"Sarah needed a sympathetic ear to mourn with her and to encourage her. With Peter overseas and Edward's death, she's decided to start managing her family's affairs. I don't know what I'd do if I lost my husband."

A cab pulled up and Jock exited. He greeted Sarah and then peered at the house with a grim twist of his mouth.

"Something's happened," Anne said. They hurried to meet him at the front door. He trudged in as if weighed down with lead, Aunt Sarah following close behind. Anne's hand went to her throat. "What's happened?"

"Josiah Fischer sent me a wire today from Boston. After I saw Mitch Bellamy and heard his stories, I hankered for more action so I asked the BNS for a transfer."

His word parsing made Claire suspicious. "Where?"

"I thought Paris, or maybe Berlin if only to get the other side of the story."

Anne's lips thinned. "Where?"

"I need to take the job, Annie. We've no savings and I won't have a career without this position."

Jock's brows contracted as he appealed to Claire.

"Where?" she repeated.

"Cairo."

Anne sank to the floor and wailed.

Claire gasped. "Why?"

"Boston needs the news," he sighed. "Lots of reporters want to cover the western front. Few want to head east. The BNS thinks a man who spoke Arabic twenty years ago should go where they speak Arabic."

Anne moaned. "You cannot ask me to return to that hellhole."

Claire knelt to hug Anne. Her mother had barely survived the illness that had killed her brothers there so long ago.

His voice cracked. "How can I go without you?"

"Why can't you stay in London?" Claire asked.

Her father glared at her.

"Is this about me? Did you request a transfer because of me?"

Jock pulled out his pipe.

Claire's head swam. How could Claire's decision to attend a prayer meeting have resulted in her mother's worst nightmare? "I'll give up the BTC. Tell them you've changed your mind."

"Too late, darling," he said in a weary voice. "They made their decision. I can't afford not to take the job and Fischer's son wants to come to London. I won't let anything happen to you, Annie. Come with me. Surely it's more modern now."

"It's a disease-ridden place of misery. It robbed me of my sons. I won't go."

"But Mama, how can I go without you?"

Anne startled. "You're not going. I won't lose another child."

"What about my job?"

Jock packed tobacco into his pipe and scratched a match. "You'll stay with your mother. You made your choice. We'll live with the consequences. I hope you and your God are happy."

"That's not fair."

"Go away," Jock ordered.

She fled to the drawing room. Aunt Sarah joined her.

"Shh," Aunt Sarah whispered, drawing Claire to her. "You'll be fine."

"How?" Claire choked on her sobs.

"Haven't you learned anything yet about faith?"

Chapter Fifteen

Summer 1915

Claire opened the thin envelope with a Cairo stamp dated June 17. Two dried flower petals fell into her lap: faded red poppies as fragile as a butterfly wing. Jim wrote in tiny script to fill both sides of the onionskin paper. She rubbed her glasses clean but still squinted to read the words:

> *Arrived safely in Gallipoli despite misses from U-boats. Found a squalid mess of soldiers, misery and, above all, flies. Joined the YMCA workers on a scrap of beach and barely brewed the first cup of tea before artillery shell hit. Broke my arm and while not as badly injured as most of the soldiers on the forlorn spot, they reassigned me.*
>
> *Now working in Cairo for Mr. Jessop. Weather hotter than England. Desert is different from anything I've seen before.*

She carried the letter into the library where her father's packing cases were being filled and handed it to him. "Jim Hodges is in Cairo with the YMCA."

He scanned it. "Excellent. Fresh from the Dardanelles, he could be a good source. Technically he's not a clergyman, so he may be able to talk more than army chaplains."

Claire sat in her uncle's shaggy leather chair, still smelling vaguely of his hearty cigars. "I'll miss you, Papa."

He grunted.

"I don't know what I'll do without you. How will I be able to work?"

"You should have returned to Radcliffe." He straightened. "I'll speak to Conroy but don't get your hopes up. He doesn't want women in the newsroom."

The last weeks had been a misery of broken hopes and unhappiness. Her mother refused to help Jock pack, so he pressed Claire into service. She drew up lists and scribbled notes to tradesman as her father closed out his London life. She helped arrange his transport and traveled to the BNS to take dictation and type. The journey to Port Said at the top of the Suez Canal would take two weeks; Jock wrote up features in advance so his byline would appear in the Boston papers even as he traveled.

Normal life went by the wayside. OC sent her final essay with comprehensive notes and a personal message. "We miss you at the BTC and pray God's blessings upon you." She'd had no opportunity to join them for prayer, but once her father sailed Claire planned to be a regular visitor. She needed OC's wise teaching and Biddy's comforting encouragement.

"Jim saw U-boats," she said.

"They're out there."

"Are you afraid?"

"Did you see where I put my new Arabic dictionary?" Jock pushed aside a stack of books and papers. "I wish I had my old one from Harvard. Beware what you study, it may come back to haunt you."

She thought of the morning's Bible passage: "Study to shew thyself approved unto God, a workman that needeth not to be ashamed, rightly dividing the word of truth." Her study of truth had gotten them into this situation, and no one in her family approved of her behavior. Guilt weighed heavy.

"Here it is." He handled the leather volume with bemusement, paging through it and murmuring foreign words. "I've not spoken this language in twenty years. I can't imagine why anyone thought my rusty ear useful. *Anaa laa afham,* I'll say that a lot."

"What does it mean?"

He grinned. "I don't know."

Claire made a face at him.

"It means, 'I don't know.' "

"You're incorrigible."

He set the volume aside. "Humor me, darling. It's unbearable otherwise."

She flung herself into his arms, shutting her eyes to focus on the physical reality of her father. She couldn't keep track of the perils awaiting him: U-boats, illness, war, bad water. He was a strong man but anything could snatch him away.

This must be how every woman felt sending a man to war. It gave Claire no satisfaction to share in the suffering of millions. Her world centered on irritating, exciting, exasperating Jock.

"What will we do without you, Papa?"

He rubbed comforting circles on her back. "I wish you both were coming with me. Your mother will come around, but you'll need to be the strong one for a while."

Claire rubbed her cheek against his linen shirt and wrinkled her nose against the familiar tobacco scent. "We may never see you again."

He held her away to examine her face. "Your glasses are mussed. Drop by the office a couple weeks from now.

Conroy will bluster, but maybe he'll change his mind once I'm gone. I'll leave a note advising the Fischer boy the BNS can use your skills and insight."

Claire had no hope the cold and hostile Mr. Conroy would change his mind.

Jock rubbed his jaw. "Your reporting skills are improving. Why not try writing articles for women's magazines either here or in America? It would give you clip sheets to demonstrate your ability."

"I want to write real news, Papa, not simple stories for silly women."

He answered gently. "Nellie Bly blustered her way into dangerous spots to get her scoops. You're smarter than she is, but just as proud. Can't you write to entertain or enlighten a female audience? Surely your Christian scruples agree?"

"Do you think I've set my sights too high?"

Jock sighed. "Ultimately, no; for the time being, yes. Why not try your mother's *McCall's Magazine*?"

Claire needed to reconsider the idea once she recovered from her father lecturing her on Christian scruples.

He shut the trunk. "What can you tell me about Peter? Where is he?"

She shook her head. "France. He made me promise not to tell anything else or he wouldn't write to me."

"His mother is satisfied he's keeping out of harm's way. What's your gut feeling?"

Terror. Since she couldn't say that, she told him the other half of the truth. "I pray for him a lot."

Jock gazed at her a long moment, sighed, and patted her on the shoulder. "You keep doing that if it helps."

On the last day of June, Claire and Anne escorted Jock to the boat train at Waterloo Station. To the end he pleaded with Anne to come, but she remained resolute. "Egypt took my sons and dreams. It cannot have my daughter."

"What about me? Do you think this is easy for me?" Jock asked.

She kissed him good-bye and spoke not a word on the ride home.

The day after her father sailed, Claire left the house on a tranquil sunny morning. Green leaves graced Belgravia Square's plane trees and children followed by their nannies carried kites to fly. She tried not to imagine the U-boat threat to her father sailing along the French coastline toward the Strait of Gibraltar's left turn into the Mediterranean Sea.

Her mother and aunt were joining Sylvia to roll bandages, but Claire had a more important task.

She walked to the Underground station near Westminster Abbey and rode it to Fleet Street. At the BNS office, Mr. Conroy stared in disbelief. "You're a fine stenographer and typist, Miss Meacham, but I don't approve of women in the newsroom. Take your skills and apply them to women's magazines where your kind belong. Good luck."

"You've so few copyboys and no one can take dictation like me."

"We have employed two soldiers invalided out. They'll be sufficient for now." He escorted her to the door. "We'll forward any mail for your father to your home."

She held out her hand. "Thank you for your time. Please let me know if you change your mind."

He sniffed and opened the door.

While not surprised, Claire still trudged away with slumped shoulders. She examined each corner newsboy as she plodded through the crowds to the Underground. Ten-year-olds in flat caps with knee socks pulled to their knickerbockers worked in the newspaper business while Claire's sex made her ineligible for a lowly spot despite proven ability.

Maybe she should seek out the suffragettes after all.

Claire caught the trolley to Clapham Common. If she couldn't report the news, she planned to enroll at the BTC.

The parkland stretched before her when she disembarked. Two boys ran past flying toy airplanes and Claire thought of Peter. She whispered a prayer, as always, for his safety and protection. He'd be home soon on leave, something to look forward to in the empty days that stretched ahead.

As she strolled across the grass toward number 45, Claire saw an angular figure with a little girl on his shoulders. Claire ran to catch OC and Kathleen.

"Ach, look who is here this day, my Scallywag. We've missed you, Miss Steno." He swung his daughter off his shoulders and onto her feet. She squinted at Claire.

"I've been preparing my father to travel overseas. He's sailed and taken my job with him, so now I've come to enroll."

Kathleen tugged his hand.

"Walk with us," he invited. "Let's admire God's beauty as found in nature. My lassie is an appreciator."

Claire took Kathleen's other hand and they matched their adult strides to the little girl's short legs. OC nodded at Claire and they swung their arms, swooping Kathleen into the air. Her infectious laugh matched the pretty day and they continued until Claire's arms ached and Kathleen demanded to totter on her own feet.

"These last months have been a time of deep reflection and prayer for the college," OC said, "as well as for Biddy and me. The war presses daily upon us; some of our students have gone to fight. Others, like Jim, have gone to serve. I've prayed and pondered before our Lord about my own role."

"But your teaching is so important to me and others."

"We are no more than broken bread and poured out wine in our Lord's service."

Claire nodded. He'd used the imagery before.

A flight of swallows swooped through the sky. Kathleen chortled and OC smiled down at her. "At New Year's I pointed out my verse to Biddy, 'I am ready to be offered,' but we did not yet know where. I have volunteered to go to the front as a chaplain for spiritual first aid. I sail to Egypt in October to serve as a chaplain in the YMCA."

"But what about the Bible Training College?" Her dismay came out as a wail.

"We are closing it on July 14. We will take our annual holiday to the Yorkshire Dales and then I sail for Egypt."

"What about Biddy and Kathleen?"

"We hope they can join me in due time, but it's not yet clear."

Claire touched Kathleen's silky locks. "My mother refused to go to Cairo because my brothers died there when they were Kathleen's age. Why take your family to such a deadly place?"

"We go where our Lord sends. I can see you have much anguish on this subject and I am sorry. Trust God. We believe and obey him." OC checked his wrist watch. "My Scallywag's walk is done. Come to the school. You need Biddy's listening ear."

Two weeks later a final service marked the closure of the Bible Training College, "for the time being," OC said.

He said he expected to reopen the college after the war ended but spoke of hope and his vision of service for the meantime, focusing, as always, on Jesus. Eva Spink sang Biddy's favorite hymn, "God Be with You till We Meet Again."

Speaking on their behalf to God, OC prayed a final benediction: "We thank thee that there is no good-bye. We ask thee that thy crown and seal may be upon us until we meet thee face-to-face. Amen."

OC bade Claire good-bye. "Our Lord has done a good work in you and there will be more opportunities to come. Will you join your father in Cairo?"

"I'd love to." Claire's outburst surprised her.

He opened his palms toward the ceiling. "We leave Claire's hopes and dreams in your hands, Lord."

Hopes and dreams, pride and ambition—Claire considered them as she traveled home. Without a job and without the BTC, her days stretched empty. All she had to look forward to was writing letters, Nigel's visits, and surviving a war.

It wouldn't be enough.

Chapter Sixteen

August–September 1915

Claire read three newspapers a day, caught up her diary, applied herself to Bible study materials, and examined a variety of women's magazines. Most of the magazine articles concerned subjects in which she had no interest or skills. How could Claire invent pastimes for children or tasty recipes? She could interview Aunt Sarah on knitting but couldn't explain how to knit, much less describe a pattern.

Claire tossed away *McCall's Magazine*. Hopeless.

Anne set aside her letter. The library windows were open on the warm Belgravia morning, and a policeman blew a whistle on the street below.

Claire ran to the window. The bobby directed a chimney sweep to the proper house. No news.

"Perhaps you could write a feature about being an American in London during the war," her mother said.

Claire picked up the *Times*. "I'd like to write about the German U-boat sinking the SS *Arabic*, but I'd need to visit the White Star offices and get quotes." Even as she outlined how to write the story, Claire knew she'd never get the chance. Michael Fischer had undoubtedly covered it for the BNS. "Or the zeppelin raids."

Aunt Sarah set aside her knitting. “You like to be useful—perhaps you should consider nursing.” She checked the diamond-encrusted watch pinned to her charcoal-gray dress. “I’m on my way to the solicitor’s office. Don’t wait lunch.” She left.

“Your aunt is working for the family business; perhaps she requires a secretary?” Anne rubbed her hands.

Claire wanted to be at the heart of the news, hunting information, investigating stories, checking historical documents. She didn’t want to sit in a mansion planning menus when newsworthy events occurred. Last week she’d convinced Mr. Able to drive her to East London to see homes bombed in the zeppelin raid.

“Couldn’t we go to Egypt?” Claire whispered.

“With U-boats patrolling the English Channel?”

Claire gave up. She could please no one, not even herself.

The only bright spots during the boring weeks were the nights Nigel came to dinner, usually accompanied by his officemate Major Cecil Hollister, whom he called Holly.

Holly quickly established himself as a suitor to Sylvia and pursued her aggressively. He usually spirited away the young widow directly following dinner to go dancing with a fast crowd.

Claire hardly knew the man, but Holly’s self-satisfaction and hurry troubled Aunt Sarah. By the time Peter replied to her letter with the advice to direct his solicitor to examine Holly’s credentials, Sylvia wore a new enormous diamond ring.

Aunt Sarah disapproved, but Sylvia made plans anyway. “I need to enjoy life while I can. He’s a baronet. Holly will give me all I’ve ever wanted.”

"Could you not wait at least to introduce him to Peter?" Anne asked. "We hardly know him."

"It's the times, Aunt Anne. No one has a long engagement." Sylvia set her lips and ordered fabric samples.

One evening, Nigel leaned against the carved mantel in the library and described the latest army politics. Aunt Sarah rang for tea and picked up her knitting needles, while Claire pressed for information from any war theater. She missed the daily BNS briefings.

Her fingers brushed across the velvet sofa as he spoke. A squiggle to the right for "I" and curves and lines traced his words. Claire could picture how she'd write up the information.

Nigel noticed her fingers. "I can speak easier with your father gone. I couldn't tell you much when he was here for fear I'd leak classified information."

"What makes you think you're safer with us?" Anne crossed her legs and smiled sweetly.

"With the latest U-boat sinkings you must be relieved you stayed behind," Nigel said, hunting for any conversation topic Anne wouldn't squelch. "I'm glad you didn't put Claire's life at risk. She's much safer in London."

"With the zeppelin raids? The war hasn't reached Cairo. We'd be perfectly safe at Shepheard's Hotel with the *memsahib* officer's wives." Anne examined her nails.

Aunt Sarah's needles paused.

Nigel shuffled in his polished boots. "Jock is living at the hotel where the senior officers billet?"

"Journalists and archaeologists like it too. Tea?" Anne poured tea and served biscuits. The women made forced conversation until the clock struck 8:30.

Aunt Sarah gathered up her knitting. "I'll say good night. Thank you for a most illuminating conversation."

"I've other matters to attend to," Anne said. "I'll return in a moment." She left the door ajar.

Nigel released his breath in a gust. "Brandy?"

Claire poured him a drink from the tray in the corner. He gulped it and held out the crystal tumbler for a refill. Claire disapproved but poured.

"Your aunt's fair dinkum, but your mother makes me nervous. She doesn't like me." He rubbed his fingers through his short hair. "It's been a grim week, but then they all are. How are things here?"

"Quiet. I feel useless. My aunt suggested I become a nurse. What do you think?"

"Empathy isn't your strong suit. You're skilled as a stenographer. Do you have nursing experience? Nursing soldiers is filthy physical labor."

His words stung. "Jim thought I considered myself too good for manual chores. Do you agree?"

"Hodges wasn't right about much. Why should you perform manual labor?"

"We washed dishes together one night at the BTC. I broke several pieces."

"Why should a fine woman like you wash dinner dishes for a bunch of Bible-thumpers? Crackers." He sloshed the golden liquid.

"The Bible says we're not to consider ourselves more highly than we ought. I'm concerned I might be too proud to do the things God asked me to do." Her voice hushed as she realized her father had suggested the same thing.

"Garbage. You're too fine a woman to get your hands dirty." He joined her on the sofa. "I'm pleased you have more time to spend with me."

Claire wrinkled her nose; his pungent cigarette tobacco bothered her. "We spend all your free time together."

"We could spend more." Nigel's voice became husky, emphasizing his New Zealand accent. "If you married me, we could spend every night together."

"Marry you?" Claire froze.

"We get along well together. We're both lonely, and I'm in the army. Should I go down on my knee? I'd rather leave you behind as my wife than a pretty girl I never got close enough to enjoy."

Claire's eyes grew wide, and she trembled. While she enjoyed the outings they shared, she'd never thought of marriage. She didn't know him well enough to consider spending the rest of her life with him. But maybe he feared he didn't have much time left. "I don't know what to say."

The heavy oak door banged against the wall. "No is a fine answer." Anne marched up to Nigel and indicated the glass. "How many?"

He cleared his throat. "Two."

"How many drinks before you arrived?"

"Does it matter?"

Anne drew her eyebrows together and her face hardened. "No is the answer to all your questions. No."

"Did you lead him on?" Anne demanded at breakfast the next morning.

Claire sighed and tapped the top off her hard-boiled egg. She'd not slept well after Nigel's unexpected proposal. Surely she would have recognized a man in love? She'd only kissed him a few times.

"He's a soldier far from home. Perhaps this is how they propose in New Zealand." Aunt Sarah poured tea into their cups.

"It's the times," Sylvia yawned. "Desperate Tommies beg anything wearing a skirt to marry them."

"That's hardly fair, Sylvia, and obviously untrue, but we know nothing about him. Who are his parents? What do they do?" Anne stirred three sugar lumps into her tea. She rarely took any.

"His father is a doctor near Christchurch and he grew up on a farm outside the town. He won a scholarship to Oxford and has been in England since 1910." Claire knew little else. They discussed books, historic sites, and current entertainment when together. He'd never visited the BTC and thought prayer and Bible study indulged hobbies of no consequence. She frowned remembering his dismissal and shifted uneasily in her chair.

"Are you giving up your dream of being a reporter?" Anne struck her egg so hard it fell onto the table. She shoved it away. A maid removed the debris.

"No." Claire knew that much. But, she realized, while Nigel teased her about being Nellie Bly, he'd never asked her why she wanted to be a reporter. Her heart sank, yet again.

"I suspect he's lonely and sees Claire's kind heart." Aunt Sarah buttered her toast.

"That's not enough to make a marriage," Anne said.

Claire set down her spoon. "I'm as bewildered by this as you are."

"With this war continuing, you should grab Nigel while you can. He won't be around forever," Sylvia advised. "We could have a double wedding."

"Not without my father," Claire said.

"Jock will be furious. Why did he wait until after your father left?" Anne asked.

Aunt Sarah reached for the marmalade. "Nerves. Praying would help you decide, Claire. Don't be too hasty, especially if you're unsure." She frowned at her own daughter. "Perhaps Peter can advise you. He'll be home soon."

Claire helped Sylvia dress for her second marriage on September 20. This time Sylvia wore a simple two-piece suit of pale blue silk and a determined expression. Resplendent in his dress uniform, Nigel smiled at Claire over Holly's shoulder as the army chaplain read the marriage service in Aunt Sarah's drawing room. Claire hid her shyness in a white rose bouquet.

This groom's fingers did not shake and he said his vows in a laconic, though firm, voice. Sylvia, however, hesitated before she pledged her troth. Her eyes glistened and Claire wondered if she, too, thought of Edward. Claire turned away when Holly claimed his bride with an amorous assurance to put those memories to rest.

"Edward was a better man," Peter growled later at the reception. He'd returned to England early that morning on weekend leave before reporting to specialized training at an airfield north of London. He pulled her spectacles from his breast pocket and handed them to her.

Claire took his strong arm, thankful for time with Peter, as cocky as ever but with shadows under his eyes. "Edward was her first love. How are things with you?"

"Worse than you'll ever hear, though I found a Stone Age arrowhead the other day. Artillery churns the chalk beneath the soil and unexpected objects emerge. I'll leave it with you. Get it out from time to time to remember me."

She shivered. "Please don't talk that way."

"When I kick the bucket, spend my money on a beautiful item that has nothing to do with war. Buy Uncle Jock a new sailboat and sail it on Narragansett Bay. That will make me happy."

Claire stared at him, her bones turning to rubber. "When the war is over, we'll buy one together, and I'll sail with you. We can go anywhere in the world."

Peter studied her. "You've grasped truth more clearly than anyone in this family. You've seen the casualty rates. Why aren't you at the BNS?"

"The city editor barred my admittance and the young BNS editor doesn't care."

"It's your last name they're afraid of, as they should be. Newspapers need to inform the public. Get back to the BNS or find another place to write. Surely Uncle Jock trained you well enough before he left. I've been afraid you might give in and marry Nigel."

She stiffened. "Would marrying him be such a bad idea? He's your friend."

He glanced over his shoulder to where Nigel and Holly were toasting each other. "I like Nigel, but I love you. He may be clever but he's miserable and afraid: a bad combination. Don't let him drag you into his unhappiness."

"Is he unhappier than the rest of you?" Claire whispered.

Peter sighed. "Nigel's talking about transferring to an ANZAC unit and heading to the Middle East. He says he'll be happier with his own kind. It will keep him out of France, but after the Gallipoli disaster, who knows what will happen in Palestine with the Ottoman Turks. Surely you've read your father's dispatches?"

"Of course."

Peter kissed her forehead. "Don't sell yourself short. You're educated enough to be a foreign correspondent, but you need to toughen up and apply yourself to your dreams.

You'll make a great reporter, but you have to fire up your ambition. Don't settle."

"Easy for you to say; you're a man."

"Don't be angry with me. Write a novel, write a letter to the editor, and send something to America. Try a different newspaper." He took her arm. "Don't be like my sister."

They strolled into the dining room where Claire, once again, sat beside Nigel at a wedding supper.

"See how happy Sylvia and Holly are." Nigel snaked his arm along her chair and whispered into her ear. "You could make me even happier if you'd say yes. I need something to believe in if I'm to survive this war."

"God's the only one who can give you peace."

Nigel sighed.

"Do you think I'm leading you on?" she asked. He'd taken to stealing kisses when they were alone and Claire demurred but enjoyed them.

"No." Nigel sobered. "You're too honest and good. What if I write your father and ask for your hand?"

"You would ask him?" Claire set down her champagne flute. She'd like to know her father's opinion.

"How about a secret engagement until I get an answer?" He sipped the champagne. "I need hope. You love me, don't you?"

She considered him.

"Claire? Changes are afoot. I'd like hope at least if you won't marry me right now."

Jock told her to be kind to soldiers. Beside her sat the dearest one she knew besides Peter. "I couldn't be married without my father. But a secret engagement..."

Nigel kissed her, full on the lips in front of the family.

"But..."

Holly shouted, "Hear, hear! The Colonial finally gets into action!"

Nigel lifted his triumphant fist into the air.

"It's certainly about time," Sylvia simpered.

"But..."

He kissed her again. Claire blushed, but couldn't help noticing Peter's shock and her mother's glare. She hoped God, at least, would understand.

Claire wasn't even sure, though, she understood herself.

Chapter Seventeen

October 1915

"Please stop into the BNS newsroom and check on a few items for me," Anne said the Monday after Sylvia's wedding. "I suspect not all your father's mail is coming through."

Anne had said not a word about Nigel's behavior at the wedding.

But Claire knew she hadn't forgotten.

Claire took the Underground to Piccadilly Station and walked up Fleet Street, marveling at the change in her independence since she'd arrived in London. She traveled freely on the trolley or Underground and could call a cab if needed. Dropping by the office was a simple task.

Claire's heart sang and her breathing quickened when she entered the tall stone building and rode the lift to the newsroom. The clatter of typewriters called and a yearning to report the news caused her to stumble on the doorstep. She squared her shoulders and lifted her chin when Mr. Conroy approached her.

"I'm here for my father's mail," Claire said.

"I'm glad to see you." He shuffled his feet and cleared his throat. "Have you come to work?"

"Have you changed your mind?"

He gestured around the newsroom where five typewriters sat idle. "Take dictation or type, you choose. I need all the help I can get, particularly with the new boss. I'll double whatever your father paid you."

Jock had paid her nothing. "Starting when?"

"Today. Are you available?"

The soggy spirit and worry over the secret engagement lifted. Claire stuck out her hand. "I'd love to. Just pay me the going rate." She returned to her old desk shaking off memories of Nigel and Jim's welcome the year before. The door to her father's former office was shut, but the rattle of the telegraph machine reminded her that even without the men, news went on.

Claire announced her job that night at dinner. Nigel said he understood but his short words and clenched jaw suggested otherwise.

"That sounds like an answer to your prayers." Aunt Sarah rang for champagne.

And Anne?

"What an excellent idea. As your father says, when the lust for news is in your blood, you're never rid of it. Once a reporter, always a reporter."

"Mr. Conroy's only letting me take shorthand and type."

Anne's lips twitched. "That's all you did today?"

Claire grinned. "I corrected grammar and assisted with a couple stories."

She loved being back in the newsroom. Reading the wire stories spurred her love of current events. Asking questions, finding answers, brainstorming with reporters for ideas, made her feel appreciated. Jock had taught her how to get to the heart of a story and Mr. Conroy praised her efforts with a sigh of relief.

Still the only woman in the newsroom, Claire focused on preparing copy to get through the censors and into the five o'clock overseas cable to Boston.

When the BNS owner's son, Michael Fischer, entered the office, the staff put down their heads and attended to their tasks. The usual reporter joking died away and few engaged the young boss with questions or comments.

One day Fischer called her into Jock's former office. At twenty-five, he was only a few years older than Claire. Dressed in a proper black suit, he tapped his thumbs together as she entered his office. His ears stuck out from either side of his ruddy face and his lips were thin, particularly as he regarded her. "They say you attended Radcliffe. I'm a Brown man myself."

Claire nodded. "How can I help you?"

"Is it possible you altered my copy when you typed it yesterday?"

She caught her fingers so they wouldn't shake. "I typed many stories yesterday. Which one?"

He leaned closer. "You don't deny altering copy?"

"If it's grammatically incorrect and not inside a quote, yes, I change it." She'd also rearranged sentence order to put the most important news at the top.

"Who gave you permission?"

"My job is to ensure the stories are as correct as possible so they don't need editing once they reach Boston." She watched him a moment before reminding him, "British spelling can differ from American."

Fischer blinked rapidly and pursed his lips, looking more like a nervous school marm than a dynamic newspaper editor. Uncertain in the newsroom, Michael Fischer's elevation to editor had been a foolish decision by his father, the BNS owner.

Mr. Conroy had noticed Claire altered copy with curt nods of approval. "You make my job easier."

The young man slid a piece of paper across her father's former desk. "The paragraphs were rearranged in this one. Did you do it?"

Claire cleared her throat. "You made a factual error and the predominant facts needed to appear in the lede. I corrected the story and made alterations for clarity."

"I don't like what you did."

What motivated this man, newsworthiness or his pride?

It didn't matter.

"Voters elected President Wilson in 1912, but he didn't take office until 1913. Since you weren't here and I'm American, they asked me to verify." She used her mother's polite smile to soothe him.

His brow furrowed. "I see." He took his chin in hand to ponder the story, Claire thought, before he surprised her. "Are you available for dinner tonight?"

Her hostility shrank. "I'm sorry. I'm meeting my"—Claire hesitated—"my beau."

He stood abruptly. "I understand. Thank you for clarifying. Please ask the next time you change my copy."

"Certainly." Claire fled, her face flaming as much as his. No wonder Mr. Conroy banned flirting.

Other than exchanges with Fischer, who seldom came out of his office, she got along well with the reporters. She returned home each night tired but exhilarated. Nigel didn't like cooling his heels waiting for her, but Anne had begun playing chess with him. Literally.

Watching them battle across the chessboard, Claire wondered if she should tell her mother about the secret engagement.

"What do you like about him?" Anne asked one night after closing the door on the departing Nigel.

"He's gallant and attentive," Aunt Sarah said. "He's interested in Claire and he makes a perfect escort. Just because you don't care for him doesn't mean Claire shouldn't."

Claire sighed. She'd better keep the secret.

She read Jock's reaction to her job in a letter over her mother's shoulder.

Good for the BNS, but I need Claire in Cairo. The stack of papers, story ideas, and interviews pile up and I can scarcely get my work done. Darling Anne, won't you join me? I miss you dreadfully and life is empty without you. I need your keen ears, your knowing eyes, and your good judgment. Please. Come to Cairo? For me?

Anne looked at Claire and shook her head. "I won't take a chance on losing another child in Egypt."

Aunt Sarah set aside her knitting. "Is it such a gamble?"

Claire crossed her arms. There must be a way to convince Mama to take her to Egypt.

A risky idea formed and she tossed off a reply. "Nigel wouldn't agree to my going anyway."

Anne folded the letter into its overseas envelope. "What do you mean?"

"You know he's asked to marry me."

Anne paled. "We said no."

Claire adjusted her glasses. "It's not a real engagement, it's a secret one. Sort of a promise to be engaged."

"Knowing my thoughts and feelings, you pledged yourself to him?"

"He's a promising officer."

"It's easy to get your head diverted by a uniform, but I thought you were more sensible." Her voice rose. "I told him no."

"He needs hope for the future and encouragement. Papa said to be kind to soldiers."

"Your father never meant you to get engaged out of pity. That's no way to begin a relationship." Anne rose and paced. "What happened to the young woman determined to be a reporter?"

"I thought you didn't approve of my being a reporter."

"You need to follow your dreams. Why do you think your father allowed you in the newsroom?"

Claire replayed the events from that long ago breakfast. "You tricked him?"

"I planted the seed and your skill proved valuable." Anne threw the letter into the air and stalked to the window. "I'd rather have gone to Egypt than lose you to such a weak man." She spun on her heel. "Do you even love him?"

"I'm fond of him."

"That's not good enough. You must love your husband with your whole heart and be willing to do anything to be with him. Nigel only attends St. Paul's to please you. How can you contemplate a life with such a man?"

Claire shrank and stuttered. "You didn't follow Papa to Egypt."

"Is this about my not going to Egypt?" Anne's eyes blazed. "You think I don't love your father enough to go with him?"

"I know you love Papa."

Anne trembled. "You've insulted me and defied my wishes. You've apparently tossed away your vaunted religious scruples which, may I remind you, got us into this mess, for a charming drunk in a uniform. I can't believe I'm hearing this."

"You don't like Nigel. You didn't like the BTC. How can I make you happy?"

Her mother closed her eyes and took several deep breaths. "Be the person you're meant to be. If it's a reporter, fine. If it's marriage, fine. But marry a man who sees deep into your soul and wants only the best for you, no matter the cost to him. Do you honestly believe Nigel is such a man?"

Claire's mind screamed no while her heart whimpered maybe.

Aunt Sarah set aside her knitting and stood. "Given your arguments, why are you still in London, Anne?"

Anne gasped.

"Aren't you the woman who couldn't wait to escape Newport and marry the dashing reporter who would show you the world? Why aren't you in Egypt?"

"You don't understand; the memories—"

"I am sorry you lost Phillip and John so long ago."

Anne flinched and Claire's eyes grew wide.

"I have a son likely to be shot out of the sky. I didn't lose two little boys, but a child I've loved for twenty-four years is in harm's way. I wish I'd sailed with Henry on the *Volturno* so I could be spared this pain and worry."

"But you would have drowned," Claire said.

"If so, Peter would be running Herrington Limited and not flying over France. Would I not give my life for my child? Anne?"

"Too much."

Sarah reached for her.

"I've watched Claire and listened to her," Sarah murmured as Anne wept on her shoulder. "Your daughter prays and wants to please you. Her heart may be too soft toward Nigel, but she wants to do right by all. She's here only because of you, Anne, but maybe it's time for you to return to Egypt and for Claire to taste more of the world for the sake of her dreams. I only wish I'd sent my daughter with Jock."

Tears pooled in Claire's eyes and she struggled to swallow.

"So hard," Anne whispered.

"I know, but you've clung to your grief a long time." Aunt Sarah glanced at Claire. "Let me take you to your room."

The sisters shuffled out the door.

Claire dropped onto the sofa and rubbed her eyes, deflated and unnerved. In trying not to hurt Nigel's sensitive feelings, she'd split apart her relationship with her mother. How could she possibly make it right? "Dear God, what a mess," she whispered.

Anne was correct. A secret engagement did not honor her family or her God.

Claire should have remembered Nigel's lack of enthusiasm for God and disinterest in the Bible. "What should I do, Lord?"

She lifted her head. She'd seek counsel.

As October drew to a close, the leaves changed color and slid to the ground in a rustling sigh. Claire traveled to 45 Clapham Common, where Biddy welcomed her into the echoing mansion she shared with Kathleen and her capable BTC friend, Mary Riley.

"Oswald arrived in Alexandria."

"An uneventful trip?" Claire asked.

"He basked in God's hands." Biddy led her downstairs to the kitchen where she turned on the stove under the tea kettle. "The troop transport ship was so crowded he could only find privacy in a lifeboat. There he prayed, read, and wrote letters."

"When do you sail?"

"When God wills." Biddy sat beside Claire and rested her hands in her lap. "What is on your heart, dear one?"

Claire outlined the challenges of recent months. "I don't know what to do about Nigel."

"Are you prepared for prayer to change you?" Biddy lifted her hands. "We give you these concerns, dear Lord, and thank you for what you will bring to Claire."

Claire laughed. "Direct as always."

"Jesus knows your heart. It is foolish to pretend otherwise. You are a different woman than when you arrived at the BTC."

"How can I know if God wants me to marry Nigel?"

"Do you have peace about marrying him?"

"No."

"Then tarry with it. Do not act until you have peace," Biddy said. "Is your heart such you can tarry?"

"He's so lost, I want to help him."

"You cannot be God's providence to Nigel. You make his life more difficult if you get in the way of our Lord meeting him in his need."

Claire sighed. She'd thought encouraging him to join her at St. Paul's would help Nigel. She'd thought not disappointing him in front of his friends would please him. But making herself a crutch couldn't possibly work. Claire polished her glasses and wondered how to get out of the secret engagement. How would he react if she broke it off?

Biddy picked up her Bible. "Let's discuss the passages you've been studying. We'll start with the psalms."

Claire smiled. The psalms always put her life into the proper perspective.

Besides, Nigel would be in France on army business for another two weeks, anyway.

Chapter Eighteen

November–December 1915

When she arrived home several nights later, Claire found a letter from Peter.

> *I've been in a crackup. Plane came down in a field, startling a milk cow. Turned tail up, but I escaped before it caught fire. Caught a horse providentially trotting by and rode it to our lines. Casualty station patched me up: torn scalp, wrenched shoulder, three cracked ribs. Grounded until new plane arrives, headed to Paris R&R. Mummy mustn't know. Love, Peter.*

She tried to picture the biplane's nose buried in the soft French mud so deep the tail stood straight up. But then it caught fire. Was he burned? Claire shuddered and dropped her satchel.

"R & R in Paris," she whispered, trying to banish the reason why from her imagination.

Aunt Sarah and her mother were chatting in the library, a cheerful fire warming the room and the heavy drapery shut against the chill November night. A squat teapot wrapped in a cozy waited on a tray before the sofa. "I'll ring for hot soup. We've cheese and crackers here. Tea?" Anne asked.

Claire warmed her hands at the fire. "Thank you."

"What did Peter say?" Aunt Sarah's knitting needles slowed.

"He's on leave in Paris for a few days."

"What a shame he couldn't come home to say goodbye." The knitting needles returned to their clicking dance through the yarn.

Claire narrowed her eyes and looked between the sisters. Fabric samples covered the sofa beside Anne, who handed Claire a cup of tea. "Your father cabled. He's deliriously happy."

"Why?"

"I told him I would come to Cairo."

Claire squealed. "When can we go?"

"That's the question. Will you come with me?"

She stared at her mother, incredulous. "How could you go without me?"

"What about Nigel?"

She'd been weighing Biddy's warning about not being Nigel's providence and to tarry until peace came about her decisions. Claire might have been uneasy about marrying Nigel, but she had no doubts about traveling to Egypt. "I'll figure something out."

Once she'd decided, Anne Meacham did not delay. She threw herself into collecting and packing the items she'd need in Egypt, particularly clothing. She also delegated tasks.

"You managed your father's voyage; arrange our transport. I'd like to be with him by New Year's Day."

Without telling her mother, Claire approached another efficient woman making travel plans. They would sail December 10.

By the time Nigel returned from fact-gathering on the battlefields, the Meachams were in a flurry of list checking.

Haggard, hollow-cheeked, and exhausted, Nigel came to Belgravia immediately.

"What about us?" Nigel demanded. "How can you go off to the ends of the earth if you love me?"

"The army can send you away at any moment." Claire held her fingers to keep them from shaking.

"If I get orders I must go. You're choosing to abandon me."

She'd expected him to be upset, but at the word *abandon*, Claire's stomach lurched. She couldn't look at him. "My father needs my help. My mother doesn't want to travel alone."

"You've just taken up a job. Why is your mother suddenly so keen to go?"

"I don't *know*," Claire stuttered, her throat thick with guilt.

"She's done this on purpose. She doesn't want us to be together." Nigel slapped his hat against the sofa. "Please tell me you're not going to Egypt because Oswald Chambers is there."

The absurdity made Claire laugh. "I'd like to see him, but he's stationed at a YMCA camp. I'll be in Cairo with my father."

He lowered his voice. "Tell me you're not running away from me."

It was so close to the truth, Claire wavered. She lifted her chin. "I'm merely a typist at the London BNS. Mr. Conroy and Michael Fischer will never allow me to do anything else. In Cairo, I might get a chance as a reporter."

"Nellie Bly triumphs again." He tossed his hand in the air. "If I transfer to the Middle East, will you marry me? Your father can give his blessing in person."

She owed him honesty. "I need to think and pray more about marrying you."

"Maybe this will help." He took her in his arms and kissed her, long and thoroughly. Claire's heart beat so fast, her knees weakened. She pushed him away, grabbed her handkerchief, and sneezed.

"You won't get a kiss like that in Egypt without me."

She knew.

"If you really loved me, you wouldn't go. You'd say goodbye to your mother and stay here to marry me. Doesn't your Bible say to cleave to your husband?"

Claire had debated the question a hundred times. She liked spending time with him. She respected him. But she couldn't imagine standing before the Hunt painting at St. Paul's and pledging her life to Nigel no matter what might happen.

Logically, then, she shouldn't marry him.

But what if her rejection caused him to volunteer for a dangerous mission and he died? How could she live with that?

"Can I give you a ring? At least claim you for my own? You'll meet a lot of men in the Middle Eastern theater before I arrive. I want the world to know you're mine."

"You're coming to Egypt?"

"I'll put in my papers to transfer to an ANZAC unit." He shrugged. "With any luck the Gallipoli retreat will be done by the time I get there."

Events were changing too fast. She shifted to reporter mode and sought facts. "When? Where?"

He kissed her. "Sometime in 1916."

Claire didn't know what else to do, so she kissed him back.

Nigel presented a box to Claire on her departure morning. "Open it on Christmas and drink a glass of wine in my honor."

She'd left a gift with Sylvia. "Will you ever forgive me?"

He hugged her tight. "I'll miss you terribly. Write using symbols I can read."

She reached for her handkerchief. Nigel tipped up her chin. "We'll meet again. You'll be a soldier's wife one day."

Claire shut her eyes tight to hold back the tears.

He kissed her and she melted in his embrace, doubts screaming even as her mother came down the stairs.

"Mr. Able has loaded the car. It's time to go." Anne held out her hand. "Good luck, Nigel."

He shook her hand, "Thank you, ma'am." Nigel saluted as they drove away. Late that afternoon, they boarded the SS *Herefordshire.* A mail packet ship prior to the war, she transported people on long hauls to Port Said, Egypt, before cruising through the Suez Canal to India. Most of the passengers were attached to the military and headed to the Middle East.

Just before dinner the first night at sea, a little girl scurried across the dining room and flung her arms around Claire's knees.

"Who's this?" Anne laughed.

"Kathleen Chambers. Here's her mother, Biddy, and Miss Mary Riley traveling as Kathleen's nurse."

"How lovely to meet you. Where are you headed?" Anne asked politely.

"We're joining my husband at a YMCA camp near Cairo." Biddy extricated her daughter from Claire's legs. "Would you care to have tea with us tomorrow?"

"Indeed." After agreeing to tea, Anne drew her daughter to the captain's table, their seating assignment for the evening. "You didn't seem surprised to see Mrs. Chambers. Did you know she'd be on board?"

"I didn't think it would matter." Claire watched the trio greet their tablemates and wished she could join them, rather than sit in a place of honor in her finest new clothes.

"You shouldn't lie, darling. You're not good at it." Anne tossed open her damask napkin.

She bit back a retort and answered calmly. "I found a ship to Egypt when we wanted to sail. I liked the idea of having a friendly face on board."

Anne glowered. "Did you know her husband worked in Cairo?"

"I knew he was in Egypt."

Anne twisted the thick napkin. "Your father will be furious, if he doesn't already know. Is that why you agreed to leave London?"

"No." Claire sighed.

Early the next morning Claire donned her life jacket and met Biddy on deck to admire the rising sun.

"Oswald writes of spectacular sunrises over the desert," Biddy said. "His letters read fair poetic in description and enthusiasm. I feel close to him when I watch the sunrise."

"Where will you live?"

"Oswald had a bungalow built on the Egyptian General Mission compound near Zeitoun army camp."

"What troops are stationed at the camp?" Claire pulled her knit cap over her ears.

"Mostly soldiers from Australia and New Zealand; many fought in the Dardanelles."

"Jim Hodges was injured at Gallipoli."

"He's at YMCA headquarters in Cairo, now. You'll see him. I know he enjoyed the time he spent with you at the BTC."

The frigid wind became too much by the fourth lap and they spied white caps on the rough seas. A sailor paced past. "Keep your eyes peeled for a U-boat," he said. "The Huns sank a ship in the Channel yesterday off Calais."

Claire's heart lurched, but Biddy looked unperturbed. "God's will goes before us."

When Claire opened the door into the lounge beside the dining hall, Anne Meacham sat in a chair anchored to the floor next to Mary Riley while Kathleen danced. "Your charming daughter has been telling me about seeing Daddy in the desert."

"Yours has done the same." Biddy joined her.

As Claire swayed with Kathleen, she listened to the two women she admired most in the world. Why had she worried? Anne and Biddy were calm, efficient women cut from similar cloth. They might not agree on religious matters, but otherwise they were well matched.

"I understand you lived in Egypt," Biddy said.

Claire gulped. Maybe not. Her cunning mother preferred the subtle.

"My husband worked for a newspaper in Cairo many years ago."

"You must know information I could use. The weather, for example."

"Ferociously hot in the summer. We vacationed near Alexandria during the hottest months, where the breeze off the Mediterranean helped."

Mary leaned forward. "What types of food did you eat? I'll be doing most of the cooking at Zeitoun."

"Whatever the servants served. The children"—Anne stammered—"loved dates and other fruits we bought at the bazaar."

Biddy gazed at her, clear-eyed but sympathetic. Anne returned an appraising, challenging inspection.

Claire could hardly breathe.

Anne gave a curt nod. "I lost two boys to cholera. I'd never take a child to Egypt. They went so fast." She twisted her hands. "Playing in the garden with the groundskeeper and the next minute gasping and…"

Biddy reached for her hand.

"They were dead by nightfall. I should have died too. Jock quit his job and we left within a month. I stood on deck and watched the sea as we ploughed toward home. I wanted to throw myself overboard and join my children."

Claire flinched.

Biddy did not move, her eyes intent on Anne. "What happened?"

"I couldn't do it. The day before we boarded the ship, I learned I carried another child. Claire didn't deserve to die because of my grief. But if I hadn't been pregnant, I would not have survived the trip to Boston." She reached for Claire. "I'm so sorry, darling. You saved my life, so I could give you yours."

Claire blinked back tears and hugged her mother.

"You have suffered much grief." Biddy opened her hands toward the roof. "We give you this sorrow, Lord, and ask you to heal it."

"I need a cup of tea." Anne rose. "Good morning."

She didn't leave her stateroom until dinner.

Claire met Biddy each morning to walk, pray, and discuss the Bible. Afterwards they joined Mary, Kathleen, and Anne for breakfast and casual conversation. They shared books and on Sundays attended the church service together.

One morning after breakfast, Anne watched Biddy and Kathleen struggle along the ship's rocking deck. "Does the woman have any flaws?"

Claire laughed. "None. She's wonderful."

"You're hardly an unbiased witness. Her clothes aren't fashionable, but she dresses the baby adorably."

"What difference does it make if she wears fashionable clothes? She's headed to the desert to live in a bungalow surrounded by soldiers."

Anne slipped her gloved hands into the arms of her coat and took tentative steps down the heaving deck. "For her it probably doesn't make any difference. But you only get one chance to make a first impression, and so we'll wear the latest fashions. We'll make those British *memsahibs* drool with envy."

"Why?"

"You may be coming to take dictation and type, but I'm coming to spy. Your father needs me to sweep into society and learn their secrets." Her lips curled into the smile Claire loved.

Claire took her mother's arm against the December wind. Whitecaps rippled across the cold ocean. High above, a sailor scanned the horizon with large binoculars.

Anne cleared her throat. "This voyage can't be over soon enough."

The next night, traveling under wartime blackout conditions, they sailed through the Straits of Gibraltar. The relatively shallow Mediterranean Sea made it easier to see a stealthy periscope before a torpedo launched and Claire knew their chances of surviving a ship sinking were better in the warmer Mediterranean. But she refused to fret.

"Worry is impertinent. Don't you believe God knows the practical details of your life?" Biddy asked.

Of course she did. Most of the time.

Christmas morning Claire opened Nigel's gift. As she feared, it contained a beautiful ring: gold with a winking blue sapphire that matched his eyes.

"Lovely," Anne said. "What will you do with it?"

"The safest place for it is on my finger."

A raised eyebrow.

"There is no formal engagement," Claire reminded her.

"You're old enough to make your own decisions. It's a pretty ring."

Claire slid it on her right ring finger, where it weighed heavily.

On day seventeen the air changed. Humanity's odor wafted from the shore along with a dozen spicy scents Claire could not identify. Warships steamed south in the distance, undoubtedly part of the Gallipoli retreat. The day before landing in Port Said, they sobered at the still burning wreckage of a Japanese ship and a cargo vessel. "U-boats," muttered a sailor.

When they passed the commanding statue of the Suez Canal's architect, Ferdinand de Lesseps, at the mouth of the canal, Port Said's low harbor came into view. Claire leaned on the railing, scribbling impressions into her diary as she tried to describe the new scenery, sounds, and smells of the African continent. Clad in a pale pink linen dress, Anne carried a parasol to protect her complexion. By the time the ship docked, they saw Jock wildly waving an off-white pith helmet. Claire and Anne hugged each other.

"Aren't you glad we're here, Mama?"

"Yes, darling. Wherever Jock lives is where I want to be."

Anne blew a kiss to her husband while Claire surveyed the crowd. A tall lanky man stood beside Jock, gladness written all over his face.

Obviously, her father knew Oswald Chambers was in Egypt.

Chapter Nineteen

January 1916

With exotic scents, sights, and the heat, Egypt more than provided the adventure Claire craved.

The sunlight emphasized the harshness of the land, while shadows splayed from the minarets and colorful eastern buildings vied for space with monuments to British bureaucracy.

Claire's head swiveled as they traveled through Port Said in an open horse-drawn carriage locals called a calash. Men dressed in white robes and wearing red cylindrical hats with golden tassels confidently strode the sidewalks while women shrouded in black scarves slunk into darkened corridors. Hordes of uniformed soldiers swarmed the streets and military ambulances rattled between.

The flies were endless.

Tanned and beaming, Jock embraced it all. His pipe went in and out of his pocket seemingly at will and his voice boomed with enthusiasm. "I want to show you everything."

"Yes!" answered Claire. Anne ducked beneath her fancy parasol.

They spent the first night at a hotel along the palm tree lined shore. "To help you acclimate," Jock explained. They dined in a local restaurant on *sayadeya*, bluefish cooked with rice, onion, and tomato sauce, and baked in earthenware. She'd never eaten chickpeas before, and new spices appeared with each dish. Claire savored cool yoghurt with a tang of cucumber and a date and honey baklava so sweet her teeth hurt.

Through it all, her father poured wine and shouted for waiters in a slippery tongue full of incomprehensible sounds. "You've no idea how I missed you," he finally said in English.

Anne gazed at the high columns, fawning servants, and overwrought potted palms. "It's like I remembered."

"Bad? Good?" Jock tapped the tabletop.

She covered his fingers. "I'm happy to be with you."

Their gaze—Claire closed her eyes. Nigel's adoration might have been similar, but Claire knew she would never match his fervor. She swallowed her discomfort.

"Wait until you see Shepheard's Hotel," Jock said. "It's as glamorous and busy as ever. Claire will be the belle of the salon."

Anne tensed when a high-pitched call ululated through the air at dusk. A melodic sound, it strung on for several minutes. Claire cocked her head, a shiver of unease slipping down her spine. "What is it?"

Jock didn't take his eyes off his wife. "*Salat al-maghrib,* the Muslim call to prayer at dusk. You'll get used to it."

"We'll hear calls like this five times a day?" Claire asked.

"You get used to it."

Anne shook her head.

On their way to the train station the next morning, they passed plodding camels and donkey carts clogging the roadway. The gritty breeze stung Claire's eyes. She couldn't decide whether to keep cleaning her spectacles or remove them completely.

But she wanted to see the scenery, to hear the staccato murmurs, and savor the late-December heat on her pale skin. She tugged her hat lower to block the wind and peered at Port Said's living riot.

A police officer wearing white gloves directed the cars, buggies, carts, and camels toward the train station. They joined travelers and beggars thronging the entrance. Black-skinned porters wearing long white robes hauled mountains of luggage. Jock led them through the raucous crowd to a first-class train compartment.

He shut the door and merciful silence descended. Anne sank into a soft leather seat and Jock opened a flask. "This will help, darling."

"It better not be spirits."

"Cool water from the hotel."

Claire cleaned her glasses and pressed her nose against the dusty train window. Soldiers in a medley of uniforms, portly Egyptians, ragged supplicants—the world milled about the platform. A conductor with a bushy moustache served tea in a china pot. When a policeman ran alongside the train, the crowds stepped away. A long whistle shrieked and the train lurched forward. Claire bounced and pulled a map of Egypt from her bag.

Jock chuckled. "How old are you?"

She grinned. "Old enough. I'm thrilled to be here."

"Good."

The train tracks paralleled the Suez Canal, flowing like a blue thread against the white desert to the east. Packet and cargo ships moved through the water, along with a large Australian troop transport filled with shouting soldiers.

Claire and Biddy had discussed the book of Exodus and references to Egypt during their voyage. Bible lands stretched before her, the place where Moses demanded freedom for his people.

Even in late December, the sun beat down. Camel trains moved along the eastern side of the canal and conical structures, tall and white, dotted the western landscape.

"Pigeon houses," Jock explained. "Farmers raise pigeons for food and communications."

"Like at the Marne?" Claire asked.

He nodded. "Carrier pigeons were invented in Egypt thousands of years ago. Maybe another story idea? Take that down."

"I'll remember. How far away is Palestine?"

"Northeast a couple hundred miles. Perhaps we should consider an article we'd call 'War Comes to the Holy Land.' Or have you abandoned your interest?"

She heard the challenge. "I study the Bible and pray daily."

The pipe came out. "Did you know your friend Chambers is in Cairo?"

Claire stilled. "Yes."

He took his time lighting it, so much so Anne looked up.

"I see Hodges from time to time. He'll call. He travels to Zeitoun often."

"Zeitoun?"

"The YMCA cooperates with the Egyptian General Mission. They run a rest and recreation area for the ANZAC soldiers near the Zeitoun camp and Chambers is in charge."

"Is Zeitoun far from your office or the hotel?"

He sighed and looked out at the Nile. "It's a distance. Why?"

"I'd like to visit."

Jock shook his head. "I'd hoped you were done with them. Did you see his wife on the ship?"

"Yes." Claire's fingers flexed but she wouldn't drop her eyes.

"Biddy Chambers is a lovely woman," Anne said. "I enjoyed her daughter."

"Have you become one of them too?"

"I liked her. She's unpretentious."

"I doubt you'll see much of them. The Shepheard's Hotel *memsahibs* will keep you busy. I hope you're confident in your bridge game and prepared for charity events."

"Not a problem. Our wardrobe should draw attention."

He grinned. "That's my girl."

Shepheard's Hotel in old Cairo, a mile inland from the Nile, served as the central meeting spot and favorite residence of British officials in Egypt. Jock rented a suite overlooking the hotel gardens. Jock and Anne shared a sumptuous boudoir with a balcony. Claire had a smaller chamber on the opposite side of the drawing room.

Claire noticed a brand-new portable typewriter on the desk near the window. "For me?"

Jock nodded. "It's a portable machine for my personal typist."

"Your reporter in training. When can I start?"

"It's hard to say what you'll be doing."

"You said you needed me. I took notes on the boat in case you wanted information about journeying to the Middle East."

"Troop transport ships would be of greater interest." Jock sighed. "Censorship is just as strong here as in England. I'll examine what you've got, but all copy has to be cleared through the British army. Our cables go to the army censors first and then on to London, who censors them again."

"When can I start?"

"Not tonight."

Claire refused to consider it might be another broken promise, but exhaustion swept over her, and she longed for the solace of her room.

Anne stood in the center of the room, her elbows tight against her sides. "It's a beautiful place to call home, Jock. Thank you."

"Shall we go down for a drink? I'll show you around?"

"I'm tired. Let's order a light supper up here." Anne removed her hat. "Claire and I will make our entrance tomorrow."

Claire gathered her possessions. "Nothing for me. I'm to bed. I'll unpack tomorrow."

As Claire went to her room, Jock took his wife's face in his hands. "Ah, Annie. I've missed you so much."

A bed shrouded in white mosquito-netting dominated the room. Claire moved past the small table and armoire to the window. Shutters closed out the soft Cairo night, allowing only a whisper of sound from the street three floors below.

She pushed open the shutters. The city spread before her in a labyrinth of boulevards, cramped passageways, slums, and stone buildings. Theater lights beamed to the north and when the traffic silenced she heard the dull clump of hooves.

Claire closed her eyes and took a deep breath of the cooling air, her senses tingling. "Thank you, God, I could come."

A dim light shone around the corner of the building and she heard her parents' voices. A rattan chair scraped across the balcony. She didn't mean to eavesdrop, but her ears caught an important question.

"I'm delighted you're here, but what made you change your mind?"

"Did I misinterpret your plea?" Anne asked.

"No. I need you."

"How much have you been drinking?"

Claire stifled a gasp.

The silence lasted a long time. "Too much, but not enough to cause damage. I've much to do. I need to keep my wits, but being back here brought nightmares."

Claire smelled his tobacco and reached for her handkerchief. She must not sneeze.

She lost her mother's murmured response to the buzz of insects.

"I'm sorry, Anne. I stayed in Alexandria the first couple weeks, trying to find stories to satisfy the syndicate without having to be in Cairo. The Gallipoli retreat provided plenty of copy, but eventually they required me here. I've kept busy, but the nights were hard."

"Have you been to the cemetery?"

Jock swore. "No."

"To the old house?"

"Of course not. They're gone. Nothing can be gained by stirring up those memories."

"Mrs. Chambers has an adorable toddler. I didn't know what to say when I met her, remembering the boys agitated me so."

"What was she like?"

"Friendly and practical. You've nothing to fear."

"I couldn't believe it when I saw her husband, but he's doing well in a terrible job. With the appalling venereal disease numbers, the generals want the men to stay at the camps away from the fleshpots. Firing them up with religion the way Chambers does helps."

"Claire will be fine. She has a level head on her shoulders, even if Nigel is trying to snatch her."

"He's still in London?"

"As of our departure, but headed out here. She cried as we left."

Her father's voice changed. "Is she attached?"

"She's confused. Peter sought me while home on leave. He said she'd be better away from Nigel. I'm terrified of Egypt. I don't want to risk another child, but I had to weigh the possibility of losing Claire to Nigel and perhaps to New Zealand if we stayed in London."

Claire ground her teeth.

Anne laughed. "Besides, I missed you. Even with zeppelin raids, London lacked excitement without you."

Jock's throaty voice whispered. "I knew you couldn't live without me, darling."

"I've never wanted to. We'll go down together."

Claire closed the shutters. Nigel's blue sapphire ring sparkled in the lamplight.

She slipped it off her finger and hid it in the bottom of her trunk.

Chapter Twenty

They dressed with care before their entrance into Cairo's British society.

"Women will want to know the latest styles. Don't say much at first. We need to figure out who's important and who's not," Anne said as she admired her reflection in the mirror.

"May I wear my glasses?"

"Naturally. We'll tell them spectacles are the rage in London these days." Anne twirled in a soft emerald dress with a high neck, fitted waist, and full skirt. She settled a wide-brimmed straw hat onto her white-blond hair and held out her elbow.

Claire wore a two-piece white organdy dress edged in black embroidery. The skirt boasted four tiers of lacy fabric and the blouse's shawl collar came to a vee on the bodice. The dress made her feel elegant and light as they sauntered arm in arm down the grand stairway.

The diners hushed in the tearoom at their entrance and murmuring slipped through the room.

When the maître d' approached with a bowing *salaam*, Anne's cultured voice carried. "We're just in from London. My husband is waiting for us."

Two junior officers stood at attention when they passed. Claire blushed as she struggled to keep up with her mother. Women in elaborate hats peered at them; waiters paused to watch. This inspection caused more butterflies than Sylvia's caustic scrutiny.

"Please, God, don't let me trip," Claire whispered as they advanced to where Jock sat.

Jock stood and kissed their hands. "Perfect."

Anne drew off her dazzling gloves with admirable flair. "Who am I impressing?"

"The general's wife, Mrs. Murray, sitting by the window in the beige frock. She likes to play cards and bargain, but has no patience with the natives. Worm your way into her inner circle."

Anne arched a brow. "I do not worm. I charm."

He winked and pulled out her chair. A waiter immediately materialized with a teapot and thin sandwiches arranged on a tiered silver tray.

As Anne poured, Jock assessed the important women in the tea room, one by one. Claire and Anne discreetly examined the women Jock indicated. Sitting bolt upright as trained by Sylvia, Claire waved a delicate fan and examined the airy room crowded with round tables covered in white cloth. Ornate columns of blue and white striped stone rose to vaulted ceilings. Open arches faced the inviting garden and a grand piano graced the northern corner.

Jock straightened his cutlery. "People know I'm a journalist and can't decide if they should befriend me or not, that's why you're valuable. See if you can learn army plans. You're my domestic ear. I can handle the rest."

"I presume you're including Claire in this task?" Anne acknowledged a beaming woman at the next table before sipping her tea.

"I prefer to work with Papa." The last twenty minutes had gone well, but Claire had no illusions about her social capabilities.

He lowered his voice and nodded at Claire. "We'll work from the drawing room the first few weeks and then shift to the office. You need to pace yourself in Egypt's weather. It's too easy to get sick here."

"I'd hoped for a chance to report. Surely it's time for me to earn a byline."

Jock sighed. "That's harder than you know."

"Why? I will not be deterred, Papa."

"Here comes the first *memsahib*," he said.

A large, buxom woman approached, dressed in yards of ruffled lace and a bonnet suitable for Ascot twenty years before. "Thelma Middleton," Jock said sotto voce. Her daughter, Cecily, who appeared close to Claire's age, wore a sailor suit and an unbecoming hat. Introductions were shared, Mrs. Middleton gushed over their clothing, and Anne promised to play bridge one afternoon in the future. As the two paraded away, Anne shuddered. "Easy, but this could get dull."

"Two weeks max and then you can do anything you want. What do you think, Claire?"

She watched the next woman advance in their direction. "When can I go to the office?"

"After you've written two insightful stories about the Shepheard's Hotel *memsahibs*."

"I'll get my pencil."

"You need to get both sides of a story and prove to me you can articulate them," he said. "Until you've spent time and spoken with the *memsahibs*, you won't know anything about the British woman's view of Cairo. Start with this woman."

Lucretia Patterson spoke in a breathless voice. "I adore your dresses, but tell me who you are and what you're doing here."

Claire blanked.

"We've come to be with my husband in this Godforsaken place," Anne said. "And you?"

"I'm here for the same reason. Do you like to tour?"

Anne hesitated. "Maybe later."

Lucretia leaned closer. "A better question: did you bring anything new to read?"

Claire straightened her sunny linen dress and sashayed down the main stairs to the salon a week later. The usual murmur like water over stones stirred as she scanned the assembly with an unsteady confidence. She reminded herself to behave like Sylvia—only friendlier—so she acknowledged Cecily's shy wave.

Across the room a man wearing a dusty brown uniform stood.

Claire rocked back on her high heels, bit her lip to keep from calling, and scurried toward him. She dodged chintz chairs, overstuffed sofas, and a phalanx of startled women.

"Is it you?" She practically hopped in glee.

"Yes, but who are you?" Jim Hodges laughed. "I came to find an earnest reporter wearing glasses. Instead I see a glamour girl."

Heads craned. Claire didn't care. Jim's round face had thinned, but smile lines radiated from the corners of his eyes. With freckles faded into his suntanned skin, he appeared worn but triumphant. "I met your father on the street and he sent me with his blessings. He'll be late."

She straightened her skirt as he seated her, trying to calm the flutters in her stomach. Claire ignored the whispering *memsahibs*. "You're different. What's happened?"

"Malaria. I've been down twice. I hope you're using your mosquito netting."

"What makes you think I have one?"

He gestured at the surrounding. "Good question. You're making progress as a reporter."

"It's debatable." Claire made a face. "I've been stuck in this hotel as my mother sorts our possessions. Papa dictates in our drawing room, I type up the dispatches and send them from the hotel's telegraph office. Tomorrow he's promised we'll go to the office. I'm dying to get out."

Jim leaned back in his chair. "Then you've not seen anything of Cairo?"

"Nothing. Most of his interviews take place in spots I can't enter, like the officers' mess. I suspect he's confining us to the hotel on purpose."

"You need to get used to the climate," Jim said. "Jock Meacham knows what he's doing. Locals are impressed the newspaper syndicate sent a reporter who speaks Arabic."

She shrugged. "He's not fluent. He uses an interpreter."

"There's more to your father than meets the eye. How do you know he's not fluent? Do you speak Arabic? "

Electric fans whirred overhead. Sunlight glared through the windows facing the street. Claire fretted. She should know better. A good reporter double-checked her facts. "He said he was rusty when he left London."

"I suspect it's come back to him. Would you care to walk to the Ezbekieh Gardens down the street? It's only five minutes away."

"I'll get a hat and let my mother know."

Jim awaited her in the airy stone foyer. His khaki uniform resembled a British officer's minus the tabs indicating rank and the leather belt across his chest. He wore a pith helmet—a dusty white desert hat resembling a wide-brimmed, inverted canvas soup bowl. An artist's thick paintbrush poked out from under his arm.

When she asked about it, Jim laughed. "I should have known by your lack of a fly whisk you're a newcomer in Egypt." He waved it before her nose. "It's used to vanquish insects. I'll protect you."

Claire took his proffered elbow. "Papa's been too busy to teach me anything about Cairo life."

They paraded through the wide front porch where several porters *salaamed* and walked down four steps to the sidewalk. A swarm of beggars surrounded them, including a child missing a hand. A one-eyed crone snatched at Claire's dress. Two men thinner than skeletons lay at her feet. Claire clutched Jim's arm.

"*Baksheesh?*" they cried.

"*La'a shukran*," Jim answered.

A hotel doorman rushed over to kick away the beggars. The crowd recoiled, muttering and growling.

"Keep walking. Don't make eye contact," Jim said. "They'll leave us alone."

"What did you say?"

"They asked for a gift. I said 'no, thank you.' They're people made in God's image. I don't want to hurt them."

The warm air, languid palm trees, babbling foreign tongues, and exotic buildings disoriented Claire. Donkeys trotted down the avenue pulling overloaded carts, while honking motorcars swerved around them. Soldiers jostled along the pavement; sweet smelling smoke rose from their thin cigarettes. Further down the street, electrical lines powered a trolley past a park.

Claire spied soldiers walking down an alleyway toward women swirling in colorful garments. "What's down there?"

Jim blushed. "It's the reason the YMCA is at Ezbekieh Gardens—to keep soldiers out of the Cairo fleshpots. The Fishmarket district—it's off-limits to troops—starts just east of the American Mission. I doubt you'll go near it, but if so, be careful."

"Why?"

He paused a moment to gaze at her. "You don't want to be captured for the white slave trade."

Claire's mouth popped open and her eyes went wide as she craned to see over his shoulder.

Jim tugged her across Shari Kamil Street in front of the French club and entered the park, a green oasis surrounded by a high plaster wall topped with a metal fence. The street noise faded as they strolled among shaggy ficus trees. Palms dotted the landscape, and they passed an open stage. Green bee-eater birds trilled in the bushes.

Jim nipped a magenta bougainvillea blossom. "Let's make a new memory."

She held it to her nose. "These flowers have no scent."

"I'll remedy that next time," he said, laughing. "How's your family? Nigel?"

Claire updated him on her relatives but didn't want to discuss Nigel. "He's the same."

Jim described his work at Mr. Jessop's YMCA headquarters. "Mostly paperwork at the moment because of my health. I see OC several times a week. He's doing a great job at Zeitoun."

"Is it far?"

"Seven miles north of here. Perhaps I can escort you on the trolley?"

"I don't know what my father will say." She touched a golden flower she didn't recognize. "He's not happy OC's in Cairo."

Jim flicked his whisk at an insect. "The kingdom of God needs OC's ministry with the ANZAC units. The soldiers appreciate his humor and how he doesn't mince words. Let's hope your father doesn't intrude. How's your spiritual life?"

"I completed OC's correspondence courses before I left London."

"Congratulations. Have they made a difference in your understanding of God?"

Claire wrinkled her forehead. While God complicated her relationship with Nigel and her family, her Bible study helped in other areas. "I was terrified of the U-boats before we sailed, but then I read a verse about God knowing all the hairs on my head and the number of days in my life. If he cares so much about me, do I need to fear the future?"

"For I know the thoughts I think toward you, saith the Lord, thoughts of peace, and not of evil, to give you an expected end." Jim's eyes gleamed.

"Exactly," Claire said. "God isn't surprised by what happens to me, so why should I worry?" She bit her lip, wishing she felt as confident about Peter's brushes with death.

Crows cawed from a tree overhanging a pond. Two men wearing long white robes poked at a furry rodent beneath a wide banyan tree.

Jim directed her down a gravel path. "Jesus spent his first years here in Egypt. Moses probably dressed in a thobe like those men when he demanded Pharaoh let the chosen people go. Without a war, the Middle East would be an excellent spot to study the Bible. God feels closer here."

"How close did he feel at Gallipoli?"

Jim waved the whisk. "Your father asked the same question. When you're under fire and people around you die, you have to decide, 'Do I believe what I say I believe, or is it a lie?' "

"What did you decide?"

"I believe God."

"You sound like Biddy." Claire laughed.

They passed through a shoulder-high reed mat fence into the YMCA camp. Jim pointed out the swimming pool and toured her about the facilities. Claire had heard about the camp from the *memsahibs* at Shepheard's Hotel; many of them volunteered at the tea canteen. Lectures were held nightly at an arena big enough to seat several thousand men. With an open-air cinema, library, and a roller rink, the YMCA maintained a busy schedule.

"What's your most important work?"

Jim's eyes flashed with zeal. "Making certain the soldiers know they don't face death alone. They need to hear the gospel."

Claire thought of Peter and Nigel; two men who wanted her to believe for them. "Don't ever forget to tell them."

"OC won't let me."

Claire's soul hummed. She could hardly wait to hear OC preach again. She'd just have to think of some way to convince her father.

Chapter Twenty-One

January 1916

A muezzin's thin cry pulled her out of sleep as it had each morning since Claire had arrived in Egypt. She pushed open the window shutters to relish the cool morning air. Far to the east, a thin pale line marked the rising sun's arrival. Below her, the city stirred to life.

Robed men aimed their bowing prayers east toward Mecca, while British soldiers on early duty hailed both horse-drawn and automotive cabs. A street sweeper pushed his twiggy broom down the sidewalk, shadowed by a crawling beggar. Claire smelled orange blossoms as the sky lightened. She reached for her Bible, the leather binding cracking in Egypt's arid air.

When Jock knocked thirty minutes later, Claire tied back her curly hair with a scarf and joined him in the drawing room. A turbaned servant served them a British breakfast. Jock liked to work at the office before the day's heat became overpowering. They'd be gone by the time Anne awoke.

The BNS's office, dusty like all of Cairo, lay a few blocks from Shepheard's Hotel. Three Western reporters from a news syndicate and a London paper shared the noisy quarters. Two English-speaking Egyptian typists and four interpreters were available and several message runners waited outside. The locals bowed when Jock entered and were careful not to look directly at Claire, the only woman present.

Claire retrieved her pad and with familiar lines and squiggles marked the date—January 18, 1916—as her father began dictating

"Word has come to us of a battle in the deserts of Mesopotamia. It's a fight for the heart of the Bible lands. Sixteen hundred British and Indian casualties occurred as they fought an overpowering force of Ottoman warlords in the dry creek beds.

"Following so soon after last week's disastrous Battle of Sheikh Sa'ad, this maneuver marks another escalation in a war spanning the globe with bloody brutality."

"Can it be any worse than France?" Claire asked.

"Depends where you are." Jock paced between his desk and the window. "If you're an Australian soldier reeling from the Gallipoli disaster, you don't want to head into the desert. Meanwhile your mother's learned fresh reinforcements will arrive soon from Australia and India, so obviously the generals expect trouble."

In addition to taking dictation, Claire read and organized telegrams, prepared wires and sent them, filed, and occasionally dusted. While she recognized her importance to her father—getting the wire copy out on time and editing for grammar—Claire chafed at not being able to report herself. Jock tapped his fingers one morning before the other reporters arrived.

"Reporters write two kinds of stories: hard news and soft news. It will be difficult for a woman to obtain hard news, so you should focus on stories appealing to women. How to recognize a quality rug, for instance."

"But you won't let me go to the bazaar by myself, so how can I find such a story?"

Jock rubbed the back of his neck. "Keep your eyes open at the hotel. Maybe one of *memsahibs* writes mysteries or is an archaeologist like that Mrs. Emerson. What interests you?"

"I want to know what's happening in world events."

"Then you've come to the wrong place." Jock adjusted the shutters over the window. He rifled through a book of maps on the filing cabinet, pushed a chair under a desk, and finally stood before her. "Egypt is a backwater in this war."

Her heart sank. "Then why are we here?"

"It's the only choice Josiah Fischer gave me. His son wanted to cover the war in London. I could come here or lose my job."

Claire leaned her head in her hand and closed her eyes. No wonder the inexperienced Michael Fischer ruled the London newsroom. She described her exchanges with the novice editor. "Was I wrong to clean up his copy?"

Jock shook his head. "Conroy's a good editor; he'll make sure the stories are acceptable to Boston."

"We'll find scoops here and impress the BNS."

He sat on the desk beside her. "We walk a fine line in Cairo with the British army. The censors will toss out an errant reporter without a second thought. We need to be careful. I can't afford to lose this job."

"You're a well-known reporter. You can get another job."

He regarded her, as if weighing an idea. Finally he shrugged. "Maybe, but all we have is my pay. If the BNS fires me, I don't have enough savings to ship us home."

Claire's hands dropped into her lap and her mind raced. "I'll get another job. Stenographers are in high demand. Or I'll write stories myself and the BNS can pay me, two writers instead of one."

"Thank you, darling, but the BNS isn't ready for a woman reporter yet. The best way you can help is by doing what you've been doing. Keep me on track, cable my copy on time, and snoop out information I can string together into a story."

She nodded, yet again wondering about the fine line between spying and reporting.

Jock and Claire spent their mornings at the office and filed the news cable to Boston at Shepheard's Hotel when they returned for luncheon and an afternoon rest. Jock usually arranged interviews and meetings during tea time and into the evening, always in male-only settings. Anne and Claire dined with him late, if at all.

Anne spent her mornings making arrangements, attending to her correspondence, and reading. Once Jock set out on interviews in the afternoons, she sidled to the hotel salon and played cards or met other women for tea. Her friend Lucretia called to discuss books and tell stories and occasionally brought Cecily Middleton to make a foursome for cards. Claire learned to play bridge to keep from total boredom.

Her mother seldom left the hotel. "I'm not ready yet," she said. So Claire joined Cecily on Thomas Cook tours originating in the hotel lobby. She visited the pyramids, Egyptian Museum, the Citadel, and took a cruise down the Nile in a felucca.

On Sundays Anne refused to attend the Anglican Church—"too many memories"—so Claire walked with Cecily and others to Ezbekieh Gardens for services with the YMCA chaplains. Cecily was happy to meet Tommies away from her mother's sharp eyes. Claire enjoyed the service and looked for the Chambers family each week, so far to no avail.

But at dusk one afternoon Claire found her mother at the window facing the direction of the Old Cairo Cemetery. Anne clenched her jaw, breathing heavily. When the Muslim

Salat al-maghrib called, she trembled. "You must think me a coward."

"No."

"The sights, the heavy air, the ripe scents, the miserable cry, they remind me of what we lost." Anne trembled. "But I can't stay holed up in this hotel. I'll go crazy playing bridge with brainless women every day, even if I pick up information your father wants. I need to take myself in hand and be useful."

"Doing what?"

Anne shuddered. "I don't know."

A knock sounded. Claire opened the door to a porter with a silver tray. She read the note and spun around. "How about a tea party with Miss Kathleen Chambers?"

Anne's relief mirrored her own. "Perfect."

They met the Chambers family at the agreed-upon time in the grand foyer.

Claire introduced Anne to a healthy and tanned, albeit as thin as ever, Oswald. He carried Kathleen in triumph—"I can't get enough of my lassie"—while Biddy examined their surrounds with keen-eyed expectation.

"I have a special treat for you, Miss Kathleen." Anne took the child's hand and led them to the hotel terrace.

Murmurs spread as they strolled to their table. The blonde, blue-eyed European child wearing an enormous bow in her hair caught every British woman's eye.

Clad in the khaki YMCA uniform, OC slipped the flat hat from his head and pulled out chairs for the women. "We've been shopping today. I wanted Biddy and Kathleen to experience the souk."

"It reminded me of Ali Baba's cave," Biddy said. "Unimaginable riches piled wherever I looked. I need to learn to haggle the way Oswald did."

"Were you at the Khan el-Khalili?" Anne asked.

"You know it?" Oswald stowed his fly whisk.

"Many years ago we loved to stroll through that market. It's a wonderland of cramped aisles and magnificent rugs. Spices from all over the world, and we bought tiny cups of the densest coffee I've ever tasted."

Claire's lips parted. "Can we go?"

Anne's smile faded. "Ask your father when he has time. How large is your bungalow?"

"Not very big." OC answered, as cheerful as ever. "Two rooms. We live mostly outside."

"Indeed?" Anne raised an eyebrow.

"They tell me it will be too hot in summer to stay indoors. This wee home is sufficient."

After the waiter took their order, Anne pulled a book from her bag to read aloud for Kathleen.

"Your mother likes children," OC murmured.

"Yours in particular. What exactly are you doing at Zeitoun?"

"We offer resources for soldiers stationed at the army camps nearby, mostly ANZAC troops. The large hut—which is actually a tent—is devoted to letter writing, entertainment, and classes. It's crucial these men hear the gospel rather than be offered the concerts and motion pictures most YMCA huts provide."

Anne glanced up from the book. "The men accept a Bible study in lieu of movies? It hardly seems sufficient entertainment for a soldier."

"Mostly they need a place other than their tents to socialize. We provide tea and biscuits. In the evenings, we hold a prayer meeting. More soldiers join us every night." His face lit up as he spoke.

"Are soldiers interested in God?" Claire asked.

"The possibility of death concentrates their minds. I also visit hospitalized soldiers. I've been asked to teach a Bible class one night a week at the Ezbekieh Gardens down the street. We stopped by the park on our way here."

Claire's heart lifted. "Then I'll be able to hear you."

"On Wednesdays."

"How do you spend your time, Biddy?" Claire recognized her mother's "spy" tone.

"I keep the bungalow, help the soldiers, care for Kathleen, pray for Oswald, and take shorthand. Kathleen is a great attraction on the compound."

"Soldiers appreciate a friendly face—and a child in particular," OC said. "They're lonely. Many don't know what to say in letters home. I spend hours in the hut listening and advising. We welcome help. Perhaps you'd like to visit, Mrs. Meacham?"

Anne crossed her arms. "This is not religious activity? I could merely chat?"

"You would please the soldiers greatly," Biddy said. "You don't need to attend Oswald's class unless you want to."

"But I could attend the class, couldn't I?" Claire's heart pounded. "Mama, could we go out once a week?"

Anne pressed her lips flat. "How do we get there?"

"Take the trolley to Zeitoun, twenty minutes from here," OC said. "You walk across the desert another fifteen minutes to reach our compound. Kathleen managed fine this morning. You're welcome anytime."

Claire bit her lip. Once her father heard of the scheme, he'd quash it. But at least she could hope for Wednesday nights at the gardens.

Tea arrived and Anne directed Claire to pour. The food brought smiles.

"Falafels at Shepheard's Hotel with a Scotsman," Anne laughed. "Who would have thought it?"

OC lifted his cup to her with a friendly nod. "Indeed. Cairo is full of surprises."

Chapter Twenty-Two

February 1916

Jock pushed back his chair after lunch and reached for his hat. "I've got an appointment in half an hour with BEF headquarters. Get those notes we worked on this morning organized, Claire, and we'll finish the whole thing when I get back. Fischer's been demanding this story, and I promised it tonight."

"How late will you be?" Anne asked.

"No later than six. We need to catch the late-night cable." He kissed them and left.

Anne went to play cards and Claire hurried upstairs to her typewriter. She'd taken extensive notes.

The room was freshened and orderly, the scarlet pillows on the settee and chairs plumped, fresh flowers arranged in a vase on the table. Her shrouded typewriter waited on the desk under the window with her satchel beside it. Claire switched on the slow electric fan overhead and drew up her chair. She opened her bag. No notebook.

Claire pushed aside the flowers on the table and dumped out the contents of her satchel. *Baedeker's Guide to Egypt*, a local map, handkerchief, coin purse, several fat pencils, smoked glasses for the sun, Peter's arrowhead, and a tiny YMCA New Testament OC had recently given her.

No notebook. She scrabbled through the pile on her desk. They were all filled, the most recent dated ten days before. She couldn't find the one she'd worked in that morning at the office.

She closed her eyes to think where she might have dropped it.

The hotel switchboard put her phone call through to the BNS office, where the duty typist found it on the floor. "I'm on my way," she said, stuffing everything back into the satchel and then dashing out the door.

Out on the street, a doorman searched for a calash. "Sorry, miss, you must wait."

The bright sun lit up everything like a spotlight and Claire clipped the smoked lenses onto her spectacles. In the languid afternoon, not much moved on the street. The local beggars had shifted into shade and even the doorman hovered under the hotel canopy.

It was only a couple blocks east and two blocks north. Claire could hurry there and back before the next cab appeared. "Never mind," she called to the doorman and set off.

"*Memb!*" he shouted, but she didn't look back.

No one strolled the broad sidewalk along the avenue; the rug shops and restaurants were shuttered against the hot afternoon sun. Claire squashed down her hat and crossed the street. Odd to see it deserted, but then she'd never been out at this hour and certainly never alone.

The tall buildings provided some shade as she hurried past the closed American Mission skirting the north end of Ezbekieh Gardens. Jock had warned her never to go out alone, but really, it was just a few more blocks.

To the east stretched the cluttered and colorful Fishmarket district. A group of uniformed soldiers swaggered out from an alleyway, a swirl of gauzy skirts and veils called out to them. Sweet hashish smoke hazed the air and coins jangled on a moneychanger's table. A dusty soothsayer swathed in rags reached a thin hand toward her as a dozen silver bracelets slid down her arm with a clink.

A loud hiss behind spun Claire in surprise as a toothless crone pushed a cart along the sidewalk. Claire stepped aside and wrinkled her nose at the pungent foul scent. A water carrier followed with a small cask nestling on his right shoulder. He held a tin cup in Claire's direction, "drink?"

Sweat trickled between her shoulder blades, but Claire shook her head and turned north. Her eyes grew wide as a pompous man with a flowing shiny moustache wearing a white thobe and black fez approached her. "Are you lost, madam?"

"Hey there, leave the lady alone," shouted one of the soldiers. The money changer clattered his coins onto the table and leered. "*Piastre?*"

"Fortune? I find in the sand?" A thin, turbaned man swiped his hand across the sidewalk, smoothing tawny dirt and writing with his finger.

"Welcome to the Fishmarket," the Egyptian man continued with a mumbling accent. "You will take a cup of tea? My beautiful shop is right here. We have beautiful rugs and always appreciate to meet beautiful ladies."

Two women with kohl-lined eyes peered at her from behind the thick Turkish carpets. They giggled and one beckoned with a sensuous turn of her arm.

"No, no, thank you," Claire stuttered. The soldiers turned her way and she smelled the anise alcohol so popular with the poor. "I must be going." Claire picked up her skirts, but the shop owner grabbed her arm and tugged her toward the shop.

Fear surged. "Dear God, help me," she said, and dug in her heels to lean away. He grabbed both her forearms and tugged.

She lurched to the left, her heavy satchel striking his arm. When he paused, she kicked him in the knee and screamed, "Take your hands off me!"

His grip relaxed and Claire pulled free, but he caught the strap of her bag. The veins in her neck felt like they'd popped as she shrieked, "Give me my bag! Police!"

He dropped his hands. "No, no, no. Very sorry, miss."

"Unhand the lady!"

Two soldiers started in her direction. Claire fled.

"Wait, miss. We'll take care of you." The soldiers shouted, the crone hissed, and Claire ran, the satchel tripping her as it bounced against her leg. She snatched it up and nearly fell.

A bellow of laughter, a chorus of high-pitched squeals, and her hat flew off. She dared not stop.

"No need to flee, miss, we'll save you!" Cockney voices called after her. Claire did not slow nor look back.

Two blocks later she arrived breathless and sweaty at the BNS door. She burst into the office and crumpled into a chair.

The duty typist hurried over. "Miss? Your notebook?"

Claire turned the pages to that morning's notes. She smoothed her trembling hand over the shorthand and gasped a raspy rush of adrenaline.

Boston needed the news. Claire pushed the damp hair from her forehead and took a deep breath. She'd get it to them, one way or another. That's what being a reporter meant.

"Please call me a calash," she told the hovering typist. "I'll wait."

One afternoon after Jock left for a series of interviews that would take him late into the night, Anne said she had finally mined all the pertinent information from the Shepheard's Hotel *memsahibs* and won enough card games. "Let's spend our time constructively," she said. "Let's catch the trolley and see how Biddy's getting along."

They caught the trolley in front of the hotel, sat in the car reserved for women, and disembarked at Zeitoun. Ancient fortune tellers squatted in the sand, calling out to them. Claire shuddered and hurried past. They trailed a group of soldiers across the desert headed east, but Anne seized her arm when the soldiers slowed to a saunter. "Let them get ahead. We don't want to ruin your reputation."

"Isn't that why you're here?"

"Of course." She caught Claire's eye. "I admit I'm curious. This is the perfect place to fact-gather for your father."

"As I expected."

To the north stretched the army range, where white bell tents stood in rows as far as they could see. Several stone buildings looked official, with officers coming and going. Far to the east billows of sand, dirt, and smoke marked maneuvers. Sunlight glittered off rifles as units marched in their direction. Horses pulled wagons and the air rang with shouts and martial clatter. Claire had never seen anything like it before, but Anne hustled her along. "The last thing we want is to be mistaken for camp followers."

They picked their way past a motor pool, water tower, and a jumble of fallen stone pillars carved for a forgotten pharaoh. Native launderers stirred enormous black vats over outdoor fires. The air jangled with snorting horses and calling native voices against the background of an active military camp. Eventually they reached a humble compound surrounded by a whitewashed wall.

It felt like the edge of civilization. Tawny, barren never-ending wilderness stretched to distant hills in the east. Inside the walls, a large YMCA sign stood beside a dusty brown circus tent. The sign towered over the desert landscape, a jaunty red triangle with blue lettering on a white rectangle.

"This is it?" Claire shared her mother's incredulity.

A two-story stone building sheltered by spindly trees was the only permanent structure she saw except for a low-lying primitive bungalow.

Anne stopped. "How dreadful."

"Biddy's undoubtedly made it welcoming inside," Claire said.

"Do you see any color other than the YMCA sign? How can a child be raised in such a grim place? Let's get our spying out of the way before they know we're here."

"Biddy and OC won't care."

They peered into the cavernous hut, twenty feet high. A Union Jack stood on the stage in front and benches marched in rows to the rear. A handful of soldiers wrote at wooden tables. The air held a musky scent from the heat, but it was several degrees cooler than outside.

"Hundreds could fit in here," Anne said. "This is much larger than I expected."

A soldier rose as if to greet them. Anne waved him off. "What does the sign say?"

Claire stepped closer to read a sign announcing a blackboard lecture at 7:30. Subject: "Religious Problems Raised by the War."

Anne sniffed. "Your father would agree. Let's see if Biddy is at that miserable bungalow."

She was.

"What a pleasant surprise. You must want a cup of cool water."

They sat at a square wooden table before the bungalow. Straggles of brown hair slipped her hair pins as the red-faced Biddy pumped water. Her long-sleeved white blouse was dusty and her dun-colored skirt brushed the top of sturdy boots. "Kathleen will rise soon from her nap and be pleased to see you. I'm thankful you're here."

Anne's face twisted as scanned the view from the bungalow. "How are you managing?"

Biddy indicated the outdoor kitchen. "An assistant helps Mary with the cooking and cleaning. I'm grateful for him. We live simply. Since we don't have a floor, it's easy to complete the housekeeping. I merely smooth the sand and I'm done. It's a good life for which we thank God."

"But it's sandy and brown," Anne said. "You're a refined woman. How can you tolerate this?"

Biddy pushed the locks of hair off her sweat-beaded forehead. "God called us to Zeitoun. We find joy in our surroundings. We're glad to be together again." She waved her hand toward the east. "Sunrise is such a glory and the stars at night are breathtaking."

Claire didn't think her mother believed Biddy.

Biddy described activities in the compound, including a French class taught at five o'clock. "Many of the men will end up in France, so there's great interest. Do you speak French? They welcome practice and a woman would be of great interest. The men arrive after dinner."

OC returned from visiting a hospital as Kathleen woke from her nap. They drank tea and ate fruit and sandwiches, talking about the ministry and their reaction to Egypt.

"My head and heart are swelling with anticipation for what will come from this new development in the desert,"

OC said. "This feels like the BTC on a much bigger scale. But that is just like God, don't you think? Something always 'better to come?' "

"How can this be better than the Clapham Common mansion Jock told me about?" Anne asked.

"It is not the material surroundings that matter, Mrs. M. We have much to be thankful for."

"The soldiers already have helped make the compound nicer," Biddy said. "They've been collecting stones for paths and enjoy playing with Kathleen." She touched the little girl's hair. "And she loves to play with them."

At five o'clock, the Meachams joined the French lesson in the main hut. Fluent Anne fell into conversation with the teacher. After a short grammar lesson he dismissed the soldiers to practice and eager young men surrounded Anne. Several tried to engage Claire, but she slipped away to chat with OC.

"Religious problems raised by the war?"

OC nodded. "Many, don't you think?"

"Yes, but what of the soldiers? Do they have questions?"

"Here come several now."

Three sunburned New Zealand soldiers entered. Two grilled OC while the third listened with skeptical interest. He leaned forward when OC made his signature comment, "I can see this is challenging to you. Why don't you brood on these scriptures and see what comes?"

"Brood? Like a hen?" One soldier guffawed. "You either have the answer or you don't."

"It's not my job to convince you," OC said. "If you meditate on the Scriptures with an open heart and mind, the Holy Spirit can show you elements of your life I'll never know."

"What things?"

"I do not know what God is impressing on your heart. I don't know your past or what you consider about your life. The word of God is alive and active and cuts to the marrow. Allow the Lord Jesus Christ to speak to your heart through his word, and you will understand things you never realized you knew before."

"What do you believe, miss?" the soldier asked.

Claire used Biddy's answer. "I believe God."

OC winked at her.

Anne joined Claire and Biddy in the tent at 7:30 to hear OC's talk. She didn't say much but nodded several times. She always appreciated a well-thought-out argument.

They exited the hut into a sparkling desert night. Biddy headed to the bungalow where a light burned in the window. Anne held out her hand. "This has been enlightening, Oswald."

"I'll have a soldier escort you to the trolley. Come again, Mrs. M."

"I shall."

When they arrived at Shepheard's Hotel, a coterie of British *memsahibs* met them. "We've a fashion show to plan. Will you be up for a bridge tournament tomorrow?"

Anne chatted without making any promises and quickly extricated herself from their requests. As they rode the lift up, Anne cleared her throat. "What will we tell your father?" She pushed open the door.

A halo of tobacco smoke hung about Jock's head when they entered the suite. "Where were you?"

Anne flung open the windows. "Really, Jock, if you're going to smoke in here, open the windows."

"I've been waiting at least an hour."

Anne perched on the arm of his chair. "The spying is amusing, but I need more constructive activities while you're out. Can you arrange your appointments for Monday and Wednesday afternoons and evenings?"

Claire set her bag on the desk.

"It shouldn't be too difficult. What will you do?"

"The ANZAC soldiers are worried about France." Anne nodded at Claire. "We've been investigating. We learned soldiers want to learn French. I could teach a class and we'd help them practice conversation."

"Have you been to the camps?"

"The YMCA handles recreational activities. Young men need help putting their ideas together to write home. Claire and I could help with that as well. Twice a week would be sufficient. We could walk to Ezbekieh Gardens."

"Not alone at night. It's not safe."

"Soldiers are everywhere, Papa. We'd never be alone," Claire said.

Her parents exchanged a look.

"If we left in time for tea," Anne said, "we would be safe in broad daylight. I'm certain we could find an escort for our return to Shepheard's Hotel. We'll talk with Claire's friend Jim. He's usually there, isn't he?"

Claire saw the appeal in Anne's eyes. "Yes."

Jock glanced between them, suspicious. "I'll go with you. I'd like to see what they're doing at the gardens. Maybe put together a story."

"What a lovely idea, darling. The class is at five on Wednesdays. You could sit in and chat with the men yourself."

Jock nodded and reached for the ashtray to knock out his pipe.

Claire marveled at the two of them: married twenty-seven years, a skeptical man and a charming woman. Until now, she had never recognized how her mother manipulated her father. By sidestepping the most critical question, Anne ensured Claire would get to hear OC lecture twice a week.

It wasn't quite honest, but it got Claire what she wanted, at least until Jock figured it out.

Chapter Twenty-Three

April 1916

"Let's go." Jock bolted down the tiny cup of thick Turkish coffee. "Boston needs the news and you're helping me this morning."

Claire stuffed the fly whisk into her bag. She could hardly wait to finally participate in real news-gathering.

The horse-drawn cab, a calash, jounced through Cairo's streets dodging camels, motorcars, pedestrians, and four carpenters carrying a fresh coffin as they headed west toward the Nile River. The Kobri el Gezira bridge with its two massive stone lions loomed.

"Where are we going?"

"A hotel near the Pyramids. Remember, you're working, no emotions."

Claire schooled herself to observe until the cab drew up to the former Mena House Hotel—now a field hospital for the Australian army.

"How many handkerchiefs will I need?" She clenched her stomach at the anticipated smells and sights.

"You'll be fine. I met a surgeon last night willing to let us visit. Keep your eyes open. I'll need your observations."

She nodded, pleased he wanted her thoughts, but frustrated too. Jock had used—"stolen" in his parlance—several of her descriptions from a night tour they'd recently made to the pyramids on the Giza Plateau. She'd read her words in the dispatch with a pang of pride and jealousy. Her father was the journalist—the BNS paid him—but she longed to see her name as a byline.

For the present she'd take what she could get.

Set in an oasis northeast of the pyramids, the Mena House Hotel-turned-hospital was surrounded by dust-encrusted greenery: palm trees, desert flowers, and spikey grass. Convalescents lounged in the sunshine, tended by nursing personnel.

"Remember, the Brits call nurses 'sisters,' and while hospitals don't mind visitors, the army doesn't like reporters poking around."

Observing and note taking didn't worry Claire; she feared disgracing herself when confronted by injuries. Carbolic soap's pungent smell greeted them as they entered the hospital and nausea threatened. She wrinkled her nose and adjusted her spectacles, anything to distract her weak stomach.

Matron—the senior nurse—led them to Dr. Travers on a circuitous route. Jock and Claire peeked into the grand ballroom crammed with iron bedsteads filled with men. Sisters wearing snowy headdresses and aprons moved among them. Stoic orderlies maneuvered the patients out of beds and through doorways. They found the doctor finishing up with a patient.

A bald man in a rumpled uniform, Dr. Travers signed a chart and then shook Jock's hand. He acknowledged Claire with a raised eyebrow and escorted them down a mural-lined corridor.

"Please let your readers know how well we care for the soldiers," Dr. Travers said. "Critics think Egypt a harsh climate, but people flocked here before the war to recover from a variety of ailments. It will be hot in a few months, but right now with the clear air and warm days, this is the healthiest spot for many of these men."

Jock kept the physician talking, prodding him into wards and places the doctor wouldn't have taken them if he had been paying attention. So intent on his own agenda, he didn't realize Jock wanted to examine nooks and crannies.

With the big windows open to fresh air, the hospital's smells didn't affect Claire as much as she feared. Not fretting about herself meant she could draw closer to the patients and scribble observations into her notebook.

They heard singing as they neared the end of their tour. "Ah, the YMCA is here," Dr. Travers said. "Helpful chaps stop in daily to talk with the patients."

"May we join them?" Jock asked.

The doctor waved them into an open lounge facing the pyramids.

Three dozen patients sat in wheelchairs or on benches. Medical personnel stood along the wall as two men in YMCA uniforms led a chorus of hymns. "I wonder where he's been." Jock reached for his pipe, remembered his location, and dropped his hand. "Look how brown Hodges is."

"Mesopotamia," Jim said an hour later when they exited the hospital together.

"Can we give you a ride to town?" Jock asked.

"Yes, but I can't discuss army maneuvers. I filled in at a mobile YMCA canteen accompanying a desert-fighting unit. Headquarters sent me because I'm an American, but I doubt the characters I saw in the desert cared."

Claire retrieved her notebook as they climbed into the calash.

Jim had sailed up the Suez Canal and caught a ride with an army unit to a forward encampment. He took the place of a YMCA secretary for a few weeks and manned his hut providing tea, reading materials, and paper to write letters. He also supplied a listening ear and "took a page from Oswald Chambers and taught a Bible study nightly."

"Did you see any action?"

"No, though an airplane flying by made our hearts race. Tension died down after the battle for Hanna and the troop reorganization. When the secretary came back, I returned to Egypt."

"How did you like the desert?" Claire asked. "Did you feel isolated? Frightened? What did you contemplate?"

His smile crinkled on the left side. "I meditated on my closeness to the land where Jesus walked and where Jacob wrestled with God and watched angels climbing a ladder."

Jock snorted. Claire frowned. According to the Bible, Jacob wrestled with God near Jerusalem. She wondered if Jim meant to hint where he'd been.

"Soldiers need reassurance their government and their God haven't forgotten them. My job is to put their minds at ease. I accomplished what I set out to do."

"Did you carry a gun?" Claire asked.

"I'd never carry a gun."

"Did you travel overland through Judea?" Jock asked as they entered Old Cairo.

"I'm not a copyboy anymore, Mr. Meacham."

"Jock."

Jim nodded. "I've seen the world since I left your employ. Reporters need to know some things, but not everything. I have confidentiality requirements."

"Thank you. Interview over."

Claire put away her notebook.

"I took a train ride and visited Jerusalem."

Jock froze. "How did you get past the Turks?"

"I'll send over the report I wrote. Mr. Jessop won't mind. I've a gift for Claire." Jim pulled a small carved cross from his pocket and laughed. "They tell me it's made from the original."

"You've been carrying this around waiting to see me?"

He pulled out another half-dozen. "I bought a bagful. Many of the men I visit want a reminder of their faith. Biddy put a hole in hers to make a necklace."

"Do I need to ask your intentions?" Jock retrieved his pipe.

Jim ignored him. "What do you hear from Nigel?"

"He's transferred to an ANZAC unit and due in-country any time," Claire said.

"I hope he comes to OC's compound at Zeitoun."

"So do I," Claire said. "We need to encourage him. He rarely mentions war in his letters."

"Censorship issues, probably."

Claire's lips parted. "I never considered it. Peter is careful too. How dangerous is your job, Jim? I pray for you daily."

"Please continue." He flushed and then recited, "I do not cease making mention of you in my prayers, asking God to give you a spirit of wisdom so you might have eyes to recognize the glories God has bestowed upon you."

She recognized a Bible passage. "Thank you."

"Intentions?" Jock snickered.

"Only good ones."

They dropped Jim at YMCA headquarters. He shook Jock's hand. "Look up a British cartographer over at the Arab Bureau, name of Lawrence. He's got interesting ideas about Arabia and the desert nomads. Don't tell him I tipped you." He waved as the calash merged into the chaotic traffic.

"Jim's become a cagey character. I'm impressed."

Claire polished her glasses. "He's trying to be helpful, as always."

"They won't let reporters in but they give YMCA padres free run."

"Perhaps generals realize soldiers need spiritual comfort more than they need reporters?"

"Hogwash," Jock said, but he didn't sound convinced.

Claire pushed open the shutters for air and climbed under her bed's mosquito netting. She closed her eyes—anything to ease the headachy dizziness—and dozed off.

To nightmares. The Sphinx peered down his missing nose and a searing wind threw sand in her face. A piercing wail slipped through her ears like ribbon following a needle and she gasped. Claire tugged at her dress, her throat burned, and heat radiated from her pores. Her eyes were stuck shut, or else she'd gone blind. Pain sliced through her brain and a million spiders crawled over her skin. "Water?"

"Take only a sip, darling."

The silky liquid sizzled against her lips. Claire struggled to sit up. She wanted to dunk her head into the tiny glass.

"Sips, darling, just tiny drops." Anne's voice came from a distance as her cool hand touched Claire's forehead. "She's burning, Jock."

Her father's answer echoed, moving farther and farther away, abandoning her to the fire. Claire pried open her eyelids to see Anne's face framed by fuzziness, light crackling between black and white. The dazzle seared her eyes and she slumped onto her tender pillow again.

A buzzing spittle: "Peter! The plane!"

More heat, a blazing bonfire and soothing tears. "Sit straight and don't eat so many sweets," Sylvia's directions taunted but Claire couldn't move.

Nigel begged, "I need you."

Jim whispered. "Riches, glory, opened eyes."

"She must take this down!" Papa shouted.

"Claire?" Anne's wail spun around and around the boiling pot.

"It is well with my soul," sang Biddy and then OC made everything clear: "O death, where is thy sting? Thanks be to God, which giveth us the victory through our Lord Jesus Christ."

Still the Sphinx leered, the sands scraped, her body shuddered, the muezzin screamed, the darkness dropped and then fell still: a long black line of silence into eternity.

"You must have picked up an illness at the hospital," Anne explained when Claire finally woke. "One of those random Egyptian fevers, but we were terrified."

Her head felt heavy, her brain clotted, but she sat up.

"It hit you so fast," Anne continued. "Your temperature soared and you slept fitfully, moaning and crying. You kept muttering about the sphinx and airplanes and fire. The doctor couldn't do anything, so I finally sent for Biddy and Oswald. They came immediately and were so kind to pray for you. I'm beyond grateful."

Claire grasped the chair handles lest she float away, but she no longer burned with fever and her headache had faded to a dull whisper. The typewriter sat on the drawing room desk and she tried to remember what she'd been typing when her poor head started spinning five nights before. "Did Papa get the wire out?"

Anne dropped into the chintz chair. "You're obviously Jock's daughter. Jim sent it for him. Jock can hardly wait until you're healthy, though I suspect you'll be distracted."

"Why?"

The animation in her face faded. "Nigel has called daily."

"Oh." Claire shivered. "I thought I dreamed Nigel."

"No. He's reported into his unit outside Cairo, but will call tomorrow. Are you looking forward to seeing him?"

Claire closed her eyes, as enigmatic as the Sphinx.

Chapter Twenty-Four

Claire propped a pillow beneath her head as she opened a week's worth of mail. She started with the fattest and most anticipated envelope, mailed from France. A sheet of paper, printed on both sides with advertisements, fell out. "*The Wiper Times of Salient News.*"

She read one and burst out laughing.

"What's that you've got?" Anne asked.

"Peter enclosed a newsletter, the *Wiper Times.* Listen to this ad: 'Building land for sale. Build that house on Hill 60. Bright—breezy—and invigorating. Command an excellent view of historic town of Ypres. For particulars of sale apply: Bosch and Co. Menin."

"Why is that funny?"

Claire paused. Didn't her mother remember *Wiper* was soldier slang for Ypres, the site of heavy destruction?

She scanned the letter. "He says some soldiers found a printing press and have made up these silly newspapers for the soldiers. It's a joke. This refers to no-man's land, suggesting the price is right if someone wants to buy a spot."

Anne looked over her shoulder. "I hardly think that's funny."

"Soldier humor." Claire shrugged. "It gives them something to do when they're not under fire."

"Is Peter under fire?"

Of course he was, constantly. He'd crashed several times evading bullets and nursed a bruised shoulder, at least that's what she read between the lines when he reminded her of sailing mishaps long ago.

Claire examined the envelope. "Written on YMCA hut stationery. He's safe if he's behind the lines with them."

She looked up when the silence lengthened.

Anne had crossed her arms. "Sure you don't want to tell me anything more?"

Jock burst into the suite, his face alight. "Ready to work?"

"She's scarcely out of bed, not even dressed," Anne scolded.

Claire quickly stuffed the letter back into its envelope and yawned. "What's up?"

He prowled the room like an impatient tiger. "I've met Hodges's cartographer. He's spent years in the desert and has fixed opinions on the British. He's not only a British officer but an Oxford classics graduate who carries *The Odyssey* with him in the original Greek." Jock reached for his pipe. "The trick will be figuring out how much I can write without getting him into trouble."

Anne straightened the pillows on the sofa. "He sounds like your kind of character. Did you conduct the interview in Arabic?"

Jock grinned. "He'll be here soon and you'll see. He refused to come to the office."

Claire grabbed her mail and hurried to get dressed for the first time in a week.

A slight man shorter than Claire and Anne, Lieutenant T. E. Lawrence shook their hands and gazed at them with pale aquamarine eyes. His fair hair and high tenor gave him an immature air, but his descriptions of the desert and those who lived there, as well as thoughts on the political situation beyond the Suez, mesmerized.

"I spent time with the Bedouin who lives in the desert air and winds, under the sun amid open and empty spaces," Lawrence said. "He focuses on the heavens above, the earth beneath his feet and hence grows close to his God. The desert is part of him."

Claire glanced at her father. Jock's face gave away nothing at the mention of God. "What's your take on Kut?"

Lawrence crossed his legs and arms. "What is the term you use—off the record? I cannot provide military intelligence to a journalist."

"Make note of it," Jock said to Claire. "Go ahead. What's happening?"

Lawrence waited.

"Off the record. Put down your pencil, Claire."

"I marched with an Indian force to Basra. It was difficult and we had to be brutal to get there. We defeated the Turkish army in several battles and felt superior to their weak forces. When we finally met bold Turkish troops they defeated us. Kut's long misery came about because of that desert battlefield.

"What should have been done?"

He shrugged. "Townsend might have pulled it off if the British had more aeroplanes, but the War Office resisted. Beyond that, who knows?"

"What will happen next?" Jock asked.

"Our army won't be able to take Kut from the Ottomans."

A knock sounded; Anne answered the door. Nigel entered carrying a bouquet of flowers.

At the sight of a uniformed officer, Lawrence moved to the window with his back to the room. Claire's head swiveled between her father's disapproval and Nigel's happiness: trapped.

"You look much better." He handed the bouquet to Claire.

"Perhaps you and Nigel would like a moment alone," Anne said. "She's not been out of the suite yet, Nigel, but she could manage tea downstairs in the salon. I'll get her shoes."

Nigel noticed the other officer shunning him. Claire handed her mother the bouquet, slipped on her shoes, and led Nigel to the door. Once it closed behind them, he took her in his arms for a long, languid kiss. "I've been dreaming of this moment for months."

She tried, she really did, to enjoy the rush of pleasure, but the tobacco scent and her news sense distracted. Half her brain remained in the drawing room, anxious to hear the mysterious Lieutenant Lawrence of Arabia's insights.

"I can't believe your mother gave us the opportunity to be alone," Nigel said. "I've missed you so much."

Claire smiled at his happiness and then gasped. "This is madness. I shouldn't be kissing you; I've been ill. Let's go downstairs."

"Not yet. I've waited too long for this madness."

She gave herself over to the next kiss, savoring his broad shoulders and strong arms. A thrumming began deep in her heart and she felt light-headed. "Enough," she breathed.

Nigel put his arm around her waist and led her to the lift. "Who was he? A rival?"

"A soldier needing privacy. We were interviewing him off the record."

"He made that clear. What a shabby uniform he wears."

"It doesn't matter."

"Everything about you matters to me." His eyes beamed with happiness and his blond hair gleamed. Compared to most soldiers in Egypt, he looked healthy and strong. His forehead wrinkled. "Is your heart still fixed on me?"

Claire couldn't tell him she wanted to postpone this meeting so she could hear the rest of the Lawrence interview. "I'm happy you're safely here." She hugged him and the lift opened.

Nigel's resplendent uniform, all parts polished and ironed, spurred whispers of admiration when they entered the main salon. Already exhausted, Claire negotiated their way to a small round table under a potted palm. She ordered tea and Nigel requested a gin and tonic. He explained why at her raised eyebrows. "I've been advised this drink will ward off malaria. Anything will be better than the plonk the troops drink."

She smiled at the slang. "We should tell Jim. He's had malaria twice."

"Jim Hodges? Why do you see him?" Nigel tapped his fingers.

Claire rallied. "Let's start over. Tell me about your trip. When did you arrive?"

"A week ago. My commanding officer sent me through France to observe on my way. Many ANZAC units are destined for France." He ran his finger behind his collar. "I worried they'd leave me there, but I brandished my orders and after a couple days escaped. It must have been a beautiful countryside once, but it's hell now."

"How?"

"Entire forests are splintered to nothing. The Alleymans send blind pigs continually."

She knew Alleymans were Germans, but blind pigs?

"Mortar bombs. They've caused enormous shell holes that fill with fetid water after the rains. You never know when the cry will sound signaling a gas attack, much less bombardment. I've never seen anything like it. If that's how civilized man behaves, I want to be a Maori in the bush. The countryside at home at least is green."

"Were you afraid?" The drinks arrived and Claire poured a cup of tea.

"Any sane man would be jittery. They're thrashing soldiers on the western front." He took a long pull on his gin and tonic. "I hope army life improves in this theater. I'm stationed at Heliopolis for the time being."

"You're near Oswald Chambers at the YMCA station at Zeitoun. My mother and I help on Mondays."

He closed his eyes. "I should have known. Chambers is here? Do you still pray with him?"

"When the opportunity arises. The YMCA uses chaplains to aid the soldiers, both practically and spiritually." Claire's tone sounded prim to her own ears.

Nigel sighed. "What does your mother do?"

"She teaches French to the soldiers and plays with the Chambers's little girl Kathleen."

"What does your father think?"

She shrugged. Jock still didn't know. "Tell me about the rest of your trip."

He described the train ride to Marseilles where he boarded a military hospital ship headed to Alexandria. The witty Nigel she loved shone as he described the journey, but his remarks revealed a bitter disquiet. "We managed to outrun several U-boats, no thanks to the navy." He'd spent a week in Alexandria and arrived in Cairo the day after Claire fell ill.

"I like being with my countrymen. I never fit in with the high command in London; they suspected men of cowardice if we weren't begging to go to France."

Claire itched for her notepad. She'd not heard such honesty while in England and knew her father would be interested.

Stop. Nigel sat across the table from her. She couldn't treat her beau as a news source. But he had recent information, so she asked her question anyway. "How is your experience different with ANZAC soldiers?"

His cheek creased. "They speak my language; they know our beautiful land. It makes a difference." Nigel picked up her hand. "I like seeing my ring on your finger."

She had dug out the pretty gold ring from her trunk after her sickness. The blue stone sparkled on her right hand, but Claire felt like an imposter when she wore it. "It's a beautiful ring. Thank you."

"We don't have much time, Claire. I don't know how long the ANZAC battalions will remain in Egypt. We won't be going to Gallipoli, but it's likely we'll end up in France."

She closed her eyes, shaken on several levels. "But you just arrived."

"I'm a cog, not a person. My mates need me to be as informed as possible if we're to stand a chance of surviving. I must master my unit and the command's expectations." He grimaced. "No one can imagine the horror of France."

They spoke of England and his visit to Claire's family. Peter had been promoted; Sylvia was redecorating her wealthy husband's flat. Nigel had traveled to Oxford to attend services for several friends at Christ Church Cathedral. "I'll never go to Oxford again. Death haunts the grounds and ghosts walk the hallways. Did you miss me?"

"Naturally, Claire said. "When we sailed across the Mediterranean, I tried to imagine the clear blue waters you described off Christchurch. I thought of you and prayed for your safety."

Anne entered the salon. Several women detained her as she walked in their direction and she chatted briefly.

"Mama has quite a time with the *memsahibs*." Claire sipped her tea. "They want to enlist her in their schemes."

"She, no doubt, manages them fine."

"I do," Anne said, "though I tire of their frivolities. You're pale, darling. You must go back to bed. When will we see you again, Nigel?"

He regarded her warily. She'd seen his drink.

Claire tried to help. "Nigel heard gin and tonics ward off malaria. We should tell Jim."

"You'd need to drink too many to make a difference." She lowered her voice. "That's why half these women are useless by the end of the afternoon, the men too. Of course, they're easy to beat at bridge when they're drunk. The Muslims have the right idea. No alcohol."

"But they're immune to malaria," Nigel said. "To have a fighting chance, we need to do something."

"Indeed. Daily quinine tablets are more effective, that's what we take. I'll put this on our tab. Claire needs to rest. Jock wants her to take dictation later."

Nigel stood and kissed Claire's hand. She followed her mother to the lift and looked back. He raised a fresh glass. Claire sighed. Her energy, physical and emotional, vanished.

Chapter Twenty-Five

May 1916

It took Claire two weeks to recover from her fever; she spent most of the time catching up with Jock's backlog of ideas and scratched notes. Triumphant when he gave her permission to write the rough drafts to save him time, Claire struggled to capture concise yet colorful descriptions for the BNS.

"An article is only as strong as the weakest source of information," Jock said on reviewing her draft. "This is helpful, but I want a list of information I lack. Include historic details."

Several times she added allusions to Moses, which he retained, saying "Perhaps you know my readers better than I do." More than once she searched for an unwitting source at the bridge table. Claire opened her eyes wide like Sylvia, adopted a bovine expression, and casually asked the new subalterns their opinion on army maneuvers.

Jock told her not to bother. "The junior officers don't know anything."

"But they're so earnest and confident about the importance of their jobs," Claire said.

"You'll strike gold eventually. Maybe you should flirt with higher-ranking officers."

Claire winced. While guilt stabbed when she pumped innocents for information, she resented how the majors and their superiors patronized her. She wanted to be taken seriously, and it especially galled her when she realized she knew more than they did.

Anne studied her latest manicure. "A pretty young face could elicit important information from vain old men."

"I hope you're not referring to me," Jock growled.

Anne laughed. "It bears considering, Claire. Employ your sex to your advantage."

To do so felt demeaning and dishonest. She didn't want to.

Once Claire regained her strength, she and Anne returned to Zeitoun.

They sought to arrive by three o'clock to share tea with the Chambers family. Afterwards they tarried in the main hut where they took pens in hand and wrote what the men couldn't express to their loved ones. The British army's capitulation to the Turks discouraged and frightened many. Claire frequently used the excuse of polishing her glasses to blink away tears.

"You're performing compassionate acts," Biddy said. "Compassion is putting empathy into action and these young men need your encouragement."

Maybe so, but Claire still felt bereft. She often stayed up late reading psalms until her tears dried and her heart's patter relaxed. High above the streets of Cairo, her room provided a haven of solace.

The intense war news terrified. The French army's redoubt of Verdun turned into a bloodbath of outrageous proportions. As news of the battles filtered through, more soldiers joined Anne's Monday French classes at Zeitoun and Wednesday nights at Ezbekieh Gardens. "But what vocabulary should I use?" Anne asked. "Military terms?"

"Whatever they need," OC advised.

Sylvia's husband, Holly, shifted to the continent to an unspecified location. Peter's once descriptive letters became terse messages on postcards, usually referencing raw French wine and poor quality bread. No more *Wiper Times* or jokes. He grew ever more remote and Claire's heart ached for the closest relationship to a brother she had. When he scribbled "nearly Edward," she stepped up her prayers even more.

Soldiers discovering Claire's newspaper connection pumped her for the latest bulletins from the western front. Some afternoons she ignored the wire before catching the trolley. Knowing the latest casualties sabotaged her ability to remain cheerful.

Jock warned her not to pity the soldiers—they didn't want it—but Claire struggled to hide her worries. She met many teenage soldiers and she agonized over their futures, both physically and spiritually. "Come hear Reverend Chambers's lecture," she urged them.

An Auckland wrangler jerked in surprise. "Why?"

"You need to know what you believe before you face the Bosch."

"They say you're a reporter, miss. Have you information?"

"Everyone needs to be prepared. I could be in a trolley accident, for example."

He nodded. "One of me mates copped it last week; seems like a thin line divides life and death."

She agreed, touched by the beauty of his words, haunted by the gut-wrenching fear of sudden death. She needed her fan in the oppressive, sweat-smelling heat, another distraction.

When Nigel entered the hut one night early in May, Claire excused herself in relief.

"Let's walk." He took her hand to walk into the desert.

The first stars prickled the night sky and a tendril of soft breeze brought a sweet scent. Claire shivered. "We heard this morning enormous sandstorms are moving this way. They're called *khamsin* and push the sand so high it blots out the stars."

"They can't be worse than the trenches."

Claire switched topics. "It's too bad you arrived in time for the awful heat, rather than the more pleasant spring weather."

He shrugged. "Heat, lice, drills, death. It's all miserable."

"Bad day?"

"I lost two men to heat stroke. You'll get soldiers at the lecture tonight."

"Why don't you come? God's word is like water to a parched soul. I'm reassured after OC reminds me of what it means to live in this eternal tension."

"What do you want for us, Claire? To spend our lives attending Oswald Chambers's Bible meetings?" He saluted a soldier walking past.

"It's a start. When you come to Cairo we can tour the Egyptian Museum and the pyramids. The war has taught me life is fleeting. Let's enjoy the times we have and pray God gives us a future."

"Together?"

She slid her hands into the pockets of her practical black skirt. "I'm struggling to find my place today. I can't envision a future until the war ends."

"I can't wait so long." His voice sounded rough and she couldn't read his face in the shadows. "If life is fleeting, we must seize it while we can. *Carpe diem.* We're both here, now, why can't we be married? I'll speak to your father. You love me don't you?"

"Of course," Claire said automatically, knowing she wasn't truly in love with him. She didn't know how to express her reservations without hurting his feelings.

The thought she might be lying needled her conscience. What did love for a man mean to her? His touch thrilled, his presence excited her, but their recent conversations made her wary. Why didn't he ask what was important to her?

"The brass hats bottle me up in meetings and training; some nights I fall into my cot without eating. I barely got away tonight. I thought I'd escape the paper tyranny coming to Egypt. Instead they pump me for information."

"What do you know they don't?"

"I'm not allowed to talk to reporters."

Claire laughed. "You're the second person to sidestep me tonight."

"You'll hear soon enough. Let's walk farther into the starlight."

"It's nearly time for OC's class. Let's join them in the devotional hut."

He kicked at the sand. "I know this means a lot to you, but I can't get behind it."

She heard his exasperation, but for her own peace of mind, Claire needed to hear the lecture. "Then I'll say good night."

"I've traveled a long way and rather than walk with me, you'll go to a Bible class?"

"I need to hear what OC says. How else can I endure the news?" Her heart throbbed.

"Are you sure Chambers isn't why you came to Egypt?"

Claire crossed her arms. "You know I want to be a reporter. That's my goal. I didn't know I'd have a chance to hear OC's lectures in Egypt, but since I can, I want to. This isn't about my feelings for you. It's about my soul and my dreams."

"Seems to me you're mixed up between journalism and God. If you want to be a reporter so bad, why don't you get a byline with any periodical? You're stuck on the BNS, but I wonder if you're just afraid to try. "

"You need to prove your skill to get the opportunity." Claire spun on her heel and stalked away, his words stabbing her pride. She bit her lip, though, knowing he was right. Fear of rejection kept her from pursuing other writing assignments. She should check other opportunities.

Claire headed to the devotional hut.

Most nights when Anne finished teaching the French class, she spent time with Kathleen in the bungalow. After putting the little girl to bed, she'd rejoin the letter writers or attend OC's lecture. "I may not agree with him," she'd told Claire, "but I find his ideas more stimulating than the *memsahibs*'."

That night Claire found her in the devotional hut with Biddy. OC sat in a corner examining his Bible—full of intricate and clearly written notes and diagrams.

"What happened to Nigel?" Anne asked.

"He didn't want to come."

It was clear Biddy saw too much, so Claire took out a Dixon pencil and her silver pen knife. As she sharpened the yellow wood, silence stretched in the mat hut. "Is his absence a problem for you?" Biddy asked.

"Will I always be torn like this, between what a man expects of me and what I want?"

Anne burst out laughing. "Yes."

Biddy smiled. "What does God impress upon your soul?"

"I want Nigel to know the peace I get from studying the Bible and praying," Claire said. "War and thoughts of

France unnerve him, but he won't admit it. I know only one solace and he's not interested."

"We're all afraid of death," Anne said, "but we have a choice: to confront fear and deal with it, or to wallow in terror."

"Which do you do?" Claire asked.

Anne's voice trembled. "I try not to wallow in the terror, but I'm afraid of dying, too, especially in Egypt."

Claire dropped her pencil. "I apologize, Mama. I shouldn't have brought it up."

Biddy rubbed Anne's shoulder.

"The Egyptians made death a public spectacle," Anne said. "This land is covered with shrines to pharaohs who died millennia ago. No one can live here and avoid the macabre."

OC stirred. "Death is a great dread. It is easy to say God is love until death has snatched away your dearest friend, then I defy you to say God is love unless God's grace has done a work in your soul."

Boots crunched in the sand heading their way and pots clanged in the outdoor kitchen. Wind shuddered the mat hut as if it breathed.

"Exactly, Oswald," Anne said. "Who can trust in a God of love when he allows children to die?"

Biddy reached for her, but Anne stood. "Not only my children, but those boys here right now, destined to be killed. It's a travesty. Where was God then? Where will he be tomorrow?"

"Weeping with those who weep," Biddy said.

"All our dead leave an aching void behind, Mrs. M." OC spoke gently. "We grieve with you and we will grieve for those who go before us. It's the nature of life. But for those who are in Christ Jesus, physical death stings but has no eternal meaning. We will live beyond this place and moment in time."

"But what if we don't want to live without those who die? What sort of a God rips a child from a mother's breast?" Anne's voice rose and her eyes flashed.

"I bid you to consider Hebrews 5:7. Jesus Christ offered up prayers and supplications with strong crying and tears unto him that was able to save from death. We who remain behind must put our hope in him for our future."

Two soldiers entered the hut.

"I will not hope for a future I cannot see. I will tend those still alive tonight." Anne left.

Claire rose, stricken. "Should I go to her?"

OC shook his head. "Mrs. M needs to meditate on this idea. Talking with the young men will help."

More soldiers filed in. OC greeted them and placed his Bible on a small table. Biddy moved to the rear of the hut to take dictation and Claire mechanically collected her pencil and pad. Drained and weak, she scarcely heard OC's prayer.

Her mother didn't speak to her the rest of the evening.

Chapter Twenty-Six

Summer 1916

Early in June, Nigel arrived at the suite wearing an immaculate uniform. "I've come to do your bidding on this one matter and then we'll tour the Egyptian Museum."

Claire returned to the typewriter. "I need to fix a mistake before I'm done." She made the correction, grabbed a hat, shoved the fly whisk in her bag, and took the copy with her. She cabled the story from the hotel's telegraph office and they exited into a stunning heat.

"Calash!" Nigel shouted.

The doorman, clad in red pantaloons with a white vest and turban, raised empty hands. "Sorry, *sahib*."

"What a miserable day," Nigel muttered. "How about a drink before we start?"

Claire stirred the air with her fan. "Let's walk down the street. A cab will come by the time we get to the French club or we can catch a trolley at the Opera House."

"Are you mad? This is a sunstroke day even if it's only ten o'clock in the morning."

"You don't mean to imply only mad dogs and Englishmen will be out?" Claire teased.

"We're not English," he said in his thickest accent, "but I know one of us is a headstrong American."

"The best kind."

The listless hordes on the sidewalk raised their hands as Claire and Nigel passed. Nigel shoved several aside with his strong boot; Claire murmured, "*La'a shukran.*"

The ragged skeletons receded, their tone less demanding.

"Impressive. What did you say?"

"No, thanks. Jim taught me."

"Do you see much of him?"

"Occasionally at Ezbekieh. He's busy."

Nigel grunted. "I wonder if his do-goodism amounts to anything."

Claire swatted the whisk at an errant fly to defuse her pique. "I think so."

Nigel hailed a calash at the corner and they climbed aboard.

The breeze stirred by the trotting horse helped as perspiration dripped down her spine. As they traveled down Kasr el Nile Street, she glimpsed pinched alleys deep in shadow where children played and men pondered chessboards. On the savagely bright main street, European-styled shops nestled beneath sheltering canopies; few people ventured out.

Claire reached for her handkerchief. Thick hookah smoke and personal detritus left a gagging stink. Nigel sat like a statue, the only way to endure the brutal heat while wearing a uniform.

Ten minutes later they arrived at the walled Old Cairo Cemetery. Nigel jumped from the calash and assisted Claire as she alit. She paused to collect her thoughts and emotions before asking a question at the gatehouse.

They walked along rows of granite headstones in a long line of grass to a tidy corner. Palm trees rimmed the interior and colorful birds called from the bougainvillea. A line of simple wooden crosses marked recent military burials. In the quiet empty cemetery only a dozen Europeans gathered around an open grave.

Claire found the simple marker: *John and Phillip Meacham, July 25, 1893.*

Tears stabbed and a mournful heaviness swept over her. Here lay the brothers she never knew. All the good and the bad in her life originated in the modest double grave. So much had been lost because of those early deaths; so much hidden. Claire sank to her knees and sobbed, gut wrenching cries from an agony she didn't know she carried.

Arms curved around her and Nigel dropped his head to hers.

"I never imagined I'd be affected like this," she whispered.

"No man is an island," Nigel quoted. "Any man's death diminishes me, because I am involved in mankind." He kissed her forehead and released her.

Claire fished a handkerchief from her bag. She squinted. "Flowers?"

"Someone tends the grave. Your brothers are not forgotten. Let's sit on that bench in the shade." Nigel ran a finger around his collar. "Egypt reeks of death, just like France."

The whole world worships death these days, Claire thought. She shifted to the nearby bench; her bones like water, her eyes and nose running.

They sat in the stillness of the quiet spot, motionless in the beating heat, time feeling meaningless and eternal. Claire had no energy to move. So small the bump of earth to have affected so much. One faded photo and this spot were all that was left, save for the yawning pain.

"Are you satisfied now?" Nigel asked.

Claire raised her head and scanned the cemetery. The boys had lain in that solemn spot for twenty-three years, alone, yet not neglected and certainly not forgotten by her parents nor her. Their shadows, once so slender in life, loomed large in death and influenced events throughout Claire's existence. Her heart ached at the thought.

But, Claire's brain protested, the needs of the living must always override those of the dead. While she couldn't forget them, she didn't have to let their deaths control her life.

On that day, she owed Nigel the attention he craved. "Thank you for understanding. I'm ready to go now."

They traveled in silence to the Egyptian Museum of Antiquities near the Nile. Nigel handed her out of the calash and straightened his tunic. "This, finally, feels right."

They strolled up shallow steps between two massive pillars into the rotunda. Nigel paid the piaster each for their summer entrance fee, slipped his hat under his arm, and paused to examine four colossal statues.

"I'll be back," she called, hurrying down the hallway to knock on the director's door. When he opened, she sprang into French, "*Please, sir, may I ask you three questions for an American newspaper?*"

The same sneer she'd met before. "*Non.*"

"*S'il vous plais?*"

"*Non.*"

"*Another day then, au revoir.*" Claire didn't take it personally; after three months of effort, her request for an interview had become a game with the snooty French curator.

"One of these must be Ramses," Nigel said when she rejoined him.

She'd not seen him so happy since he joined the army. Claire pulled out her *Baedeker's* and read aloud: "Amenhotep, the son of Hapu, a sage of the time of Amenophis III."

"Smashing!" He grabbed her hand. "Let's see it all."

While she preferred to linger over fly-stained notecard descriptions and contemplate unusual statuary, Nigel moved swiftly between exhibits. "Think how old these are. They've been here forever. Time stands still before such gods."

Time. Arid Egypt, timeless with brown sands and ancient structures, spoke of savage slavery and anonymous souls to Claire. In and around the monuments to the dead, living people moved, bled, and begged. Claire could appreciate the craftsmanship, but her mind wandered to the individuals. Reading the Bible had taught her God's eyes were on the very sparrows and he knew the hairs on each person's head—today, tomorrow and yesterday.

The Egyptian pharaohs cared nothing for their people and saw them as tools.

She shook the grim thought from her mind. Nigel deserved her cheerful attention. "The man in this wall art is carrying a fly whisk."

"Obviously insects have always been with us. I wonder what those hieroglyphs say. They resemble shorthand to me, can't you read them?"

She relished his cheeky joy. "Alas, not in Egyptian."

They gazed at colorful frescos: a bejeweled woman holding an *ankh* sauntering beside a staff-carrying nobleman with elongated head.

"Their features are so stylized, I wonder if Egyptians saw differently than we do," Claire mused.

"Maybe it's you," Nigel said. "You view the world through your own lens. You see life as if God orchestrates events from above. You don't notice the ugliness of mankind when it lies at your feet in front of Shepheard's Hotel."

She stared at him, incredulous. "Those beggars are made in the image of God. They may be poor and ill, but it doesn't give me an excuse to treat them like animals."

"The world is full of poor people. You must examine the big picture, change society from the top down. You can't help everyone."

She polished her glasses. "Jesus said the poor will inherit the kingdom of God."

"He also said the poor will always be with us, so we should get used to them. You insist upon bringing up God all the time. Your attitude is as stylized as what these painters portrayed on the walls." Nigel stomped off.

Claire replaced her glasses with a sigh as he entered the next gallery.

Nigel tapped on a dusty glass case at a faded red flower. "They found this poppy in a tomb buried three thousand years ago." His face twisted. "Poppies spring up on land near freshly buried corpses. I hate poppies."

"They were a gift for Demeter, to remind her of Persephone left in the underground. Poppies symbolize remembering the hopeful in the midst of the difficult."

Nigel snorted. "Are you allowed to believe in Greek myths?"

"Myths are part of our cultural heritage, no matter our spiritual beliefs." Even as she spoke Claire winced. She'd fallen into lecture mode.

"You studied history. You know religion is a way for uneducated people to make sense of the world."

She bristled. "Uneducated people like me and OC and Galileo and Sir Isaac Newton?"

"Other than you and Chambers, those men were products of their time. They didn't know any better."

Claire retrieved her whisk and brushed the dust off the exhibit case. "Do you like anything about my beliefs?"

"Loving your neighbor. Particularly the one standing next to you."

A guard shuffled up to them. "Monsieur, the museum, it closes now."

Nigel put on his hat and took Claire's arm. "We're done here. People are only bones disintegrating into the dust."

"No." Claire pushed away his hand. "The soul lives forever."

He walked away.

"What's wrong?" Claire asked when she caught up at the museum entrance.

Nigel sighed. "We're leaving to practice maneuvers near the Suez Canal."

"Ismailia?"

"How did you know?" He frowned. "Did your father sniff it out?"

"OC is running a YMCA hut at the Ismailia camp this summer."

Nigel sighed. "Of course he is. Will you visit?"

"Only if it's newsworthy."

"It will be."

The Middle Eastern theater grew complicated in June, when the grand Sharif of Mecca led a revolt against the Turks and established the Kingdom of Hejaz on the eastern side of the Red Sea, mostly along the route of a railroad from Damascus to Medina.

Jock examined the wall map. "Where's Jim these days?"

"Up in the desert with the troops."

"Keep track of that man of mystery."

"Jim?" Claire laughed. Other than his current location, he was as mysterious as a puppy.

"What do you know about him?" Jock asked. "Why was he in England?"

"He came to study with Oswald Chambers at the Bible Training College."

Jock rubbed his chin. "Why would a penniless young man from Ohio come to London? His story doesn't ring true."

Claire had tried to pry Jim's secret out of him without success. Like Jock, he lived in the present or the future; he never spoke of his past.

"You get a sense for truth when you're a reporter, and something about him isn't quite right." He grabbed his hat. "I'll grill him next time I see him. I'm off to badger the brass."

He dropped her off at Shepheard's Hotel.

Claire greeted the doormen and headed directly to the telegraph office to send off the day's wire to the British censor. The sweet-faced Egyptian who ran the office handed her several in return, including one from the BNS owner Josiah Fischer. Claire ordered tea in the salon and slit open the wire.

"Needed: Positive story, preferably religious, rush STOP."

Jock easily could write about the YMCA ministry at Ezbekieh Gardens. Claire could provide the information. She could talk to OC, even chat with her mother's friend Lucretia who ran the teas. She considered the telegram.

"Are you saving this seat?" Biddy touched Claire's shoulder.

"For you." An idea struck. She folded the telegram in two. "I'd like to interview you concerning Ezbekieh Garden activities."

Jock was too busy these days, but Claire recognized an opportunity. She would write and file the story herself.

Chapter Twenty-Seven

July 1916

They caught the early morning train north in July, changing at Benha station and traveling east. The syndicate wanted news about the Suez Canal and the morale of soldiers preparing for desert battle.

Most were camped near Ismailia, the midpoint of the canal. Jock had arranged for Anne and Claire to accompany him before the family vacationed on the Mediterranean coast.

"You'll like this story," Jock said. "Your friend Chambers is popular out here. It's amazing what the man accomplishes."

Claire knew. The Zeitoun compound had closed in May when OC trekked off with the troops to Ismailia. Biddy, Kathleen, and Mary Riley had joined him the previous week at the YMCA huts adjacent the camp.

"So you've decided YMCA stories are worth covering?" she asked. He'd not said a word about the Ezbekieh Gardens story she'd written and filed with the BNS—listing the author merely as Meacham.

Claire tried not to reflect on her actions, but she couldn't help wondering if she needed to confess this act as sin. Still, she'd been writing Jock's drafts for over a year now and he seldom made changes.

On the other hand, Claire's prayers now hit the wall and bounced back at her, unconnected to God. OC said sin was the reason when God seemed far away. But she'd just been doing her job, helping her father during a busy time. The only difference was he didn't know.

At least that's what she told herself.

"Fischer wants anything positive, though he'd like more hard news. I'm hoping to find both out here. Keep your eyes open."

Anne pressed a dampened handkerchief against her neck and waved her fan as the train crossed narrow canals and rattled past dusty villages. "Our holiday?"

"The job never ends with the news business, but I'll try. Maybe you'll like Ismailia; it's the headquarters of the Suez Canal."

Having read Ismailia's pathetic description in her *Baedeker's Guide to Egypt,* Claire doubted it. "What's your plan?"

"We'll look up Chambers and poke around. I've lined up interviews for Monday with the army brass and we'll head to Port Said on Tuesday. You'll need to scout for information around the hotel, Anne."

"No problem."

After a quick luncheon at the Ismailia Grand Hotel, they taxied out of town to the Ismailia camp, even more primitive than Zeitoun. They hurried in the relentless sun toward the brand-new hut made of native reed sporting big YMCA letters nailed to the side. A line of men marched across the desert from a collection of white triangular tents to the northeast. Claire laughed when she spied OC in his sun helmet directing the men toward the building, a determined Kathleen beside him with a ribbon in her hair imitating her father's movements.

Swarms of flies rose, forcing their whisks into action. "This is a nightmare," Anne said. "What is the stench?"

Horses, latrines, gun smoke, men; it mixed into a potent brew that sent both women scurrying for handkerchiefs. Jock tugged his hat lower and opened the lightweight hut door.

They found Biddy inside the airy hut organizing a book table. Her sunburnt face wreathed into a smile, and she hugged both women. "What a lovely surprise. We prayed God would send workers to help."

Anne recoiled. "What do you mean?"

"Oswald has begun free Sunday tea for the soldiers. It should be a lovely afternoon."

"Free?' " Jock asked. "I thought the YMCA charged for their canteen services."

OC and Kathleen entered the hut, which smelled of warm reeds in the hot air. "It's lovely to see you, Miss Steno and Mrs. M." He held out his hand to Jock.

Jock shook it and nodded at Claire. "Notebook." He addressed OC. "We're interested in what's been happening out here in the desert. You're serving tea?"

Claire scribbled their words.

"I wanted the men to be able to celebrate the Sabbath in a meaningful way," OC said. "A friend gave us five pounds to pay for a free afternoon tea and the men enjoyed it." He touched his wife's arm. "Biddy and Mary arrived in time to help. Four hundred men joined us last Sunday."

Anne stepped forward. "You made them serve tea and cakes in this heat? Don't you have servants?"

Biddy stiffened. "It's a joy to do the tasks God puts before me. Mary and I serve willingly. The YMCA baker in Port Said supplied the cakes and soldiers help us." She brushed a hand past her sweaty forehead and nodded toward three Tommies carrying in steaming urns. "We're hot, but the soldiers labor harder every day than we do."

"Did you come to see me?" A tiny voice piped from behind OC.

Anne crouched to hug Kathleen. "I certainly did. I haven't seen you getting your hair done at the hotel recently."

"We came to see Daddy," she said.

"Lovely."

"We're happy to be together, Anne," Biddy said. "Mary and I enjoyed our rest at the Swans' house in June. It's time for us to be useful again."

Anne glared at OC. "Do not wear her out, do you hear me?"

OC put up his hands in mock surrender. "Certainly, Mrs. M. I treasure Biddy far more than you do. I could not pour out to the men if Biddy did not pour God's love into me first."

Anne whisked her indignation at an assortment of flies.

Jock observed the conversation with a deepening line between his eyebrows. "How does your ministry function out here? Is it similar to what you've done in Cairo?"

"Yes. I lecture from the Bible in the evenings. The hut has pens and paper, opportunities to write home. No more French lessons." He nodded to Anne.

Jock frowned. "They don't need French?"

"They're too exhausted from the fierce sun to study the language by nightfall. Indeed, the YMCA warns the secretaries to rest in the afternoon. God keeps us for his own purposes and we are thankful."

"So how does this work?" Jock asked. "You teach them and run your hut?"

"Join us for tea and see for yourself. You're welcome to attend the evening lecture."

"What a fine idea," Anne said. "Claire, take that teapot from Mary. We can help serve."

"I need her to take notes," Jock protested.

"Give him your notebook," Anne told Claire. "He can take his own notes this afternoon. Here come the troops now."

Half an hour later, sweat dripped down her back and Claire knew her face must look as red as the tablecloth. She'd removed her hat and while Anne took up a position beside an urn of tea, Claire handed out plates of what the British liked to call buns. While she kept smiling, Claire drank to the bottom every glass of water she could get.

The work may have been physically grueling, but her spirits soared at the happiness expressed by the men.

"Coo-ee, Miss, you from London?" asked a tanned and dusty soldier in a crowd of five.

Claire grinned. "Worse. I'm an American."

"Blimey, I never met an American before!" He whistled. "What you doing here?"

"Making sure you know God loves you."

He laughed. "The OC tells us all the time."

Claire pointed to her father. "Tell that man about it." They joined Jock on a rough bench nearby where he was conducting interviews.

"He's a good man to come here and give us tea," one said.

His sunburned mate gobbled three cookies whole and nodded. "Last week one of our mates went west and we were pretty down when we came in. The secretary listened to us and asked if we wanted prayer. Who wanted prayer when we wanted our mate back? We said aye to be polite and it helped, him talking about the big guy in heaven. Too right, it did."

"I like the little tyke," said a burly man with a crease in his forehead. "She stands up on a chair and tells us what for and we all salute. She reminds me of my little one back home. I last saw my Sally 385 days ago." He downed his tea and looked away.

"How's the training going?" Jock asked.

"Tough," the first man said. "But I come here at night and listen to the OC and I think, it was worth it enlisting to hear him talk about God."

Jock dropped his pencil. "What?"

The Tommy swallowed a big bite of his bun and chewed, watching Jock through narrowed eyes. "I were a wrangler before, out in the bush. I looked at the stars and didn't know anything. I'm headed up the line. I can ride my horse all the way to Beersheba and then to Jerusalem if I have to, no matter what. Whether I live or die, I know my life be in God's hands. I ne'er knew that before."

Claire paused, plate in hand, to watch her staring father process the sunburned man's statement of faith. The wrangler stared right back until Jock nodded and shut the notebook. "Thank you. I'll be thinking of you."

The man from Australia got the last word. "You should be thinking of yourself, sir, if you don't already know."

"Another Yank comes!" called OC as they finished stowing the baskets filled with used tea cups and plates into the YMCA car.

Jim Hodges swiped the hat off his head. "I heard reporters were in the camp and hoped I'd find you."

"Where have you been this time?" Jock asked.

"Filling in as needed. The heat gets to people pretty quickly."

"Mesopotamia?"

"Just along the canal with the troops. Are you staying to hear Oswald preach?"

"Yes," said Claire, as Jock replied, "No."

"My subject matter is the Sermon on the Mount," OC said. "Perhaps you know the passage?"

"Blessed are the pure in heart, for they shall see God," Jock murmured.

"Exactly."

Jock glanced at his wristwatch. "Thank you, no. The heat depletes my wife and I asked the cab to pick us up at five o'clock. We need to return to the hotel." He nodded to Jim. "Claire may remain if you'll bring her to the hotel afterward."

"I'd be pleased to escort her."

"Thanks." Jock gave Anne a long look. "My wife and I have much to discuss." He led her to the waiting taxi. OC helped Kathleen and Mary into the YMCA car. They would return to the house in Ismailia to finish cleanup and to put Kathleen to bed. As the driver drove away, OC waved farewell and went into the hut to prepare for that evening's lesson.

Claire watched after her parents. "How many soldiers come to the Sunday evening meetings?"

"A couple dozen. Why did your parents leave?" Jim asked.

"My father just discovered how well my mother knows Biddy. We've hidden our trips to Zeitoun so he wouldn't forbid them. He thought we were at Ezbekieh Gardens twice a week."

"Didn't you learn your lesson in London?" Jim sighed.

Claire stiffened. "My mother finessed this one."

Jim knocked back several flies with his whisk. "Oh, Claire, how can your conscience let you get away with such behavior?"

She squirmed. "My mother didn't want to upset him. I honored her wishes."

He shook his head. "And when you pray?"

"I don't pray about it." She tried to swallow the guilt.

"Maybe you should."

He opened the hut door and escorted her to a backless wooden bench in the rear near Biddy.

Claire and Jim sat shoulder to shoulder in the crowded hut, sweat dripping, and fly whisks busy on mosquitoes as night fell. She couldn't help thinking of Nigel as OC explained what poor in spirit meant—to desire nothing but to follow Jesus into his kingdom. Her pencil slowed.

"What are you thinking?" Jim asked.

"Will Nigel ever understand any of this?"

He searched her face a long time before speaking. "Only the Holy Spirit can determine the true state of a man's heart."

Claire's chest tightened and she had difficulty swallowing. She swatted mosquitoes savagely.

Afterwards, soldiers flocked around OC, their sunburned faces alight with enthusiasm and questions. Biddy and Claire examined their notes together and then closed their notepads.

A faint breeze blew from the direction of Ismailia proper, bringing a hint of water off the canal. "Shall we walk while OC and Biddy finish?" Jim asked.

"How long?"

"Maybe half an hour. Let's admire the stars."

They ambled into the dark desert expanse.

Behind them, the camp spread wide, dotted with lantern lights in the white bell tents. But before them, the black sky touched the sand and stars glittered like brilliant diamonds. The cloak of night brought peace, but the Bible teaching sparked ideas Claire wanted to discuss.

"'Blessed are they that mourn, for they shall be comforted.' I appreciated OC telling us we shouldn't expect difficulties to be magically removed but should instead ask him to walk with us through them."

"Have you suffered more sorrows?" Jim's tenor voice brushed against the velvet night.

"My cousin's husband, Holly, died in June. I grieve more for Sylvia than for him, which makes me feel guilty. The whole world groans with death and mourning."

"It can be difficult to encourage people when they fear dying and it confronts them daily."

"Nigel won't discuss death. My parents never mention my brothers, yet their grave lies not far from where we live. How can anyone, particularly now, not try to come to terms with death?"

"Does it frighten you?"

"Not as much as it used to and not for me personally," Claire said softly. "The Bible says death no longer has a sting. I know I will go to heaven when I die."

Jim clasped his hands behind his back. "For those in Christ Jesus, death is no more than closing your eyes on this world and opening them in the next. But if you don't have assurance, death means nothingness."

"Nigel thinks death is an endless void. Because he cannot see heaven or touch God, he won't believe."

"Many feel the same."

"How do you answer them?" Claire clasped the solid flesh of his forearm.

Jim stopped, his face shadowed. "Like OC said tonight, you can't pretend grief or sorrow won't happen. But it's not for us to say God made a mistake in allowing a death to happen." He sighed. "I remind myself of that every single day."

A thin breeze blew sand across their boots and she heard a dog barking. The lights of Ismailia, a few sparks on the near horizon, marked life.

He spoke slowly, almost to himself. "We know not the time of our birth nor of our passing. God determines the day. We submit ourselves to him, knowing his choices are perfect whether we understand or not."

"But you told me once God knows the good plans he has for us."

"It's still true." He hesitated. "Has anything been settled between you and Nigel?"

"Not officially."

"Is it your intention to marry a man who doesn't share your beliefs?" Jim paused. "He's certainly a clever and polished officer."

Claire viewed the sky. "What is marriage supposed to be? My parents are a loving and well-suited team. OC and Biddy are affectionate and serve in harmony." She confessed the truth. "Nigel's lonely and afraid. How can I reject him?"

Jim didn't speak as they crunched across the rocky sand. Claire watched the sky and touched his arm to point.

"A shooting star," he said. "What will you wish?"

"For the end of the war, so men won't fear death any more. How about you?"

"I pray you'll figure out what you truly want and who you really are."

Chapter Twenty-Eight

Fall 1916

The Meachams spent the summer traveling almost a month along the Mediterranean near Alexandria and then a cruise down the Nile to Luxor for August. Jock interviewed military and civilian officials on an array of subjects and filed stories from obscure telegraph offices five days a week for the Boston syndicate.

Claire typed and edited his stories on her portable typewriter.

They toured hospitals in Alexandria where the last of the Gallipoli patients were being released for repatriation or convalescent hospitals in Cairo. Anne ferreted out ships' movements and orders to France, earning praise when she discovered a general's wife anticipated leaving Egypt soon.

Jock wormed stories out of soldiers and itched to investigate the Sinai Desert. He also tried to discover who might take the general's place.

Claire interviewed young men about their thoughts on leaving sunny Egypt for the muddy trenches of France. "'Twill be hard, but we need to get on with it, miss, so we can go home," one New Zealander explained through lips cracked and crusty from the dry wind.

Shepheard's Hotel forwarded mail. Aunt Sarah joyfully wrote of Sylvia's pregnancy, even as she acknowledged the loss of the child's father. Peter scribbled three letters detailing a close encounter with the infamous Red Baron and described the horror of dropping a bomb inside the cockpit of his own plane. He managed to toss it over the side before the ticking stopped.

Claire passed her hand over her eyes after that letter and doubled her prayers.

> *It's not going to matter much,* he wrote. *Only three of us from the original unit are still alive. Make sure you buy Uncle Jock that sailboat I owe him. Still carrying my arrowhead?*

In her satchel, all the time.

In Luxor, Anne spent her afternoons on the Luxor Hotel veranda and caught whispers of illegal antiquities trading after tea with Mrs. Emerson. Claire and her father rode horses through the Valley of the Kings, and they sat on the toes of enormous statues of pharaohs. They wrote about a hostel where missionaries relaxed on furlough and joined organized tours with soldiers on R & R.

The syndicate liked their copy. "Keep up the good work. YMCA stories and positive influences on the soldiers are popular here."

Mostly, though, Jock watched his wife with concern.

In early September Anne tossed down her book and held out her hand. "I'm better. Let's go back to Shepheard's."

Jock booked passage to Cairo the next day.

"You seemed fine," he explained to Claire at the BNS office upon their return, "but your mother needed to get out of Cairo. It wasn't healthy for her."

"Physically or mentally?"

"Look at me, Claire."

Abashed, Claire raised her eyes to his face.

"You may be twenty-two years old, but you don't have the right to question her grief. Losing the boys broke her. We need to be kind. Can you sit with this grief and not judge her?"

Claire's jaw dropped. "I'm not judging her. I'm trying to understand her struggles. My brothers died a long time ago; why can't she let them go?"

His eyes blazed. "I hope to God, your God, you never lose a child. You've no idea what she's been through."

"I apologize. But how is her grief any different than anyone else's? Sylvia's lost two husbands."

"It's not. It can't be, but it's hers. She couldn't handle the anniversary of their deaths in Cairo's heat. We're past the date and the weather will be better for six months. She'll be fine."

Claire wanted to ask Jock about his grief. He bent down, however, and retrieved his pipe.

Weep with those who weep, she thought, wondering how she could fulfill Jesus's command when her father stowed his emotions away. Only Jesus could fill the two boy-sized holes in her father's and mother's heart. Claire didn't know how to help them see the truth.

"The Chambers girl helps," Jock mused, his head wreathed in sweet tobacco smoke. "That was one of the low moments of my marriage."

Stunned, Claire dared not move.

Jock groaned. "Why did my Annie suppose she couldn't tell me you volunteered at Zeitoun? Did she fear I'd ban her from seeing the little girl? Will they return when the army starts up their school of instruction at Zeitoun?"

"Yes, with reinforcements," she finally stuttered. "I've heard from Eva; she and Gertrude Ballinger and Gladys

Ingram will arrive soon. Many BTC regulars have come to Egypt to assist the ministry."

Jock's brows rose. "Single women? How do they get into the country to work with the YMCA? What pull has Chambers got?"

Claire opened her silver pen knife to sharpen her pencil. "I don't know. What will we do about mother?"

"You're welcome to visit Zeitoun. But your mother must go with you." He opened his pile of mail from Boston, which included several months' worth of his story clippings.

Claire's heart raced, but after Jock scanned a dozen, he tossed them to her. "Your mother likes to read these. Once I've written something, I'm done with it."

Claire collected the papers and slid them into a folder. What no one saw, no one knew.

An idea whispered through her brain and quickly evaporated. "Except for God."

The British Army opened an Imperial Instruction School at Zeitoun in early October when the weather eased. Machine gunnery school continued, along with classes Nigel couldn't discuss. "I'm lecturing again on what I saw in France, but I don't know how pertinent my information will be for much longer."

"Is your job changing?" Claire asked one Monday night.

"This school is focused on desert warfare. The camp's certainly healthier now the Australian Light Brigade moved with their mounts to the canal."

"I thought you liked horses."

"I love horses in clean green paddocks far from living quarters." He whisked at a fly. Claire didn't know how to encourage him out of yet another dark mood. The division seemed to be widening now they spent more time together and he grew increasingly frustrated with her.

"Are you determined to stay tonight or can I lure you away to dinner?" Nigel asked.

"He's talking about what our religion has done for us that we couldn't do for ourselves. I want to hear it. We'd both benefit from a Bible study."

"No, thanks. Do I get a kiss good-bye?"

Claire lifted her cheek for his peck and watched him stalk away.

Over the summer Claire studied the book of Ephesians per Biddy's suggestion. She'd reached a stomach-lurching halt at the passage admonishing men to be the heads of their wives as Christ headed the church.

The question leaped at her. How could Nigel be her spiritual head?

She and Nigel enjoyed museums and dining out; they could discuss history for hours. But he wasn't interested in the God who held her heart, much less the Bible she read daily. He stoutly refused to listen to OC's preaching and only visited the YMCA hut to find her. Once there he tried to remove her as quickly as possible.

When Claire asked his opinion on biblical passages, Nigel refused to participate. "I heard enough about the Bible as a kid. No, thank you, mate."

Nigel preferred the blithe and bonny life found away from camp. She didn't blame him.

Claire and Jock spent the fall touring military hospitals, talking with the matrons and willing patients. "Scraping the bottom of the barrel," Jock groused. "If they're here, they don't know much."

The 14th Australian General Hospital at Abbassia barred Claire from entering, which puzzled her. "Doesn't it specialize in dermatology?"

"Skin disease, yes," Jock said. "Ask your mother to explain venereal disease. In the meantime, let's see if we can scrounge up news at one of the other Australian hospitals."

She stopped him. "I know what causes venereal disease, Papa."

He shuddered.

They met OC as they walked up the front steps of the 1st Australian General Hospital and exchanged greetings. "You YMCA secretaries get around." Jock shook his hand.

"It's part of our job," OC said. "Many of these men are discouraged because they've been left behind while their units headed to France."

"They want to fight so badly?" Jock asked.

"The men want to do their best so they can finish the war and go home. Thank you, by the way, for allowing Claire and Mrs. M to join us Sunday afternoons to serve tea. It's popular with the men."

At Jock's nod, Claire retrieved her notebook. "You're continuing the setup you began at Ismailia, then?"

Her father could have asked her these questions, but Claire wrote down the answers, anyway.

"Perhaps Mrs. M told you we served nearly one thousand Tommies last Sunday."

Jock dropped his pipe.

Both men bent to retrieve it.

"Anne mentioned the crowd. She was done in by the time she arrived home."

"We appreciated her assistance. She and Biddy covered the tables in white cloth and placed a wee flower posy in the center. Mostly Mrs. M poured tea and chatted with the men. It's significant work."

"She's not strong, Reverend Chambers," Jock said. "The weather is hard on her. If she exhausts herself, I'll insist she stay home."

"I'll let Biddy know. And you, Miss Steno? Did you toil too hard?"

"Not at all. I'm pleased to help." She eyed her father. "I could see how it cheered the men to spend time with us, particularly with my mother."

OC winked at her. "Nevertheless, we'll be careful not to overdo the teas. Good day to you both. I'm headed to Abbassia." He tipped his pith helmet at Claire.

"Smooth." Jock watched the thin man walk away.

"They'll probably let OC into the 14th," Claire said.

"I'd be interested in hearing those conversations."

They interviewed several soldiers, chatted with the matron, and heard more stories from Gallipoli, now months in the past. Jock then discovered a physician with a vexing problem they'd seen among battle-scarred patients.

"Numerous soldiers who survived the Dardanelles battles suffer from a peculiar nervousness," explained Dr. Clarke. "Doctors in England describe it as shell shock. Men who've survived battle struggle with panic, an inability to sleep, and can become catatonic. We keep them comfortable and watch them. It's a terrible ailment without a cure."

"They're malingering cowards?"

Dr. Clarke frowned and bade them follow. They peered through window slits at men locked in tiny rooms, empty save for thin mattresses on the floor. "It's like a jail cell," Jock said. "Is this necessary for men who are merely ill?"

Claire took ten pages of notes, growing increasingly uncomfortable as they viewed men oblivious to their presence, even when they entered their rooms. The soldiers rocked, howled, curled up into fetal positions, and ignored the sisters and orderlies attending them.

In a large room housing several soldiers, one man trembled so badly he could not stand. He fell to the floor, twisting and grunting, with staring wide eyes. Trembling began at his feet, roared through his body to his face, and then started over again.

Claire closed her eyes.

"No emotion," Jock whispered. "You can't testify if you don't watch."

Claire addressed the sister beside her. "How do you care for them?"

"We see they do not hurt themselves, but I do not know beyond that. The private only sustained a flesh wound; we can't explain his behavior." She folded her hands and frowned.

"All this reaction from a flesh wound?" Claire whispered.

The sister shrugged. "They pulled him out of a collapsed trench in the Dardanelles. He cannot speak and flinches at the slightest sound."

"Are they troubled by loud noises? Can you peg it to anything?"

The sister shook her head. "We don't know. We try to keep them clean and fed. They'll go home someday, but I don't know how. It's a long journey to Australia."

Jock's eyebrows contracted in disbelief. "What's done to help them?"

"Massage, baths, food, soothing hands. YMCA chaplains call regularly. Some doctors suggest hypnosis, but no one knows. 'Tis a real shame." She clapped her hands and two orderlies picked up the soldier, walking him between them to his bed.

"Have you seen enough?" Dr. Clarke asked.

"What's the high command's reaction to this?" Jock asked.

"Unsympathetic, but then, they're trying to win a war. I doubt you'll get anything past the censors, but if you do, please emphasize how well we care for the men."

Jock and Claire slumped on a bench outside the hospital, stunned.

"What have we come to?" Jock asked. "We'll need to investigate other army hospitals to learn more on this story. Terrible." He jerked his chin. "Look who's coming."

Nigel waved his fly whisk. "I ran into Chambers and he told me you were here. May I take Claire to dinner, Jock? Heliopolis sports a fine restaurant she'd enjoy."

In his neatly pressed uniform, properly tucked tie and shining boots, Nigel appeared a vision of glowing health compared to the men they'd just seen. Dazed, she wanted nothing more than to crawl into her quiet room at Shepheard's Hotel and shut the door.

Claire stared at her skirt as her brain tried to process what she'd witnessed. She brushed at a spot and sighed.

"If you don't want to go, just say so," he said.

Jock cleared his throat. "It's been a grueling day, Nigel."

"Claire?"

She knew he wanted her to jump at the chance to spend time with him at a lovely outdoor restaurant, but Nigel would expect her to be charming and fun, to distract him from the war.

Claire couldn't be the young woman he wanted this night. She removed her glasses to polish.

"I see." He clicked his heels. "You're not flexible enough to change for me, so we will stay with our prior arrangements. I will see you on Saturday. Good day, sir."

Nigel marched off.

He periodically saluted Tommies as he headed toward Heliopolis. Claire put on her glasses with a heavy heart.

"Is he always so thoughtless of your feelings?" Jock asked.

Claire remembered Nigel's tenderness in the cemetery last summer. "He's a lonely man who wants to be released from the pressure like everyone else. I don't blame him. I should have dined with him." She leaned against her father, limp. "But I can't tonight."

"What does your holy book say about love? Charity is kind and not envious, bears all things, believes all things, hopes and endures. Maybe Nigel doesn't know how to love."

Claire shook her head. Nigel had endured a lonely childhood in the bush, with his doctor father always gone and his mother battling with hired hands. Perhaps Nigel struggled to be tender because he never experienced it himself. But while Claire could be sympathetic, she wasn't his answer.

Jock hugged her. "You made the right call."

Time would tell very soon; Claire knew it in her bones.

CHAPTER TWENTY-NINE

November 1916

Jock suggested Claire vent her emotions by writing up the treatment of shell-shocked soldiers at the hospital. He submitted the story to the BNS under her name. Army censors returned the article with REJECTED stamped in red.

They'd expected it, but Claire's hopes plummeted at the dismissal. "Would they have accepted it under your name?"

He shook his head. "Probably not. I can't afford to get on their wrong side, so I took the chance they'd let your writing through. They know you work for me."

"You used my article as a sacrificial lamb?"

"With great risk comes either great reward or failure. Consider your notoriety if they'd published the article."

"That's not sufficient and you know it. When will I get a byline?"

He hesitated. "I'll watch for another opportunity; in the meantime try a soft story." He handed her a telegram from a British women's magazine. "Talk to the women here at the hotel; find out how they're coping in Egypt. They'll love it and you should get a byline, even if not the one you want. You're more than capable."

Three days later, Claire found herself muttering as she scanned her notes, hunting for the lede by asking her questions: "Who, what, when, where, why and how?"

Mildred Murray, a bridge partner of Anne's, sat for an interview. Unfortunately, she'd been married to the head of the British forces only four years and her perspective was limited. Claire knew her husband's job was on the line, which made the interview awkward.

She next tried Colonel Middleton's family. Cecily sat beside her mother, twisting her new engagement ring as Mrs. Middleton discussed the depravity of Egypt and the constant insects. "I don't know where we'll find quality satin for Cecily's wedding dress."

Anne's friend Lucretia Patterson provided better copy but Claire couldn't quote only her. It took imagination to put together a rational story worth reading. Claire rolled a fresh sheet of paper into the flat black typewriter.

"Don't get us thrown out of the hotel." Anne lounged on the sofa and waved a fan. "Emphasize their stiff upper lips and concern for the Tommies. Lucretia has run the canteen at Ezbekieh Gardens since it began."

Claire knew. The army wives treated the soldiers as pets and vied to help them in creative ways. So many new soldiers arrived daily in Cairo, the women never ran out of things to do.

Anne snickered when she read Claire's draft. "I see their names on top, which they'll love, but your story is bland."

"I prefer hard news."

"It's easier to write." Anne tossed the pages to her. "Mildred is childless and Thelma's fixated on a wedding, but Lucretia's two sons are in France."

"She's terrified. Her husband feels guilty the boys are fighting while he's safe in Cairo."

"Safe for how long?" Anne asked.

"Until they move into the Sinai."

"Try focusing the angle on how a mother functions when her sons are in danger and her husband is preparing for war. Many British women probably struggle with the same fears." Anne picked up the newspaper and marked a story.

"What have you got?" Claire leaned over her shoulder.

"Water concerns for Bedouins. Someone's moving in their direction. It's an idea for your father to investigate."

Claire took the chintz chair across from her mother. "Do you ever tire of spying in the background?"

"We're a team. He uses my skills to develop his leads. It suits us. Why?"

Anne adopted her husband's values and served as a "help-meet" like the Bible described. Nigel complained Claire's job distracted her from paying enough attention to him.

Her parents enjoyed the same books, argued over the news, debated current events, and laughed together. They respected each other and provided a lively duo for the dinners they attended. Her mother's wit could tease Jock from gloomy moods, and her father paid close attention to Anne's needs and desires. Theirs was the type of marriage she wanted; it made her feel safe.

She did not feel safe sharing her fears or dreams with Nigel. The cleverness she'd admired in London carried a bitter edge these days and she had to force herself to remain cheerful when in his company.

Worse, when she prayed, God seemed far away.

Claire examined the pretty ring on her finger. She'd miss Nigel as a convenient escort, but he was safe in Egypt. She didn't need to worry about sending him to the trenches in France with a rejection ringing in his ears.

A copper coin landed in Claire's lap.

"A piaster for your thoughts. You're mournful," Anne said.

"What does it take for a successful marriage?"

"Respect on both sides."

A knock sounded and Claire answered the door. She signed for a telegram, set the piaster in its place on the silver plate, and handed the wire to her mother.

"Sarah, Sarah, Sarah," Anne murmured. "You're too busy to write a decent letter, so you send a wire?"

Claire gathered her papers. She'd finish her rewrite after dinner. "Has Sylvia's baby arrived?" As she slipped the papers into a folder, she realized Anne was silent. "Mama?"

Tears ran down Anne's cheeks. The flimsy telegram fell to the floor. Claire retrieved it and gasped.

Peter was dead.

"What happened?" Nigel spoke gently as he rubbed her hand.

"Shot down in a dogfight near Verdun. He survived the crash, but was badly injured. They transported him to hospital in London, but he didn't survive. At least the family could bury a body this time." After a week, Claire had no tears left to cry.

"Did they sing a requiem for him at Oxford's cathedral? Or worse, the grotesque hymn 'God Moves in a Mysterious Way'?"

She recoiled at his tone. "I've no idea."

"Seems to be a common occurrence. I'm sorry. Peter was a fine mate. You'll miss him."

Claire felt carved of stone, her face a mask. "We will."

He stared out at the garden sparkling in the Cairo sunshine. "Will you go to London?"

"Of course not. Our work is here."

"Work to do, people to convert, songs to sing. That's my Claire. Time for anyone but me."

A scarlet bird chittered through the bushes. She watched it maneuver from branch to branch. It cocked its head in her direction, tapped its clawed foot and then launched into the blue sky. She watched it soar above the outbuilding, slipping through the air to glide onto the fronds of a towering palm tree.

He cleared his throat. "I've got you now; what shall we do?"

A rust-colored bird trilled from a star jasmine and sped to the palm. Claire made up her mind.

She pulled her hand from Nigel's grasp and tugged the blue ring from her finger. "You're right. I don't have enough time for you. I don't believe I make you happy. Thank you for this ring, but I'm returning it. I wish you the best and will always pray for you."

Nigel went rigid. "That's it?"

"I think so." Claire stood.

He tugged her down into the wicker chair and his gin and tonic sloshed. Two officers at a nearby table frowned.

"I don't want to make a scene," Claire whispered. "Remove your hand and let me go."

"Claire, you don't know what you're doing. This is grief. Why throw us away because you're mourning?"

She closed her eyes and saw Peter's open, honest face. She heard his voice and remembered his teasing. Claire recalled his rough hands teaching her to sail when they were children. As close as the brothers she'd never met, but dearer because she had known him.

They'd loved each other with a special bond that gave and forgave and gave again.

Peter always tried to understand.

Claire clenched her eyes shut, but moisture slipped under her lashes.

"I say," a deep voice asked, "are you troubling this woman?"

"She's lost a family member," Nigel replied. "She's having trouble dealing with it."

She nodded. She couldn't help Peter anymore. Her letters, Bible verses, prayers, meant nothing now. Claire folded her arms onto the table and put down her head.

An undersized hand patted her shoulder. "Don't cry, Miss Steno. God will take care of you."

Claire raised her head, sniffed, and gazed into Kathleen Chambers's darling face.

"What are you doing here, Kathleen?"

Nigel grunted. "Here comes her esteemed parent. Let's go."

Kathleen twirled and her freshly washed curls waved under a wide white ribbon. "Daddy took me to the beauty parlor."

Her eyes and soul ached, but Kathleen could not be quenched, at least not by Claire. She acknowledged OC, who carried packages.

He stopped. "We're intruding."

"Yes." Nigel stood. "Claire needs to leave. Nice to see you again, padre."

OC knelt beside his daughter. "Claire is with a friend, but I commend you for greeting her."

"Why are you crying?" Kathleen asked. "Are you hurt?"

Claire touched her chest. "My cousin died and my heart hurts. Thank you for asking."

OC took Kathleen's hand. "I give you John 16:33. Good day. Let's find a seat and eat ice cream, my Scallywag." He led his daughter to a table on the far side of the tea room.

The officers at the next table eyed them again.

Claire scrambled in her bag while Nigel fidgeted. She pulled out the palm-sized New Testament and flipped through the pages.

"You carry a Bible in your bag along with maps?"

She read the text aloud: "These things I have spoken unto you, that in me ye might have peace. In the world ye shall have tribulation: but be of good cheer; I have overcome the world."

Claire savored the words. Jesus had overcome the world; he knew about her circumstances and her dilemmas. He loved her through them all.

Nigel pushed the pretty ring across the table to her. "I bought this for you. Keep it. I hope you're happy with your books and your wise man. Happiness, Claire, will never come as long as you ignore the people who love you. By the way, our orders arrived. We leave for France in the new year."

He settled his officer's hat on his head, gulped the rest of his drink, and stormed out of the dining area.

Claire stared at the palm tree's green fronds. Two red birds chattered, chased each other among the leaves, and then flew away.

Chapter Thirty

Winter 1916–1917

Two weeks after Claire bid Nigel farewell, a simple bouquet arrived with a question scrawled on the card: *Won't you reconsider?*

"No." Claire might lack a gallant escort for the winter festivities, but her prayers now flourished with joy and intimacy. She no longer had to look over her shoulder for Nigel while chatting with soldiers at Zeitoun. Guilt didn't dog her steps. The burden of trying so hard to no avail lifted.

She felt clean and honest and vowed to speak only the truth to young men, even if it was uncomfortable. She'd seen in her relationship with Nigel how futile it was, in OC's words, to try to be God's providence for another person.

Including Peter.

Jock never said a word once the grief hit them all. He tightened his jaw when news of plane crashes and aerial dogfights crossed the wires, but he never mentioned Peter's loss once he wrote Aunt Sarah and Sylvia a condolence letter.

Anne and Claire grieved together: sharing letters with the women in London, remembering happy times, and trying to make sense of the unimaginable loss. Claire mined her diaries, hunting stories about Peter she could share with the family. She showed Peter's letters to her mother now that confidentiality didn't need to be kept.

"We suspected as much." Anne sighed. "It's hard to know how much to pry into an adult child's life. You want only the best but fear asking too many questions will push them away." Her eyebrows went up.

"I'm done with Nigel," Claire said. "We can't be the person the other wants us to be."

Anne nodded, rose, and patted Claire's shoulder. "No matter what you do, I will always love you. Never forget that."

Claire could only nod, dumbfounded. Her mother had never before said she loved Claire.

Winter arrived in December with an abrupt change in weather. Rain poured down in thunderous outbursts, flooding the land and causing OC to post a sign outside the YMCA hut: "Closed during submarine maneuvers!"

It swept through the streets of Cairo, cleansing them from the usual litter and sweetened the air for momentary optimism as 1916 wound down. The residents at Shepheard's Hotel expected the war to end in 1917.

Claire took encouragement from OC's blackboard message scribbled at midnight on New Year's Eve: "1917, a great New Year to you all. 'And God shall wipe away all tears.' Rev. 21:4."

She prayed he was correct.

Her father differed.

"The war will only end if the Americans enter, and it's unlikely since we reelected Wilson on the slogan, *He kept us out of war*."

"How can it go on?"

He waved his hand. "Use your eyes. Soldiers aplenty in the Middle East. I wonder if it'll continue until we've killed every able-bodied man on the planet."

Claire looked out the office window where a contingent of off-duty men wandered the street. Many units had moved to the northern end of the Sinai, but the camps outside Zeitoun still crackled with machine gun firing practice and the groans of men learning to dig trenches. Aunt Sarah wrote of teenagers being called up to France and she fretted her newborn grandson might grow up to be fodder for mad Germans.

"I hope Sarah's not prescient," Jock said. "At the rate they're killing each other in France, no men will be left by the time Sylvia's baby grows up."

Claire shuddered.

He struck a match. "Maybe this effort in the desert will amount to a breakthrough. I haven't seen Lawrence in months, but I know he's out there. Word is your camel corps friends were a great success."

"Will you be writing another story?" Claire couldn't keep the scorn out of her voice. "Or do you need a ghostwriter?"

Claire had spent a long, smelly day interviewing members of the Imperial Camel Corps after an invitation from a regular at OC's devotion hut. She'd written a story which she later learned Mr. Fischer at the BNS loved. Jock, however, had attached his name to it before the wire was sent.

He puffed on his pipe but it wouldn't light. "Boston wanted an unusual angle on the war. The ICC story was perfect. Ghostwriting is an honorable profession."

"Not to me."

He sighed. "The BNS hasn't paid a bond for you. Under the regulations all copy has to be sent in my name."

Claire slammed shut the file drawer. "Why?"

"The government has to accredit war correspondents. The BNS paid a $10,000 bond for me to work here. I must prove I'm worth the money." Jock fumbled in his desk drawer and pulled out a pipe cleaner.

Claire slapped her forehead. "When did this happen? Why didn't you tell me, Papa? Is there any hope of my getting a byline? Mrs. Rinehart made it to the Belgian front and wrote for the *Saturday Evening Post.* Why can't I have such a chance? Don't I write well enough for the BNS?"

He inverted the pipe over the trash can to knock out the old tobacco. "I don't know why you're so fixated on the *Boston Daily.* The British military wives magazine liked your article even if they didn't print it. The YMCA has magazines you could write for. If you stick to soft news, you'll be a shoo-in. Don't mention the war in your copy and the censors will pass it."

She threw herself down in a chair and glared at Jock—who paid no attention as he cleaned his pipe. "You take advantage of my abilities."

"I sired them and paid for your education." Jock poked and twisted the pipe cleaner. "I may need to buy a new pipe."

The book of Proverbs warned about anger, but she didn't care. "Would you have treated John or Phillip like this?"

His head jerked and his jaw tightened. "I won't answer such a vulgar question."

"I'm as informed as the other reporters. I know the history. You wouldn't treat a man the way you treat me."

Jock shrank before her, his shoulders hunched and his hands dropped into his lap. He stared at his empty pipe. "You may be correct."

Two reporters burst in with rumors about a battle in the desert. Jock swept away his pipe cleaning paraphernalia and spread a map of the Sinai Peninsula across the desks. They ran their fingers along the few roads and trading routes crossing the barren land. In spite of herself, Claire joined them. She recognized place names Jim had mentioned in the past.

Jock was in his element. "Rafah, near the coast along the trade route. Check your notes, Claire. What units are in the area?"

Claire flipped through a November notebook. "First and third Australian Light Horse brigades and the New Zealand Rifle."

"Is Nigel with them?"

Stung, she answered frostily. "I don't know."

"An Ottoman garrison is up there, a couple thousand soldiers. If the New Zealanders take it, the BEF will conquer the Sinai Peninsula." Jock locked eyes with his colleagues. They nodded.

"Next stop Jerusalem," Jock shouted. He grabbed his straw hat and headed to the door, the other reporters following. "I'm off to headquarters. I'll drop you at the hotel. Type up the notes from this morning and see if you can frame another article out of the heroic camel brigade information. I'll get the details to fill in. Boston needs the news."

The hotel suite was empty when Claire entered. Anne hadn't mentioned an appointment when Jock and Claire left.

Nothing was out of place. The newspapers were neatly stacked, ready to be sent to the rag picker. Three newspaper articles were spiked onto a nail on the desk for Jock to examine, but as Claire glanced through them, nothing seemed pressing.

Vaguely disturbed, Claire took the cover off the typewriter and organized her notes. She translated the circles, swoops, squares, and curious shorthand marks into straight English and typed them up. She remembered Nigel teasing her about hieroglyphics. Perhaps the Egyptian Museum of Antiquities director would grant her an interview if she wrote to him in hieroglyphics.

Nigel would laugh if she succeeded.

Stop.

Claire refused to contemplate Nigel or where he might be.

She finished her transcription and retrieved her Imperial Camel Corps notes. Flipping through the pages and remembering the story, she seethed yet again that it had been taken away from her. She'd been proud of that article, of how much she'd been able to describe to give readers a feel for life in the desert with camels and artillery. "Papa should not have taken the credit for my story," she muttered.

But in the neat Shepheard's Hotel suite, she heard her bitterness and stopped. Perhaps pride was at the bottom of her irritation with her father and her lack of a byline. One of her objections to Nigel had been his refusal to recognize her writing skills and the importance of her dream. He'd humored her and called her Nellie Bly but never asked why she wanted the byline.

Why would God have given her skills and background if he didn't want her to use them?

Claire pushed open the shutters to contemplate the dusty city with her bleak January thoughts. Out in the desert cameliers were clambering off their mounts and lying on their bellies to shoot an enemy. They didn't care how smart or educated she was; they performed their duties and wanted to be entertained when they picked up a magazine, not lectured.

When readers opened a newspaper, they wanted information. They weren't reading to flatter a writer's ego. A line from the book of Romans flitted through her mind, warning her not to think of herself more highly than she ought. If her goal was to flatter and call attention to herself, why should she be published? How could God use her ability if she sought to feed her pride? Claire's stomach clenched. She'd been going about her career all the wrong way. No wonder she felt so unsatisfied.

Claire opened her Bible; the Psalms always helped: "Why art thou cast down, O my soul?... Hope in God: for I shall yet praise him."

Her sin, pride, affected God. She remembered that from OC's first lecture. Claire rubbed her face. Here was sin worth confessing. No wonder her spirit felt cast down.

What could happen that day to make her want to praise God?

Knowing she was forgiven once she confessed, Claire stood at the window, confessing and thinking until the door opened and she heard her mother's voice.

Claire went to greet her.

Anne dropped her drawstring purse when Claire entered the drawing room. "Darling," she gasped. "You're home." She twisted her hands and indicated her guest.

Biddy shut the door and removed her hat.

"It's Tuesday," Claire said. "You only come to town on Wednesdays."

"I made a special trip today." Biddy smoothed her skirt.

Anne picked up the candlestick telephone. "Tea is coming. I'll ring down and order for a third. I'd no idea you'd be here."

"Papa got a hot lead. Have you two been out?"

"Yes." Biddy sat at the table.

Claire knew this game. She sat at the desk and they watched Anne.

"A battle?" Anne said after hanging up. "Who won?"

"He went to find out. Where were you?"

Anne appealed to Biddy. Biddy didn't speak.

Anne closed her eyes and rubbed her hands. Claire watched, fascinated. She'd rarely seen her mother so discomforted. "Is it a secret?"

"It shouldn't be." She met Claire's eyes. "Biddy accompanied me to the British Protestant Cemetery. I decided to visit my boys." She slumped onto the sofa and covered her face with her hands.

Claire's lips parted. "How was it?"

"Hard. Almost as hard as burying them. Their names are melting with age on the gravestone, but it was time for me to face their death and visit them again."

"Why didn't you take me?" Claire whispered.

"I needed a woman who could understand the pain, another mother. Biddy encouraged me that grief and tears are not signs of weakness, but of fond remembrance. I honor them when I weep for their lost lives."

Kind eyes shone at Claire. Biddy nodded.

Claire knelt before Anne and smelled her lavender scent. "I'm so sorry, Mama, for your loss. For our loss."

Her lips trembled. "I've faced it, the finality of their death. We left flowers." She paused to collect herself. "I want to remember them."

"I saw their grave with Nigel. We honored your loss."

"Did you leave flowers?" Anne asked.

"Last June," Claire said.

"Then who left the yellow chrysanthemums we saw today? Jock?"

"The answer will come when God knows you need it," Biddy said.

"I hope so." She gazed at her daughter. "Thank you, darling, for caring about your brothers."

Claire buried her face into her mother's lap. Anne stroked Claire's hair until a knock brought their tea.

Honesty, grief, and truth restored her soul. If only she'd remember the lesson.

Chapter Thirty-One

Spring 1917

Jock burst into the drawing room. "Look who I found coming out of Ezbekieh Gardens."

Claire hugged Jim. "You're so thin."

He joined Anne on the sofa. "Another round of malaria. I'm headed south to Luxor on furlough for a couple weeks, Mr. Jessop's orders. Fortunately, the Y has new reinforcements. Eva is here, as sprightly and fun as ever. OC laughs each time he calls her Sphinx."

"I remember how you liked Eva," Claire said.

Anne's lips twitched.

Claire ignored her. "They came to tea. Miss Ashe is as reserved as ever."

Jim removed his cap. "She and Gertrude Ballinger have set up a little hut on the side of the Benha railway station, chatting and serving tea and cakes. Tommies love them."

Jock knocked the ashes out of his pipe. "Where've you been to come down with a malaria relapse?"

"The usual places."

"What's it like out in the desert?" Jock asked.

"Hot, windy, desolate, thirsty, and grim. How's life in Cairo?"

"Not so bad," Anne said. "How are the soldiers holding up?"

"They're stoic. It's sobering in the desert with not much to do in the evenings. Our huts don't offer much, but we provide a respite from the miserable tents and the never-ending flies, lice, and general grubbiness. You saw Ismailia. The Sinai's the same."

Anne scratched at her hair. "How can we protect ourselves from lice when we're in the Zeitoun huts?"

Claire scratched too. "Don't sit too close?"

Jock found new tobacco and snickered. "Do-goodism has its dangers."

"The Tommies burn lice out of the seams of their clothing with matches. We wear our hair shorn close to help matters," Jim said.

"Did you see Lawrence?" Jock asked.

Jim shrugged. "Hard to know. He's been in Arab mufti lately."

Jock laughed. "Where were you?"

Jim pulled a simple olivewood carving from his pocket. "Here's a present for Claire. I considered dousing it in frankincense or myrrh, but none was available where I spent the last couple months."

Claire pretended to sniff the poppy carving. "You're hopeless."

Jock examined it over her shoulder. "Check to see if it says 'Made in Jerusalem,' on the flipside. The American Colony sells tourist trinkets." He scrutinized Jim. "You get much razzing because you're not in an army uniform?"

"Not as long as America stays out of the war. YMCA secretaries are considered part of the army, even if we're not."

"Especially if you're at the front lines with them?"

Jim tipped his head.

Claire poured him a glass of water. "How close to the front have you been?" Perspiration beaded his forehead. His cheekbones stood out and his hand trembled when he took the tumbler.

"Close enough to be uneasy, but it's for the good of the men." He winced. "OC sets a tough example for the secretaries. We all want to be as successful as he is, but Oswald drives himself to extremes. While most of us rest in the heat of the day, he visits hospitals. He's up before dawn and the last one to bed. I don't know how he does it."

Claire agreed. The man seemed indefatigable and always cheerful.

"I don't like how he drives Biddy." Anne crossed her arms. "She slaves to accomplish the tasks he assigns her."

Jim held out his glass for a refill. "He makes her lie down with Kathleen in the afternoon."

"Perhaps that's why he's imported the other women," Jock said. "To protect his wife."

Claire placed cookies and a handful of dates on a plate and handed them to Jim. He needed fattening up.

"Thanks." He devoured a cookie in one gulp and drank more water. "The BTC in London prepared workers for one purpose: to present Jesus to the world. OC expects us to do it. Students have gone on to missionary work throughout the world. I may take the message to America. It's not surprising Eva and the rest came to Egypt. The YMCA needs them here."

Claire refilled Jim's glass and, recognizing Jock's signal, opened her notebook.

"How can you continue with death all around you? What makes you so sure?" Jock asked.

Jim finished the cookies. "We're given a choice: we believe in a God of love or we do not. We believe he sent his son to die on the cross for the sake of our sins—that we could have fellowship with the creator of the universe. I believe God loves me and sorts out events in my life to his glory, not mine. I don't want to live in a world where death is an end rather than a beginning."

"You must see senseless death?"

"Yes." Jim hesitated. "I'm sorry for the losses in your family. Claire wrote about your nephew. I'm sorry, but until I know otherwise, I choose to trust God acts in ways I cannot explain." Jim closed his eyes and whispered. "I understand personal grief."

Claire spun his words across her page. She didn't know how her father could use them. Watching anguish cross both men's faces hurt. Her mother dabbed at her eyes.

Jock cleared his throat. "Thank you for your honesty, and we accept your condolences. I can't share your religious views, but appreciate how you try to encourage others."

Jim acknowledged Jock's words. "I must be on my way. Bessie Zwemer will play the piano tonight, Claire. Care to join me at the gardens?"

Claire retrieved her bag and after kissing Anne's wet cheek, left with Jim.

While they waited for the lift, Jim mopped his forehead with a khaki handkerchief. He paled under his tan and his hand shook.

"When do you go to Luxor?" Claire didn't like his sickly pallor.

"Tomorrow morning."

They crossed the salon in silence. Claire's yellow linen dress drew no attention in the hotel these days. Recent travelers from England brought the latest fashions and Claire was no longer a trendsetter. She preferred the anonymity.

"What can you tell me?" Claire finally asked.

"I saw Mt. Sinai," Jim said. "A more forsaken land would be hard to imagine. No greenery; only red boulders and dust and tall, craggy, frightening mountains. I'm not surprised Moses took off his sandals when he stood on holy ground."

"What were you doing there?"

"Recovering from a malaria attack at a monastery. I spent a week watching the sun and clouds move across the mountains. The sky seemed enormous and God almighty."

Jim dropped piasters into the hands of the beggars when they left the hotel. The first star appeared in the east and the local call to evening prayer trilled. Jim halted and they stood in silence. Officers passed them on the sidewalk and grumbled. Well-dressed *effendi*—high-society Egyptian men—and fancy women paid no heed as they entered restaurants across the boulevard.

Only Jim and Claire waited.

The shaggy palm trees whispered as cars traveled past and Claire could smell the pavement's dirt. She wrinkled her nose at the greasy beggar scent and turned her head in the direction of a nearby cafe where skewered lamb sizzled over an open grill.

When the last syllable melted into the dusk, Jim took her arm and they continued down the street.

"Were you praying?" Claire asked.

He recoiled. "No, were you?"

"No, but why stop?"

"We don't live in a bubble. The pitiful people I gave money saw us wait until prayers were done. It shows respect."

Claire glanced back. Thin arms beseeched European pedestrians. "I don't think they noticed."

"I knew. Was I too direct with your parents?"

"They respect straight talk. I didn't realize you carry burdens of your own."

"I'm human. I carry plenty."

"I'd like to know."

Jim eyed her. "I wonder."

OC spoke that night at the Ezbekieh Gardens. Claire joined Biddy and a rosy Eva in the middle of the packed audience.

"What a glorious setting," Eva said. "What a magnificent night."

Two rows of Tommies grinned at her.

"You've made a conquest," Claire teased.

Biddy chuckled. "They're admiring more than one."

Eva sat up straighter. "Do you know how OC described tonight? He said 'the new slip of a moon over a most superb afterglow is exquisite.' Don't you love such images?"

"Is Oswald always so poetic?" Claire asked.

Biddy examined her pencil tip.

Eva's merry laugh drew more attention and Biddy hushed them. Bessie prepared to play.

OC spoke on "A Fatal Error of Indignant Integrity," the attitude of the prodigal son's older brother. Claire took notes and squirmed over what it meant to resent God's gifts to others.

She glanced at the rapt Eva and envied her spot at the YMCA camp. Claire wished she could join the merry Zeitoun comrades on a daily basis. Kathleen provided unending entertainment. The wise OC dispensed godly insight. Biddy was the source of great comfort—or pithy remarks.

But Claire's job was to take down information and help her father shape it into news. She attended bridge games and dinners in the salon. She mingled with army officers as she searched for fresh ideas. She lived in a beautiful hotel with plenty of water and no chores. Was it such a bad life?

She nudged Jim. "What's my purpose?"

"To take shorthand?" he whispered.

This wasn't a joke to Claire. "Should I leave my parents and serve God with the YMCA like Eva?

"Let's discuss this later."

Claire picked up her pencil.

Afterwards, they drank lemonade at the canteen. Eva drew admiring soldiers with her vivacious conversation. Jim, Claire noticed, watched the young woman with appreciation.

She batted away her irritation. Eva's friendly presence cheered everyone. What was Claire's problem?

"I don't believe Sphinx came seeking a husband," Biddy said, "but I suspect she'll find one before she leaves Egypt. She works hard. I'm pleased she could enjoy herself tonight."

Claire wanted to glare at Biddy's inscrutable smile.

"Do you miss your friend Nigel?"

"I miss feeling wanted." Claire admitted before she could stop herself. "I'm not significant to anyone now."

"Like tonight's older brother?"

"In a half-dozen different ways. I don't suppose there's room for me in the bungalow?"

Biddy touched Claire's cheek. "God has put you into a special position with a significant opportunity. You have far more places to go than our little compound."

"Where?"

"Just because you cannot see where God is leading you, does not mean he is not leading you. God bestows talents for his purposes. You need to trust him. One day you'll get your fatted calf, and then you will know his perfect will."

"Will that be the day I finally get a byline?" Claire hugged Biddy. "I want you to celebrate with me."

"I will be delighted to rejoice with you if God wills."

Chapter Thirty-Two

Late spring, 1917

Before he left for Luxor, Jim suggested Claire interview Miss Ashe and Gertrude Ballinger at the Benha railroad station.

Jock traveled with her and waited as she interviewed the two women she'd known at the BTC. They served tea and cookies to hundreds of soldiers journeying between Alexandria and Cairo or out to the Sinai Desert.

"Egypt differs from your native Ireland, Miss Ashe," Claire said. "What motivates your dedication to service in such challenging conditions?"

"The love of Jesus Christ, none other." Clad in a severe black dress, Miss Ashe spoke in formal tones. She intimidated Claire. No surprise, the native assistant jumped when she asked him to bring more boxes of English biscuits.

"And you, Gertrude?"

A pretty woman with merry eyes, Gertrude seemed to pluck the answer from her full apron pockets. "I agree with Miss Ashe. We trained for these tasks at the BTC."

"Pouring tea?" Claire didn't remember either of them serving in the kitchen.

"Ministering to those in need by being our Lord's hands and feet." Gertrude handed Claire a ladle. "Won't you join us?"

Jock smoked his pipe while Claire served. "I need a number, Papa. Count how many soldiers come through in an hour."

"One hundred thirty-seven," Jock said when they rode the train home to Cairo. "Those women will be worn out before this war ends, especially the old one."

"She'll say the joy of the Lord is her strength. Nothing slows down Miss Ashe."

Claire enjoyed writing the article and sent it off to a magazine in London: *Red Triangle: The British Empire YMCA Weekly*. When her copy of the magazine arrived with a small check a month later, Claire was speechless at seeing her own full byline for the first time: "Claire Meacham, Egypt Correspondent."

"Your name looks good in print," Anne said.

"I hope we'll see it often. They told me to send more." Claire planned to write up Zeitoun and to interview a YMCA chaplain after a hospital call. The next time Jim showed up, she'd craft a story about his adventures too.

Buoyed by the excitement of a byline, she took Anne to the Egyptian Museum to request an interview yet again. Claire knocked one more time. The director opened, crossed his arms and spoke in French.

"*I will only answer questions in French.*"

"*Mai oui.*" Claire followed him into the office and pulled out her prewritten questions. Anne sat beside her with a polite smile. "*What is your greatest difficulty in overseeing a museum of antiquity during a war?*"

He pursed his Gallic lips. "*Your French is good.*"

Claire waited.

"*Your question is excellent.*"

Claire wrote a description of the man in her notebook.

"*You take shorthand in French?*" The pince-nez nearly popped from his eye socket. "*I think you must be a serious journalist.*" He then answered her questions.

"That went well," Anne said as they caught a calash to the hotel. "Your father will be interested in his answers."

"Do you suppose I can submit this to *McCall's Magazine*, or do I need to give it to Papa for the BNS?"

The calash horse clopped through the cosmopolitan city streets. The tired smell of a dusty, disorganized museum blew away in the spring breeze and with it Claire's inhibitions. "I'll try to sell it myself, first. If all else fails, I'll give it to Papa."

She watched a group of self-satisfied Egyptian men enter the Café Egyptian with its all-female orchestra, the golden tassels on their cylindrical hats swinging.

"Is it seeing 'Claire Meacham' that means the most to you or the opportunity to write a hard news story for the *Boston Daily*? I saw how you successfully snuck in the Ezbekieh Gardens story." Anne popped open her parasol and pretended to be intrigued by a military haberdashery.

Claire's throat caught and she stuttered. "Does he know?"

"He seldom rereads what he writes. Your great-aunt keeps the clippings. The mistake you made was in language choices and interviewing Biddy," Anne said. "I didn't say anything, hoping you'd become—what is the word Oswald uses, convicted? Did you intend to betray your father's trust?"

"I had to prove I could write. I knew he didn't have time to write it. Josiah Fischer wanted the story immediately. An opportunity arose and I took it." She wanted to cry.

"Did it confirm your confidence in your ability?"

Claire shook her head. "I've felt so guilty, I didn't know what to do. If I told him I'd forged his name, he might fire me. And yet I proved I'm good enough to write for the BNS."

"Have you submitted other stories?"

"No."

Anne sighed. "He is too busy and the article was good. I'll absolve you if you promise never to do it again."

A line from a psalm popped into Claire's mind: "Against thee, thee only, have I sinned." It referred to God, but Claire also knew she had sinned against her father. It would be easy to take Anne's suggestion and not face Jock, but Claire's soul knew what she needed to do. "I won't do it again," Claire said slowly, "but I need to confess to Papa."

"Suit yourself."

Jock heard her out. He read through the *Boston Daily* news clip Anne provided. "Looks fine. Don't do it again without telling me first."

"Please forgive me, Papa. I wanted to prove I could write well enough to get a BNS byline."

Jock pulled out his pipe. "The only mistake you made was not telling me. I need to know all stories sent; the bond is in my name."

The heaviness in her heart loosened. "You're not going to punish me?"

"How is this any different than what you've been doing?" Jock couldn't find his matches. "The only difference between this and the copy you've been drafting is you sent it out without my knowledge. Of course I forgive you! I couldn't do this job without you."

Grace, Claire thought. Unknowingly, her father extended grace to forgive her sin. She felt free for the first time in months.

Meanwhile, the pace picked up for the BNS.

When President Wilson learned of German Foreign Secretary Zimmerman's telegram to Mexico suggesting they join the German side of the war in exchange for vast lands in the United States, American neutrality ended. On April 6, 1917, the United States declared war on Germany.

Jock and Claire interviewed British officials who expressed relief the Yankees were joining the war effort.

"I'd love to witness our boys arriving in France," Jock mused as they traveled home from BEF headquarters.

"Could we? Imagine the stories."

He laughed. "Your grandfather was right. Reporting is in your blood."

The driver's whip cracked and they swerved around a donkey cart. "How soon before the Americans get to France?"

"Pershing's methodical and won't rush over sooner than he has to. I'd say the end of the year."

"Eight months?" Claire thought of Nigel and other Zeitoun soldiers. "Millions could die."

"They probably will. Fischer said Wilson plans all-out war, much like Sherman in the South. He'll stop at nothing to be the savior of European civilization."

"Don't you like the president?" Claire waved her fly whisk.

"You'd like him. He's a strict Presbyterian who believes in his God-ordained opinion."

She winced. "Is that how you see me?"

He tapped her knee. "Can't you take a joke?"

"Not on this subject." She admired the blooming purple jacarandas. Cairo's air held no haze. Her stomach grumbled. "Are we done for the day?"

"I can file the copy after lunch. Have you other plans?"

"I'd like to play with Kathleen's new kittens."

Jock laughed. "War news bothering you so much you need kittens?"

"With any luck, the kittens will include a blue Manx, a white Persian, and a rusty tomcat—in honor of America entering the war."

"Take your mother. She'll enjoy the spectacle." He chuckled all the way home.

A favorite of the Zeitoun compound, Kathleen's cherubic features, precocious conversation, blue eyes, and fair curls tied with a bow, thrust her into the center of gatherings.

Kathleen liked to sit on her father's knee during tea and dip dry rusks into his cup. OC petted his daughter, relished her pronouncements, and thought her an endless joy.

Many soldiers using the YMCA services agreed and brought her gifts. "We've a fair menagerie," Biddy said, laughing. An Australian soldier provided a donkey and several men stood by to help Kathleen learn how to ride.

OC waited under the shaded veranda with them to watch Kathleen kick her mount and trot along the pathways. "What do you think of my lassie, Mrs. M? Does she not have a fine seat?"

"With such a coterie of admirers, she'll never fall. Such attention isn't good for her, Oswald. She'll be disappointed sooner or later."

"Ach, yes, but not today. We'll leave her to her fun." He selected one of the kittens and tickled its chin. "This one likes to hunt lizards. I'm hoping she'll learn to leap for flies."

Anne stroked the kitten in Oswald's hand. "I've been worrying about the soldier you found under Kathleen's window last week. Who was he?"

"An Aussie homesick for his family." OC handed her the kitten. "He enjoyed hearing Kathleen lisp her prayers. We can't fault a man for missing his children and he thanked me for understanding."

OC dangled his fly whisk for the second kitten, who batted it. "He returned after the lecture and asked to peek in at the sleeping bairn. He placed his hand on Kathleen's head and whispered a prayer."

"I wouldn't be so generous," Anne said.

He dashed a hand across his forehead. "I cannot deny a man such a small thing. She may need plenty of prayers before she leaves Egypt. Come; let me show you recent changes."

Many soldiers showed their appreciation for the Chambers family by improving the compound. Whitewashed stones outlined flower beds and pathways. A wooden clothes-drying frame stood alongside a walled garden while a lone Italian cypress supplied spindly shade near a bank of desert flowers. Between the long bungalow and the devotion hut, OC had erected a white bell tent for his personal study.

The tidy compound was an oasis of calm: the sand raked, the few flowers neatly pruned. The wild desert and the war loomed beyond the wall, but inside order reigned.

"We have a new scheme afoot." OC led them to a large foot-deep indentation beside his tent. "Since we will spend the summer here, we've decided to build a dugout. It will be a place for me to study in the mornings and where we can escape the afternoon heat. I'm grateful."

"You're building this?" Anne paced the ten-foot square.

Claire pulled out her notebook. "Ways YMCA secretaries cope with Egyptian life."

"Not me. I lack such skills. I've drawn the design and our carpenter Sidrak Eff oversees the digging and construction. The soldiers are agog with curiosity, wondering if it's to be a swimming bath like the one in Ezbekieh Gardens."

OC adjusted his cap. He had hollows under his cheeks, lines on his tanned face, and his belt had been taken in several notches. Claire knew he labored long hours but she had not recognized the physical effects before. He looked far older than his forty-three years.

"Can you not get away this summer?" Anne asked. "Couldn't Biddy and Kathleen accompany you on one of your weekly trips to Alexandria to lecture? You could take a short holiday near the coast."

He gestured toward the horizon where a billow of dust indicated military maneuvers. "The men won't rest as they march across the desert to Jerusalem. Perhaps we shall spend a few days at the shore, but we need to prepare the compound for summer. There's talk of my accompanying the army to the Holy Land. I want a place for Biddy to rest and find quiet. The dugout will be for her as well as me."

Ten guests sat around the table at tea that afternoon. Eva recounted silly stories of Egypt's surprises. "I can't get the proper wrist action with this fly whisk."

They picked up their whisks to demonstrate, resulting in peals of laughter. When OC pulled out a volume, the conversation shifted to books.

"I have been enjoying this thrilling story," he said. "Rider Haggard's *The Brethren* takes place in Palestine during the Crusades. It has been enjoyable to read, particularly interchanging it with Marmaduke Pickthall's *Children of the Nile.*"

"You're reading Rider Haggard?" Anne said. "I thought he wrote fiction. King Solomon's Mine gave me goose bumps."

He brushed his hand across the cover. "I enjoy a rollicking story."

"I'm surprised you read anything besides the Bible."

"God's word is the most essential book to read, but he has given men and women creativity in the arts. God gives us the beauty of his creation—we've had glorious sunsets this week. He gave man an eye to create, whether in the written form, the musical form, or art. I am an appreciator. Fine art makes me love the ultimate Creator more."

"Have you been to the pyramids?" Anne asked.

"Four times. They are particularly stunning at night, don't you think?"

"Absolutely."

Anne stayed behind after tea to "help" Kathleen run the hut where soldiers purchased sundry items. She'd put the little girl to bed at the proper time, instructing her to say her prayers loudly in case of eavesdroppers. Claire wandered over to the large hut to converse with soldiers. OC would lecture in an hour.

New soldiers arrived and others returned. OC garnered love and respect from many. His lectures provoked conversations and deep thought. Men caught Claire by surprise with their practical applications. One soldier in particular stood out.

She knew him only as Moe, a dark man with furrowed brow. "My orders came through, miss," he said. "I'm headed to France with the last group from New Zealand."

Claire knew he'd hoped for Jerusalem, if only to see the holy city. "Are you worried? U-boat threats are much reduced now."

"It's in God's hand," Moe said. "The way I see it, God may have created me just for this task. The whole purpose of my life may be to serve in the army, so I could hear Oswald Chambers preach in Egypt and then die in France."

If he'd punched her in the midriff, she couldn't have been more shocked. "What do you mean?" she stuttered. "You can't believe your sole purpose in life is to die in battle."

He squinted with his left eye closed. "Jesus died so I could have eternal life, miss. If it's God's will for me to sacrifice my life in France, then I'll accept it."

"You aren't frightened at the thought?" Aghast, she fell back in the chair.

"I don't want to die, but I belong to the Lord Jesus Christ. That's enough. I need to finish my letter."

Blinking tears, horror welling, her mouth open in shock, Claire left to mull over what he'd said. She didn't have faith like Moe's. She didn't want to believe God would create her only to be killed.

She crouched in a corner, shaking with wet eyes wide and surveyed the hut; dozens of young men, many no more than teenagers, scribbled letters or conversed in small groups. Moe's stoic pragmatism enabled him to go with a free spirit to whatever grim horror awaited him in France. Claire couldn't grasp such a foreign idea. "What will make my heart so secure, so willing, Lord?" she whispered.

She waited until a peace she couldn't explain seeped into her soul and her mind, but it ruffled and took a long time to set. Biddy's words echoed: "I believe God." She whispered it again. No matter how incomprehensible his acts, if she clung to that stated truth, she could gain confidence.

"Could you help me write to me ma?" asked a private with acne.

"Certainly." Claire picked up her pencil and joined him.

Later, as she listened to a young man describe the kick from machine-gun firing, Claire took mental notes. Jock had trained her to defuse emotion with work. He could use this information. After she asked several questions and helped frame a description to his girlfriend, she noticed an officer enter the hut.

Nigel scanned the crowd. When he saw her, Claire handed back the soldier's letter. "It's good," she told him.

His jaw went slack as he staggered to his feet. "Good evening, sir."

"Stand down, private. I'd like to steal your assistant."

The young man saluted. Nigel returned it.

"A moment, please, Miss Meacham?"

Claire dragged herself to join him in the starlit evening. They sat on a bench not far from the entrance. "I figured you'd be here. I've missed you."

"I thought you'd sailed by now." Her heart hammered and she tensed as she tried to marshal her emotions into coherence. Moe's words returned to stab.

"Soon. They say absence makes the heart grow fonder. It's been true of me. You?"

The stars filled the sky, an astounding display of lights so far from earth. Insignificant though they made her feel, Claire knew the heavens were friendly because their Creator told her so—the Creator she conversed with daily, who filled her with hope and encouraged her despite the war. The God Moe trusted with his life, no matter what. She could do no less.

"I've thought and prayed for you. You're a fine man, Nigel, but unless you've changed and are interested in God, we have no future together. I'm sorry."

"I've attended the lectures hoping to understand. I was particularly interested in Chambers's take on Job."

Claire's heart leapt. "What did you think?"

He shrugged. "Not convinced, but it filled lonely evenings." Nigel looked her in the eye. "I can't believe in God like you, Claire. I've come to say good-bye. I'll join my unit the end of the month and that should be the end of me."

Her mind reeled, her body froze. "Where?"

"The Somme." He picked up her empty hand. "I left you the ring without any ties. Maybe you could put it on sometime and remember me?"

"I'll wear it and pray for you every day."

"If anyone has a line to heaven it's you." Nigel kissed her palm. "Good-bye."

Claire hugged him. "I'll be praying, always."

"I know you will."

Nigel broke away, straightened his tunic, saluted, and strode out of the compound.

Claire watched until his erect figure blended into the desert night beyond the stars and then he vanished.

Chapter Thirty-Three

Fall 1917

"Do you have an itch for the real story?" Jock asked after their second summer in Luxor.

"Only if I can report it."

He batted away Claire's answer. "My two years are nearly up, and Fischer wants me in Paris to meet the American doughboys by the first of the year. I suspect your mother's health would improve if we left Egypt. Will you come with us?"

"I wouldn't want to stay here without you."

"Do you want to be a reporter, Claire, or a disciple? Your YMCA friends probably could find a spot for you. You could sit at Oswald Chambers's feet and assist him and his womenfolk. Would such a life satisfy you?"

"No. But I could write their stories."

He chuckled. "What's in your diaries?"

Claire had filled nineteen diaries since they arrived in Egypt, each written in shorthand. Those leather-covered volumes covered the ups and downs of her emotions over Nigel. She'd poured out her anguish over Peter's death, meditated on Bible studies, and recounted the idiosyncrasies of Egyptian life.

"My whole life is in my diaries."

"It's the mark of a writer, darling. You write to figure out what you think about an incident; expressing emotions in words on a page helps process them. But the quest for news can send you into dangerous spots. Will you come to Paris?"

"Certainly."

"You'll leave Chambers behind? Or is he moving to France and you haven't told me?"

Claire laughed. "He's staying in Egypt." She thought of the diaries filled with OC's lecture notes and the study skills he'd taught her. She'd miss OC and Biddy, but she'd go to France with her Bible.

And God. OC and Biddy both taught God would be enough.

Claire knew the truth.

Jock's replacement, a fresh-faced young man from Chicago, arrived in September.

Hal Dunlop slapped Jock on the back, admired Claire before shaking her hand, and stepped into the office with cheerful aplomb. "What a great place."

"How long have you been in the business?" Jock asked.

"Five years at the *Chicago Tribune*." Hal roamed the room, peered out the window, opened and closed file cabinets. "*Salam*," he said with a bow to the two interpreters who watched with wide eyes.

"They speak perfect English." Jock introduced the mainstays of his tenure in Egypt.

"I'm glad to meet translators." Hal shook their hands. "I've worried about the language. Mr. Fischer said you spoke Arabic."

"Rarely. It mostly helped to follow what locals thought they could say without my understanding. You'll be in the desert most of the time with the BEF. The ANZAC troops speak a different version of English, but you should be able to understand them."

"The difference is the accent, right?" Hal said. "I can't wait to get out there. I sailed with this guy from Indiana, Lowell Thomas; he's hunting a rogue British officer in the desert."

"Lawrence?" Claire squeaked.

"Major Lawrence could be a wild goose chase if you went searching for him," Jock said. "The command doesn't know what he's up to at the best of times and you could dry up your army sources if word got out you admired Lawrence."

Hal swung a chair out from beneath a desk and straddled it facing backwards. Chin on fist he grinned at Jock and Claire. "Reporters want to go to France where the action is with the doughboys landing. How did you get the transfer?"

"Would you rather be in France?" Jock asked.

"Naturally. Careers will be made on the Continent. So how'd you do it?"

Jock retrieved his pipe. "Old family connections."

Hal grinned at Claire. "Any chance with a young family connection?"

Claire blushed.

"Depends," Jock drawled as he lit his pipe. "You a religious man?"

"Not on your life."

"You've time. Warfare has a way of focusing the mind; otherwise I'd say no chance."

"Perhaps you'd like to join me tonight at Ezbekieh Gardens and learn about the off-hours of the men you'll be covering?" Claire asked.

"You got it, princess."

Jock hadn't lit his pipe yet and choked into a coughing fit. Claire enjoyed thumping him on the back.

Hal Dunlop took dictation and knew how to type. He had the skills Claire had learned painstakingly over the years and took over most of her job. She still traveled with the two around Cairo as another set of eyes, but as the battles formed up in the desert, they needed to investigate closer to BEF headquarters at Port Said.

"I'd like to be on hand when they enter Jerusalem," Jock said. "But I doubt it will happen soon enough. I'll take Dunlop, show him the ropes, introduce him, and be back by mid-November to help pack up."

"How much packing will we need to do?" Anne asked. "We give away our clothes, buy my sister a rug, and stash the papers into trunks. One day, maybe two."

"You can shop for the best rug, haggle, and enjoy yourself. Your friends at Zeitoun will always welcome your assistance."

They kissed him good-bye. "Keep safe," Claire said.

"You've still got a job, Claire. I'll send wires. Write up article ideas and set up the list of contacts for Dunlop. A journalist never has a day off."

They waved the men off at the train station. Jock smoked his pipe like an enigma while Hal leaned out the window like a kid off to camp. "He'll run your father ragged," Anne said. "But Jock will enjoy a final adventure in the field."

As the train chugged away, Claire examined her mother. Anne seemed to have shrunk, her features thinned, her arms more stick-like than rounded. She reached for Claire's elbow and put on a jaunty smile. "I'm treating you to lunch at Groppi's and then we'll visit Kathleen."

Anne and Claire rode the trolley out to Zeitoun and followed the well-worn path across the desert. "Perhaps we can find a car for the trip home tonight," Claire suggested, suddenly conscious her mother needed to walk slowly.

"You don't need to baby me, no matter what your father said. If I can't manage I'll tell you. Deal?"

Relief flooded Claire. "Deal."

They met OC sitting on the rock wall surrounding the compound. "I'm surveying the premises," he said. "While they write orders to send me with the troops, I'm trying to imprint this Eden in my mind."

"If this was the Garden of Eden, I'm not surprised Eve ate the apple," Anne said.

OC laughed. "No, it was a little northeast of here in Mesopotamia, but I will leave my heart here with my little Scallywag and her mother." He nodded at Kathleen gamboling in the dust with the puppies.

"You're off to see Jerusalem, then?" Anne asked.

"If God wills."

"I'll commiserate with Biddy." Anne called to Kathleen and they headed to the bungalow.

OC watched after her. "Perhaps," he murmured.

"When do you go?" Claire asked.

"It's not clear yet. I traveled to town today to purchase my kit. I'm excited at the prospects."

He spoke in his usual even-tempered way, without the coltish excitement of young soldiers itching for battle. His face was drawn, his cheeks and forehead lined. As with her mother, Claire recognized frailty. Did Egypt drain them all of energy and health? Even his braces—suspenders—were loose on his bony shoulders.

"What ails you, Miss Steno?"

"I should ask you the same thing. My father, my mother, Jim, now you, everyone appears thinner and less vital than they did in England."

"Two years in the desert takes the meat off your bones. Only you and Kathleen bloom. You've had a lift in your spirit these last months. I'm happy to see it."

"I made a hard decision."

"Did the Lord lay it on your heart?"

"Yes."

He brushed sand off his trousers. "When we are devoted to the right things, we can hear his voice better."

Claire agreed. She was stronger and more confident in both spiritual and day-to-day matters since she'd ended her relationship with Nigel. The Bible's words came alive now when she read them.

OC swung off the wall. "Trouble nearly always makes us turn to God. His blessings are apt to make us look elsewhere."

His words, as usual, bore pondering. "Who will run Zeitoun while you're gone?"

"Biddy, until the YMCA sends another secretary. God will provide."

"Will we see you again?"

"Ach, I don't know when I'm leaving. You may be gone before me."

"We sail December 8. I asked Biddy if I could serve the YMCA like Eva instead of going to France, but she said no. She thought I'd be more useful reporting with my father."

"God gives each of us gifts for his purposes, Claire. We don't always know what they are, but we can trust him with our lives. Some are called to be teachers, some apostles, and so forth. The body of Christ has room and need for all."

"Even a reporter?"

He smiled. "God has given you a sound mind and opportunities. Travel where God leads you, not where another wants you to go. Keep your heart bent on him." OC paused and cocked his head to the side as if listening. "I give you Isaiah 1:18."

"Which says?"

He winked. "I see it is tea time. Come now, and let us reason together, saith the Lord."

OC taught with calm words and a solid, though occasionally mischievous, tone. His words smoothed like a benediction over Claire, confirming what she'd suspected. OC maintained God wanted to communicate with her; she just needed to bring her heart to him, submitted to wherever he took her for his purposes.

Across the desert, a line of men in khaki uniforms headed toward the compound. Claire shaded her eyes. "What's your lecture topic tonight?"

"I've taken to the minor prophets these days, and a phrase from Hosea haunts me: 'I will have mercy and will save them by the Lord their God.' That's the only answer for us. Remember it." His loving eyes smiled at her as if he, like Biddy, could read her soul.

The sun dipped to the west and dappled the sky with splendor. "Saved by the Lord our God? I'll never forget." She watched the colors deepen and change to burgundy and indigo as OC stepped away to greet the newly arrived guests.

As the men trod the rocky sand toward the bungalow, Claire idly wondered if she'd ever have another chance to speak with OC again, to hear such wisdom applied to her personally.

She chided herself. Of course she would.

Chapter Thirty-Four

November 1917

Claire worked each morning on tasks Jock assigned and projects for the *Red Triangle.* The editor assured her he'd take more stories once she arrived in France. While she still dreamed of getting a BNS byline for a hard news story, she'd write the necessary soft news to prepare. Seeing her name in print thrilled and encouraged her.

She and Anne traveled to Zeitoun daily for tea. They spent time with the family, helped the soldiers, and listened to OC's lectures. It made for a change of pace and helped fill the hours without the voluble Jock—who was having a "smashing" time in the desert as General Allenby's troops fought through Gaza headed to Jerusalem.

Jim Hodges, now assigned to headquarters, frequently traveled with them and provided a strong arm for Anne.

"The doctors decided I've had too much exposure to malaria and I need to leave Egypt," he explained as they rode the trolley together. "They suggest I transfer to the European theater this winter."

Anne rubbed her hands together. "Does such a plan make sense? Why spend the winter in Europe after living in Egypt?"

"One might ask the same of you, Mama," Claire said.

Anne ignored her.

"I could choose winter in Europe or go home, Mrs. M. I'd rather help, so I asked for headquarters in Paris."

"Do you speak French?"

"*Oui.*"

"This is too much of a coincidence," Anne said. "Claire and Jock are going to France."

"Not you too?

Anne looked away. "I'll be spending time with my sister in Belgravia Square."

"The YMCA offered London, but I'd like to be where the Americans are fighting. I'll probably be pushing papers, but it'll be sufficient for me."

"Do I need to ask your intentions?"

He grinned. "Honorable. When do you sail? I thought I'd travel on the same ship."

"December 8," Claire said. "I'll get the details for you."

"Thanks. I knew Miss Steno would come through."

Jim spent long hours conferring with soldiers in the YMCA hut. "I pray with them," he explained. "Their fear of death makes them want to ensure they're right with God, as it should."

Meanwhile, OC's posting to the army front line took longer than he anticipated, and Claire thought the delay a good thing. Increasingly tired and haggard, he pushed to keep up his ministry pace. One day in late October he mentioned an ache in his side but insisted it was a mere stomach ailment, common to many in Egypt. He spent the day in bed.

He did not improve the next day, or the day after.

More than one person encouraged him to see a physician at the Red Cross Hospital, but with a battle raging to the northeast, he didn't want to bother overworked army doctors. Any free bed would be needed for soldiers injured in the fighting, he explained.

"Really, Oswald," Anne said. "You look ghastly. If you don't want to bother an army doctor, why not see a civilian in Cairo? I'm under the care of Dr. Milton, but Dr. Garvey is equally good."

He waved away her concerns and asked others to take the evening lectures. A concerned Biddy led the Sunday morning service, which OC said was excellent practice for when he joined the army units.

"I don't like this," Anne said. "He's acting like a martyr. Why won't he see a physician?"

Claire didn't know.

A grim-faced Jim arrived at Shepheard's Hotel Monday afternoon. "OC finally agreed to go to the hospital. They performed an emergency appendectomy. We need to pray."

Anne jumped up. "Is Biddy with him?"

"She insists upon staying to nurse him. They're holding a prayer meeting tonight at Zeitoun. Do you want to go?"

Anne decided to stay in. "Mary will see to Kathleen," she said, so Claire and Jim went together.

Dozens of people knelt in the hut. One man led them in prayer for the "officer in charge, OC." Eva played hymns on the pump organ and they prayed and sang throughout the evening. By the time Jim escorted Claire back to Shepheard's, word came the surgery was successful.

"God answered our prayer," Claire explained to her mother.

"We'll see."

News of OC's illness traveled fast. Claire received a wire from her father asking about him. She showed it to Jim. "Why does he care?"

"News, of course."

She wired Jock the particulars. He replied, "Prepare obit."

"I won't," she told Anne in defiant tears. "That's a lack of faith. Biddy has a word he won't die."

"It never hurts to be prepared," Anne finally said. "I'd start writing."

Information from the hospital swung from hope to fear. OC rallied, he failed, and he recovered. Biddy remained by his side. Prayer continued at Zeitoun. A week into the ordeal, Eva brought Kathleen to see her father.

"He's doing better," Eva said when Jim, Claire, and Anne arrived at Zeitoun. Night was falling across the desert; they no longer came for tea during this trying time. Anne spent the evening at the bungalow rocking Kathleen while Jim and Claire volunteered in the main hut. They gathered at nine o'clock for desperate prayer. OC's lungs had hemorrhaged.

"It's not good, darling," Anne said on the ride home.

"Biddy has a word." Claire clung to her hope. She could not give in to fear.

"What word?" Anne asked gently.

"God impressed a verse upon her; you know the way OC always has one. It's 'this sickness is not unto death.' "

"What if she's heard wrong?"

"Oh, Mama." Claire buried her face into her mother's shoulder. Anne held her all the way to Shepheard's Hotel.

They were at breakfast on November 15, when a knock came. Jim entered, ashen-faced. "Oswald Chambers died at seven o'clock this morning."

They cried together.

The next afternoon Claire and Anne traveled with Jim by calash to the British Protestant Cemetery. Anne flinched when they arrived at the high-walled cemetery, but she straightened her shoulders and joined the crowd waiting beside the entrance.

Under an overcast sky, Claire's shoulders bowed, numb and heavy with grief. She could hardly remember him without wanting to cry, though she knew OC would say he had gone to a better place.

Why would God let Oswald die so young?

On November 16, 1917, the army buried Oswald Chambers, a YMCA chaplain, with full military honors.

Four coal-black horses with mounted riders pulled a gun carriage from the hospital where he died. OC's casket rode on a carriage draped in a Union Jack flag with an arrangement of white chrysanthemums. A long double line of one hundred uniformed soldiers marched behind as escort, their shouldered rifles aimed backwards and down.

Biddy, Kathleen, and Mary Riley rode in a car behind the cortege.

Claire and Anne wept when they saw the little girl, dressed in impeccable white, climb out of the car holding her mother's hand. Biddy nodded at the Meachams and waited as six muscular soldiers lifted the coffin onto their broad shoulders.

The men shuffled through the entrance to a freshly dug grave. The cemetery was crowded with people: soldiers from several armies, British *memsahibs,* doctors, and other civilians from around Cairo. The native foreman from Zeitoun stood with another Egyptian. Claire and Anne listened from several rows back as first Bessie Zwemer's missionary father Samuel spoke, and then a Scottish chaplain, William Watson, read the service.

They sang Psalm 121 from the Scottish Psalter and then a hymn, "For All the Saints Who from Their Labors Rest."

The British rifle team sounded a three-shot volley on command, and soldiers lowered the coffin into the ground. Claire shuddered as dirt landed on the coffin with soft hollow thuds. A bugler played the haunting "Last Post."

The mourners covered the grave with flowers. A soldier tapped a wooden cross marker at the grave's head: "Oswald Chambers."

Biddy hugged them wordlessly and departed. Claire and Anne held handkerchiefs to their eyes and waved as the car drove away. "Eva is taking Biddy and Kathleen to Luxor for a couple weeks to mourn," Jim explained.

"Will we see her before we leave?" Anne asked.

"I believe so." He hesitated. "Anything else you would like to see here?"

Anne's eyes widened.

Claire waited.

"I don't know." Anne's voice wobbled.

Claire selected two white flowers from OC's grave. "He won't mind. Let's say good-bye."

Anne leaned on Jim's arm as they shuffled to John and Phillip's grave. Claire let the petals drop while Anne touched the headstone with her fingertips. "They were so little. We had them such a short time. Poor Kathleen only knew her father four years."

Would the sorrow ever end?

Tears engulfed Claire and her heart ached as she put her arms around her mother.

"Biddy reminded me they were not alone in this graveyard," Anne choked out. "We never suspected her husband would join them in the Egyptian ground. Please don't die, darling. I couldn't go on."

"No, Mama, but the same is true for me. Get well in London."

As they returned to the hotel, Anne recovered enough to ask Jim a question. "How did you know the location of the grave?"

"I've paid my respects when we've buried soldiers in the cemetery. When I had flowers I left them. It seemed the honorable thing to do."

Anne kissed him.

Jock returned to Cairo the next morning and accompanied Anne and Claire to Zeitoun for a memorial service. No Biddy or Kathleen, but nearly a thousand people packed the hut, few with dry eyes. Gladys Ingram sang "Jesus Triumphant," at Biddy's request. Testimonies, stories and remembrances lasted for hours. It was an evening filled with crying, laughter, and the conviction they'd see Oswald Chambers in heaven.

They closed with the hymn "God Is Our Refuge and Our Strength," chosen to remind them of OC's focus.

Even Jock wiped away tears.

"I may not have agreed with him, but he was an exemplary man." Jock hugged his daughter. "I know this is hard for you."

She nodded.

"But when we get home, you need to write. The syndicate will want the story of a YMCA chaplain laid to rest."

"Must it always be about news, Papa?" Weariness swept over her and Claire couldn't bear the thought of her pencil or typewriter.

"It's the only way to endure sorrow, darling. Spill your heart on the page for this one and tell people what happened."

Claire wavered.

Her father kissed her on the forehead. "You owe it to him."

She sighed. What could she possibly owe OC?

Her faith.

Chapter Thirty-Five

December 1917

"No tears?" Anne sat beside Biddy on the bungalow porch the day before the Meachams left Cairo.

"I've none left." Biddy touched the soft petals in the bouquet Anne brought her.

"And you, darling?" Anne hugged Kathleen to her side.

"Daddy's with Jesus. He's quite near us."

Claire gasped. How could a four-year-old put such a concept together?

Biddy nodded. "Her confidence is a wonderful source of comfort and strength."

"My sympathies, Mrs. Chambers," Jock said. "Claire told me you didn't expect his death. She said God gave you a word?"

She answered slowly. "Through all the days of the illness and its crises, the word which held me was, 'This sickness is not unto death, but for the glory of God.' And there were times when it seemed the promise would have a literal fulfillment. But God had a fuller meaning."

"How can God be glorified in a death?" he asked.

Biddy spoke quietly. "We will see."

Eva cleared her throat. "The Zwemer family treated us so very well; Bessie had a vision."

"A vision?" Anne frowned. "What can you mean?"

"We were sitting in the garden and Bessie said she saw Oswald standing at the end of the table. He gave her a word to be radiant for Jesus." Biddy set the flowers on the table beside the teapot.

"Did you see him?" Anne leaned forward.

"Bessie believed she saw him and it brought her comfort," Biddy said. "I'm told dreams will come and I anticipate seeing him, but for now I have a great expectation of heaven. It feels closer, more intimate. Perhaps you've reached the same conclusions about your sons?"

Color drained from Anne's bereft face. "Maybe."

Biddy took her hand. "I wish you this comfort, Anne. Hard though it is to lose Oswald, I know I'll see him again. Such knowledge is a balm to my heart."

"When do you return to England?" Jock asked.

"Mr. Jessop asked me to stay on at Zeitoun. I'm here until the end of the war."

"Biddy! You can't be serious," Anne exclaimed.

"Dear, Anne, yes. I must finish the task God gave me to do. Oswald has been released, but not me. We'll miss seeing you and certainly bid you God's blessings as you travel. I'll be praying for you." She reached for Claire and smiled. "Of you, I know God will do much if you let him."

OC had said something similar the last time she saw him. Claire's heart contracted. Who knew when they'd see her again? As Claire hugged Biddy good-bye, she wished she'd done the same the last time she'd seen Oswald Chambers.

Gloom.

Claire contemplated nothing else as they set sail. The Mediterranean sky hid behind a dreary fog cover, which suited her. Claire traveled in a cocoon of aching sorrow. It was as if in casting off Egypt, they fled their past and embraced a future dark and colorless, cold and muddy, dank and saturated with blood.

In the pagan sunshine of Africa, Claire had acquired insight, growth, and spiritual understanding; now they sailed back to a civilized Europe shrouded in destruction. Heaviness and foreboding bore down on her as she watched Jim shaking from malaria symptoms, Anne sleeping long hours, and Jock endlessly pacing the deck with his pipe.

The loss of OC's wry wisdom, clear teaching, and spiritual leadership in Claire's life hollowed her stunned soul—though she'd anticipated the separation when they planned their departure for France. But she knew how prodigiously Biddy and OC wrote letters. If Claire had a question, she had expected to write and receive an answer.

Biddy remained, but with so many responsibilities, how would she find time to write?

Claire ran her hand over the leather cover of her Bible. Biddy would manage the same way as always, only without her husband.

"Pig-headed," Anne muttered at dinner the first night they sailed. "She can take her child home to England. Why stay in the miserable desert with mourners begging for answers to impossible questions? She needed the Luxor trip, but she didn't need to be responsible for a busy ministry."

"What would you have her do?" Jim asked. "She's poured her life into the YMCA ministry at Zeitoun. The war isn't over. Why should she give it up? They'll be cared for; no one who loved OC would allow his family to suffer."

"I wonder," Anne said. She retired early to bed and remained there. Claire and Jock brought meals.

Jock stalked the deck while Claire and Jim huddled on chaise lounges under an eave on the starboard side. Swathed in blankets, she stared at the fog, her soul slumping.

"Refreshing to breathe moist air, isn't it?" Jim said.

Claire drew the plaid blanket closer to her face. "How will we survive winter in Europe after living under Egypt's sun?

"Long underwear. I wore it in Ohio."

Claire couldn't remember what she'd left in the trunks at Aunt Sarah's house. The clothing would be three years out of style. She'd need to hunt through the shops or find a dressmaker. She closed her eyes. She didn't care. Claire wanted to wallow in her grief.

"He wouldn't approve, you know," Jim said.

"I don't want to hear this."

"God allows for emotion, Claire. The psalms revel in one emotion after another. What you cannot do is sulk into bitterness or anger. OC's death is a terrible thing, but don't you believe God ordained it?"

She seethed so much she sputtered her reply. "Why take OC at the height of his work? So many met God because of him. Why would God end his ministry? I don't understand."

"I don't either, but I have a choice. Do I trust God or don't I?"

"I don't want to trust God. I don't like him right now."

Jim laughed. "Honest enough! How long until you will be willing to consider him a friend?"

She averted her face. "I don't know."

"I can't hear you. If you're mad at God, yell loud enough so he can hear you."

Furious, she sat up to shout. "What's wrong with you? Don't you mourn your great teacher? How can you be so callous?"

She stopped short at the tears in his eyes.

"How do you know I'm not grieving as much as you?"

The ship plowed through the murk, bellowing its fog horn at regular intervals. Claire sank back into her blankets.

Weep with those who weep. Those words were engraved on her soul. "How do you hope in God again?"

"By praying. You tell him your feelings, when you're angry, when you're sad. You don't shy away from them and pretend they don't exist. You pour them out and then you read God's word for consolation. He can't comfort you if you refuse to admit you need comfort."

Claire tugged her knit cap lower, removed her spectacles, and rubbed her face.

"Our faith is based in terrible pain and tragedy. Without Jesus suffering on the cross, our sins wouldn't be forgiven. We need to remember God's agony. He loves us, yes, but his son's death on the cross saved us, not God's affection for you and me."

Jock marched past on his umpteenth trip around the ship. "What's happening?"

She jerked her head in Jim's direction. "He's counseling me."

"Your intentions?"

"Positive. She needs to grieve."

"I imagine you do too. God knows my Annie is a mess."

"Yes, sir, she also needs to grieve. Perhaps she'd like to join us in remembering Oswald Chambers?"

"She's worried about Biddy. I can't imagine why. A more confident and resourceful woman would be hard to find, except when Anne isn't ill." Jock pulled out his pipe.

"How do you deal with grief, Jock?"

Claire caught her breath. The horn called, underscoring the drama of Jim's question.

Jock didn't answer until his pipe lit. "I suppose you apply yourself to what's essential, which in my case means reporting the news. I've kept writing and hunting for answers. In time, the pain dulls and you don't notice it as much. With any luck, you forget."

"Do you think grief changes a person?"

"Of course it does. I can't imagine what the world will be like when this is over. The fields of France will yield fine harvests for generations from the bloodshed. How will those countries who detest each other live side by side? I hope you saw Europe before the war destroyed it. I doubt it will ever be the same again. Good day." He headed down the deck.

Jim opened his Bible. "Let me read a passage to you. 'And God shall wipe away all tears from their eyes; and there shall be no more death, neither sorrow, nor crying, neither shall there be any more pain.' "

She ached from the crying. "OC wrote that verse for New Year's Day. I've shed more tears in 1917 than in my whole life."

"OC anticipated our resurrections with Christ at the end of time. It's true for him now. The question is, do you believe it?"

Rage burst from her mouth. "Do I have a choice?"

"You always get a choice. Do you believe God's word or not?"

The fight melted from her bones. She put back her head and let the tears roll. Claire only wanted the pain to disappear. She didn't want to face Jim's quiet questions. She didn't want to think. She wanted to climb into the bunk with her mother and pull the pillow over her head forever.

Her parents must have felt like this when they left Egypt last time: devoid of hope. But she had hope. She'd see OC again. Biddy and Kathleen counted on it.

If a four-year-old could make the connection, Claire could too.

"It hurts too much."

Jim spoke slowly. "While nailed to the cross, Jesus declined the wine offered on a sponge because he didn't want the wine's medicinal affects to dull his mind. He wanted to experience the agony his death would vanquish. If we give our heartbreak to Jesus and don't try to avoid it, he will comfort us."

Weep with those who weep, Claire thought.

"Are you willing to give him your pain, Claire? Do you love him?"

She knew who he meant.

"Are you willing to be broken to accomplish his ends, to feed his sheep?'

"I'm a would-be reporter. I don't know how Jesus's question applies to me."

"No?"

She was willing to be broken if that really was what God required, but she didn't know if she could bear any more death.

Claire put on her glasses and glared at the sea.

She needed to brood and cry—and probably pray—before she answered him.

Chapter Thirty-Six

London, December 1917

The liner docked at Le Havre, France, and a number of passengers disembarked. Some joined the armies, others sought civilian affairs. Jim hugged the Meachams good-bye and caught a train to Paris. YMCA headquarters expected him.

The Meachams sailed to England.

Mr. Able met them with fur coats at Waterloo Station as they disembarked from the boat train. He organized their luggage into the motorcar on the wet December noon. "Madam waits at the house."

Anne clutched the soft fur to her face and nestled into the back seat.

Jock sat beside Mr. Able. "How are things?"

"Challenging, but Madam is coping. Mrs. Sylvia's little boy is a charmer."

Claire leaned over the front seat. "What's life like in England now?"

"Sugar and butter are rationed. Coal is limited. Madam has closed down most of the house. It's me and the cook and the nanny. A cleaning woman comes in once a week."

"Tell us about Peter, please," Claire said.

"What a sad day." Mr. Able swung the motorcar wide around a corner. "His plane crashed after a heroic dogfight.

He'd broken numerous bones and was badly burned, but the casualty center at the front stabilized him and sent him home. Madam and Mrs. Sylvia saw him at hospital, but he died several days later. They awarded him a posthumous Distinguished Service Order medal."

Anne stirred. "How did my sister take it?"

"The light went out," Mr. Able said. "Until young master Donald arrived. She dotes on him."

"Babies will do that for you," Anne said.

London's gray skies lowered to earth and mixed with chimney soot leaving a dark day fighting sleet. Despite the nonstop honking of brass bulb horns, traffic moved slowly.

"Why did we imagine England preferable to Egypt?" Anne sniffed.

"No malaria," Jock said. "Americans and rest. Your sister."

"Maybe I should go to Paris with you."

"As soon as you're my strong Annie again."

She sighed. "I dream of Newport. I want to walk the cliffs and breathe the clean sea air. I want American food and the view out our front window." She put her hands to her face. "I just want to go home."

Jock fiddled with his pipe. "I'd love to give you your wish, darling. But I can't take you home yet. Sarah's home is the next best thing."

Claire watched London out the window. While she understood her mother's yearning for the safety of America, Claire wasn't ready to leave Europe. Too much remained to be seen. Too much history needed to be written.

A veteran with one pant leg pinned up maneuvered down the sidewalk on crutches. Other pedestrians stepped around him without a second glance.

Too much needed to be restored.

⚜ ⚜ ⚜

The mansion's white walls were dingy; mourning crepe hung over the entry. Aunt Sarah, dressed in absolute black, greeted them at the front door.

Sarah invited them into the house and clutched Anne so tight Claire feared the two women would fall over. From Uncle Henry's library, a thin wail rose and she led them into the warm room. "Here's our adorable Donald."

Anne picked up the chunky one-year-old, his face red from hollering. Robust like his late father, Holly, he gurgled with wide blue eyes. "Sylvia must be so proud!" Anne exclaimed. "He's a bonny fellow."

"It depends if you like babies, doesn't it, Aunt Anne?" A nervous rail of a woman, Sylvia advanced into the room and studied her child. She wore a slender black skirt and a crimson silk blouse. Her once fine hair was shingled into sharp lines and scarlet lipstick slashed her lips. Lush perfume lingered.

"Darling, we're sorry for your losses." Anne dumped the baby into Jock's surprised arms. Anne hugged Sylvia until her niece's rigid body relaxed into weeping.

Claire took the now-wailing baby and toured the room. Blankets covered the sofa and thick curtains blocked the light. The fussy room smelled of baby, dust-swathed corners, and tea-rimmed cups. Uncle Henry's books were safely stowed behind glass, but little else of him remained.

Other than the liquor tray. Jock poured a brandy and sipped while the women crooned.

The baby's squalling faded to a whimper and they lowered their voices to match. When Mr. Able announced dinner, they tried be festive, ignoring the empty seats.

Sylvia ate little, gulped wine, and ignored the baby. While carefully made up, Sylvia's eyes were dark circled and her fingers fidgeted with her hair. Holly's enormous diamond glittered from her right hand.

"It's too bad Nigel couldn't join us." Sylvia pushed away her plate. "He didn't much care for Egypt."

Claire's fork clattered from her hand. "You've seen him?"

"He came on leave. He had a miserable trip; boat nearly torpedoed, and then orders to the Somme." She shuddered. "He took me to Holly's club, but it wasn't the same. You should have married him when you had the chance, Claire."

"When was he here?" Claire sipped her wine.

"Three weeks ago. We've invited him to come whenever he can get away."

"How lovely of you to open your home to a soldier." Anne patted her sister's hand.

"I'm thankful one young man remains alive."

"Yes, but for how long?" Sylvia poured more wine. "We'll travel to Newport when the war ends or the U-boats go away. All the men are dead. America is our only hope. Perhaps you'd like to come with us, Claire? You've still not snared a man and Europe has few left."

Surrounded by so many soldiers in Egypt, Claire hadn't considered the ramifications of a war killing an entire generation. The fighting took place far from Cairo and she'd only faced wounded soldiers during hospital visits. She'd not lived in the misery of England, where every robust male between sixteen and forty-five served on the battlefield.

"An interesting idea. Scholars argue the South hasn't reclaimed its prosperity because they lost so many of their leaders in the Civil War," Claire said.

Sylvia raised her chin. "There you go, spouting off another historical fact. It's no wonder Nigel strayed."

Claire probed her heart at Sylvia's stabbing words. She didn't want to be obligated to Nigel and his expectations, but in her sophisticated yet unhappy cousin, Claire recognized tremors of insecurity.

"Any mistakes would be Nigel's," Jock said. "We wish him the best of luck, particularly in the Somme."

"He feared the Somme," Claire remembered. "He didn't want to go to the slaughterhouse." She gasped and put her fingers to her lips.

Sylvia rose. "Thank you for reminding me. Merry Christmas." She left the room.

"My daughter is hurting and confused. Please forgive her." Aunt Sarah rang for dessert. "Nigel left a letter for you, Claire. I'll get it for you."

Claire tucked the letter into her Bible to read and think about later.

They spent the remainder of their time collecting provisions for France, taking Anne to a physician who prescribed total rest, and on the final day, visiting Peter's grave.

The stark granite headstone recorded his name, dates, and "beloved son, brother, and uncle."

Jock squeezed Aunt Sarah's hand. "I wish you had inscribed nephew too."

"He knew you loved him." She brushed a brown leaf from the lush green grave.

How could this white stone on a bump of lawn be Peter? Claire bit her lip until it bled, trying to reconcile his lively mind and droll sense of humor hidden under the earth. It would have been better for him to have been shot out of the sky; she could picture such a noble end.

Wearing new clothing in serviceable black, Claire stepped away from the grave, more determined than ever. No one should face death without knowing about heaven.

Jock's hand shook as he lit his pipe.

Whether they wanted to believe in it or not.

Chapter Thirty-Seven

January 1918

"I wish I could go with you." Anne tucked the black wool scarf around her husband's neck.

"Get yourself strong, and then you can come. Enjoy the baby."

She clung to Jock. "Promise you won't let the war end before I get to Paris? I want to celebrate with you in that beautiful city."

He laughed. "Do the world a favor, then, and get well soon. This war has gone on too long."

"I'll take care of him," Claire said.

"Try to keep him out of trouble and if you need me, wire. I'll come no matter what he says."

Claire and Jock closed the car door on her words and Mr. Able drove them to the train station.

On the other side of the English Channel, Claire gathered her new heavy winter coat around her chin. The weather in France sent icy fingers all the way to her chattering bones.

"The ship will send the trunks on. We've got a couple hours; let's see if we can learn anything." Jock belted his new "trench coat," a khaki calf-length gabardine covering with a thick woolen liner. With epaulets, multiple buttons, and a large belt, the trench coat was the latest and most practical fashion for officers and other professionals along the front, according to the Burberry shop clerk.

Claire suspected Jock purchased it hoping to fool authorities into letting him advance to the front lines instead of remaining at the rear. He delighted in it so much, however, she didn't have the heart to quell his enthusiasm.

She grabbed her satchel with a new map of France tucked inside, and they treaded the gangway into chaos.

Cranes and longshoremen toted loads from transport ships. The oily ship smell, raucous seabird calls, and salty ocean moisture pervaded the busy dock. Farther down the quay, they found a line of ambulances waiting to offload patients to a ferry. Soldiers stood in formation, nursing sisters scurried and a moaning fog horn underscored it all.

Jock identified himself to an officer. "I'm with the press. Can you tell me what's happening?"

The tall man scrutinized Jock. "No."

"Are these men headed as convalescents to England?"

"Yes."

"What battle?"

"Does it matter anymore? The stalemate continues. Poking your head above a trench can get you a hole in your brain. The snipers are vicious, the weather atrocious, the trenches disease-ridden pigsties, and we're still here."

Claire scribbled down the answer. His litany of misery continued, framed within a cacophony of noise, stench, injury, and deprivation.

"Very good, sir," Jock said, shocked. "Your name?"

The officer frowned. "I can't possibly give you a name. You shouldn't be here. No press allowed." He whistled for a military policeman.

Jock tugged Claire away. "Let's see if we can find other news ideas."

They watched ships unload cargo, spill out soldiers, and fly jaunty Union Jacks. The industrious longshoremen ignored them, except for a craggy Frenchman leaning against a crate. His thick accent bewildered Claire.

"You'll need to do better," Jock said as he guided her to a convenient YMCA hut.

"My mother taught me Parisian French."

Once inside they huddled beside the warm stove. The YMCA secretary served them tea and a bun. "Where did you come from and where are you going?"

He jerked to attention when Claire mentioned Oswald Chambers. "Here's his book on Job: *Baffled to Fight Better*," he said. "I've used it with discouraged soldiers."

Jock paged through it. "Did you know he'd written a book, Claire?"

"He and Biddy edited and prepared it for printing last spring." She read over his shoulder. "The only book he ever wrote. We'll find one and cherish it."

As they waited for a taxi to the train station and on to Paris, the fog lifted and a line of sleet came down. "Tell me again why we left Egypt?" Jock grumbled.

"To see the Americans."

"Doughboys. Spotted any?"

She shook her head at first and then laughed. "A secret landing spot is up the coast. That's what the Frenchman said."

Jock grunted. "You understood more than you thought you did."

"Maybe."

The weather moderated as they traveled inland. The Paris outskirts began with humble dwellings huddled along the railroad tracks, which changed to stone houses growing winter vegetables in walled gardens. Soon apartment buildings with iron railings grew tall and Claire glimpsed the enormous Eiffel Tower. The train roared like a dragon into Gare Saint-Lazare and she pinched herself.

The City of Lights, cloaked in blackout conditions, waited.

Her father called a cab in passable French and gave the woman driver directions to Rue Cler, not far from the imposing tower. A bulky middle-aged woman wearing a stained apron met them at the address, handed Jock a heavy key, and led them up narrow stairs. The syndicate provided a compact apartment for them with Madame François, board included.

"A far cry from Shepheard's Hotel, but we may not spend much time here." Jock opened and closed the doors to both bedrooms. "Which do you prefer?"

"I'll take the smaller one, since we expect Mama."

Jock knocked his pipe. "Do we?"

Claire froze. "What don't I know?"

"Sarah's taking her to lung specialists in London. We didn't want to risk misunderstanding health information by bringing her to France."

"What?" Claire dropped into the shabby leather chair beside the window. "How could you let me leave my mother?"

"Sarah's taking charge. I need you here. We'll be out in the countryside, on the move. The baby will keep her occupied, which is better than sitting alone in a cold Paris flat."

She tugged off her glasses and rubbed her eyes. "I cannot lose my mother. It's too much."

"Then you'd better pray."

Jock answered a knock. "The trunks. Excellent. We'll unpack and be on our way."

They walked several blocks to the syndicate office near Les Invalides hospital, a center for French veteran affairs. Two American reporters shared the BNS offices with them. An interpreter smoked thin cigarettes in the corner and a chic matron, Madame Ouellette, managed their business and answered the telephone.

"You may draw funds as needed from the American Express Office not far from Gare Saint-Lazare," Madame Ouellette said. "I can arrange a motorcar for you. Do you need a driver? Mr. Hull and Mr. Jackson drive themselves as needed."

The Meachams shook hands with the two Americans. Mark Hull and Alf Jackson would contribute to both the Boston syndicate and the *Stars and Stripes* newspaper, slated to begin publication February 8.

"We've plenty to do," Mark explained. "We'll pool resources using our ideas, along with wire information sent from home. We've a connection in the *Stars and Stripes* office on Rue Sainte Anne. The paper's designed to keep the doughboys informed and entertained. Our syndicate is one of several to provide stories from America."

"How old are you, Miss Meacham?" Alf Jackson asked.

"My name's Claire and I'm nearly twenty-four. You?"

"Twenty-five. Mark's the old man at thirty." He blanched. "Begging your pardon, sir."

Jock pulled out his pipe. "I'm conscious it's becoming a young man's war."

"What's your beat, Claire?" Mark asked. "What've you done before?"

"I assisted my father in Egypt. I covered obituaries, women's stories, religious issues, and war events when possible. I attended an interview with T. E. Lawrence."

Alf Jackson coughed. "Did you make it to Jerusalem with him?" He elbowed Mark.

"No. We left Egypt before Allenby took the city. I haven't seen Major Lawrence in months. Last I heard, he roamed the desert in Arab mufti."

Alf was intrigued. "He wore an Arab headdress?"

"Yes, and robes. He likes to blend in. How much time do you spend in Paris proper?" Claire's heart raced, but if she let these men patronize her, the job would be impossible. "If you're writing a paper for the troops, are you censored?"

Jock leaned on a filing cabinet and puffed his pipe, amused.

"Most of our stories are for the BNS. We hope we can travel to the front lines, but since we're not in the army, they may stop us. The new army paper may give us more access."

"Any contacts at the YMCA?" Claire asked.

Jock laughed.

"No. Why?" Mark asked.

Claire smiled. "They get around too."

They spent the morning discussing their jobs, how to divvy up assignments, where the best restaurants could be found, and what Claire should focus on the first week in Paris. She agreed to investigate the local YMCA headquarters for useful information for soldiers on leave in the city. She'd attend a French press conference with her father and report on English-speaking church services.

She had a copy of *Baedeker's Paris and Its Environs* in her satchel and knew she'd be able to get around.

The American reporters sat up in surprised respect when she demonstrated her shorthand proficiency. "Can you take dictation in French?" Mark Hull asked.

"I've done it. We'll see how I manage with the locals."

Jock chuckled as they walked to a French army briefing. "You did beautifully, darling. Those two men were eating out of your hand. I'm not sure how much time we'll spend with them."

"Why?"

"The American army has shifted its headquarters further south, closer to the front line at Chaumont. The wily General Pershing lives out of a railroad car. The question is if we should spend time there or hang around here with the French." Jock rubbed his neck. "I'm glad Peter taught you how to drive those last Newport summers."

She stopped in surprise while he walked ahead.

Jock reversed his steps. "Didn't you learn how to drive?"

"Yes, but I haven't driven an automobile since before the war."

"Come now, Claire. Once you learn you never forget, right?"

She went blank. "I don't know."

He shrugged. "Maybe it won't make a difference."

Chapter Thirty-Eight

February 1918

"Did you write any significant obituaries in Egypt?" Mark Hull asked Claire one February morning. "I checked the records and didn't see your byline on anything."

"I wrote about Oswald Chambers's death last November."

Mark shuffled through the newspapers on his desk. "Here's the byline: Jock Meacham, Egypt correspondent."

Claire seized the paper and scanned the story. Her face grew hot with rising bitterness as she read her grief-fueled words. He'd had no right to steal her story.

"Chambers was well known and many readers wrote to the paper." Mark raised his eyebrows.

"I wrote it. I don't know why my father's name is on it."

She removed the cover from her typewriter, determined to hammer out the minor story about ration coupons for the troops in Paris and hygiene issues with the influenza season.

Madame Ouellette set three letters on the desk beside Claire. Jim's didn't surprise her, she'd heard from him already. Rather than stay at a desk job in Paris, headquarters sent him on the road driving a YMCA canteen truck to isolated stretches of the front line. He'd volunteered for the dangerous duty, which he claimed involved boiling water for tea and making coffee.

She sighed at his description of bumping over rutted roads and trying not to spill the truck's contents while he ducked errant artillery.

Claire examined the envelope for more information. How close to the front had the YMCA sent him?

"I should be in Paris soon and I'll stop in to see you."

She shook her head. Jim was still a man of mystery.

The second letter came from a New Zealand encampment in the Somme River Valley.

Claire set it aside. Ire with her father seethed; she'd never be able to read Nigel's letter without overreacting in some way. She dashed away tears of frustration.

While she debated what to do, Jock bustled in demanding her for dictation. Claire gathered her materials and closed the door when she entered his office.

He blew on his hands to warm them. "Paris may be beautiful in the spring, but it's freezing today. What's up?"

"I'm here at your service."

"Why are you sulking?"

"Mark found my Oswald Chambers obituary. Why is your name on the byline?"

He plummeted into his chair.

"You told me things would be different in France. Does the BNS know about me? Am I on their payroll or are you still paying my wages?"

Jock sighed.

"I quit, Mr. Meacham," Claire declared. "I'll go to London and live with my mother and find a real job. I refuse to be treated like a child."

"They needed a story—"

"Stop. I don't want to hear this. You have no excuse." Claire slammed the door behind her, stuffed the notebook and mail into her bag, tugged on the knit hat and coat, and stormed out of the office. Mark called after her, but she ran down the steps without answering.

She stalked across the street and down the crushed gravel path through the Invalides parkland toward the Seine River. The gray sky glowered overhead, clouds gathering as if they would pounce, and a thin cold wind whistled past the tall stone buildings.

Claire marched without thought, stomping and sobbing. She'd been proud, had done her best, knew she wrote well—and her father had stolen her material.

Too harsh, her mind argued. He didn't steal anything.

Oh, yes he did, her emotions spat.

She slumped onto a park bench and rubbed the tears off her cheeks, her hands freezing in the February weather. She tucked them into her pockets. Snow would fall soon. Papa would be frantic.

Claire bolted upright. Let him be afraid.

She found an open tearoom and ordered a pot of tea and what passed for bread and butter these days. Sloughing off her coat, she pulled out her pocket Bible and read sixteen psalms before her emotions calmed down enough she could think.

She refused to consider her father.

She'd read her mail instead.

Claire tugged Nigel's frayed letter left with Aunt Sarah in December from her Bible to reread his words before she opened the newest mail.

Dear Claire:

I thought of you so often as we sailed to Europe, remembering your kindness to me, and how you only wanted the best. With orders into the trenches sobering a man, I remembered the moments of historical glories we discussed and how much faith you had in me and my ability to do well.

You meant a lot to me, and the hole of not having you in my life feels more profound here in London. I walk the streets recalling every conversation, every turn of your head, every wrinkle of your brow as you thought through an argument, an answer, a story. You have been a gift to me and it was only when you weren't mine anymore I recognized how precious you are, and how you tried to care for me.

I'm frightened, Claire. When you get to France you'll understand. I appreciated your prayers in the past, and I'll need them in the future. I think about what you've said of God and wish I shared your faith. I have a little Bible here, a gift from the YMCA. Sometimes I open it and think of you.

Please know how much your friendship has meant to me, and I will always love you.

Nigel

She didn't open the letter often, but when she saw it in her Bible, she thought of him and spoke a prayer for his safety.

Claire slit the new envelope with her butter knife:

Claire:

I've two days leave in early March. I'd like to call on you. I'll come to the newspaper office. It will be amusing once more to see where the news is reported.

Nigel

Apprehension and hope swelled, along with a shameful pride that he wanted to see her and not Sylvia. Of course she'd see him.

Unless she rejoined her mother in London.

What would she do now she'd quit her job? Maybe she should get a job at the YMCA and stay in Paris? She didn't need to drive a canteen truck like Jim; headquarters needed her stenography skills if nothing more.

"Yes," she whispered.

Claire poured hot tea into her cup and nestled in the chair as she unfolded the final letter. Across the top, the elaborate stationery read: "Y.M.C.A. For God, For King, and For Country." An engraving of two palm trees, a cannon, and pyramids was centered beneath, making Claire long for the warm sunshine and friendship of Egypt.

Instead, she read *Dear Claire,* and a paragraph of shorthand in Biddy's neat penmanship.

Two full pages of encouragement, stories, insight, and wisdom from a wise woman who must have stolen time to write. Claire's joy grew from deep within; her lips stretched to a smile full to bursting and she sighed.

She needed Biddy.

Kathleen flourishes and has yet another new kitten. She asks about her father from time to time, but seems to accept the reality he "went to another place," and she will see him in due time. She encourages me greatly with her childlike faith.

I end with these words of Oswald's for you, my dear one: "If I put my trust in human beings first, I will end in despairing of everyone; I will become bitter, because I have insisted on man being what no man ever can be—absolutely right. Never trust anything but the grace of God in yourself or in anyone else."

I send you greetings from Eva and Mary Riley as well.

Lovingly,

Biddy

Claire slid the onion skin letter into its envelope. Biddy lived far away and yet she saw Claire's heart. OC died, and yet his words continued to minister.

Jim's challenge echoed: "Do you trust him?

Had God had sent her to Paris for his purposes at this time?

She nodded.

Did it matter who received the glory in writing a newspaper article?

Who on the planet needed her more than Jock?

Well, maybe Nigel.

Claire's pocket New Testament opened to her favorite section: Romans 12. She reviewed advice from the apostle Paul on how to live peaceably with her father.

She rubbed her cheek and recognized the truth. She needed to apply herself to the tasks God called her to do, whether her father respected them or not.

Chapter Thirty-Nine

March 1918

The Tuileries Garden beds were orderly and weeded on that March morning. Claire loved seeing the crocus, daffodils, tulips, and hyacinths of her childhood. Europe looked so colorful compared to Egypt, her eyes ached. Colder, too, but aesthetically far more refreshing.

To the south loomed the magnificent Louvre, one of the largest buildings in the world. The three-sided former palace faced north to the gardens, where she sat wrapped in her coat watching passersby. When she spied a man wearing a YMCA uniform headed in her direction, Claire straightened her beret and waved.

"What a wonderful surprise." Jim took her hands. "Are you French yet?"

"What do you mean?"

"I like this French tradition of greeting each other with kisses on both cheeks."

"I'm not that French," Claire said.

"Neither am I. Let's shake hands like Americans. Shall we speak English?"

Claire laughed. "We are speaking English."

"*Tres bien.* I've gotten so accustomed to switching back and forth I can't tell the difference anymore."

He looked terrific. Tired, but so much healthier than in Egypt. He seemed taller, more assured. She couldn't articulate the difference, but while war had broken down most men over the last three and a half years, Jim acted freer and more confident. Intriguing, really.

"I'm so happy to see you."

He gazed deep into her eyes. "What's happened? I'll walk with you. Tell me."

"All the way home? What were you doing?"

"Nothing as important as walking you home."

They strolled through the Tuileries as she described her disappointment with her father, her letter from Biddy, and her ultimatum. "I went to YMCA headquarters and asked for a job, but by the time I arrived at the apartment, Papa had wired Boston and convinced the BNS to pay a bond for me as his assistant. They hired me as a stringer."

"What's a stringer?"

"I'm paid by the story. Now I have a bona fide role and if he won't buy a story, I can appeal to Boston." She displayed the dark green armband with the red C marking her as a correspondent.

"If being a stringer doesn't pan out, try the Y. They've a paper like the *Stars and Stripes*, called *Trench and Camp*. The soldiers love both."

"I've been contributing to the *Stars and Stripes*. They like my female point of view."

"I've enjoyed your articles; unique voices always interest me."

They reached the Place de la Concorde where Claire directed him toward the Seine. Jim stopped instead and revolved: the Champs-Élysees straight as an arrow to the Arc de Triomphe; the Tuileries and Louvre to the south. He chuckled. "It's hard to imagine a guy from Cincinnati is in such a beautiful place."

"Will they have trouble keeping you down on the farm, now that you've seen Paree?"

He sobered. "I'll never return to the farm. But I should send a postcard home. They'll never believe where I've been."

"You never speak of your family. Are you from a farm?"

Jim considered her, a searching scrutiny. She waited.

"No."

"No, your family doesn't live on a farm?"

"Exactly. Let's cross the bridge."

They watched barges plying the river. Claire pointed to the two towers of Notre-Dame. "My father tipped the janitor and we climbed up to pay our respects to the gargoyles. It reminded me of *The Hunchback of Notre-Dame*."

"Which you probably read in French," Jim chuckled. "I loved *The Three Musketeers* as a kid; we brandished swords for months after reading it."

"You meaning you and a friend, or you and a sibling?"

He grinned. "Yes."

She pushed his arm. "Have you seen some of the historic locations here in Paris?"

"General Pershing recommends soldiers use our resources while on leave, so the YMCA sponsors motor tours of Paris and walking tours through the Latin Quarter. They're trying to keep the men out of the brothels, for good reason." He glanced at his wristwatch and held out his elbow. Claire linked hers and they continued along the river. She shivered when a gust of wind blew and leaned closer.

Jim patted her arm.

"Alf Jackson told me American soldiers ask him why he isn't in uniform. Has it happened to you?"

"Who is Alf Jackson?"

"An American reporter."

"Is he a close friend?"

"He and Mark Hull are reporters with us at the BNS office."

Jim shrugged. "Most times I ignore the remarks. I'm here to honor Jesus, not myself, in the YMCA work. On days I feel defensive I mention Gallipoli. Soldiers whistle and usually change the subject. Of course I then need to confess the sin of pride."

Claire understood, too well.

Boys in school uniforms ran through the park and several women pushed perambulators. A man dressed in rags rummaged through a rubbish bin, and several officers in overcoats hailed a taxi. Rain threatened.

"Listen, Claire, you need to know I met Nigel. He's nervy, the way men get before they snap. He wasn't congenial like he used to be. War would affect him that way, of course, and the trenches are the closest place to a stinking hell I've ever seen, including Gallipoli."

"I've been praying for him." Her words sounded feeble.

"Good. He hopes to come to Paris on leave. I've been praying for him and for you. Rumor has it the Germans will launch a big push as soon as the weather improves. They want to move before the American army enters the war. Paris, of course, is their goal."

"I hope I'm here when he comes. We leave tomorrow to interview the American commanders in Chaumont before they get too busy."

Jim peered at the sky. "I need to return to the YMCA. I'm in town to pick up supplies and have the truck's engine checked. I leave at daybreak tomorrow for the front."

Her stomach turned over. "How close to the front?"

"Close enough to see the poppies." He touched her cheek, his finger warm against her skin. "Maybe I'll bring you a posy when I come back."

Claire held his hand against her cheek. "Please don't take a risk. I don't need flowers."

His lips smiled, but not his eyes. "Not even to make a memory? God bless you. *Au revoir.*" Jim kissed her hand and walked off.

Claire watched after him through tears. "Please, watch over him, Lord."

Poppies, of course, flourished on fresh battlefields.

Jock and Claire traveled by train to American Expedition Force Headquarters in Chaumont, one hundred forty miles southeast of Paris and near the American lines.

"We should have come last month," Jock said. "I don't mind being here if the battle begins, but I'd hate to put you in danger."

Claire set aside the March 8 edition of the *Stars and Stripes* containing a short overview of Parisian history with her byline. "I can handle it."

They'd arranged meetings with American officials and would spend three days in the area, hunting stories and information shareable with American newspapers. General Pershing, whom Jock knew in the past, maintained tight control of military information and press interaction. "Black Jack may not talk to us, but it's worth a shot."

They left their gear, which included Claire's portable typewriter, at an inn not far from the train station. Dressed in his belted trench coat, Jock flagged a taxi driven by an elderly man and directed him to the French barracks taken over by the American Expeditionary Forces.

"*I am new on the job, Monsieur Officer, sir, but I will take you where you want to go. The AEF?*" the taxi driver replied in French.

Jock nudged Claire. "Ask him his profession."

He was a farmer, waiting for his fields to dry in hopes of planting. He did not know American women were in the military.

"Tell him to take us to the front."

"What?"

"If he's an innocent, we may get a chance to see something. Offer francs if he balks."

The man shuddered at the request and requested an extra thirty francs, which Claire handed over. He made the sign of the cross and drove down the cobblestoned street, heading east into the countryside.

Jock studied Claire's map. "Lorraine, Burgundy, Champagne, this must be wine country." The rolling hills showed signs of spring: yellow mustard between rows of pruned vines. According to the contour map, the land sloped to the Rhine River one hundred fifty miles away.

The driver muttered at the potholed and mushy country road.

"I don't like this," Claire said. "Where are we going?"

"We need to find action. You can't stay tied to a desk and imagine you'll find anything newsworthy. This is the reporter's life. Always observing." His hand shook.

"Are you okay?"

"Pay attention to the scenery. We're hunting information."

The ancient cab lurched from side to side like a raft in a swollen river. Flocks of sheep and the occasional cow appeared in the mucky fields smelling of rich soil. They saw no one, military or civilian. The only sound was the car's sputtering engine on the still day.

Far to the east, however, Claire spotted a line of smoke in the sky. She tapped the taxi driver on the shoulder. A squeal of brakes and he hauled the wheel to the right. The taxi came to a standstill, and Claire climbed out.

The dozen planes flew far enough away, Claire couldn't make out their markings but they appeared evenly matched in numbers. They soared through the sky in a twirling, evading motion, their engines revving with a buzz while staccato machine guns spit bullets.

Before her, a dozen orange and golden butterflies rose in a cloud of delicate wings from a hedgerow. Cows mooed, and a hare raced past. The air didn't move and tranquility reigned at her feet, but in the distance, death and destruction roared.

She couldn't help but think of Peter.

Jock leaned against the car beside her, mesmerized by the dogfight.

"They act like demented dragonflies, battering their wings through the sky." He reached for his pipe.

The driver shouted at them. A white spurt and one of the planes spun out of control, black smoke fouling the air as the plane plowed into the ground. They both flinched. Claire tasted bile.

But the aeronautics didn't let up and two planes bore down on a slower one barely skimming the field. The *rat-a-tat-tat* sounded closer as the planes dove for the kill. As the prey smashed into the ground, Claire screamed. Jock's hand fell heavy on her shoulder and then he pushed away, storming out into the field.

Claire pursued him. "Please, Papa."

Jock pawed at his eyes. "He insisted on flying, even though I warned him not to. He was headstrong and wanted to be a hero. This is where it led, to death in France."

"They got him to hospital in London," Claire cried. "Aunt Sarah and Sylvia saw him. He knew about her baby. He didn't want to die."

"But he's still dead. Just like the others. All these wasted deaths. They pile too high." He gasped.

She leaned against his shoulder, weeping, and Jock reached for her.

"Why would God allow this?"

Scoured and brittle, she clung to her father. "I don't know."

To the east, the biplanes buzzed in circles around the crashed plane. A machine gun burst was shot into the wreckage, sending up black and red flames. Claire closed her eyes against the sight until she realized the engines were growing louder. Then she opened them wide.

A plane broke off from circling and turned in their direction.

The driver's anguish finally translated into Claire's ear. "He says we need to leave."

Still watching the planes, Jock threw his pipe to the ground. "Get into the car. Is there no one else on this ridge?"

The driver gunned his ancient car engine and swung the wheel. The car rocked in the mud and the plane's thunder deafened as it sped closer. "*Se dépêcher!* Hurry!"

Jock pushed her down to the floorboards. "It'll be a fine thing if we're killed by one of our own."

The earsplitting buzz filled the air. The car banged back and forth, hitting deep ruts in the road. The driver slumped low over the wheel and muttered prayers as he pressed on the gas.

Around them, fields spread wide open, but ahead a copse afforded hope.

The driver swore and prayed, and still the plane zoomed closer. The car bumped and sped, swerved and hopped. Claire closed her eyes to pray.

Rat-a-tat-tat, rat-a-tat-tat. Jock covered her with his heavy body. The car skidded yet again. The driver downshifted with a groan and—*foosh*—a roar squeezed Claire's mind and body.

The biplane swept low over them. The motorcar's pounding reverberated in her body. She smelled her father's fear and tasted blood. Claire knew only one thing: she didn't want to die on a lonely French country road.

The sunlight darkened, the car spun to a stop, and the plane's angry engine swung away. Jock sat up and Claire lifted her head. The driver sobbed in the front seat, while above them a crow scolded from a tree branch. The biplane climbed above the small wooded area. The air filled with the smell of fuel.

"Your coat is black. He probably didn't see you against the car. He must have thought I was an officer and aimed at my trench coat."

"Don't ever do that to me again," Claire shrieked.

Jock's voice and hands trembled as he groped in his empty pocket. "I won't. The best reporters are the ones that live to tell the story."

Chapter Forty

Mid-March 1918

Claire pulled herself up the stone office steps. Interviewing Russian émigrés exhausted her. They complained in perfect French recounting what they'd abandoned, how little they'd escaped with, and didn't she admire their jewelry?

Jock had no patience, but insisted she try. "One day you'll get a Romanov and the world will be thrilled."

"Do you mean Mama?"

"It's the same thing."

The Russians sophisticates were too polite to say anything, but she saw in their faces distaste at Claire's dress (her reporter uniform: simple black mid-calf skirt and a white shirtwaist), hair (a loose chignon), hat (round crown) and old leather bag (serviceable and soft with plenty of room). She told herself she didn't care, but remembering the glory of her entrance at Shepheard's Hotel provoked nostalgia. At twenty-four, she felt worn out and unattractive. Black clothing suited her mood.

Claire opened the door to find Madame Ouellette shouting into the black stick phone. When the woman saw Claire, she hung it up and exclaimed in French about the arrival of "the young god."

Maybe Claire wasn't hearing correctly after the Russian accents.

"*Voilà*!" The secretary pointed to Claire's desk.

And there he relaxed behind her typewriter, a cigarette between his lips, feet on the desk, and a grin on his face.

"Nigel?"

He swung his legs down and rose to hug her. "Nellie Bly in the flesh! Did you get the story?"

"I did."

Jock came out of his office smoking his new pipe. He waved his hand. "Unless you got something newsworthy, we don't need the Russians today. You can write it tomorrow."

"Can you come?" Nigel asked.

"Yes. Where?"

"I dropped by the YMCA and picked up tickets to see the Sweetheart of the AEF. Care to go with me tonight?"

Claire unbuttoned her coat to examine her clothing. "I'm not well dressed."

"You look gorgeous to me."

Claire noticed Alf and Mark were trying to ignore the medaled officer in their midst. Nigel's vigor and pressed uniform, polished boots, and rakish cap were a reprimand to their wrinkled dark suits and pale faces. Madame Ouellette beamed.

Nigel's uniform smelled of danger and stirred Jock's enthusiasm; she could sense it repressed behind his smoke. "Did you want to join us, Papa?'

All four men went still. Claire knew the thrill of feminine power for the first time. Was this how Sylvia silenced a room?

Jock coughed. "Not tonight. Please get her home by midnight, Nigel."

Like that, they were off in a cab. Bewildered by how fast events moved—calculated, as usual by Nigel—Claire needed facts. "When did you arrive?"

"Early today. I found a room with a bathtub, sent out my uniform to be cleaned, ate a decent meal, and took a nap. I'm a real man again, not an animal."

"How's your unit? What is the Somme like?"

"I refuse to discuss the war."

Claire blew out her cheeks. What should she talk about then? The weather? "Have you seen much of Paris?"

"Just out the window of the train and the taxi. When we crossed the Seine, I spied Notre-Dame on that island."

"Are you here for long?"

"Three days."

They dined at a café serving thick soup and little else. They discussed European history, Paris sites, and their respective voyages to France. Claire's stomach twisted as she filled it with soup. What did he want from her?

Charming, witty, even a bit provocative, Nigel acted "nervy" in Jim's apt description, but also haunted. Efforts to get him to talk of his experiences were staunched by his open hand. "No war."

After three attempts to deepen the conversation, Claire narrowed her eyes. "What are your thoughts on the spiritual life now you've been at the front?"

He threw a handful of francs on the table. "Curtain time. Let's get decent seats."

Soldiers were queued up outside the YMCA theater off the Champs-Élysees, but Nigel stepped to the front of the line. He sheltered Claire against the crush when the doors opened and hurried her to a box seat. "Elsie Janis," he explained, "has been selling out the theaters in London. She arrived in France last week."

Most of the men in the crowd were eager Americans, stomping and clapping as they waited. When the lights lowered, they hushed. A petite woman spotlighted in white entered the stage and shouted, "Are we downhearted?"

The nearly-all male audience roared, "No!"

The band struck the first note and Elsie Janis swung into "When Yankee Doodle Learns to Parlez Vous Francais."

Nigel stood and cheered, his eyes shining, his throat hoarse. "Brava!"

While not a homesick soldier, Claire understood. Magic.

Three hours later, Claire pushed open the apartment door.

"How was your evening?" Jock swirled the amber liquid in the short glass.

She noted the brandy bottle within reach. "Pleasant. Elsie Janis put on quite a show. The men were appreciative. And you?"

"I had a letter from your mother today and I've been thinking about her. Once I was a strong young man ready to take on the world for the love of a beautiful woman. I can scarcely reckon how many years have passed since I claimed her as mine. Has Nigel done the same?" He sipped.

She'd kissed the captain good night at the street door, but retreated at his hunger.

"The Russians can wait another day. I'm exploring Paris tomorrow with Nigel. He wants to see the Eiffel Tower and Notre-Dame. He plans to wear mufti to blend in with normal people."

"He loves you, he loves you not?"

Claire hung up her coat. "Have you been plucking daisies? What's the answer?"

"Do you love him?"

She stacked the newspapers. "I loved the man I met in London. The vivid enthusiast who wanted to change people's lives, the idealist who adored his homeland and wanted only the best." She sank into the chair opposite. "That man doesn't exist anymore."

"War does that to men ... and to women."

"I've prayed for him daily since I last saw him, Papa. I ask God to lift the gloom shrouding him, the blinders that don't allow him to consider God has a purpose for his life he can't see. I tried to talk to him tonight, and he shut me down."

"Of course he did." Jock finished his drink. "God can't be an answer to a man who faces death day and night on the front line. He lives with the reality of bomb craters and poison gas; thinking about heaven could get him killed."

She sighed. "He watches the sky during the day because it's the only visage other than collapsing trenches. To poke your head up, even wearing a helmet, exposes you to snipers. I can't imagine living with fear gnawing at you every second and in one minor error, a breach of curiosity protocol, you could be dead."

"Why don't you get the other glass and drink a brandy with me?"

"My mind needs to be clear when I see him in the morning."

Jock contemplated the bottle. "You can't solve what ails him, darling. This is who he is now and who he will be in the future. If he can last until Christmas, he can return to New Zealand and put this behind him, but the war will never go away."

She rose to straighten her father's overshoes beside the door, then fluffed the faded pillows on the couch and refolded the blanket. Claire righted the tilted lampshade. "Will the war always haunt us?"

"My father never recovered from Gettysburg."

She bit her thumbnail. "But he redeemed his life and made the best of it."

"He moved to Boston after the war, made a family life, and produced a newspaper. But the war haunted him. Remember his agitation during the fiftieth anniversary of Gettysburg? He had a life before the Civil War. Nigel doesn't know what he wants."

"Or where he wants to be," Claire said. "He's as rootless as the Flying Dutchman and now flitting away from substance. Maybe tomorrow I can pin him down to honesty."

Jock got up and set his glass and bottle on the square table where they ate meals. He kissed her on the forehead. "He can take care of himself. Guard your heart."

They admired the Eiffel Tower shut away from tourists and imagined the radio waves it sent throughout the world. A BNS story wired to Boston might have sailed above her head in dots and dash clicks even as she craned her neck at the structure.

Nigel grinned. "Fair dinkum, it's a marvelous world. Technology is king and should be used for good."

"Machines have advanced in the last four years."

His face fell. "We've become adept at killing more efficiently. What would it be like to fall from such a height?"

"I'm glad I won't find out."

A ragged laugh. "At least that way you could control your end instead of waiting for a stranger's bullet to hit you."

Claire cleared her throat. "Why don't we talk about what's bothering you?"

"I don't want to. Let's go to church." They took the metro to Notre-Dame and walked the aisles between services. The glorious stained-glass windows had been removed and stored at the beginning of the war, and the light filtered through temporary glass with a yellow tint. "Not as grand as I expected, though I love the flying buttresses."

They sheltered in a tiny bistro late in the afternoon, flushed from the cold and hungry.

"I study maps all day. Tell me what you've been reading." Nigel rubbed her hands between his, trying to warm them both.

"After *The Three Musketeers,* I finished *Madame Bovary,* both in French."

Nigel nodded. "Excellent, a book about love."

"More like lust," Claire said. "I didn't care for it. I finally received a copy of OC's book *Baffled to Fight Better.* I can hear OC's voice when I read it, and it helps." She choked up.

"You loved him."

"All of them. I miss Oswald and Biddy, but I have notebooks filled with lecture notes. I review his teachings if I start feeling lost." She inspected the ceiling, hoping to keep the tears in place. "I pick out a quote and send it to Jim when I write him. It helps me, and him, to remember."

"Hodges. You're always interested in Hodges or Chambers or anyone but me. Where is the do-gooder now?"

His face red from the cold, Nigel withdrew his hands and leaned back in his chair, his eyes challenging her.

Claire considered her words, wondering how much she owed him and why the conversation kept veering off at cross-purposes. As a Christian, she needed to love him as herself, so Claire tried to imagine what she'd want to hear or do if she'd left behind the mud of northeastern France for three days in the capital city.

He snapped his fingers in front of her face. "Where did you go, Claire? You're off in your dream world again."

"I don't know where Jim is. I remember you often, Nigel. I worry for you, pray for you, wonder how this war is affecting you. I'm helpless to balance the horrors you've experienced. I wonder how you'll be changed when it's over."

"I won't survive." He swirled the tea in his cup. "I'll die in a miserable trench wondering about the futility of heroics. Homer and Xenophon were crazy to write of the glories of war. There's nothing heroic in the Somme; it's do your best and wonder if you'll survive a general's stupidity. I have no hope."

"But where there's life, there's hope. You can't give up because it's grim."

"Claire the plucky poppy stands up despite the slaughter all around her. The little red flowers flourish in the sunshine and remind us tomorrow will be another day."

"The poppy flourishes after the seeds lie dormant for years," Claire said. "It's when events churn the soil around them they germinate. What does the poppy teach? A glimpse of the future, life goes on, beauty can survive ugliness, and hope exists in the world. I defy your cynicism."

He crossed his arms. "You've become a philosopher. I attended Oxford with mates who wrote exquisite poetry glorifying death. I reject them. No glory can come from a twisted body machine-gunned to bits and left to rot in pieces on barbed wire. You do not know, Claire, and your pretty words cannot gild an ugly, horrible act of a god you believe is loving."

"This war doesn't come from God."

"Then why doesn't he end it?"

"It's the result of free will and men choosing to be evil."

He lit a cigarette. "Tell me then, why do I need to be the sausage in other men's free-will grinder?"

"I don't know," she whispered. "I don't know."

"I sit in the trench staring at the sky and curse a God who leaves me to die like an animal, like a mole, a sightless, bald creature whose only purpose in living is to aerate the earth and eat worms. That is my destiny, and I wonder why I studied civilization's great literature. Why I listened to music that moved me, why I sought the love of a woman who spurned my fears and fed me Bible stories. I meditate on nothing beautiful, because everything leads to death."

She clutched her fingers together and willed herself not to cry. "But where there is life, there is love and the hope of comfort."

"Why don't you come back to my hotel with me, Claire, and I will show you a thing or two about love and comfort."

Claire's jaw dropped.

He held out his hand in invitation.

Chapter Forty-One

April 1918

April in Paris brought flowering trees and sweet spring air. French housewives opened windows and swept out the debris of a war's winter. Birds trilled their love songs, inspiring the hushed sighs of lovers.

April in Paris for Claire brought only regret.

The German's big spring offense hurtled at the Allied forces. Nigel's unit in the Somme Valley fought a ferocious onslaught as the German army made a final thrust toward Paris and the end of the war. A savage gun rained artillery casings onto Paris, blowing up the Tuileries rose garden and destroying a church during Good Friday services.

"This is bad." Jock read the wire bulletins at the window. "They're urging families to flee south to the countryside. The German army is within seventy-five miles of Paris. A two or three day march and they're here."

"I didn't say good-bye," Claire whispered.

Jock shook her. "Use your head, Claire. Nigel's not mooning over you in the trenches. He must be losing men left and right. You need to focus your mind on what's coming. You must separate your private emotions from your job."

She nodded. "I know. Germans are coming. What do you want me to do?"

"Join your mother in London?"

She dropped her bag on the desk. "Why?"

"If you're not paying attention to your job, you're a liability to me and I need to send you away to safety. Are you reporting or reacting?"

She retrieved her notebook.

"Go down to the park and interview the mothers. Find out why they're staying or why they're going and how they react to the bombing. Be back in an hour."

Claire found half a dozen women to chat with and most were resolute they'd stay in their homes. They were soldiers' wives, proud of their country but exhausted by the war.

A defiant woman with ruddy cheeks and black eyes gave her the best quote: "My husband writes we are safe in Paris; the men will fight to the end to preserve us. I am not worried. I am a resolute Frenchwoman. France will stand."

Claire wrote the words down in French, but as she closed her notebook her mind wandered away again.

Why had she slapped him?

She'd stormed out of the restaurant, self-righteous and indignant, done with the man. But what did it mean to lay down her life for a friend? Should she have prayed and thought of another way to reach Nigel in his misery?

It gnawed at her he returned to the front with her stinging rejection.

She remembered the Bible passage telling people not to worry when they appeared before a judge, God would provide the words needed. Claire had prayed for wisdom before spending the day with Nigel. She'd asked God to fill her mouth with his words.

If her prayers resulted in this end, could she be satisfied their discussion had been part of God's will?

Claire sighed; she had to believe it, but she wished her last sight had not been his shocked face after the slap. She wished they'd parted in peace.

An explosion to the east, another shell.

She prayed Nigel would come through his battle whole. It was the least God could do, now Claire had botched the chance to send him to the lines confident and secure in God's love.

The bombardment continued through April with no set pattern, though as many as two-dozen large shells hit each day. People went about their business with relative calm, until reports came the Germans were advancing on Amiens, a major rail center near the Somme.

The battles raged fast and furious until the Germans arrived in Albert on their way to Amiens and tarried to loot stores of clothing and food.

"Curious," Jock said as he discussed the situation with Claire. "We've heard rumors food is in short supply in Germany. Maybe the Bosch are running out of steam. The pressure on Pershing must be huge for the Americans to start fighting."

Claire saw American troops daily, particularly at the YMCA events. They stood out on the streets: tall, healthy men in new uniforms with energy in their steps. Young Frenchwomen pursued them down the street *ooh la-laaing.* General Pershing's command arranged for dances and other entertainments to include American women hostesses. The general thought female volunteers providing a wholesome evening were a "good tonic for the homesick American soldier."

They welcomed Claire.

Jim spent the last two weeks of April in Paris getting briefed and preparing for a new role along the western front once the Americans went into action. "I'll be running supplies to huts near the front lines," he said. "It will be mobile, but without much support. Headquarters handpicked me for the job."

"Because of Egypt or did you volunteer?" Claire asked. "Are you healthy enough?"

"You remember OC said God doesn't give us strength for tomorrow, he gives us strength when we need it. God will use my weaknesses to display his strength and I'll be fine."

He remained thin but his face had more color and the malaria symptoms were gone. Claire saw him at Sunday services and in the evenings at the cinema run by the YMCA. They'd enjoyed movies starring Mary Pickford, Charlie Chaplain, Fatty Arbuckle, and Buster Keaton.

One night Claire scanned the soldier audience and wondered how many would survive the battles coming on the western front. In the face of their youth and vigor, she felt ancient. Claire sighed. Would the killing never end?

"Hey, Claire, could you rewrite this for me? We need to edit official information for the *Stars and Stripes* using words soldiers can understand."

She read through the press release Alf Jackson handed her and snickered. "Why can't a staff member do this?"

"They talk in multiple syllables," Alf said. "Soldiers like it plain."

She cranked a sheet of paper into her typewriter.

"Use slang if you know it. That's the best way to make a soldier read the article."

Claire laughed and set to work.

"Claire?"

She looked up. Jim stood in front of her desk, his face white and his eyes worried. Jock stepped out of his office.

She lifted her hands from the keyboard. "What's happened?"

He exchanged glances with Jock. "I have bad news."

The shaking began in a stilted tiny way from her core. It traveled to her shoulders and she gasped, but it made no difference. Claire clutched her midriff. She didn't want to hear, but she gave a curt nod.

"Nigel was killed last week. They buried him with others from his unit at the Somme."

Her ears buzzed and her vision went fuzzy. She struggled to take in the information. Jock said to concentrate on facts and not let emotions take control. Her mind raced through the five Ws and quit on "how?"

"He took a bad hit to the gut while trying to save one of his men." Jock spoke softly.

"How do you know?"

"I called your father to tell him," Jim said. "The Red Cross sent the message to Nigel's family, but he'd made arrangements for his possessions to be delivered to me at the YMCA if anything happened to him in France. One of my colleagues brought in his kit this morning."

"Why you?"

"He trusted me to pass them on to the people he cared for."

Cared. Jim spoke in the past tense. Nigel's wit, insight, and love were gone, buried in a muddy grave probably being trampled by German soldiers as they spoke. Those long legs would never be propped on a desk, his resonant voice would never read aloud, those lips would not kiss. He'd never fling the typewriter carriage in triumph and type another story.

A thousand years older, heavy and broken, Claire marshalled her thoughts. "Where is his kit?"

Jim knelt beside her. "It's here. I didn't open it. I brought it because you needed to know. Maybe he left an item for you."

The typewriters stopped. Madame Ouellette muttered in French from the doorway.

"You don't need to do this, darling," Jock said. "Jim and I will go through Nigel's things. We'll give you anything pertinent."

"I want to see what the Germans destroyed. We'll open it together."

Jim carried in the khaki canvas bag with *Nigel Bentley-Smith* stenciled in white paint and then retrieved a leather trunk. He untied the rope and slid the bag's contents onto the office table. Jock and Claire gathered around, while Mark Hull, Madame Ouellette, and Alf Jackson stood a respectful distance away.

Binoculars in a leather case, mess tin, wire cutters, a tin mug—paraphernalia necessary for a man living on the go. Blanket, pay book, knife, waterproof cape, extra clothing, a tunic. His shaving kit, towel and soap, flint and a metal canteen. Claire sniffed the bar of soap. It didn't remind her of Nigel. Nothing meant anything to Claire.

The man came alive in the trunk. A black-and-white photo of Claire taken in London rested on top of a folded officer's trench coat. Books, papers, a half-burnt candle, tea and biscuits, had been stowed in the trunk. At the bottom they found a packet of Claire's letters and newspaper clippings tied with a faded red ribbon. Claire pulled out a stained YMCA pocket Bible from the corner.

She handed it to Jim.

"No one knows the state of a man's heart, beloved, except God. Let him be the judge."

Claire picked up Nigel's tunic with the shiny brass buttons. She rubbed her face on the wool and cried.

Chapter Forty-Two

May 1918

Anne arrived three days after they learned of Nigel's death.

Thin, with new lines on her face and her fair hair now completely white, she stood tall and turned loving, yet fierce, eyes on her child.

"The trouble is you never had sufficient time to mourn Oswald's loss, Peter's grave and now Nigel's death. I'm not surprised you're upset and depressed. God knows we've been through difficult times and it will get worse before the war ends."

Claire clung to her mother. "Maybe so, but what now? Do I wear black?" She gestured to her skirt. "I already wear black. My losses are no different than millions of women."

"Why not write to his mother?" Anne finally suggested. "Think how much a letter from you would mean. Emphasize his positive characteristics and what you loved about him. Don't tell her you broke it off with him. Let her think you loved her son all the way to his death."

"I did love him."

"Then you can write honestly, can't you?"

Claire didn't know. Everything about her life seemed untethered. She wasn't sure what was important and what didn't matter. She had failed Nigel in the most important thing: understanding how dearly he was loved by God.

"Papa said writing is the best way to deal with grief."

"For a writer that's true. If we ever return to Boston"—Anne paused to correct her word—"*when* we return to Boston, we'll open a trunk in the attic stuffed with your father's writing. I learned how deeply John and Phillip's deaths affected him only by reading those words. He couldn't speak them, but he could write about his love and his grief. Don't discount the power of the written word to provide consolation."

Claire pulled out her handkerchief to polish her glasses. "He wrote it down?"

"Yes—which is why he never speaks of their loss. As far as he's concerned, he poured out his emotions on paper, and thus the mourning was complete."

Anne carried the used teacups to the sink. "I don't agree with him, of course."

Claire savored the sounds of her mother in their apartment. Anne would organize. She would take care of them. Claire removed the cover from her typewriter. Mrs. Bentley-Smith deserved a letter.

While Claire typed, Anne muttered. "Really, Madame François is terribly overworked. I can take care of my family now." She cleaned the apartment, chided Claire and Jock for the state of the bathroom, purchased food, and brought in flowers. "Biddy was right, as always: flowers cheer up the room."

Against her heartwarming chatter, Claire typed a lengthy remembrance to Nigel's mother.

Jock watched from the doorway as she finished her project. "Does this mean you're ready to return to the office?"

"Tomorrow." Even as she signed her name to the bottom of the letter, Claire's hands shook. Reviewing the past reminded Claire of Nigel's spiritual state. The grief of missed opportunities gnawed.

Jock pulled Anne to him. "What will you do without us?"

"I'll teach French at the YMCA."

Jock tipped his hat. "That's my girl."

The American army began arriving in France in enormous numbers. Claire and her father were on hand to greet several shiploads near Le Havre in mid-May.

Marching down the gangplank singing "Yankee Doodle Dandy," they resembled gods coming ashore. Hale, hearty, and disciplined, their arms swung in unison. They toted packs and carried guns across their shoulders. Focused and determined, they marched to the railroad station and traveled to training areas southeast of Paris.

"I haven't seen such robust men since the war broke out," Jock said.

Claire admired their sturdy shined boots. "Maybe they only send the healthy ones."

"I wonder." Jock rubbed his chin. "Let's wait around. Maybe the sick ones come ashore at night."

His reporter instincts were sound. A ship arrived late in the afternoon, but no one disembarked. Military personnel came and went while Jock and Claire waited near the pier in the shadows of a brick building. As the moon rose, ambulances arrived. Jock wandered over with questions.

"Who are you?" asked a driver.

"An American from Boston. It's a proud sight to see the doughboys march onto French soil. How come this bunch didn't march to the train?" He checked his watch. "Will they catch the next one?"

"Not on your life. This is the sick boat. Influenza's on board; half the soldiers died. The rest won't be mustering any time soon."

Claire retrieved her notebook.

"What are you doing, miss?"

"I"—Claire faltered at Jock's scowl—"need to write a note."

The thin man ran his tongue around the inside of his cheeks, studying Jock and Claire. He shouted for the military police.

An hour later a bright light shone in their faces as they sat in a tiny room before an American colonel. "John Patrick Meacham," he read from Jock's identification papers. "Claire Anne Meacham. Both with the Boston Newspaper Syndicate. How do I know these papers weren't forged?"

"You're holding our passports and our pink press cards. We're wearing our reporter armbands." Jock leaned back in the chair.

Claire clutched her hands and stared at the floor.

"Miss Meacham," the colonel asked, "what were you doing on the pier tonight?"

Claire raised her chin. "We're covering the doughboys' arrival. We watched several boatloads arrive and were seeking quotes."

"At night?"

"We'd noticed a ship docked but no troops disembarked. We wondered why, so we walked over to observe." She kept her voice level and tried to sound bored.

"And you learned?"

She answered without blinking. "The ambulance driver said the soldiers were ill, which is why they stayed on the ship."

He examined her passport. "I see you've been in France a couple months. What were you doing in Cairo?"

"The paper sent us. We were in London before."

Jock stepped on her toe.

"London, Cairo, Paris. Have you been to Berlin?"

"No."

He compared the photo to her face. "What is your mother's maiden name?"

"Powell. She's from Newport, Rhode Island. We're not spies, sir."

"There's a fine line between asking questions to write a news story and spying. Can you prove you're a reporter, other than these fine cards?"

"Wire the syndicate; they'll endorse me," Jock said.

Claire cleared her throat. "I wrote an article this week for the *Stars and Stripes,* page two."

The colonel motioned to a staff member. "Get me a newspaper."

"May I smoke?" Jock asked.

"No."

When the paper arrived, Claire pointed out the article.

"Spiritual opportunities in Paris," the colonel read. "You've listed religious services, Bible studies, and a course on biblical psychology based on the teachings of the late Reverend Oswald Chambers. Do you attend any of these?"

"Of course." Jock thumped the arm of his chair. "We're good church-going people."

"I attend services at the YMCA on Sunday mornings. I also take the biblical psychology class. I studied under Oswald Chambers in London and Egypt."

The colonel inspected her with interest. "I heard him speak years ago in Cincinnati. I remember his remark about the importance of being broken bread and poured out wine. A likely motto for a disciple of Jesus Christ."

Claire nodded. "Particularly in war. Oswald wore himself out serving the soldiers in Egypt."

The colonel shuffled their papers and handed them back. "I trust anyone taught by Oswald Chambers is honest. You can go if you'll give me your word you won't mention sickness. If the Germans learned of it, more men could die." He stood.

Jock and Claire stood as well.

"The military police officer outside will take you to the Paris train. Don't come back to Le Havre."

They boarded a train with dimmed lights, filled with American soldiers singing popular tunes: "It's a Long Way to Tipperary," "Over There," and "Pack Up Your Troubles in Your Old Kit Bag."

So innocent, Claire thought, listening to the jaunty music. The Americans expected a different war altogether.

Claire leaned her head against the window and watched the dark landscape. The full moon shone over isolated farm houses, planted fields, and denuded ponds. The moonlight touched the countryside with a magic she knew it lacked. Flashes in the eastern sky indicated a battle raged. The windows rattled periodically.

She rubbed her forehead. While he lived, she could go days without thinking of Nigel except when she read his name on her prayer list. Now with his death, her mind circled, asking the eternal question: why?

But why should Nigel have been spared when so many died? She clenched her fists. If she knew she'd see him in heaven, she wouldn't keep replaying her guilty words.

Guilt. She and OC had discussed guilt once. True guilt caused repentance from an act or decision. Assuming responsibility for negative behavior she could not control caused false guilt.

God alone knew the state of Nigel's heart. Claire needed to leave her regrets with God. She could not be faulted for Nigel's death.

Jock brought sandwiches. "You know, darling, you didn't need to be so forthcoming with the colonel."

"You wanted me to lie?"

"There's a difference between lying and not telling more than necessary. You should have answered his specific questions with yes and no."

Claire lost her appetite. "If I had not suggested he find my article, we might be sitting in jail on spying charges. You prefer jail?"

"Something new to write about," Jock said. "They wouldn't have kept us for long."

"You're incorrigible." She faced the window.

"Excuse me, ma'am, but is this gentleman bothering you?"

Claire peered at the doughboy sitting in the seat ahead of her.

"Where are you from, soldier?" Jock asked.

"I'm talking to the lady, here."

With a voice not quite deep enough, the teenage soldier's uniform hung from bony broad shoulders. Claire put humor in her words. "He's bothering me, but he's my father. Thank you for asking. Tell me, where's home?"

"San Pedro, California."

"You've come a long way," Jock said. "Can we interview you about your travels?"

"I'd like to hear them, too," Claire said.

Her father didn't need to tell her. She found her notebook and wrote in the moonlight.

Chapter Forty-Three

June 1918

Claire went through the motions at work. She asked her questions and wrote up the answers in perfunctory stories.

Jock didn't like it. "Where's the fire? We need more than these wooden stories of little consequence. You must be engaged, not passive. You need to ask questions and prod, not accept whatever the flunkies tell you." He tossed the copy to her. "Not good enough."

Claire rubbed her neck. Her writing wasn't good enough. She wasn't good enough. She failed her job, her father, and Nigel. Her words, indeed, had failed.

"Claire?"

She picked up the rejected story. "I'll rewrite it."

"Would it help if you traveled to the Somme and spoke to his unit? Maybe the nurses at the clearing station?"

Her eyebrows rose. "Go to the front? How?"

"I saw Jim yesterday. He's taking supplies to Nigel's unit for the YMCA tomorrow and will take us if you want to go."

"In what capacity? Only pool reporters can go to the front lines."

"He'll get permission for us to ride along for a story on the hardships the YMCA encounters trying to serve soldiers on the front line. Not a bad idea: Pershing loves the YMCA and likes it when they get good press. Folks at home want to hear someone cares about the soldiers."

"They're not Americans in the Somme."

Jock shrugged. "The YMCA is the YMCA. It will do. Are you game?"

She wondered if they might find someone who remembered Nigel. "If we can do it through official sanctions, I'll go."

"Excellent." Her father smiled. "Did you notice your questions? You were hunting answers. Maybe you just need the right story."

They rendezvoused with Jim early the next morning at Gare du Nord and boarded the train to Amiens. They'd meet a YMCA secretary at the station, offload the supplies Jim brought, and drive to the Somme River Valley near Albert, recently regained from the Germans.

"Do you usually work so close to the front lines?" Claire asked once they settled into the truck. The three shared the bench seat with Claire in the middle. Jock helped start the Ford Model T using the crank on the front grille.

Jim put the truck in gear. "Yes."

They traveled through an ancient town filled with rubble. Blocks of brick buildings had broken into pieces and fallen into the street. The Germans had fired artillery in an effort to vanquish Albert two months before and destroyed two thousand buildings. Storefronts had no windows left; tidy fires on corners kept the few remaining people warm. They bumped over fractured roadbeds in the truck. Pedestrians waved. "It's the YMCA triangle," Jim explained.

The city streets soon gave way to countryside lying fallow. Few trees remained; farmhouses were gutted or burned. As the road deteriorated, traffic slowed.

Claire clutched her fluttering stomach as they jounced over rough country roads through a landscape churned and demolished by artillery. Color gave way to gray as the land changed from fertile to desecrated. Leafless, splintered trees remained from battles. Abandoned equipment littered the fields, including trucks sunk to the running boards in dried mud.

In four years of war, Claire had never been so close to a battlefield. Here she could smell the stink of oil, gun powder, cordite, and despair. No wonder Nigel insisted on forgetting the war while in Paris. No wonder he'd feared the Somme.

She sniffed.

"What are you thinking about, darling?" Jock asked.

"The mistakes I made with Nigel."

"He made his own choices. You need to quit brooding."

"You have a lot in common with Oswald, Papa. He said self-pity is the worst sin because it disregards God and puts our self-interest first."

He grunted.

Jim drove silently, watching the road and gesturing to people he saw along the way. At a crossroad, the majority of trucks veered east, closer to the lines. They diverted left down a narrower road.

Biplanes circled overhead. "They know we're on their side today," Jock said.

Claire still didn't like seeing them so close.

Mortar fire and minor explosions pummeled countryside far away; on either side of the dusty road bits of white pocked the rich black soil. "Chalk," Jim said. "Like the cliffs of Dover on the other side of the channel. When you see a field littered with chalk, you know it's been a battlefield. The bullets churn it up through the soil. Patches of poppies mark the fields too."

Clumps of red poppies were the only splashes of cheer. The countryside reeked of utilitarian army and death. The smell worsened and a sweet rotting odor mixed with the rest, including human waste. Claire wrinkled her nose and reached for her handkerchief. Jock lit his pipe.

Eventually they reached a level spot filled with soldiers, trucks, and canvas. A Red Cross flag flew on top of a series of tents marking the casualty clearing station. Jim parked the truck.

"Most action takes place at night, so the daytime tends to be quiet. I'd start at the nursing station and then ask to speak with the commanding officer. He can answer questions or direct you to people who knew Nigel."

"Where can we find you?"

"I'll be hauling boxes to the hut." He pointed to a sandbagged tent displaying the YMCA triangle near where a duckboard ramp disappeared into the ground. "The trench maze begins right there."

"One more thing." He reached behind the seat and handed them each binocular-case sized boxes with a loop to fit around their neck. "Wear these just in case."

Claire held the gas mask and tried to squelch the dread. "How does it work?"

He showed her how the top flapped open and a headpiece attached to a white tube fit over her face. Her glasses crimped inside the face mask and she couldn't see.

"If you've time, you should remove your spectacles."

"How will I know if there's an attack?"

"Smell, people shouting. A whistle. If it happens, put on the mask and run. Don't hide in a trench, gas is heavier than air and sinks. It probably won't happen, but you never know."

While he stuffed the mask in its case, two large black rats skittered down the ramp.

Claire shuddered. No wonder the fastidious Nigel hated the trenches.

"At least the gas kills the rats. Don't worry. Artillery fire comes at night. We'll be gone by then."

Jock took her arm. "Let's start with the matron at the casualty station."

Gaunt and tired, the matron listened to their request. "Most of my sisters sleep during the day and I will not awaken them for questions from the family." She checked a ledger and her watch. "Shifts change in thirty minutes. If Jo Little is available, I'll send her to you."

"I don't know if I can do this," Claire whispered to Jock as they waited outside the tent.

"Ignore your emotions and go into reporter mode. Get your facts, write them down, and process them later. It's the only way."

A strong woman from Yorkshire, Jo Little spoke with a thick accent. She remembered Captain Bentley-Smith. "Aye, 'twas a bad one. They brought him up from the trenches with wounds to the abdomen."

She placed her hand in the appropriate spot. "He'd gone to rescue a mate before dawn. The poor boy lay on the edge of a crater. Captain Smith found him shot in the head, but alert. He dragged the boy to the trench and had just handed him down when he got pipped."

"Did he suffer?" Claire asked.

The woman's eyes flicked to Claire's face. "He were on the front line. The trenches zigzag, which make 'em awkward to carry a stretcher through, particularly with a man as brawny as Captain Smith. They brought 'im here quick, maybe thirty minutes, but the wound gaped. The doctor operated immediately. He'd lost a lot of blood."

She looked away. "They patched him well enough, and he woke. But the fever set in within a day and then he died."

"Did he say anything?"

"Ooh, they all ask that question. He had them gorgeous blue eyes, I remember, and he asked about his mate, if the soldier survived. I told him yes. He needed to know his sacrifice was not in vain, whether true or not."

"He thought of another person over himself." Claire hugged the idea to her heart. "That's what I wanted to know."

"I cannot say he thought of you, miss, but I remember his concern for his men. He died in the night. Sepsis. He's buried with the other New Zealanders down in Caterpillar Valley."

The commanding officer didn't know much else. "I put the information we had into the letter home. Did you receive the letter?"

"It went to his parents," Claire said.

"What are you doing here so close to the lines?" he growled.

Jock pulled out his card. "Press. We're writing about the YMCA on the front lines and we caught a ride with a supply truck."

He scowled at Jock. "The YMCA is vitally necessary to give the men a place to go when they're in the rear positions."

"How far to no-man's land?" Jock asked.

"Not far enough."

They conducted a full interview with Claire taking down the answers and Jock asking the questions. While polite, the CO made it clear he didn't like having Claire and Jock in his camp.

"Mind if I ask soldiers their opinion?" Jock asked.

The CO drilled his fingers. "Stick to YMCA questions and it will be sufficient. I'll send one of my men with you."

Jock acknowledged the swipe. "Can we walk down the trenches?"

"Why?"

"My colleague lost her fiancé here, as you know. Could she see his dugout?"

The commanding officer scrutinized her. "You want to see the hole in the ground where Captain Smith lived?"

She knew what Jock wanted her to say. Claire raised her chin. "Yes."

He checked the clock. "The trenches are no place for a lady. Meacham can go. May I suggest a cup of tea in our YMCA hut?"

Claire whispered. "Thank you."

Chapter Forty-Four

June 1918

"You've never been a good liar," Jock muttered as they exited the CO's office.

She wanted nothing more than a cup of tea. "Most parents appreciate honest children."

"Not in my business."

"I must be honest, Papa. If that means I'm not a reporter, then I'll be another kind of writer, or I'll write for an editor who values honesty. I've suffered too much in my spiritual life by skirting the truth. Go wherever you want. I'll wait for you with my tea in the YMCA hut. Jim must be around." She checked the sky. "But it's getting late. We need to be on our way soon."

He rubbed his chin. "It's unsettling knowing the front line is only a mile away. I'll run down, check it out and be right back."

"Do you want my notebook?"

He tapped his temple. "I'll store the quotes up here."

In the nearly empty canvas hut a soldier hunched over a letter. Claire poured a cup of tea and crept into a dark corner as far from him as possible. She wanted to think, so she turned away from the soldier.

The plywood door creaked opened. "Hey, mate," she heard Jim say, followed by a thud as he dropped a box.

The soldier muttered a reply. Jim's voice changed. "Tell me."

As the soldier mumbled his story, he broke into tears.

Claire dithered. If she moved, she'd draw attention to herself and humiliate the man. To listen was unconscionable. So she prayed.

"Listen, mate," Jim said. "It's no shame to be afraid. It would be crazy if you weren't. We're stuck in a war not of our choosing and we can't get out until it's done. If the worst happens, what will become of you?"

"I'm worm food already, sir."

"You're not worm food, you're a man made in the image of God and you're valuable to him. Do you believe?"

"Aye."

"Then you probably know Jesus's words about God's love for you. God sent his son to die on your behalf so you can live with him forever. No one comes to the Father but through Jesus. All who call upon his name will have life abundant. Do you believe?"

"Aye."

"It doesn't make going over the top any easier, but it does mean if you go over the top and don't return, you have a place in heaven with God. That's the assurance I can give you, soldier. Is it enough?"

The man didn't answer immediately, as if mulling the question. Claire scarcely heard the muffled response.

"Aye."

"God loves you, mate. Go with God."

"Thank you, sir." Claire heard him gather his things and leave the hut.

It was simple, Claire thought. If you believed Jesus died for your sins, you have a place in heaven. Nigel knew the teaching. She didn't know he didn't believe the simple truth. Maybe he was in heaven. It had nothing to do with her, it was between Nigel and God. The burden she carried in her soul lifted.

But then she heard another sound.

Jim wept.

An artillery shell whistled and struck, shaking the ground and tent. Claire gasped.

Jim jumped up, saw her, and shouted. "Get into the trench. The Jerries must be breaking through."

She ran after him out the door and down the ramp into the trench, along with others. They ran deep into the earth, the walls rising above their heads.

"If you see a stray helmet, grab it," Jim yelled. He pulled her along until they came to a soldier bleeding on the step. "Get into that dugout. You should be safe."

He stooped to examine the man. An ear-shattering rush flew overhead and he ducked. Two soldiers running along the pathway covered their heads. Clumps of dirt fell on their metal helmets.

"Didn't they see the red cross?" one shouted.

The other screamed an expletive at the Huns and they ran deeper into the trench.

Ten feet underground, Claire couldn't imagine the surface. The tents would be shredded by artillery shells. Where was her father? What would happen if the German army broke through the lines?

Claire retreated deeper into the dugout housing a cot, a table, and personal possessions. She tugged the blanket off the cot, put it over her head and curled up beneath the table.

She shut her eyes and listened to whistling and explosions. They were a mile from the front line. As she thought about her loved ones suffering through such an onslaught, Claire knew the answer to OC's question from the first sermon she heard. War must be from the devil. God would never torment his people like this.

She'd feared dying the entire war and now opportunity clamored, as easy as peering over the top of the trench. Claire clutched the blanket, trying to hide the noise, the light, and the smell of crumbling earth.

She remembered Jesus's words. "In my Father's house are many mansions; if it were not so, I would have told you. I go to prepare a place for you."

Did she believe it?

Biddy's confidence whispered: "I choose God."

Jim's question: "Do you trust him?"

She covered her ears to block the thunderous nightmare. She ached to the marrow of her bones, but Claire knew the answer: yes.

The stomach-curdling shaking eased. She took a deep breath. If she died, she died with Christ and would be in paradise—with OC if no one else.

The shelling ceased. A shrill whistle blew.

She poked her head out from beneath the blanket. An insect-like man peered into the dugout and she heard a muffled, "Claire?"

"Jim?"

"Put on your mask! It's gas!"

Chapter Forty-Five

Summer 1918

"Don't you ever take my daughter into danger again. Do you understand me?" Anne's fury over the incident at the Somme knew no boundaries. When they limped home after the nightmare at the front lines, Anne seethed and raised her hand as if to strike her husband.

"First-person stories are powerful," Jock said. "I've never been through anything like it."

"I don't care. When we return to Boston, Claire will be the social reporter for the *Boston Daily*. I obviously can't trust you to ensure she has a long and pleasurable life."

Claire stepped to the window, thankful to see flowers, blue sky, Rue Cler and no soldiers.

"We're in a war, Anne. I can't protect her from life."

She flung the dishtowel at him. "Don't start. We may be in a war, but you didn't need to take her to the front lines. You courted danger."

"No one expected an attack."

"Jim did. That's why he gave you gas masks. Thank God."

"We achieved the objective. Claire spoke to the nurse with Nigel when he died. She has peace of mind now. Don't you, Claire?"

"I'm glad to be alive."

She also was thankful to breath freely without a claustrophobic mask. Her mother placed a vase of fragrant stock beside the window. The sweet scent, her clean skin, and birds singing, however, couldn't overcome her horror of nearly being buried in the Somme's thick, chalky earth smelling of vile death.

Anne tilted up Claire's chin. "Really?"

Claire nodded. "I'll always be sorry Nigel died, but I don't feel guilty anymore. He died helping another soldier. Greater love hath no man than to lay down his life for a friend." Her voice trailed off.

"You nearly died," Anne whispered.

Claire shrugged, detached from herself, still so stunned by the artillery barrage. "God must have more he wants me to accomplish, stories to write, people to meet. My life hasn't been my own since the war started. Today I know it's simply on loan from God."

"Will you write about it?"

"I'll need a new diary to do the experience justice." She kissed her mother. "Don't be so hard on Papa. He was terrified too."

Anne crossed her arms and glared at her husband. "If you died, what would happen to me?"

Jock tried humor. "You've always looked breathtaking in black."

This time she did slap him on the shoulder as she stomped into her room and slammed the door.

As Americans streamed into France—ten thousand soldiers a day in June, July, and August—the war tempo changed. The marines won a shocking, grotesque battle in the Belleau Wood and fully inaugurated into the horrors of this war, those soldiers visiting Paris wandered in a daze.

"Pershing's disciplined them and they're a powerful unit. They're reporting signs of the Germans weakening as they throw everything at the Allies. Germany must be empty. They're finding dead schoolboys on the battlefield." Jock picked up his gear. "I'm going to poke around Chaumont for a couple days with Mark Hull."

"What am I doing?" Claire asked.

"The French army is having trouble. I want someone with better French than Jackson to attend their press meetings." He grinned. "They're susceptible to pretty women, too, so take your mother. She can translate if you run into trouble."

Claire waved him off gratefully. She'd willingly forgo news drama for a couple days.

"It's a beautiful day," Anne said. "Walk with me to the YMCA."

They donned straw hats on a sunny summer morning. Pockmarked with shell holes and broken tree limbs, the city bore heavy signs of war. Many Parisians suffered through shortages of food, but with the clouds parted and a happy breeze blowing, they saw children flying kites.

"The big push is on," Anne said, "but it's hard to imagine the Germans could still march in and take this city."

"When will we know if it's time to flee?" Claire asked. It seemed an impossible question.

"If a reporter doesn't know, how can you can expect me to know?" Anne laughed. "Let's make an arbitrary decision. If they get within ten kilometers, we'll flee."

"That's only six miles. I say we need a twenty kilometer head start."

"Twelve miles? But if they get too close, anarchy may befall the city." She sighed. "Let's change the subject. Biddy is doing well."

"Kathleen's had her fifth birthday now," Claire said. "What will they do if Germany wins the war?"

"Perhaps we should invite them to join us in Boston? Biddy worked in New York before she married Oswald. We could find her a job if she'd come."

"She'll be busy preparing OC's sermons for publication. Who knows how many filled notebooks she's got?"

"A woman as lovely as Biddy will have no end of suitors, she's not even thirty-five," Anne said. "Though it would be difficult to find a man as talented and intense as Oswald."

"She loved him so much and respected his vision. I doubt she'll marry again."

They'd reached the Seine and admired the sweeping view across the river. "I'm sorry you never saw it before the war," Anne said. "We loved strolling through the city with the Eiffel Tower lit at night and musicians on street corners. I look forward to the day Paris comes out to celebrate. We won't want to miss it."

They entered the bulky YMCA building and Anne greeted a dozen students in her classroom. Claire climbed the stairs to the office where she asked for Jim Hodges. The secretary sent her down the hall where she found him chatting with a pretty woman secretary.

"I planned to visit you today, but now you've spared me a trip." He rose from his chair.

"I beg your pardon. I didn't mean to interrupt."

"No problem. We're done praying. Let's sit outside in the sunshine on the balcony. I want to talk to you."

"Is she an American?" Claire straightened her skirt as she sat in a chair overlooking a postage stamp–sized garden.

"Crystal's a Hoosier from Terre Haute and we were swapping stories of home."

"I thought you were from Ohio."

"I knew her brother at Oberlin."

"Will you always be mysterious? Did you attend Oberlin College?"

His face tightened. "Yes."

"And?"

"I graduated from Oberlin."

"Any particular subject?" She couldn't keep the edge out of her voice. Why had he never talked about his life prior to the BTC?

"History and economics."

She twisted her face and glared. "You never said a word when Nigel and I debated world history."

A pigeon flew onto the ledge. One round eye watched, unblinking and unafraid.

"Beware little bird, you might get eaten," Jim said. "I enjoyed listening. Your conversations were enlightening."

"When my father and I were detained for being spies, I thought of you. You're a perfect 'man of suspicion.' "

He leaned on the railing. "I'm a YMCA secretary, not a spy, but I don't share anything people don't need to know. I protect confidentiality, particularly when I'm in a ministering position."

"You weren't ministering when you were a copyboy." Really, he was exasperating.

"No?" he grinned. "I took the job to serve. Anything else would have detracted from my purpose in working at the BNS."

She crossed her arms. "Was I a ministry target?"

He laughed. "I didn't have preconceived notions of my role at the newspaper. I took the one job that allowed me to take classes at the BTC. You, and your reaction to the word of God, were an unexpected and gladly received joy."

Claire flushed and, to her surprise, batted her eyelashes. At Jim?

She regained her professional composure. "What did you want to tell me?"

His twinkling eyes sobered. "I want to ask you to pray for me. I leave in the morning to man a hut at the front with the American Expeditionary Forces."

"Of course," she whispered, but her mind reeled. What if something happened to him? Who would remind her of OC's teachings? God forbid, what if he should die?

"Starting tomorrow, let's read the same psalm," Jim said. "We'll start with the first psalm and pick out an element to pray for each other. You can include the usual prayers for safety, but pray I'd hear God's call on my life. Pray I'd be led by him in my choices and in my words."

"Of course." Claire swallowed a sob. "I'll miss you."

He squeezed her hand. "You've no idea how much I'll miss you." He took a notebook from his pocket and scribbled out an address. "Write me in handwriting I can read. Keep sending me quotes from your Chambers notebooks. Tell me what you see in the psalms. I'll anticipate your letters."

She clutched his hand again and closed her eyes. "Dear God, please keep him safe. For me, if for no other reason."

"Amen," he whispered. He helped her up. "I need to pack. I'll see you soon."

Suddenly Claire needed to memorize his face, every feature, every inflection. Her lips parted as she considered how to hold him, to make him tarry. She stepped closer.

His face changed, his head tilted, and his voice went hoarse. "Claire?"

Claire threw her arms around him and hugged him tight, her heart ready to burst.

Jim stood ramrod straight. "You'll be fine," he whispered. "God walks with you, Claire. He always will. You can count on him."

And then he took her face in his hands and kissed her.

His sweet gentle kiss left a promise and took her breath away.

Chapter Forty-Six

September 1918

Jock placed the hamper into the rear seat. "Do you remember how to drive?"

"If I get scared, I'll give you the wheel." Claire checked the gas cans secured on the bumper.

He affixed the pass to the windscreen. "It's not anyone who can get an interview with the general. I'd hate for one of the sentries to shoot us by mistake."

Claire patted the red C on her armband. "We should be safe, but we're not supposed to go near danger, remember?"

"Your mother worries too much."

They climbed into the car and Claire started the engine, thankful it didn't require a crank on the warm day. They had a distance to travel.

General Pershing, an erect man with steely eyes and a precise moustache, met them in his train car office with a curt nod. When he finished signing papers, he stood, shook Jock's hand and admired Claire. "My word, Annie, you haven't aged."

Claire saw the wink. "I'm Annie's daughter, Claire."

"Annie and I raised ourselves a reporter," Jock boasted. "We've come to see if you'll give Claire a scoop. How about it?"

The general sobered. "I can't tell you anything other than our official statement: the soldiers are fighting hard, and we're confident we'll whip the Germans before Christmas."

Claire produced her notebook. "How can you be so confident?"

"We pushed them back at Soisson, though our casualties were high," Pershing said. "The Germans are on the run; they know it's only a matter of time."

"What's your take on the French line disintegrating?"

"I'm changing the question. While the American army will fight, it will not fight except as an independent American army. We trained together as units; we don't need to confuse the soldiers by mixing them with men from other countries, particularly countries speaking a different language."

She asked more questions about the battles the doughboys had fought and how they had prepared for trench warfare. Pershing answered in clipped, precise sentences.

"You travel in your own train," Claire said. "What's the advantage?"

"I can control my men and keep a clearer eye on events if I'm moving. When you see me at headquarters, you'll know the end is near."

"Any resemblance between warfare in France and what you saw in the Philippines?"

Jock startled. "Great question."

General Pershing paused, shutting his mouth. "More parties involved here," he finally said. "This is a more political job, balancing the needs of the different armies. I'm dealing with more people, more material. It's far more complicated."

Claire scribbled the answer then checked her prewritten questions. "You've ordered more than a million men into battle, ten times the size of the combined Union and Confederate armies fifty years ago. Do you ever reflect on the difference between your war and that of your West Point instructors?"

Both men stared at her. "Mine isn't over yet," the general finally said. He turned to Jock. "Where did this kid come from?"

"Radcliffe. She studied history and grew up hearing my father's stories about the Union army."

"What kind of article will you write, Miss Meacham?"

Claire folded her hands around the pencil. "I couldn't ask current operations questions lest the answers tip off the Germans, so I tried to devise questions you could answer."

"Ever thought of joining the army? We value thinkers like you." The general laughed.

Claire put on her mother's polite smile to dampen her irritation with his joke.

"One last question. My sources suggest you want to become president yourself, much like Grant after the Civil War. Any reaction?"

"You've raised a clever reporter, Jock," Pershing said. "I'm here to fight a war, Miss Meacham, and if I fail it will not be because I have a bug in my head about becoming the US president. My focus needs to be on finishing the war so my boys can go home. What happens in America in the future remains to be seen."

"Thank you, sir." Claire shut her notebook, stood, and extended her hand.

Pershing climbed to his feet and saluted. "I'll anticipate reading your article."

"Anything off the record we should know?" Jock asked.

The general straightened his uniform. "You've heard of the influenza concerns? A number of soldiers have died. I don't want to see any reporting. Troop strength is information we don't want the enemy to know."

They spent the night at an inn far from the front lines. Claire shared a room with two volunteer nurses staying in the village for a respite from their hospital lives. They didn't want to discuss the war but accepted Jock's invitation to dine.

"What's the most common injury you see these days?" Claire asked.

The question made them uneasy. "The usual," the darker and more senior woman said. "Bullet wounds, mustard gas, trench foot, dysentery. Lately we've seen influenza. We isolate them as soon as possible; it travels so quickly among the men."

"What's it like?" Jock sipped after dinner brandy.

"They come in achy and throwing up, typical influenza. But before you know it, patients get nosebleeds and their skin takes on a lavender color. We send them away from camp as quickly as possible."

"Where?" Claire wished she'd brought her notebook.

"To a convalescent hospital far behind the lines. You might inquire at the Chateau Duval up the road. They can tell you more." The curly-headed blonde reached for her glass of wine. "Any new films in Paris these days?"

"Charlie Chaplin's in one called *Soldier Arms*. It takes place in France. I saw it at the YMCA."

The dark woman cut up her potatoes. "Funny?"

"We laughed."

The nurse stared into her cup. "We appreciate a laugh these days."

They traveled northwest through the countryside the next morning, Jock giving directions from the map he'd procured the day before. When they reached a French chateau doubling as a hospital, he directed her to park. "I'll go in by myself and talk to the matron. Influenza can be dangerous, and I don't want you exposed."

"What about you?"

"I had it in 1889. I'll be fine."

"That was a long time ago, Papa."

"Stay here."

Claire reviewed her notes. The courtyard swarmed with activity. She watched ambulances drive up and orderlies carry their stretchers into the large building. Once emptied, the ambulances were driven behind the chateau for servicing. Tradesman arrived with food and nurses exited carrying basins of liquid to toss into a pit. Claire decided to take a walk.

They'd driven through fields around the estate busy with the late season harvest. A copse surrounded the chateau, giving it a detached serenity, even as Claire heard the report of distant artillery. After so many months, she didn't worry until whistling shells hurt her ear drums.

She followed two orderlies pushing a wheelbarrow and carrying shovels down a path through the trees and checked in surprise when the vista opened. She should have known.

Row upon row of graves spread before her. The orderlies deposited a white shroud into one of the long narrow holes already dug. A chaplain waited. Once they'd tossed dirt on top, the orderlies stripped off their hats and bent their heads as the padre read a short prayer from the service manual. One orderly hammered a wooden cross at the head of the grave. The chaplain checked the name and made a notation in a notebook. The orderlies grabbed the wheelbarrow and shovels to return to the chateau.

Claire slumped to the ground beneath an orange-leafed poplar tree, undone. She smelled the damp earth and shuddered at the morning chill. Nigel, Holly, and Edward were buried in humble graves like this one, in simple services without anyone standing by but the chaplain.

The orderlies tarried when they reached her. “You all right, miss?”

“His name?”

They shrugged. “Padre knows.”

“May I pay my respects?.”

They shrugged again. “Suit yourself.”

The haggard chaplain straightened when she drew near. “Are you a sister?”

“Reporter. I wondered if you’d tell me this soldier’s name.”

“Oscar Bailey, corporal, Royal Engineers. A sapper.”

Claire reached into her bag for her pocket New Testament. She removed the dried red poppy she’d saved from Jim’s last letter and dropped it on the grave. “How did he die?”

“Influenza. It’s sweeping the hospital. I’d avoid it if you can. It’s deadly.”

The chaplain held his handkerchief to his nose and paled.

Claire stepped away and whispered. “God bless you, Corporal Bailey.”

She trudged to the motorcar, praying for the family soon to receive a dreaded telegram.

Jock leaned against the hood, smoking his pipe and contemplating the building. “Did you get what you wanted?” Claire asked.

“They say more soldiers die from illness than battle wounds. You take young men who’ve seldom left their farms and you make them live in close proximity to others, disease is bound to spread. Measles killed a lot of men during the Civil War. This influenza is serious.”

Claire told him of the graves below the chateau.

Jock nodded. "Sobering. You should write it up. People will want to know."

"I'll need to interview you."

He nodded. "It will make an interesting story if we can get it past Black Jack's censors. For now, though, let's head up the road. I've seen you studying the map. Isn't Jim's YMCA canteen nearby?"

She nodded. After two months of exchanging letters, it would be reassuring to see him in the flesh.

Reassuring—that's what she told herself, but her heart pounded and she licked her lips.

Chapter Forty-Seven

September 1918

Five miles as the crow flies but a lot more difficult as the Model T traveled. Claire drove behind an ambulance crew headed to the front line where the drivers said a friendly Yank who liked to preach ran a popular YMCA canteen.

A line of ambulances came their way from the front, so Claire pulled off to the side. The Meachams ate sandwiches from the food basket and drank water from a large flask as they watched the vehicles pass. Jock filled the gas tank, nervous as the shadows lengthened.

Claire felt jittery too. "Should we go back? Or do you expect to sleep in the car tonight?"

He checked his watch. "We've come a long way; let's continue."

They drove into a dimly lit yard rancid with the scent of war as groups of soldiers tramped down the duckboards to their more forward trenches. They found the fortified YMCA hut and entered. Jim stood in front, his open Bible in hand. He acknowledged them, but continued his teaching. Claire searched the shoulder bag for her pocket New Testament and paged to the book of Ephesians.

"I'm going to find an officer to interview." Jock slipped out the door.

Jim described the armor of God and the need to prepare for the future, both physically and spiritually. The dozen soldiers murmured among themselves and several asked questions, which Jim answered without hesitation. At 5:55, he led them in prayer for safety and confidence in God's knowledge of each.

"Amen," Claire echoed.

She wandered the hut reading posters and messages stuck on the walls, supremely conscious of him, while Jim talked with individual men. By the time she'd toured the cramped hut, savoring the timbre of his voice, his questioners had left and a handful of men remained writing letters or reading.

"What a wonderful surprise," Jim said. "Are you French yet?"

She replied in French. "*What if I said yes?*"

He glanced around the room.

"Go ahead and kiss her, I'm not watching," growled the nearest letter writer.

A quick peck on both cheeks and they fell silent.

Jim cleared his throat. "Well, then. Tea? A woman from Paris sent me an excellent cake."

"You got it?"

"Yes. Pre-crumbled, so it's easy to eat."

She couldn't imagine what to say at this frivolity. Jim had never been so lighthearted before. She told him so.

He directed her to a table and poured the tea into enameled cups. The poor cake was in the same box, now battered, in which Claire had mailed it. He settled himself beside her and took her hand. "Let's pray."

"Thank you, Lord, for bringing Claire here tonight. Watch over us, keep us safe and be in my words. Amen."

They chatted while they nibbled cake and drank tea. He thanked her for the letters and described issues at camp.

"Many of the men are terrified. They know the end is near and they're afraid they'll be killed before it's over."

"General Pershing says it will be finished by Christmas."

"I pray he's correct."

More soldiers entered the hut, along with an officer. "I need to talk to you. Let me see if this officer will take charge and we can go outside." He listened a moment with head up. "Artillery sounds far enough away tonight."

Jim carried out stools and they sat a short distance from the YMCA tent and not far from the casualty station entrance. Claire buttoned up her jacket. "We're safe here?"

"We're several miles from the front. We'll be fine."

"Did you tell me that at the Somme?"

"No. I knew we were too close."

Dull light seeped from the nearby tents. Dimmed ambulance headlights periodically flashed in their direction, and the thin cusp of moon hung in the sky. It was a place for whispered confidences, albeit not solitary.

"What did you want to say?"

Jim leaned his elbows on his knees. "I've been meditating on Isaiah lately."

Claire smiled to herself. He spoke the prophet's name with an English accent.

"Several verses resonate in chapter 61, like 'the Lord has anointed me to preach good tiding to the poor.' " Jim took a breath, almost like a sigh. "Followed by 'they shall rebuild the old ruins, they shall raise up the former desolations, and they shall repair the ruined cities, the desolations of many generations.' "

"He could be describing 1918 France." Claire ran her hands up her forearms, shivering with a sudden chill. His intensity held her rapt as he continued.

"When I anticipate the future, Claire, I see a world beaten and destroyed by the arrogance of leaders who thought nothing of sending their people to slaughter. The pain and suffering I've witnessed could depress me, indeed it has, but I come to the God who put me here for purposes I can only guess at."

She nodded. "Why else have we been spared when so many died, including OC?"

"OC never cared about his life as an end to itself. He loved Biddy and Kathleen and the rest of us. He expected to teach about Jesus after the war. God must have a purpose in taking him when he did, though I doubt I'll ever know. We can't allow ourselves to despair over what is not. We must grab hold to what is and bless those around us with the good news."

Claire wanted to believe the killings they'd reported had been for a purpose, but they'd pockmarked her heart with holes of loss.

"You don't believe me?" He smoothed his rough hand over hers and squeezed, fingers entwined, comfortable and secure.

She sighed. "God gives purpose to our lives. But how do people survive a time where civilization has been destroyed? How do they live with themselves if they've killed people? Can they return home to love again when such blackness may hollow out the center of their souls?"

The YMCA hut door opened and light spilled in their direction.

Jim recoiled. He removed his hand and sat upright, his lips twisting.

His anguish frightened her. "What?"

He gazed toward the distant no-man's moonscape. Jim cleared his throat. From his hoarse words sprang a passion she'd never heard before.

"I hated Nigel taunting me for not fighting. It stirred up memories I've struggled to accept, forgive, and release. But he kept insisting I wasn't man enough to fight."

A spurt of light filled the horizon with a blinding dazzle. The rattle of machine-gun fire sputtered in the distance. A sharp cry and the moans of the wounded vied with clumping boots on duckboard headed to the relief station. Truly, this was hell on earth. "You sure we're safe?"

She sensed, rather than saw, his affirmation. "He knows the hairs on your head."

Yes, but the Germans wanted to see them too.

So they could kill her.

"Maybe we should move. It's time for me to find my father, anyway."

He grabbed her hands. "Don't go. I need to tell you what I did. It may change how you feel about me, and I need to know now, rather than worry anymore."

"What could you have done to change my opinion of you?" Claire asked.

"I killed my brother. Shot him dead between the eyes."

Another flare exploded, bathing the countryside with a reddish glow. For a brief moment, Claire saw Jim's tense face. Frozen to her leaden core, she remained silent, waiting.

He sighed. "We were duck hunting. Out in the marsh on a cool morning, we'd gotten wet and were tired and hungry. Timothy was a kid, just fifteen years old and beginning to shave, but he constantly razzed me about my faith. My mother adored her baby. The whole family thought me foolish for going to hear OC talk in Cincinnati and then taking his correspondence classes."

"Go on," she whispered.

"We were running late, in a hurry to get home for breakfast. He dawdled and taunted me. I told him to knock it off. He laughed. We were still arguing when we reached the Model T."

Two soldiers hurried by, carrying a young man between them. The guns strapped to their chest bobbed as they maneuvered the stretcher. The injured soldier cried out when they jostled him against the trench wall before climbing up the ramp. A nurse carrying a tiny torch met them, checked the soldier's wound, and directed them to a far tent. A Ford Model T ambulance arrived.

Even as she listened, Claire took it in.

"The engine got cold while we hunted," Jim continued. "One of us needed to crank it. Tim wanted to drive, but I told him to crank. I was joking when I aimed my shotgun and ordered him out of the car. He grumbled, climbed out, and reached for the crank handle."

"He complained and I balanced the gun through the steering wheel in jest, aiming at him. I knew better. I tell myself he knew it was a joke. He turned the crank, once, twice, three times and the car jumped forward. He looked up in surprise, I grabbed for the brake and the gun went off. He died with me begging God to spare him and take me instead."

Jim choked and wiped his eyes.

"It wasn't your fault," Claire said.

"I'd taught him gun safety. We both knew better. He died because of my carelessness. My mother—" He couldn't go on.

Two groups of orderlies left the casualty tent, carrying stretchers to the ambulance. They slid them into the canvas-roofed truck, one above the other. When they finished, the young woman driver climbed behind the wheel. An orderly spun the crank and the car took off with a jerk heading west to the closest field hospital.

"My mother couldn't forgive me. My whole family blamed me. When I thought of what to do, I remembered OC's teaching on forgiveness at God's Bible School in Cincinnati. When I earned enough money, I went to London to attend the BTC. You know the rest."

How many men had died senselessly in the last four years? How many soldiers had Jim counseled? Besides OC, Claire didn't know another person who worked so hard to help others.

"You're so encouraging and cheerful," Claire said. "Have you been trying to atone?"

He flinched. "I confessed the sin. I've never shied from what I did, but I left America to find a different way to live. OC knew what happened and reminded me if we confess our sins, God will forgive them. He absolved me when I couldn't forgive myself. But France has been a nightmare of seeing boys who resemble Tim. The soldier in the Somme hut could have been his twin. Off he went into the night and disappeared."

More flares.

"It's a bad night out here," Jim said. "Let's find your father."

She stopped him. "Why did you want me to know this, Jim?"

He rubbed her hand. "What will you do when the war ends?"

"If I survive?"

"One of us has to be the last man standing."

She scanned the clearing. The casualty station stood as a beacon of relative sanity amid the muddy gouged roads, nightmare trenches, and unending fighting. Exhausted men lay on the ground or hauled stretchers. Jock exited a tent and lit his pipe, a short officer still talking to him.

Claire hardly remembered a normal life of clean clothes, sidewalks, and carefree action.

She spoke slowly. "I sailed to Europe in 1914 in search of myself. I had an opportunity to work with my father, to spend time with him and learn a craft while I figured out my next step. I can't imagine returning to Boston with so much recovery needing to be done in Europe. Not only rebuilding, but helping the people understand forgiveness. They need the gospel here."

"So you'll stay?"

Jock laughed, glanced at the sky and shook the officer's hand.

"My father won't leave before he's done reporting. Maybe I'll stay to help." As she spoke the words aloud, she knew them to be true. She wanted to stay, to write, to help.

"How old are you now?"

"Twenty-four. I'm old enough to live without my parents. You don't need to remind me I can be my own person."

"Would you stay with me?"

The night hushed and Claire's heart pounded. Her lips parted and her face softened.

"You don't need to answer now. I've told you the truth about myself so you can make an informed decision. I've loved you a long time … but the war, Nigel, my past, all stood in the way. I still may not survive this war, but if I do and you're willing, I'd like you to stay in Europe to help rebuild with me. Would you consider marrying me?"

Claire nodded slowly, too dazed to speak at the first idea that made sense for her skills, heart, and soul. Deep inside, love unfolded pure and bright.

She leaned toward him, wanting to see him up close. His fingers cradled her face. Her heart pounded.

The kiss came tentative, but deepened to a satisfying hum of joy.

A headlight spun across the area, and they parted.

"I'll write," he whispered.

"Good, I found you in the dark," Jock said. His voice sharpened. "What's up? Claire?"

She brushed off her skirt mechanically, trying not to tremble, and tugged the bag onto her shoulder. She spoke slowly. "Did you get what you needed, Papa?"

Jock faced Jim. "Do I need to ask your intentions again?"

Jim laughed, free and easy. "Good. Always good. Claire will explain." He kissed her on the cheek and walked away.

"Well?"

She watched as Jim helped an orderly straighten a stretcher into an ambulance, and then ducked into the casualty tent without a backward glance.

Claire smiled at her father. "The future looks a lot more promising tonight."

She laughed at his raised eyebrow. Promising, indeed.

Chapter Forty-Eight

October 1918

Claire stopped by the Paris headquarters of the YMCA to ask about postwar plans.

"Do you know something I don't know?" asked the stout director, who recognized her. "It will take a while for soldiers to disband and return to their respective countries. They'll still need entertainment, they'll still need the canteens and we'll continue working with the Red Cross. Prisoners will need to be repatriated and it takes an internationally trusted group like the YMCA, Salvation Army, or the Red Cross to get the jobs done."

Claire anticipated the next question before he finished answering the first. "Do you anticipate having more job openings or fewer when the war ends?"

"Do you want a job?" he asked.

"Only if you need a reporter."

They talked for half an hour and when she walked down the steps, Claire knew the YMCA would welcome her skills and services if she wanted to join them. She caught the metro at the Saint Lazare train station to the BNS office on the other side of the river.

"He must go home," Madame Ouellette shouted when Claire entered.

Jock shivered. "I can't get warm. Must be a round of malaria."

"We left Egypt months ago, Papa. Let's take you home."

Madame Ouellette called a taxi and helped Claire get Jock down the stairs.

"My head, my ears, I ache all over," he moaned.

Fear kept Claire's mouth shut.

Anne met her at the apartment door. "Oh, no. Put him on the couch." She tossed a blanket over him and whirled to face Claire.

"Get into the bathtub and scrub with soap from head to foot. I'll put clothing in your valise. When you're dressed in fresh clothes, take my purse and go, go, go. Get a hotel room and don't come until I send for you. You must go."

"Mama!"

Anne glared at her. "You know this influenza kills the young. I cannot lose you. Go."

Fifteen minutes later a damp Claire stood on Rue Cler with her valise and her mother's purse. She gulped sobs as dusk fell. She'd never rented a hotel room by herself before. Something heavy banged in the purse; of course, Anne must have stuck in Jock's office key.

She'd need to collect her passport from her bag at the office, so Claire went there first.

Madame Ouellette had left already, so Claire used her father's key. She clicked on her desk lamp and scanned the empty office, the typewriters shrouded, the phone silent. A dust bunny eddied across the floor and caught on a desk leg.

Claire removed her spectacles and rubbed her eyes. Exhausted and confused, she yearned to lie down. She needed to act, but to do what?

A passage from the book of James came to mind: "If any of you lack wisdom, let him ask of God."

"Dear God, please show me where I should go. Be with Papa and Mama; heal him, keep her from getting ill and if it be thy will, keep me healthy too. In Jesus's name. Amen."

Madame Ouellette had left Claire's old battered satchel on the desk and Claire reached inside for her Bible.

She found Biddy's most recent letter and opened it.

Work at the compound continued; Mr. Jessop had taken over the printing of pamphlets based on OC's sermons. Eva and Gladys were engaged, ministry to soldiers continued.

When the war ends, Kathleen and I will return to England, thankful for a full ministry. Oswald is with me continually, in his words, in my memories. I've much to be thankful for.

Claire picked up the pamphlet based on OC's Sermon on the Mount series Biddy included in the envelope. "Blessed are those that mourn, for they shall be comforted."

"Can you comfort me, Lord, as I mourn?" Claire asked.

Nigel, Peter, OC himself.

In the empty room, she whispered her worst fear: "Papa."

She retrieved a packet of crackers and a pot of lukewarm tea left from the afternoon. She didn't need to rent a hotel room; she'd sleep on the old leather couch in Papa's office. Her coat would cover her and she'd use the old soft satchel as a pillow.

Claire opened the French doors onto the balcony off her father's office. She set her teacup on the tiny table and sat in secluded darkness.

Influenza usually killed in the first twenty-four hours. She'd know by morning.

The darkened Eiffel Tower loomed to the west and before her the City of Lights lay shrouded in wartime darkness. High above, Claire saw the first dim stars, the same stars that had beckoned to her in the Egyptian desert and reminded her of God's glory.

But also of his distance from earth. "But I know you're listening," she shouted. "I know you can do whatever you please—with me or them."

Claire squeezed her eyes shut. She didn't know what she'd do if Papa died, or if Mama became ill from nursing him. What if they both died?

Her greatest fear would be realized: everyone she loved dead and Claire left alone.

Weep with those who weep.

She knew whom to turn to. "How can you ask this of me, to take them all?"

Why keep the tears in? Claire fell to her knees and wailed.

"Is this what it means to be broken bread and poured out wine?" Claire shouted to God. "To lose everyone?"

Weariness weighed down; she was so tired of fighting death's despair. If only she could let go, release her soul and go to heaven—then the pain would end. Heaven was her anticipated goal anyway.

When she had sobbed herself to a whimper, a verse threaded through Claire's mind, in one ear and out the other, gentle, quiet, comforting: "Why art thou cast down, O my soul? Why art thou disquieted within me? Hope in God, for I shall yet praise him."

How often had Jim asked if she trusted God? How had Biddy found the courage to never doubt God or his word with OC's death?

"Do I believe my life is yours, Lord, to your glory?"

Claire nodded. She did.

And if her loved ones died? Would she still worship such a God?

Claire didn't want to consider the horror, but she needed to. Did she have any other choice than to submit her life to the God who already owned it?

"Then it will be for your purposes, Lord, that I will live. I don't know why you've spared me, but I believe you will show me the answer someday. No matter what happens, I'll write the stories so the world can hear the truth: that despite a great war gone mad to destruction, Jesus's death can redeem the life of any soul for eternity."

"Hope in God, for I will yet praise him," Claire whispered. She wasn't completely alone. Two remained: Biddy and Jim. They both loved her.

Exhausted, Claire brushed off her black skirt. She mopped her face with her handkerchief. She would trust God for whatever came.

Jock's office couch invited. Claire shut the doors and stepped to her desk for the makeshift pillow. She picked up her bag and stopped. A thin envelope lay beneath.

A telegram from the YMCA.

Claire slit it open and slumped. It could not be.

Tears overwhelmed again.

Only one remained for sure.

"They say Sleeping Beauty can be awakened with a kiss. Or is that Snow White?"

"Depends if you're a dwarf or not, Alf. Why don't we wake her up?"

Claire smelled strong tea and her stomach contracted. She didn't want to open her eyes on a new day where her worst fears could be confirmed. Better to stay asleep in a state of ignorance where her loved ones lived and she had a future.

Springs poked from the old couch and morning pried at her eyelashes. She sat up. "Any news?"

"We've always got news in this office," Mark said. "Madame Ouellette saw you sleeping and went for food. I take it you'll want breakfast?"

"My father?"

"Nothing. Did you spend the night here?"

Claire filled them in and the two reporters sympathized. "We'll find a place for you to sleep tonight; you don't need to stay on the couch."

She handed Mark the telegram. His eyes grew round. "I'll check on this."

Her heart as heavy as a pyramid, she could only whisper. "Please."

Madame Ouellette bustled in with bread and cheese. She brought a note from Anne: *Safely through the night, sick but holding his own. Stop by tomorrow: knock at the door and wait in the stairwell. Please pray. Mama.*

Claire touched the words while she tried to recall when her mother changed from antagonistic to God to open to him. It had been slow, motivated by grace, nurtured by Biddy. Claire prayed and then she wept in gratitude.

She spent the morning ignoring her emotions and typing up copy from the day before. She attended the daily press briefing with the French army. She organized her thoughts, wrote them up, and wired the story to Boston. She didn't inform the BNS of Jock's illness.

Madame Ouellette found her a room at a hotel around the corner. Claire knocked on the apartment door at nine o'clock the next morning.

A haggard Anne peeked out. "It's been difficult, but he'll survive. Terrible headache and chills, but he held down the broth I fed him last night."

"How about you, Mama?"

"Don't worry about me. Here's a list of items to purchase. Knock on the door and leave them. I'll send a message if we need anything else."

"I'll return tomorrow morning."

Anne closed the door.

And so it went all week. Claire signed the wires "Meacham," and the BNS sent her assignments. She covered the briefing for the Paris press corps, met with the American ambassador, and on a long day, traveled with Mark Hull to Chaumont to gather information on recent American army battles.

"Stealing my job?" Jock asked when Anne allowed her into the sickroom.

"Filling in for you. People hear Meacham and are surprised when I appear."

"Do you like running down your own stories and making the Boston deadlines?"

"Boston needs the news." Claire grinned. "I love it."

"I'm proud of you. How do you feel to finally get the byline you've wanted for so long?"

She'd thought and prayed about how to handle the BNS. If she'd indicated only she wrote the news, they might reject the story, but by including her name with Jock's, she figured the syndicate wouldn't pay any attention.

Her contacts came because of her father. Officials expected Jock, his name and reputation opened the doors.

The first time she'd written the byline with both names, Boston cabled asking for verification. Claire debated whether she was lying by implying Jock was on the job.

She wired Josiah Fischer the truth.

When his response arrived, she had to blink back tears. Her vindication came in square black letters on a flimsy telegram: "I don't care who writes copy. Stories are powerful. Good work."

"We're a team, Papa," she said, relating the story. "They've been bylined Jock and Claire Meacham."

Jock fumbled for his pipe. Anne took it away from him. "Why, Claire?"

"It was the right thing to do, Papa." Claire outlined what she and Mark had learned two days before. "Pershing parked his train car."

"The war should be over by Thanksgiving, then. I hope I'll be on my feet and able to report at the end."

"It's coming." The adrenaline of an enormous story, probably the greatest story of her life, rushed through Claire.

"You've done well, darling." Jock brushed the wool blanket covering his legs. "I've read your articles. You've come far from the London newsroom taking shorthand. These have been challenging years and we've not always seen eye to eye."

"True."

"But as I lay here fearing death, I thought about how earnest you've been in your faith. I worried Chambers would steal you and I'd lose my only child. That's why I pushed so hard. I needed to make sure your faith drove you and not infatuation with a zealot. We want a broad life for you, to see the world with sophisticated eyes. Religious people aren't like us."

"What do you figure now?" she asked, her throat dry, her heart tired.

"Your mother has his little book and I read it." Jock lifted his chin and met her eyes. "The book of Job is an excellent one to contemplate as we near the end of this ghastly war."

He took a deep breath. "I always liked the man, but I was jealous. I'm sorry. Oswald Chambers was an example of what we hope a Christian can be. I'm sorry for making your life miserable."

Claire could barely see him through her tears. She nodded.

His hands shook and Jock's hair had turned white but he still had questions. "So now you've experienced my job, what do you want to do with your life?"

Claire knew the answer. "I'd like to stay on and write—to help Europe rebuild."

"Do you want to work for the syndicate now you've shared the front page with your father?" Anne asked.

"Perhaps. Jim suggested I work with him, maybe through the YMCA."

Jock's eyes gleamed. "Good intentions, indeed. Whatever you decide to do, following your God, marrying a fine man, reporting, your mother and I give you our blessings."

Claire tilted her head to understand; the words she'd always longed to hear and yet…

"What's the matter, darling?" Anne asked. "We love you, nothing you can say or do will disappoint us."

Claire willed her voice to stay calm, but the shaking began anyway. "I didn't tell you the worst news. We've been checking. German advance troops overran Jim's canteen at the front line. He's been missing for two weeks."

Chapter Forty-Nine

Chaumont/Paris, November 11, 1918

Claire hadn't slept well in the Chaumont hotel bed, fretting about the day to come and reviewing questions. With the Kaiser's abdication would the German army go home—or would the generals push until every soldier died? What about people who were missing, like Jim? What value were negotiations if Jim and other prisoners didn't survive long enough to be freed?

Anne entered her room a little after five, the windows still black with the late fall dawn. Claire sat upright. "What's happened?"

"Your father received messages hourly through the night. General Pershing wants to see you both at six. The maid's brought coffee, you'd best get up."

Claire dressed quickly, pulling on the serviceable dark skirt and white shirt she'd worn most of the year. She brushed the dust off her black jacket, wrapped her hair onto the nape of her neck and sighed. Aged by the war and depleted, she could barely lift her arms. The last four years seemed an eternity of loss and brutal endings.

She flipped open her Bible to read one verse for the day. She put her finger down in Psalm 20: "Some trust in chariots, and some in horses: but we will remember the name of the Lord our God. They are brought down and fallen: but we are risen, and stand upright."

Nigel and Peter's faces floated before her; she heard OC's voice reading the same passage. "One of us needs to be the last man standing," Jim had said. Her heart sighed. She wanted to believe he still stood somewhere in France.

As she tugged on thick stockings, Claire thought of his gentle laughter and encouragement. She remembered his despair in the YMCA hut. He spoke positively even when he struggled to find good among the evil. He'd wished her well and waited so long to tell her the truth about himself, she'd nearly missed it. And then, when she finally realized what she dearly wanted, he disappeared.

Like everyone else.

Claire tied the shoelaces, straightened her skirt, picked up her notebook and walked out of her room. Suitcases were half-filled in her parents' room. Her mother handed her the café au lait, made the way Claire liked it, and she sipped the warmth.

Jock was whistling and tying his tie. "Are you ready for exciting news?"

Her heart leapt. "Has a message come? You've heard from Jim?"

He glanced at Anne. "No. Pershing wants us. Your mother's packing and will be done by the time we return. If it's the armistice, we want to be in Paris today."

"The next best news. Am I allowed to say 'thanks be to God?' "

"Of course!" Anne laughed.

Jock bolted down his coffee and took Anne into his arms. "If it's the end, we'll hurry back, grab the bags, and catch the 7:30 train to Paris. We'll be celebrating today."

"Celebrating and remembering?"

"Always."

They walked through the quiet streets to AEF headquarters a few blocks away. A horse-drawn cart piled high with winter vegetables clopped by. A soldier bicycled past; a char woman tossed a bucket of water.

"This war robbed you of so much. When we sailed to Europe four and a half years ago, we hoped to show you the Continent in its glory, to finish your education by polishing you into a charming and capable young woman."

"Polish me?" Claire thought of her tired clothes and hair unfashionably knotted at her nape.

"You were never anything but a gem to us but the war has made you a deeper person."

"I feel a million years old, Papa. I can hardly remember the girl who thought being able to take dictation fast made her valuable."

"But hasn't your skill given you a life?" He took her arm to avoid a pothole in the cobblestoned street.

"It's certainly taken me a lot of places and introduced me to many fine people." She thought again of Nigel, Jim, and OC. "All gone now."

They entered the courtyard at a nod from the sentry.

"Let's not count Jim out yet," Jock said. "Alf sent a message late last night. The AEF freed several POW camps in the last couple days. I can't imagine the Huns killing a padre this late in the game. Wasn't Jim studying German for such a time as this?"

"Ja wohl."

Claire examined her father's features in the dim morning light as he fumbled, yet again, for his pipe. His hands trembled as he lit it and took a long draw.

"I should be able to get good tobacco once more. That will be a pleasure."

Like Anne, he appeared more fragile, less a dominant force. Had Jock shrunk or had Claire grown?

"What will you do, Papa? Will you go home, now?"

Jock's cheek creased. "The treaties need to be sorted out and signed. I imagine we'll stay on another year or two with the BNS."

The pipe smoke didn't make her nose tickle in the fresh morning air. She hitched the bag onto her shoulder, removed her glasses to polish, and put them on once more. The morning gleamed brighter, clearer, but the grief remained. What did a new old world need more than people to rebuild and restore?

A soldier raised the American flag and saluted when they reached the American Expeditionary Forces headquarters. The guard escorted them in to the metal stairs leading to the main office. The general's administration clerk beamed when they entered the room. "Such great news."

"Oh?" Jock asked.

"I'll take you to the general."

They entered a paneled situation room where a colonel barked orders to a flurry of young officers. Uniformed men scribbled and conferred, the large map so long dominated by thwarted lines and multicolored pins ignored. "The press is here!" shouted the clerk.

Conversation ground to a halt as they were escorted through a door to where General Pershing sat in an ornate office. "Meacham, Miss Meacham, come in. Let's get this ball rolling."

Claire scrabbled for her pencil and notebook.

"General Foch signed papers two hours ago for an armistice between the Imperial Forces of Germany and the Allied Forces of France, England, the United States, and others.

The cease-fire will go into effect at the eleventh hour of the eleventh day of November, at eleven o'clock in the morning. This morning. Treaties will be signed in the future."

"What are the terms?" Jock asked.

Pershing indicated his chief of staff. "The terms are lengthy, thirty-five total. We'll give you a copy."

"Most important?"

"Hostilities cease this morning. All German troops out of Belgium, France, Alsace-Lorraine and Luxemburg within fourteen days; reparations to those harmed by the war to begin immediately."

Jock glanced through the list and his eyebrows flew up. "These are harsh terms."

"The Huns deliberately killed a generation of fine young men. There can be no conclusion to this war until Germany is brought to her knees. I prefer an unconditional surrender. Conciliation now can only lead to a future war."

"So this is good news?" Claire asked.

The old soldier's eyes softened. "The French will be dancing in the streets before nightfall. I fear, though, Europe will see another war before you're my age."

Jock stuck the paper into his pocket and held out his hand. "Thank you, General. We'll let the folks in America know their boys will be coming home."

"Thanks. You're among the first to get the news because you've got such a clever assistant. Reporters like her will make the world a better place." He shook Jock's hand and then Claire's.

The *New York Times* reporter greeted them in the courtyard. "What's the news?"

Jock tossed his thumb in the direction of Pershing's office. "Find out yourself."

They reached the street. Other reporters were on their way. Claire flung her arms around Jock's neck. "Is it truly over?"

He checked his watch. "It will be in a couple hours. Let's tell America." A cab drew up, and once the tardy reporters exited, the Meachams took their place.

Jock lit his pipe, eyes dancing, hands trembling. "What do you think now? You've got the front row seat on history. Ready to become a fantastic history teacher with a firsthand account?"

Claire laughed. "Not on your life. I'm telling this one myself!"

They traveled directly to the telegraph office and Jock sent the news flash to his Boston editor. He telegraphed the news to Sarah in London and his offices in London, Paris, and Cairo. The telegraph operator shouted for his colleagues as they left the office.

They picked up Anne and the luggage and headed to the train. Traveling to Paris, Jock read the armistice information and crafted the story while Claire typed up his words. They arrived at Gare de l'Est, at 10:30.

Jock hesitated. "I'd like nothing better than to be on the streets of Paris today, but I'm tired and one of us needs to man the office. I'll take the luggage and go. I want you to rejoice with the city today. Get your quotes, scream and dance, kiss strangers, and be happy."

"It won't be as fun without you," Anne said. "I came to Paris to celebrate with you."

He kissed her. "We'll celebrate tonight. I've set aside a bottle of champagne for this event." He hailed a cab.

"Where should we go first?" Claire asked.

"I'll drop you near the Place de Concorde and you can get a statement from the US ambassador. Walk down Rue

Rivoli, inquire at the Louvre, head to Notre-Dame, see if you can find someone official for a quote and come to the office. I'll make some calls and see if I can get a reaction from the various armies."

Claire pictured the map in her head. "We'll get to the office by two o'clock."

"I'll wire these stories and you can provide celebration descriptions for the deadline." He kissed them both. "I'm more than thankful we're alive and together on this day. *Au revoir*!"

The French newspapers splashed EXTRA! above the fold. Boys sold papers on the street, crowds gathered, and the bells of Paris began to toll, chime, clang, and ring at eleven o'clock. A large gun fired from the top of the Eiffel Tower and flags flew from every building.

Shouting and singing "La Marseillaise" began spontaneously and as they walked the streets, Anne and Claire saw few dry eyes. People crowded the boulevards, walking arm in arm. Soldiers danced among the Parisians, exchanging hats and singing. Women and children tossed flowers and handheld flags flourished.

Anne and Claire couldn't resist laughing and singing with the excited crowds. So many people swarmed the street, cars could not move. Biplanes flying over the city dropped slips of paper. Claire read one aloud: "Congratulations to France on the recovery of her lost children."

They pushed through the throngs to reach overflowing Notre-Dame Cathedral. High above, the big Emmanuel bell rang continually. "They say it will toll for eleven hours," a priest told them. "God is good. We are so thankful."

Claire wrote it down, but knew she'd never forget. Her heart beat fast and her feet could not stand still. She reminded herself to observe, not participate, and yet underneath lay a desperate sadness.

Anne nudged her. "Let's light candles."

"We're not Catholic."

"God doesn't care today."

In a dark corner they found a flickering bank of votive candles.

"One for Holly and Edward together, because we hardly knew them," Anne said.

Claire lit another. "One for Nigel."

"One for Peter." Anne wiped away a tear.

She struck a match and Anne's hand joined her. "One for Oswald who made the difference."

Claire reached for one more candle but Anne caught her hand. "We don't know yet. Let's have faith."

Tears started in Claire's eyes and she nodded. They hugged each other.

The enormous bell tolled, people sang, and everyone got kissed. It felt like swimming to push their way out of the ancient cathedral.

At 1:30 and still a distance from the office, Claire spied a taxi. "Come, come," the driver urged. "No fares today." Another couple joined them and they headed west.

"I hope your father ordered lunch," Anne called as they climbed the office stairs.

A typewriter clattered as they entered the office. Madame Ouellette was not at her desk.

"You're here! Boston needs the news; they're holding the front page for Claire Meacham!" Jock brandished a champagne bottle in one hand and a glass in the other.

"*Vive la France*," Claire declared. "Who's typing?"

"*Voilà*!" Jock waved at his office, where a bearded man in a dirty uniform pounded on the typewriter.

"*Vive la* American liberators." Jim grinned. "They freed me two days ago and I caught the first train to Paris. It took me longer to get here than I expected."

Claire dropped her old leather bag and ran to his arms. "I thought I'd never see you again."

He held her close. "God isn't finished with us yet, Claire. Shall we bring the world good news together?"

As she breathed in his scent—a dirty man newly freed from a POW camp—the faces of those she'd loved and lost passed through her mind yet again.

She might not be the same girl who started a job as a stenographer four years before, but she knew what she wanted now: life with a man who could find reasons for faith in the midst of tragedy, no matter where God took them. Claire and her writing belonged with Jim and their God.

She leaned back in his arms. "It won't be easy."

"We'll be broken bread and poured out wine," Jim said, "but it won't be worthwhile without you. I've asked your father. Did you decide? Will you marry me?"

"Yes," Claire said.

He reached into his breast pocket and pulled out a handful of dried red poppy petals. "I've been collecting these for months."

She caught them in her open palms and sniffed. "No scent."

Those dearly loved brown eyes shone at her. "No. But a perfect day to remember." He kissed her with all the passion and bittersweet joy of the last four years and then they clung together, peacefully home.

Jim lifted his head and smiled at Jock and Anne, beckoning them over. “Shall we celebrate the end of the war and new beginnings?”

“Sounds like a plan to me.” Jock kissed his wife. “I’ve been waiting for your return.”

“As soon as I’m done writing.” Claire tilted her head and laughed for joy. “I need to file my story first.”

-30-

“Our yesterdays present irreparable things to us; it is true that we have lost opportunities which will never return, but God can transform this destructive anxiety into a constructive thoughtfulness for the future. Let the past sleep, but let it sleep on the bosom of Christ. Leave the irreparable past in His hands, and step out into the irresistible future with Him.”

—Oswald Chambers

Author's Note

A Poppy in Remembrance is a work of historical fiction and thus a product of Michelle Ule's imagination.

The novel includes depictions of real people from history. Michelle portrayed the historical individuals with action and dialogue representing their behavior at the time.

In particular, she conducted research in the Oswald Chambers papers at Wheaton College Special Collections Library on Oswald and Biddy Chambers, to ensure an accurate depiction of their characters.

Oswald and Biddy ran a Bible Training College in London prior to World War I. They served with the YMCA in Egypt during the war and led a revival among ANZAC troops stationed at Zeitoun.

For more information about their lives and ministry, readers should examine *Oswald Chambers: Abandoned to God* by David McCasland or *Mrs. Oswald Chambers: The Woman Behind the World's Bestselling Devotional* by Michelle Ule

Other information about references, photos, and research done while Michelle wrote *A Poppy in Remembrance*, can be found at www.michelleule.com.

Michelle Ule

Biographer, *Mrs. Oswald Chambers* (Baker Books, October 2017)
Check out my website for more information: www.michelleule.com

Acknowledgments

My writing of *A Poppy in Remembrance* defies the normal experience of an author.

I have been blessed beyond measure.

I've been led in extraordinary ways and helped by unexpected people.

Here's my list, with gratitude.

The Oswald Chambers experts: Nicholas Gray, David McCasland, and Ed Rock of Discovery House Publications.

The archivist and the World War I genealogists: Keith Call of Wheaton College's Special Collections Library and Peter and Meredith Wenham.

My book friends: Jamie Clarke Chavez, Cindy Coloma, Janet McHenry, Janet Grant, Rachel Kent, Robin Gunn, Tim Stafford, Davis Bunn, Virginia Smith, Jeane Wynn, Alisha Ule, and Nicole Miller.

The extraordinary cover artist Mary Wyatt Moen.

Early readers included Linda Livingstone, Jo Miller, Nicholas Gray, Leah Warren, Kim Hurlburt, Caroline Brethauer, Hillary Cummings, Carolyn Ule, and Rachel Durham—who walked the lake with me and prayed the morning the idea came.

Long-suffering listeners who have been with me every step of the way include my family and all my Wandering Views friends!

My ever-wonderful patron of the arts, Robert Ule—who agreed to a weekend in Paris but burst out laughing when I explained it was a place to stay before touring the Somme battlefields!

Biddy Chambers—who altered the plot line of *A Poppy in Remembrance* so many times, I thought someone should write a biography about her. That person turned out to be me!

I've dedicated this book to my late parents who taught me to travel the world, love history, and that I was capable of anything if I read up on the subject.

Lastly, thanks to God, Jesus, and the Holy Spirit and the wonderful example set by servants Oswald and Biddy, with a nod to their daughter Kathleen.

Michelle Ule
Northern California 2018

About the Author

Michelle Ule is the author of five best-selling novellas, a Navy SEAL novel, an essay in *Utmost Ongoing: Reflections on the Legacy of Oswald Chambers*, and the biography *Mrs. Oswald Chambers: The Woman Behind the World's Bestselling Devotional.*

A graduate in English literature from the University of California, Los Angeles, she learned about journalism as a reporter and city editor at the *UCLA Daily Bruin.* She still reads a physical newspaper every day.

Married to a retired naval officer and proud of being a twenty-year navy wife, Michelle loves reading, music, and history. She lives in northern California with her extended family when she's not traveling the world.

You can learn more about her at www.michelleule.com, where she blogs weekly.

Michelle has written 100 blog posts related to Biddy and Oswald Chambers, and many posts about World War I events. The most widely read post is "Why Did God Allow Oswald Chambers to Die so Young?"

If you're interested in a reaction to each day's *My Utmost for His Highest,* check out her Michelle Ule, Writer Facebook page. You can also find her on Twitter @Michelleule.

For pictures pertinent to *A Poppy in Remembrance*, Biddy and Oswald Chambers and World War I, visit her Pinterest boards: https://www.pinterest.com/michelleule/

Want to know more about Biddy and Oswald Chambers? Subscribe to Michelle Ule's free newsletter where you can receive a free copy of her e-book *Writing About Biddy and Oswald Chambers: Faith Affirming Stories and Serendipities.*

Sign up at her website www.michelleule.com or at http://bit.ly/UleNews

You also might enjoy

Mrs. Oswald Chambers: The Woman Behind the World's Bestselling Devotional.

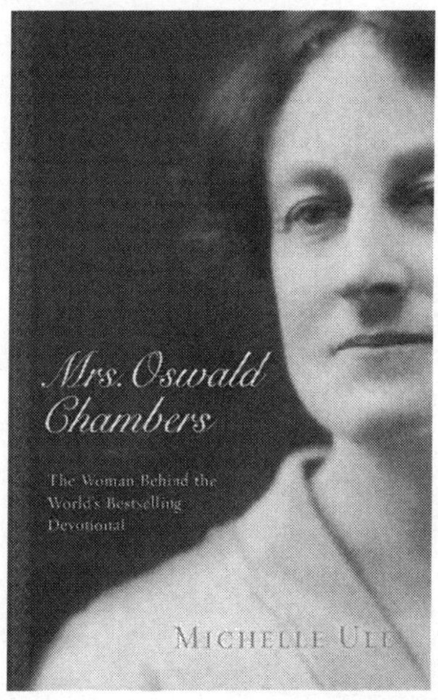

Made in the USA
San Bernardino, CA
13 March 2019